8/18/01

To: Velma, i v---

thanks to some
truly great neighbors

Bill Paul

# The Road He Chose

# *The Road He Chose*

## William Paul

*Autumn Leaf Publishing*
Atlanta, Georgia
2001

**Publisher's Cataloging-in-Publication**
*(Provided by Quality Books, Inc.)*


Paul, William, 1925-
    The road he chose / by William Paul. -- 1st ed.
    p. cm.
    ISBN 0-9709115-0-5

    1. World War, 1939-1945--Fiction.  2. United States.
Office of Strategic Services--Fiction.  3. World War,
1939-1945--Secret service--United States--Fiction.
4. World War, 1939-1945--Underground movements--France--
Fiction.  5. France--History--German occupation,
1940-1945--Fiction.  6. Quebec--History--Fiction.
I. Title.

PS3566.A82695R63 2001        813'.6
              QBI01-700370

For information, contact:

*Autumn Leaf Publishing*
1275 Peachtree Street, Suite 600, Atlanta, GA  30309
AutumnPub@aol.com

# *Dedication*

This book is dedicated to
the two greatest people I ever knew:
my Mother and Father,

\*\*\*\*\*\*\*\*\*\*\*\*\*\*
and to the
MEMORY
of
my five boyhood friends
who
never came home
from World War II,

\*\*\*\*\*
as well as
those valiant French men and women
of the *Résistance*
who never submitted to
Nazi domination.

## *Five Who Never Came Home*

I see their faces, every day
—-the five who never came home
They gave their lives, to keep us free
—-the five who never came home

I hear their voices, and ask myself
—-why was it they, and why not I?
This question I've pondered, all these years
—-but never had answered, despite my tears


Perhaps somewhere, I'll meet them once more
—-the five who never came home
What will I say, if they ask of me
—-why was it we, and why not you
—-who died to keep men free?

What can I say, I've done to deserve
—-to live so long as a man still free?
When I owe this debt, wherever I roam
—-to the five who never came home.

My hopeful prayer, and I pray it's not late
—-is to live out my days, before I must die
So to tell them one day, somewhere in the sky
—- in living my life, I strove to honor
—-the five who never came home

—-Bill Paul

\*\*\*\*\*\*\*\*\*\*\*\*\*\*\*\*\*\*\*\*\*\*\*\*\*\*\*\*\*\*\*\*\*\*\*\*\*

*For my five boyhood friends,
Claude, Dock, Bernard, Billy, and Doug.*

\*\*\*\*\*\*\*\*\*\*\*\*\*\*\*\*\*\*\*\*\*\*\*\*\*\*\*\*\*\*\*\*\*\*\*\*\*

# Acknowledgements

Although this is a work of fiction, it was written to be a *historical* novel. Thus I have endeavored to describe factually and accurately those historical events, settings, and places that indeed did occur and exist during the period from September 1939 until September 1945. In conducting my research, I read or consulted a number of books which were extremely valuable to me in either refreshing my memory of that era or in providing me totally new and apparently credible information. I would be remiss if I did not acknowledge that assistance, as well as my appreciation, to the following authors and their books :

Ambrose, Stephen E. *D-Day* (Simon & Schuster, 1995)

Astor, Gerald. *The Mighty Eighth* (Dell, 1998)

Bowman, Martin W. *Images of Aviation, Stearman* (Tempus Publishing, 1999)

Bowman, Martin. *Mosquito Bomber/Fighter-Bomber Units 1942-45* (Osprey, 1997)

Bowman, Martin W. *The Bedford Triangle* (Sutton Publishing Limited, 1996)

Bowyer, Chaz. *The Royal Air Force 1939-1945* (Pen & Sword Paperbacks, 1996)

Churchill, Winston S. *Memoirs of the Second World War* (an abridgement); (Houghton Mifflin Company, first published 1959)

Kizilos, Peter. *Quebec, Province Divided* (Lerner Publications Company, 2000)

MacLean, Charles. *The Clan Almanac* (Eric Dobby Publishing, 1990)

McIntosh, Elisabeth P. *Sisterhood of Spies ,The Women of the OSS* (Dell, 1999)

Paxton, Robert O. *Vichy France* (Columbia University Press, Morningside Edition, 1982)

Ryan, Cornelius. *The Longest Day* (Simon & Schuster, Inc. 1959)

Weitz, Margaret Collins. *Sisters in the Resistance* (John Wiley & Sons, Inc., 1995)

I wish also to express my appreciation for the abundance of information I obtained from many Web Sites too numerous to mention in detail here; without that information, I doubt that the book could have been completed for at least another year.

Last, *but far from least,* I express my grateful thanks to the following individuals, without whose help I could never have written the manuscript:

Claude Wegscheider, the Executive Director of *Alliance Française d'Atlanta,* and his staff, who first introduced me to the fascinating world of the French language and traditions.

Jean and Madeleine Colbert, the owners of the *Institut de Français,* along with the professors and other staff members of that truly great language school at Villefranche Sur Mer, France. It was they who not only gave me the opportunity to learn—on the ground—some of their beautiful language, but also to know—and grow to love—the people and culture of the Cote d'Azure.

Special thanks are due to Vicky Greco, Isabelle Mosser, Jean-François Greco, and Christian Cesari, for specific and detailed information they furnished me at my request.

David Nielsen and Marie-Françoise Carton, owners of the shop *La Salamandre* on the *rue du Château* at Eze Village, France, and their neighbor, Marie Sauvage, at the delightful small cafe *Le Nid d'Aigle,* who provided me much valuable data regarding the history of their ancient village.

My daughter, Jennifer Paul Harrison, who was my patient advisor and compassionate critic throughout the process.

Edith Brooks, my secretary and faithful colleague of more than thirty years, who edited constantly the beginnings and—most of all—encouraged me each day in this new endeavor.

Sergeant-Major Franklin Osborne (USA, Retired) and Paul Cadenhead (one of my law school classmates who was a paratrooper during World War II) for their guidance regarding the training at the Army Jump School at Fort Benning, Georgia.

My wife Janice, as well as some other members of her family, Winifred Hale of Blue River, Kentucky, and Donald and Drema Osborne of Prestonsburg, Kentucky, for their help about Eastern Kentucky.

# Author's Note

This is a work of fiction. The characters and events described in this book are either a product of the author's imagination or are used fictitiously. The same is true of those fictionalized events and incidents that involve the names of real persons who were public figures during the era of the story. Their inclusion in the book is intended only to give the fiction a sense of reality and authenticity.

# About the Author

William Paul served as an Aviation Cadet in the Army Air Corps during World War II and as a Special Agent, OSI (Office of Special Investigations) in the Air Force during the Korean conflict.

He is a retired lawyer and lives in Atlanta, Georgia.

# *Prologue*

Bill now found himself looking back again, sitting by the fireplace with his old soldier friend, as they had done so often since V-J Day.

How many times had he recited to himself the same five lines? Hundreds—maybe more?

> *"Two roads diverged in a yellow wood,*
> *And sorry that I could not travel both*
> *And be one traveler, long I stood*
>
> _____
>
> _____
>
> *I took the one less traveled by,*
> *And that has made all the difference."*

He had long wondered what inspired Robert Frost to write those words. Was it the same reason he seemed haunted by them? Bill had long since quit the search for that answer and begun concentrating on whether his own choice of roads had been the right one.

It bothered him, for it had become almost an obsession. He loved his twin, but found himself constantly reminiscing—and wondering—if he should have picked the road his brother had chosen.

Everybody had called his brother and him *identical* twins. God knows they did look alike; even now he still dreamed of Mama saying, "They're like two peas in a pod." It was hard, even for her, to tell them apart. Not only that; their voices sounded exactly alike. And both were straight-A students (as their father had always broadcast loud and clear to everyone he saw). For Bill's twin, making top grades had been a snap, even though he loathed classes and found ways, many of which were truly ingenious, to "lay-out" from school (as they called "playing hooky" from school in the South in those days) at least a day each week. But Bill had to excel the hard way, by working twice as hard as anyone else in everything he did, but excel equally with his brother he did, and without ever the hint of a complaint.

Both were developed physically beyond their years, and truly precocious, so much so that on those rare occasions when they dressed in coats and ties (usually only in church, by command of Mama) a stranger would never have guessed them to be so young. Their demeanor in public probably added to that impression, together with the fact of most of their schoolmates and cronies being one or two years older.

Each twin was an accomplished athlete, Will through a gift from God, and Bill only by pure determination and sweat. But it was Bill—as well as his twin— about whom their old football coach said, years later at his retirement banquet: "Both kids were good athletes, but there was something else that made them truly special; they had the greatest *will to win* of all the many boys I had on my teams."

In other ways they were different as night and day. When that came up, Bill usually said, "Thank the Lord for the difference." But he didn't really believe that, deep down, because Will always seemed to get the best of most things.

Yet, the two had been inseparable as young boys. Will was always in some kind of hot water, and Bill was always there to help pull him out of it, each time swearing that would be the last time—until the *next* time.

But *the day* had changed all that, perhaps forever.

# Chapter One

They were barely into their sophomore year of high school when the Nazi hordes goose-stepped into defenseless Poland that September of 1939 and butchered the valiant Poles' horse cavalry with their steel armor and shrieking Stuka dive-bombers.

They were barely sixteen when the Panzers of the modern-day Huns swept once again across the Low Countries into France, out-flanking the French and their useless Maginot Line, on which the French generals had foolishly staked the security of their great nation.

After France collapsed so swiftly, it became obvious that some in France, as well as many more in Switzerland and other European venues—many of whom laid claim to being leaders—were convinced that Hitler was destined to rule all that continent with his blood covered fist. Some gave strong indications that they were resigned to a fate of being a Nazi district for God knows how long.

The most celebrated, as well as the most denounced, was the rush to claim his spoils by the Italian dictator Mussolini declaring war on France within days of the Dunkirk withdrawal, as described by President Roosevelt that same evening: "On this tenth day of June, 1940, the hand that held the dagger has struck it into the back of its neighbor."

By then, every bright and literate young American male from age 14 to 25 was beginning to sense that the tragic events unfolding in old Europe might be forming his future too, not yet realizing that they were to evolve into the defining factors in the lives of their entire generation.

Thus they had gradually become fans of the increasingly grim evening radio broadcasts from Edward R. Murrow and his contemporaries who were describing the horrors of modern warfare from radios in parlors throughout America.

Many teen-aged American boys could tell you the most minute details of the Dunkirk evacuation, and most came to know a Hurricane fighter

1

from a Lancaster bomber, even if they didn't know the names of any of their own American military aircraft.

And almost all would thereafter remember—until their dying day—the inspiration and hope they drew from the powerful voice of Winston Churchill as the British stood alone in what may have been their "darkest hour"—later to become surely their "finest hour," as their great leader forecast on June 4 of 1940.

In the summer of 1941, Bill and his twin had both gotten summer jobs as messenger boys with the old Postal Telegraph Company, mainly because their Aunt Beth was a branch manager who had become something of a living legend with the Atlanta managers of that company during the world premiere of *Gone With the Wind.*

That event was about the biggest thing that had ever happened to Atlanta and she had been only 24 when Postal had entrusted her to run the temporary desk at the old but fashionable hotel where all the stars, Clark Gable, Vivian Leigh, and all the rest, had lodged during the premiere. Afterwards, the way she had done her job was one of the few things about her town that the stars went out of their way to compliment.

She was more like a sister than an aunt to the boys—they always called her "Aunt Sissy"—and she knew that both needed to work in the summers to help their folks make ends meet. When they took their intelligence tests for the jobs, they made their own personal *hit* with the company, becoming two of the few people in the company's history to score a perfect 100 points on the exam.

At the request of the local manager of Postal's desk at the old Terminal Railway Station (she happened to be a friend of Aunt Sissy, as well as an almost daily lunchmate) both boys were sent there to work until school started in September.

They were very pleased with the jobs. Thirty cents an hour—even though you did have to furnish your own bike—wasn't bad for two kids from their side of town; it was the minimum wage under one of the many new laws that Roosevelt had pushed through the Congress, and they were delighted to get it.

But far and away the best part, to them, was the exciting people you met there.

By this time in the war, the Royal Air Force was sending many of theirs to bases in the U.S. for training and, because of the climate, most were being trained in what we now call the Sun Belt, stretching principally from the Carolinas to Texas.

A typical example was the town of Terrell, Texas, where a BFTS (British Flying Training School) trained 2,200 aviation cadets—including

150 Americans who flew and fought with the RAF. The first class graduated in 1941.

Nineteen British cadets were killed in training there and buried in the Oakland Memorial Cemetery in Terrell, where a memorial plinth was dedicated on 16 April 1942 by Viscount Halifax, British Ambassador to the U.S., bearing the inscription, *"Some corner of a foreign field that is forever England."*

They traveled by train to and from their training bases, and many would stop by the Postal desk to send telegrams home to England while changing trains. Both brothers were entranced by them and asked them a hundred and one questions about the RAF and the war.

And neither twin failed to notice that most of these handsome and self-confident young flyers were barely older—if indeed *any* older—than they.

With that winter came the Sunday that both foreverafter called *"the day."*

They were in their last high school year on the seventh day of that December when Pearl Harbor became a living hell for a few very long hours.

As they leaned close to their old radio and tried to understand the near-hysterical voice above the static, each felt the rush of a thrill, along with a tinge of *gut wrenching* fright, that only boys—about to be vaulted prematurely into manhood—could feel about going to war.

They slept maybe an hour during the first part of that night, and talked the rest about what they and their pals, would do, and when. Will was talking flying with the Army Air Corps—and soon—but Bill reminded him of the age minimum for that—18 in the Army—and that they had just turned 17. This drew a sort of sneer about "so-called rules" from the other twin, who was already figuring how they could cover the truth about their ages.

"Even so, what about finishing our last year of school?" said Bill. "It would break Mama's heart for us to go, 'specially underage, and Daddy has always dreamed of us finishing at least high school, something he wasn't able to do."

But Will wasn't hearing much, and started yelling in the middle of the night, "That's all fine, but damn it Bill, that little piss-ant Hitler's trying to make soap out of the rest of the world, and now the Japanese have left us no choice but to go out and kick their butts. If you ask me, those little fellows have done the world a favor, because now our own lily-livers here don't have any excuse for us standing back and chewing our toenails 'til Mr. Hitler is puttin' his Stukas over New York. Next we'll be seeing them doing their damned goose-step right down the middle of Peachtree Street! Is that what you want? Is that what we want for our families? Not me!

"You know I'm fed up with school anyhow, and now's my chance to do somethin' really *worth* doin'. If we can't get into our own air corps, then let's go to the RCAF. I'll bet it wouldn't be hard to get in, in Canada, like Joe Hearn did. They don't give a hoot how old you are, as long as you can learn to fly without ripping up the airplane. Joe is only 17 and was flying a danged Spitfire, a really *hot bird*—as he described it—about six months after he quit school and went up there last year. The last letter he sent me he had just gotten what they call his first 'kill' of a Nazi bomber—a Heinkel 111. He said it was a "piece of cake"—got it in just his second combat sortie too. Not only that, he's got a really great-looking number of a gal there—sent me her picture. He drinks a beer or two whenever he wants it—a damned sight better time than we're having here, treated like we're still in diapers. Now what's wrong with that?

"You do what you want, but I'm *goin'* and I'm going *now*—not next June—and I'm counting on you not to breathe a word about this to our folks! Promise me now that you won't. You know I'll do it anyhow, so why put our folks through a lot of worry twice?"

"Are you finished now," said Bill, "or you wanta make another speech? If I didn't know you so well, I'd think you're nuts. That's a lot of bullcrap about stopping Hitler—you just see this as an excuse to quit school and do what you think you'd like to do.

"What about the feelings of our parents? Don't they count for anything? And don't call me a yellow-belly—you do, and I'll whip your butt right here and now. I'm ready to go fight—just as ready as you—but there are other things to think about too. Things like not always lying just because there's something you want. Things like the word *duty*—that our father always told us is the most important word in the English language. I think he is right about that, 'specially when it comes to our duty to him and Mama!

"Look Will, I know how you feel—I feel some of the same—-but why don't you just cool it, at least until tomorrow when we can talk with some of the other fellows at school and see what they think; and you'd be real smart to watch your mouth when we do, cause I don't want you getting some more teeth knocked out, and I'm not real charmed about losing any of mine by having to help you. Besides, remember that most of them are older than us, so they may have some good ideas.

"Now, for Pete's sake, let's shut up and get a little sleep."

And they both did *shut up*—but neither slept another wink of that night that followed *the day;* they were too charged up, because they could hardly wait for *tomorrow.*

★   ★   ★

Half a world away from the boys' modest neighborhood of Lakewood, others were also very interested in the biggest news of that day:

**England; Sunday Evening, December 7, 1941**

Four thousand miles away, at Winston Churchill's country retreat, he was at table with Averell Harriman when his butler, Sawyers, came into the room, saying, "The Japanese have attacked Pearl Harbour!"

Within three minutes, Sir Winston was on the line with President Roosevelt, who confirmed "It's quite true. They have attacked us at Pearl Harbor. We are all in the same boat now."

Churchill rang immediately his Foreign Office to prepare "without a moment's delay" a declaration of war upon Japan, as he had pledged, on November 11, to do if Japan attacked the United States.

As he later described his feelings on hearing the news, " . . . to have the United States at our side was to me the greatest joy." He was then totally confident that he and his valiant island nation " . . . had won after all. Yes, after Dunkirk; after the fall of France; after the horrible episode of Oran; after the threat of invasion, when apart from the Air and the Navy, we were an almost unarmed people. We had won the war. England would live. Britain would live; the Commonwealth of Nations and the Empire would live. Many disasters, immeasurable costs and tribulation lay ahead, but there would be no more doubt about the end."

**France; Sunday Evening, December 7, 1941**

In a *safehouse* near Grenoble, France, in the foothills of the Alps, a small group of young French *résistants* were just as interested in huddling around their tiny shortwave radio as was the British Prime Minister in using his hotline to the President of the United States.

They had been risking their lives each day, for many months, in their dogged determination not to accept the German boot on the neck of their beloved country.

Each day and night they were being hunted and hounded, not only by the Nazi occupiers of most of France, but also by their own Vichy rulers of the so-called "Unoccupied Zone" who were unabashedly collaborating with the Nazis, and so had declared these freedom-fighters to be outlaws with a price on their heads.

But tonight, nothing could diminish their elation in knowing that they now had a new and powerful ally in their struggle to regain the freedom and restore the genius that was France. They, equally as indomitable and determined as Mr. Churchill, were overjoyed, not by the Japanese blows against the Americans, but by the absolute certainty they now felt of ultimate victory, with the Americans actively at their side.

Even in the face of great danger, the French seem to ever retain their *joie de vivre,* and this night was surely a cause for a celebration of life, pronounced Jean-Pierre, the 22-year-old "patriarch" of the group, as he miraculously produced a magnum of *vin rouge* for a rousing toast *à la santé des américains.* As all raised their glasses, David the Dane, replied in English, "And to *our* health, as well!" To which in turn Bridgette, Marie-Françoise, and Frederic—those were their *noms de guerre* (their war names)—echoed, in unison: *"Nous sommes d'accord!"*

Little did they realize, in this moment of joy, what paths would cross theirs before the end of their saga.

# Chapter Two

Atlanta was a small town in the winter of '41. On this Monday, December 8, it was sunny and clear at the old school down near the state capitol building.

This was the original high school that had been built many years before for all the kids who lived outside the city limits of Atlanta but in Fulton County. As late as 1941 boys and girls still came there from diverse communities and various parts of the county that lay outside the city proper—that's why it was centrally located like it was, so the youngsters could come in conveniently from the north, south, east or west, and why it was called Fulton High—usually just "Fulton" by those who studied there.

A few years after Fulton was built, another secondary school had been constructed just north of the city in the Buckhead community; it was built to serve the high school needs of Buckhead and the *Northside* (as those areas were called in the Atlanta area—lovingly by those who lived there, and sarcastically by those who couldn't afford to). Buckhead was where the rich kids lived.

By the time *the day* had happened, most of the students who went to Fulton came from around a community south of the city called Lakewood, a poor but proud neighborhood that had not yet recovered from the hardships of the Great Depression. In spite of that, if one were looking for true examples of hardworking, God-fearing folks who truly fit the description of "the salt of the Earth," he should have started with those who called Lakewood home back then.

Lakewood was only five miles from Buckhead, measured as the crow flies, but a million or so if measured by economic status.

And Lakewood had been home to the Johnson family and their twin boys since the boys were toddlers.

It was also the home of three-fourths of the boys and girls who were talking about nothing but Pearl Harbor on this Monday that next followed *the day*. Most of the girls—but not all—were crying; and most of the boys—but not all—were talking army, navy, or marines.

A few of the boys were stone-silent, alone with their own special dreams—or fears; some were posturing, trying to pretend they had no fear, though all figured there had to be a bit in everybody, after the news in the Atlanta papers that day.

It sounded as if the Japanese aircraft had devastated Pearl Harbor and half or more of our fighting ships, and that the Philippine Islands were in imminent danger of being invaded and occupied by an enemy army. As more and more details of the extent of our grave losses became public knowledge, they certainly justified a high level of fear in the most courageous of Americans.

Fear was no stranger to any kid who had grown up in Lakewood during the depths of the Depression, especially to those like the twins who lived just up the road from the main exit from *the park*. The park had a carnival-type midway that drew to it characters from all over, nearly year round, including some of the tramps and hobos who roamed the country in desperation in the '30s, some honestly looking for work but most on the lam for many different reasons.

In the summer, after the auto races on the red dirt track, a parade of drunks would come staggering by the twins' home; all you could see were their eyeballs, peering from a face covered in a dust of the color that could only be created by the red clay of Georgia.

By and large they were decent people, but there were some with a mean streak who, flat-broke and furious after betting—and losing—the pittance they had saved from last Friday's paycheck, just had to take it out on the neighborhood. They were what Mama called "mean drinkers" and couldn't resist trying to intimidate the folks who lived near the park and its race track.

That just didn't sit well with the twins' Dad, so together, he and his boys always "dealt with it," as they put it. In the wake of those and many other challenges that were much more serious, the twins soon became afraid of few things or people, yet following their father's frequently repeated advice to: "Respect everyone, but *bow* to nobody."

Everyone in that community understood and admired the twins' family, in particular their parents and the way of living they had taught their children; and that reputation was legendary even among the kids at Fulton. So it was not surprising to the Johnson boys when they were getting most of the conversation that morning about what to do because of *the day*, even from their older friends.

About 20 of the boys had gotten to school extra early that morning and, at Bill's suggestion, after a few minutes of rambling conversation at the bus stop on the street, they gathered on what the football boys called "Rocky Stadium." That was the name they had given to the gravel-covered yard back of the school where football practices were held, since Fulton didn't have a real stadium. Rocky Stadium was also used for military drills by the school ROTC unit. About 15 of the 20 were wearing their ROTC uniforms that day; but it was only because those were the only decent clothes many of those boys owned and the main reason they were enrolled in ROTC to start with.

It was sort of an unwritten rule at Fulton that Rocky Stadium was male country, while the girls had their own special territories elsewhere in the building. There the boys felt they could speak their pieces, without the girls or teachers being around.

Bill was eager to hear from some of the fellows before classes started, but once they got in back everybody just sort of mumbled, so he spoke up. "I guess we're all wondering about the same thing this morning—*what* do we do about the war, and *when*, and *how?* So, anybody want to tell us your ideas?"

Ten seconds later he knew he had screwed up, as his brother leaped up and took the floor.

"I'll tell you what *I'm* goin' to do—and I hope some of you will be right there beside me!" he shouted so loud you could have heard him a block away. "I'm going to fly! That's where we need men if we're going to win this war. You saw what the Japs did to us in Hawaii yesterday, and what Hitler's trying to do to England right now—bomb it til the whole island sinks. They think the war is gonna be won or lost in the air, and I think they're right—except they're picking the wrong winner! Plus, all of us are young, and *young* men are what they need for pilots, so it's right up our alley, right? I say let's go do it and let's do it NOW!"

Bill was moving toward Will to shut him down by whatever it took, when a booming voice suddenly barked "AT EASE, men!" All of these *men* recognized instantly to whom that voice belonged; and they knew it was best to listen to it.

The R.O.T.C unit at Fulton had been honored, for the past four years, with every award the Army could give to such units, and everyone knew why; it was because of the dedication and leadership skills of the barrel-chested, ramrod of a man who had just stepped around the corner of the building and commanded the attention of his "men." He truly meant it when he called the boys "men"; he treated them like men, and they responded to him like real men, in ways that belied, amazingly, their boyhood.

In those days almost every high school in the South had an R.O.T.C. unit, and every unit had a regular army "Sergeant Instructor," and that was the job of Duncan Angus Macdonald, Master Sergeant, United States

Army. He was a legend at Fulton, as at U.S. Army stations around the world where he had served with distinction for 24 years; and he was a man not to be trifled with.

He was a kind man, but in appearance and bearing was somewhat awesome to many. Mr. Etchley, the rather meek little teacher of English literature at Fulton, was fond of saying of the Sergeant that "Whenever I approach this man in the hallway, I halfway anticipate that, at any moment, he will roar 'Lay on Macduff, and DAMN'D be him that first cries, *Hold, enough!*' "

The Sergeant found little humor in this but was always a good sport. Yet he could never resist pointing out again to Mr. Etchley and others that he knew well his Scottish roots, and that he most certainly was not a Macbeth, and that neither should his ancestry be confused with "those other Macdonalds" they may have heard about. He and his had been traced authentically to the Clan Donald with lands in The Western Isles, but many of his kinsmen had finally left for the New World after constantly feuding with the monarchs of Scotland since the twelfth century. His own branch had first settled in Canada, with 3 of their cousins; but they soon moved to the southern mountains of Appalachia to join their other kin who swore that it was so much like the hills of their beloved Scotland they could smell the heather if they closed their eyes on a morning after a rain.

But he was not a happy soldier at this particular stage of his career, and on *the day* his unhappiness had been immeasurably compounded.

Not only had his country he loved been stricken a crippling blow by a ruthless enemy, he knew also that he would never have the honor of serving it again in a combat zone at a time when his experience and training were desperately needed.

In the late Fall of 1936, he had been one of the first of a number of elite soldiers invited to participate in a top-drawer confidential training experiment. He was the oldest in the group, as well as the only one who had served in combat in World War I, when he, an 18-year-old infantryman, had been decorated for valor by General "Black Jack" Pershing himself.

The training mission involved a major, but dangerous, effort to develop the art of low-level parachuting, in anticipation of building much larger and more effective airborne assault forces, which many military planners were convinced would be vital in the event of future warfare. The training was being conducted at Fort Benning, near Columbus, Georgia, where thousands of U.S. paratroopers later went to jump school.

When they got to the flight line on the day of his fourth jump, the wind was high and they delayed takeoff for it to die down a bit, but finally the non-com instructor said to his Captain, "What the hell, sir; if this concept is gonna work worth a damn in combat conditions, we better train that way. I say let's go do it." His young C.O. hesitated a moment, then nodded his head and gave the signal to board the aircraft.

The wind aloft wasn't strong or steady, but it was gusting. Sergeant Macdonald was the sixth trooper of the stick out the door, and just after he plunged from the C-47 that morning, at the scheduled altitude of less than 1,200 feet, he and his chute were grabbed by a powerful gust that slammed him directly into high tension wires. It took an hour to get him down. He survived, but his right leg didn't—it was amputated that afternoon, just below the knee.

He could have retired. In fact, he was ordered to do so at one point, but after his many appeals through every channel he could find, he was allowed to stay in uniform, on the firm condition that he could serve only as an advisor in an R.O.T.C. or similar program.

That huge loss to the active duty army became the great good fortune of the boys of Fulton High. And today he had lots he wanted to discuss with these boys he was making into men.

"Excuse me interrupting, men," he said very quietly, "but I couldn't help but overhear you through my office window, and look—we all need to talk about this—but important decisions shouldn't be made in a rush—and not so as to put anybody on the spot unfairly; it's too important to do it that way. Now classes start in three minutes, and as I've always preached to you, your first mission here today, and every other day as long as you stay a student here, is to be a *good* student. I'd like to suggest we plan a meeting for tomorrow afternoon right *after* classes for all who want to attend; then everybody will have a chance to have their say, after all of us have thought about it some more. In the meantime, think about whether you should discuss some of your ideas with your parents tonight, and let's talk it out tomorrow afternoon, O.K.?

"Now, let's get to class—that's your mission right now, so be a good soldier and don't fail it."

The boys left for class.

# Chapter Three

It was quiet in the Johnson home that night, much quieter than usual.

Despite Sergeant Mac's counsel—they almost always called him *Sergeant Mac*—the neighborhood boys' grapevine had been buzzing all afternoon, and Will was the name most often mentioned. All the boys figured Will meant what he said that morning, and they were choosing sides on who would go with him. And one of the mothers had called Mama.

Normally, when the family sat down to dinner—all at once, as was their custom—the room was alive with chatter. But this night not a murmur was heard from Mama, the twins, their Dad, or three older sisters,—until the blessing by Dad and after several seemingly endless and stony-quiet minutes following his "Amen." Finally there was a sound from the end of the table, and one rarely heard in this home. Mama was sobbing.

Noah Johnson was a strong man in every way. He had not found life to be easy during most of his 57 years. Nor had he expected it to be so. He had been born to a farm life in deep south Georgia; and he had dearly loved that life, in spite of the dawn to dark work, the whims of weather, and all the other travails of those who tilled the land.

He had not gone far in school; for some reason never known to him— nor understood by him in later life—the adults who controlled those decisions in Noah's childhood just didn't think a farmer needed "book learning." But to all his children he constantly—and bluntly—pounded away at them on the absolute necessity for them to get an education if they wanted to "amount to anything in this world."

Noah's becoming something of a self-educated man commenced one day when he happened to visit the post office in the tiny south Georgia town of Sasser. As he liked to describe that chance meeting, "I went in the post office to order a case of *likker*, and saw the prettiest little girl I ever saw, standing behind the counter."

That beautiful young woman was Kathryn Brim—"Katie" to her friends and later to be "Mama" to her family. Kathyrn lived in town and had finished two years of college by the time she met Noah. They were soon wed, and she moved out to live in the farmhouse where she was to bear all of their five children without ever visiting a hospital.

Life on the farm took some adjustment for her. In later years, she often told the story about an event during the third week of their marriage, when she heard Noah calling to her from their front yard, saying he wanted to show her something. She walked onto the porch and saw him on horseback, with a huge smile on his face—and a huge kingsnake draped around one shoulder. She was hardly impressed by the *trophy* he thought he had brought to his bride; in fact she later said that was one moment when "I thought I had married a *barbarian!*" But she soon learned that whatever else Noah was, he was also a husband who would forever worship his wife.

In the 1920s most deep South farmers were still depending on cotton as their main—sometimes the only—money crop, and they lived or died each year with the success, or not, of King Cotton. Noah had been no exception. Yet he had always found ways to overcome the various and numerous enemies to cotton growing; that is, until the mid '20s when the boll weevil devastated cotton farmers across the vast fields of Georgia and the rest of the South. As Noah phrased it, "The boll weevil came and ate us out."

Suddenly he had found himself bankrupt, with a skill of no value outside a farm, but five small children and a wife to feed, clothe, and shelter. For the first time ever, he felt overwhelmed by despair. He had witnessed other farmers driven from the only life they had ever known, and he had seen their misery when forced into the life of a city wage-earner with no skills to sell.

But each challenge life had thrown at him heretofore had just seemed to make him stronger and more determined to never give up on himself or those he loved. As ever, within days, he sat with Mama and talked about the future and what to do to make it good. Mama reminded him that she had acquired skills beyond the home when she was a girl who had lived and been schooled in town so, if necessary, she could earn money too. The question was *how* and *where?* The *where* was easy—Atlanta was the only place where any jobs, to amount to anything, existed, in Georgia or the rest of the southeast in 1926.

So they went there, as Noah was prone to say later, "With five hungry kids, five dollars in my pocket, and five miserable years ahead of us."

Those first five years in the city truly had been the hardest of the 15. Noah had gotten a job driving a truck, and Mama did some office work near their rented house. They had taken that first house mainly because it had space out back for a garden.

They had brought the old truck with them from the farm, but it was in such bad shape, and gasoline cost so much, that Noah never drove it the seven miles to his job, except on those occasions when it was pouring rain. Instead, he would walk the three miles to the streetcar stop ("streetcars" were what Atlanta people called the old street railway cars). From there he would ride into town, work his truck for 12 hours, ride the streetcar back, and walk home from the stop—*six* days each week.

The first couple of years, there were nights when Noah, Mama and the kids would go out back and plant potatoes in the garden by the headlights of the old truck, since Noah seldom got home before dark. Things got a little better, but not a lot, after those first five years.

The worst part for Noah was that he never felt like a free man after leaving the farm, but always he kept that to himself, especially from Mama and their children. It was only much later in their lives that Bill and Will realized—and appreciated fully—what a sacrifice of self it had been for their father to forsake the life he loved for the sake of the family he loved even more.

Through all of that, and more, there was only one sound in his world that had ever made Noah Johnson want to cry; and he was hearing it at his dinner table on this night—his *wife* was sobbing.

All three of the girls rushed to Mama; but Mama was so choked up that all she could do was shake her head and keep crying.

Bill finally blurted out to his brother, "Why don't you say something Will? Why don't you tell them what's going on. Everybody else in this whole neighborhood knows about it, so why not *our* family too?" Will pretended, not too convincingly, that he didn't understand, and that really set Bill off. "Will, you *know* what's bothering Mama; you've been running off at the mouth all day about going out to be a big hero, and it's plain as day that Mama's heard about it. So, Mr. Hero, why don't you be *hero* enough to be honest with your own family?"

Noah decided it was time to stop this, because it was causing Mama even more tears, and calmly said, "That's enough of that, Bill. I know you mean well, but it won't help Mama any for you two to fuss with one another. She told me, before supper, a little bit of what's worrying her, but I planned for us to discuss it afterwards; but now that it's out we may as well do it now.

"I even heard rumors at the plant today, but I want to give Will a fair chance to tell us what this is all about, since he seems to be the gossip-topic of the day for all our neighbors. Will, you got the floor; tell us your side."

By then Will was pretty choked up himself. He adored his mother, and had already realized that he was indeed the cause of her tears. "Please, Mama, I'm sorry if I've caused you to feel that bad; it's really not that awful. I have to admit that I was talking to Gary Kelly and lots of other guys this afternoon, and about the war too—but is *that* why you're crying?" He muttered in a half whisper, "What did . . . "

His father stopped him in mid-sentence with a sudden change in tone. "Just hold on, Will! This is not for you to sit there and question your mother! It's for you to explain to us—your *entire* family—*here* and *now*—*without* any baloney—what you've been saying around the neighborhood today—*who* you said it to—and *why* you said it.

"Mama's not the only mother upset about this—almost every young boy's mom within a couple of miles of this house has tried to reach me or her since three o'clock today. And *they* knew lots more about what *our* boy was saying than either of us knew. So don't start trying to sweet-talk us; just get on with telling us—*exactly* and *completely*—everything about this afternoon."

"O.K., Dad; I understand. It all started this morning at school. Bill and me, and about 20 more guys, were out back of the school, before class, trying to talk about what we should do now that our country's in the war and all. Bill asked for ideas, so I had just started to have my say when Sergeant Mac butted in and told us all to get to class; it *was* time to go, so I didn't try to argue with him, but it did seem to me like what we were trying to decide is lots more important than missing a couple of classes for a day.

"I spent some time, the rest of the day at school, passing the word, for those who wanted to, to meet down at the park pavilion at 3:30 to go on with our discussion that the Sarge had stopped. When I got to the pavilion, Gary Kelly was the only one on time, but after a few minutes about eight or ten others showed. Everyone had something to say, but most were pretty wishy-washy, except for Gary. He feels like the country needs us bad and he's ready to go in now.

"The Army Air Corps is what he wants—to be a pilot—what the country needs most—and he said his brother Charley was downtown right then applying for pilot training. It takes about nine months of training—Gary said they call it being an 'Aviation Cadet.' Gary figures that if his brother can do it , then why can't *he?*

"That's the kind of thing we talked about. I guess some went straight home and worried their folks about it—and then the phones started ringing off the hook."

Bill had been squirming in his chair, waiting for a pause, "You're kind of shading things a little, aren't you little brother? 'Specially about Sergeant Mac."

But his Dad cut him off, "Easy, Bill; you can have your say, but not now. I want to ask something. Will, how old is Charley Kelly, and how old is Gary?"

After thinking a minute, Will said, "Er, I'm not sure about Charley—er, er, about 22 I think, but maybe not that old. Gary's 17, a few months older than me."

His Dad then asked, "What age you have to be to be an Aviation Cadet?" Bill interrupted, "I know—it's 18."

Noah then said, "There's a lot of difference between a 17-year-old-boy and a man 22, Will. Plus, how does Gary plan to get in when he's underaged?"

"Geez Dad, I don't know, but he swears he knows a way. You know his Mom passed away about a year ago, so maybe his Dad will help him—how do I know? But he says he knows a way. He didn't share all his life's secrets with me," Will answered with an impatient jerk of his head.

His Dad stared at him for a long moment that seemed an eternity to Will, finally saying: "Well why don't I give you a little clue. The *only* way his Dad—or anybody else—can '*help*' Gary with that, is by lying about his age—and probably having to lie under oath as well; and that's an oath before God Almighty! I'm sure *that* is his 'secret,' and I'm *just* as sure that you know that's what he has in mind. So what did you advise him. And what did *you* do and say during these conversations? Because all these phone calls today were not about Gary—they were about you."

Will took a deep breath, paused, and said, "O.K. Dad, Mama, I guess—no, I *know*—Bill's right. I have been doing too much talking. But Mama, I hope you—and *all* of you—can understand how I feel. I'm young, willing to go and do what's needed for my country—that you and Daddy always said is the greatest in the history of the whole world. And they need *young* men to fly, like the ones Bill and I saw at the Terminal Station this summer—the young English fellows who've been tryin' to keep Hitler away from their country—but they need help! I just want to do that for us—and I never wanted anything more in my life! Don't any of you understand that?"

"Yes, Will, I think I do understand," said his mother, "but you are still too young for that. If you weren't, the government would be making you register for the draft by this time, but you're not even old enough for that yet.

"I'm like any other mother; I shudder at the thought of a son of mine having to go fight in a war. But I know now that lots of our boys are going to have to do it, and when your time comes, I won't try to stop you. But right now you're too young and I *will* stop you, any way I can!

"And if you have any idea that your father or I will help you *lie* to go in, you may as well forget it. We wouldn't swear to a lie if our lives depended on it—so we certainly aren't going to do it to send you off to get shot at!"

"May I say something, Mama?" asked Bill. "This morning, Sergeant Mac urged us all to discuss this with our parents tonight, and I'm glad we're doing that. He's having a meeting after school tomorrow, and there's probably going to be a crowd there. I think Will and I should go, out of respect for him if nothing else. Do either of you have any objection to our going?"

"Not at all, Bill," said his Dad; "If there is anyone around who knows what he's talking about regards the military, it's Sergeant Macdonald. I think both of you should go; and I hope to Heaven that *all* the kids will heed his advice.

"And listen to me, please, Will; we're not trying to hurt you, son; in fact, I'm very proud of you for your attitude on this. But I think your mother put it as well as it can be said; so please think about what she just said, and take it to heart, son. Now, if anybody's still hungry, let's try to eat."

Will—now near tears himself—got up and started out of the room. His father shouted, "Will!" But Mama said, "No, Noah! Let him go for now."

They stayed at the table for a while, but no one felt like eating. The girls left without a word, while Bill and his parents just picked at their food.

Finally Mama spoke up again, "Bill, I'm sure you have some of the same feelings as your brother, but you handle things differently—you always have. I'm going to ask you to promise me two things; one, that you will not go off to this war, now or later, without at least discussing it with me and your father beforehand, and that you will do your best to get Will to do the same.

"I know you can't control the second—Will is headstrong, as we all have seen since he could crawl, but promise me you will do your best with him. Can you promise me those two things?"

Bill walked around the table and hugged his mother. "Of course I'll promise you, Mama, and I'll keep those promises too—I would have done both that you asked anyhow, even if you hadn't asked. With all you and Daddy have done for us, we sure owe you both a lot more than that.

"And listen; tomorrow, Will's going with me to that meeting with Sergeant Mac if I have to drag him. Sometimes he won't admit it, but Will respects the Sarge, like everybody else at school. I think he'll listen tomorrow.

"But I've gotta say this to both of you, 'cause I wanna be totally honest with you. I feel the same as Will in one way; at some time *soon*,—we—*me* as well as Will—have *got* to go do our share, now that the country has been pulled into this war. We'd be betraying everything about *duty* that you ever taught us if we didn't feel that way."

"We know that son" his Dad said, "and I guess I'd wonder— deep-down—about *any* young man in this country who didn't feel that way tonight; but when it's your own blood it's hard to accept it easily.

"Now this talk has been tough on all of us, and we're worn out by all this, so why don't we just sleep on it for now?"

# Chapter Four

At school the next morning there was a notice from Sergeant Macdonald, on all bulletin boards, that he had reserved the school gym for the meeting at 3:30, 15 minutes after the end of the last class, and that all Fulton students over 16 years old were welcome to attend.

The sergeant had spent most of the previous afternoon and evening on the telephone with his network of former barracks-mates who were still on active duty with the army and who had also worked during the last year or so in recruiting at different locations throughout the U.S. The basketball coach had canceled the team's practice session for the day and released the entire gym for Sergeant Mac's meeting, since most of his basketball kids had told the coach they wanted to go to the meeting anyhow. The sergeant had checked on the minimum age for all the services, as well as any educational requirements for several special categories.

He felt he was ready to meet with his "men."

At 3:18 the first boys entered the gym, and by the time Sergeant Mac came in at 3:25, it was already standing room only; five minutes later it was packed.

As he scanned the crowd, he realized that a goodly number of the crowd were girls—which he hadn't anticipated—and that many of the boys were first-year high-schoolers and no more than 13 years old. So he addressed the young kids first, "First, I want to thank each and every one of you for coming to this meeting, but it really was intended only for those who are 17 years or older; obviously we have a number here who are not that old. I'm not going to run you out, but I am going to tell you that you can only observe and listen during the meeting, but not participate otherwise, because one of the main purposes for this is to hear from those who are, or soon will be, of age to serve in one of the military services. Those are the army, navy, or marine corps, or—for the young women—the recently-formed Women's Army Corps.

"Now, the second thing I want to emphasize to all of you is this: I am *not* asking, suggesting, or encouraging any student of this school to leave school before you graduate in order to enlist in any branch of the military; just the *opposite* is the case.

"Yesterday, this place was alive all day long with rumors—and I happen to know first-hand that some of it was *more* than mere rumor—about some of the men saying they were going to quit school to join up. One of my purposes today is to do my best to show everybody here why that's not in the interest of you *or* your country.

"I double-checked the age requirements yesterday afternoon and last night by talking to three of my sergeant friends who have been in recruiting at least a year. The minimum age for enlistees in the navy, including the marine corps, is 17, but for active duty in the army it's 18; and for the WACS it's also 18.

"So now, I guess we should start taking questions—and I hope you won't be shy about asking them; no one should feel shy about saying anything that's on your mind—and we're gonna have only one rule here today—but it is iron-clad: *nobody* is gonna make *fun* of anything anyone else says. If any person breaks that rule, he or she is gonna be long-gone from the rest of our meeting! Understood? Who has the first question?"

Will and his friend Gary Kelly had come early to the gym for seats on the front row. Gary asked the first question, with more than a little arrogance in his tone, "I notice you didn't mention an age for the air force; why not?" The Sergeant half-smiled and answered, "Well, because we don't have a separate service that is an 'air force'; what we have is an 'Air Corps' as a *part* of the army, like the marine corps is a *part* of the navy; then the navy also has it's air arm, but I don't know the exact name it goes under. So the age minimum for all parts of the army is the same, and that goes for the navy as well. Is that clear?"

Gary felt a little foolish, and said, quietly, "Yes; thank you sir."

Now Will's hand was in the air, "I got a question, Sergeant Mac. Why do you say it's not in the country's interest for us to go in now?" He paused a minute and then answered , "A good question—let me answer it this way, Will; last night, I talked to three different master sergeants I had served with before I hurt my leg—all of them now in recruiting , one at Seattle, another in upstate New York, and the last in Birmingham. Each told me the exact same thing; they have been absolutely over-run with volunteers since about 4:00 Sunday, and yesterday they got wires from D.C. that it was the same at every single recruiting center in the entire country. So the fact is that they are strongly urging young men like you, who are still in high school and mostly no more than 18, to *not* come in right now. They just don't have the facilities or the training cadres—at least at this time—to *train* the people they are already getting. Their advice that they asked me to pass on to you is just this: 'Cool it for now; it's gonna be a long war, and we're gonna need you, and need you *bad,* but later, not now.'

"Also, they said they need you to stay in school and work on improving your knowledge and skills, so you can be more ready to become more than just a 'grunt' when you do come in. We're gonna have plenty of grunts coming in, by way of the draft if nothing else. And don't get me wrong— grunts are necessary and important fightin' men in an army—but I hope you Fulton men can be learned enough to fill other jobs that all our services are going to badly need in order to win this war.

"There's another thing they mentioned after I had told them of the wide interest here in flying, something I didn't know before; the Air Corps has been requiring two years of college for anyone applying for the Aviation Cadet program. While there's a rumor that—after what happened on Sunday at Pearl Harbor—this is gonna change, nobody knows if or when that'll happen. Even if it does change, it's pretty certain that anyone applying to be a cadet is going to have to pass a stiff test that requires some good schooling beforehand. These are some of the reasons, Will, that I said all of you will be serving your country better by staying in school for now.

"Believe me—we're gonna need you later, but we'd ruther have you when you've got more to offer from your *head* rather than your *back.* Next question?"

"Why do they require *any* college?" came a voice from the top row, "My cousin—who lives up in Toronto—wrote me that they don't require that in Canada or in the RAF." The Sergeant thought for a second, then replied,"I'm not sure *why* we do, but I am sure *that* we do, as of now. Maybe it's because all our pilots, navigators and Bombardiers are required also to be commissioned officers. While in the RCAF and the RAF they have what are called 'Flight Sergeants.' There might be other reasons, but the fact is that—right or wrong—this *is* a requirement and we—neither you or me—is gonna change that. I'm a soldier, folks; all soldiers don't write the regs, but all good soldiers do *obey* them."

"Sergeant Mac," said a hesitant voice, "what if you don't want to fly? I hate to admit it—and I hope nobody laughs at this—but I'm just plain scared of heights." The sergeant instantly panned the room with his laser-like blue eyes to make sure there was no sign of laughter before he answered—and there was none. "First of all, there's nothing wrong with your being fearful of heights—some of the bravest men I've ever known had the same feeling. In fact, I hope every man and woman here today will forget any ideas you ever had that being scared—about *anything*—is a weakness.

I've been plenty scared—and *plenty* of times—and I think every person with a brain has that feeling when in danger.

"But you can forget any concern that you would be required to be a member of a flight crew or to be a paratrooper. Those are purely for those who volunteer to be such. Now I can't guarantee you that you would *never* be transported somewhere by air, whatever your regular job might become, but—so far, at least—ridin' an aircraft as a main job is only for volunteers. Next question! "

"A while ago you were talking about the *ages* for going into the military," said one of the older girls. "One of my brothers is just 16. He's not here today, but he's already asking Mom and Dad to give their O.K. to his signing up for the navy; can he go in that young if they consent? He's going to kill me for bringing this next up, but I'm going to do it, anyhow, 'cause I'm worried sick about it—-he wants to lie about his age if he has to, and for my folks to back him up on it. How does that work?"

The sergeant scratched his head for a moment, then said, "Well, I guess if people want to lie, and are good enough at it, they may get away with it. But I can tell you this: Nobody 16 years old is going into any of our services—legally—no matter what they or their parents say or sign. I'm not sure what proof of age is required, but I believe that any volunteer under 21 not only must show some proof of age, but also must have the written consent of his or her parent or guardian."

The meeting went on for a couple of more hours, with Sergeant Macdonald fielding more questions than he had ever dreamed he would have to handle in one day, but he was pleased—and very, very proud of—the interest shown by the youngsters, and especially of the manner in which they had behaved themselves that afternoon. He went home that night reassured by a wonderful feeling that the youth of America was equal to the greatest challenge in the history of their country.

It had been dark and wet outside when the meeting broke up. Bill looked around the room for his brother, but he had disappeared. Probably at the streetcar stop, thought Bill. He was wrong.

Will and Gary had slipped out quietly, just before the meeting ended, and were at the Stop just in time to catch the No. 5 streetcar to Lakewood as it was coming south down Washington Street. They felt lucky that they were the only students on board, so they could talk privately.

After settling in their seats on the half-full trolley, Will turned to his friend and asked, "What did you think of the meeting, Gary? Has it changed your mind?" Gary didn't hesitate, "Not a whit, Will; I know Sergeant Mac means well, and he's a good guy—I respect him, that's why I stayed so long—but *really*—what does he know about this situation any more than lots of others? Sure, he's been in the Army a long time, and I know he was in combat in the first World War and all that—but that was 20 or more years ago! Things have changed a lot since then; the whole world has changed since then.

"I decided, two days ago, what I'm gonna do, and nothing he said has changed my mind—what about you?"

Will hesitated just slightly, then, "I feel the same as you, but my family looks at this differently from yours. My dad and mom have made it plain not only that they won't help me lie about my age, but Mama said flat-out to me that she's going to do everything she can to stop me from going in under-aged; she means it too, and there's no way Daddy's going to go against Mama in this."

Gary looked long and hard at his friend before responding to that, "Will, I don't want to cause trouble between you and your folks—but you can do this *without* their help if you want to do that.

"My brother and old man know a guy in Atlanta who says he can fix all the paperwork in about one hour, and it can all be kept graveyard quiet 'til you're on the train to Pre-Flight School. They've already talked to him about me. It's a snap—or so I'm told."

"Oh yeah," said Will, " but what does something like that cost? I'm pretty sure this guy's not doing it just for fun. I don't have any real money—and there's no way any of my family's going to help me on something like this."

Gary shrugged, "Who knows? But it shouldn't cost to find out. My old man knows this guy well—says he's a 'reformed counterfeiter'—whatever that's supposed to mean; if you want, I'll ask Pop to check it out for you."

Will shrugged too, "O.K., but tell your dad—*and* his friend—to keep my name out of this for now; if my father hears of this too soon, he may beat the hell out of somebody—not only me, but your Dad and his pal too. My Dad sometimes has a temper you wouldn't believe—'specially when you mess with his kids. Worse, he'll torpedo the whole thing if he hears about it too soon."

"How could he do that Will—I mean, just kill the deal?"

"It's plain to see that you don't know my dad" Will sort of half-smiled, "Simple—he'll go straight to the Air Corps people with it without battin' an eye. Like I said, Mama has already made it plain she'd stop me any way she can from my goin' in underaged; and my dad would back her up a hundred percent—no doubt about that."

"I think the old man's home, Will—he's been kinda sick a lot lately—why don't you stop by our house and let's talk to him?"

Will looked at his watch, "Well it's early; I can stop for a few minutes, but I've got to think long and hard about this; if I do what we're both thinking of, it's no telling what it will do to me and my family. You know what I mean?"

"I think so," murmured Gary, "but my situation's not the same. Since Mom died, Dad doesn't seem to care about much—doesn't work hardly any—drinks a lot more than before—just sits around the house most of the time. I don't think it makes any difference to him what Charley and I do—about the Air Corps or anything else."

Harry Kelley had been a master carpenter as a young man, one of the best craftsmen in the state of Georgia. Many homeowners in the wealthy parts of Atlanta regarded him as a true artisan, and much more than a mere carpenter. Harry had been very successful—financially and otherwise—until about his fortieth birthday. It had been that day, 18 years prior, when he announced at his birthday dinner that he had decided to go to night law school to become a lawyer—a longtime and burning ambition that he had kept to himself until that evening.

He enrolled two days later and for the next three years he toiled each day at his trade, then—three nights each week—he cleaned up after work and trudged off to the law school, often staying in the school law library until well past midnight.

He failed the Bar exam the first two times, but finally got by on his third attempt. He sold his business, for income for the first year or two—he realized he would not get many fees for awhile—and opened a store-front office down near the Fulton County courthouse.

Harry truly loved being a lawyer, and there were some of his contemporaries who would tell you he was a pretty good one—but he never could make a decent living at it. He had no connections to get good-paying law business, so about the only cases he got were for semi-indigent defendants in criminal cases; or parties to divorce actions, where lack of money had been a major reason for the breakup to start with—meaning that there was rarely any money left to pay a lawyer. In order to make a semblance of an income, he had to scrounge so many similar cases that he couldn't prepare and try them with anything approaching professional competence. One of his former customers—an extremely successful and wealthy Atlanta trial lawyer—said of Harry, to another lawyer- friend: "What a tragedy—to see such a magnificent *artist* hell-bent to turn himself into an absolutely *incompetent* lawyer!"

After several years, this took a severe toll on Gary's father. He started drinking, not only a lot, but at the wrong times. He missed court calendar calls, didn't return clients' calls, co-mingled clients' money with his own—at times "borrowing" from it. Finally, after being officially and severely reprimanded by the Bar Ethics Committee—and filing for bankruptcy—he quit trying to practice law and re-opened his carpentry shop with financial help from his younger brothers.

But it was never the same for Harry. It was almost like he had left his ambition and pride in the burning ashes of his failed effort to be a lawyer. Things got worse—much worse—and it had all culminated with losing his wife to cancer the year before. After that he didn't seem to care about much except his two sons, and he realized he wasn't much of a father to them anymore. That's why he had not discouraged his oldest from going into the Air Corps right away, and hadn't put up much of an argument with young Gary when he had asked for help in going in under age.

As usual, Harry was already half in his cups when Gary and Will got to his home on this dreary winter evening. He told them that it was pretty simple to get the necessary papers done for what they wanted, and that he would sure be pleased if Gary had a friend with him in the flying program.

When Will pointed out he had no money, Harry laughed and said that the guy whom he would get to fake the birth certificates and parental consent papers owed him so much dough for unpaid legal fees that "even a s.o.b. like that crook" wouldn't have the gall to charge him for what the boys wanted done. The only thing Harry asked was that Will swear he would never tell anyone, especially Will's family, that Harry had been involved in this. Will swore to that, asked Harry what information he needed, jotted it down , and left, promising to get what was needed and be back one week later.

# *Chapter Five*

Bill was waiting, and watching from the front window as his brother walked up the driveway. He sensed that Will had been up to something—probably nothing good, he suspected—by leaving the gym without a word to him. He wanted to see his brother before their Dad got home.

Before the front door had closed Will heard, "Where you been, Will? I looked for you after the meeting, but you'd disappeared."

"What's this? Have you been waiting to ambush me?"

"No—but I am anxious to know what you think about what Sgt. Mac said today, and you didn't give me much chance—make that *any* chance—to see you after the meeting. Why the disappearing act?"

"Hey—I left with Gary; he is my best friend, remember? We wanted to talk—that's all. You got any more cross-examination you want to do?"

"Yeah, I know he's your 'best friend'—or so you think. But I'm your *brother,* remember *that*—as well as your friend! You and 'your best friend' are scheming about something, and it doesn't take an Einstein to guess what it is!"

"First of all, Mr. Big, it's none of your business what we were discussing; I don't have to tell you everything I do."

"Right you are, Will, but I've got a hunch you and your so-called friend are talking something our parents are dead against; and that *is* some of *their* business—and when you're doing something that's going to cause them misery, that makes it some of mine too, whether you like it or not ! So why don't you just stop playing games and be honest for a change?"

"O.K.—O.K.—Gary and I left right after the meeting and talked about it on the streetcar coming home; then I went by his house and we talked more—we yakked a lot, but decided nothing. I think he knows what he's going to do, and apparently that's alright with his Dad, but I told him about the feelings of my folks being different, so I don't know what to do—and I told him that too.

"Bill, I don't want to go against Mama and Dad, but I really want to fly, more than I ever in my life wanted to do anything. I'm pretty screwed up on this right now—so give me a break and let me think it out—O.K.?"

"I'm not trying to give you a hard time, Will, but I've always been honest with you—and I'm not gonna change on this. Mama is worried sick about this, and I've promised her I'd do what I can to talk you out of jumping the traces and lying about your age and all. Yeah, I'll leave it alone for a while—but there's no way I'm going to leave it alone for good. I hope you can understand, 'cause that's how it's gonna be.

"And I hope you'll just think about something else—and this is all I'm gonna say right now: You're fighting a losing battle, because even if you manage to get *in* the Air Corps, it won't be for long. You know Dad—he's not gonna let you defy him and Mama like that, and get by with it. He'll have you *out* in no time, and that's just gonna embarrass you. Why cause *yourself*—not to speak of our parents—all that misery for nothing? Just think about it Will—and that's all I'm gonna say tonight—but I hope you will think about *that,* if nothing else. Good night—see you later."

☆      ☆      ☆

About an hour later Noah Johnson pulled in the driveway, and came in the kitchen door of the Johnson home, kissed the cheek of his wife, who was at the stove, sat down, and asked, "What did Sgt. Mac say to the kids this morning?"

She looked at him, "I don't know, Noah; Bill got home an hour or so before Will, and I heard them talking out front—sort of loud, as if arguing—but about what, I don't know. The truth is I'm afraid to ask, Noah." She was silent for a moment and he saw tears slowly rolling down her cheeks again, but she finally managed to get out, "I don't think I've ever been so worried, Noah. You know how bull-headed Will can be, and I just know he's planning to try to go in the Army, no matter what we say, and—*my God,* Noah—he's just a *child!* What *are* we going to do?"

"Well honey, let's try not to jump to any conclusions until we have a real reason for it. As soon as supper is over I'd like to sit down with the boys and hear what happened at Sarge's meeting this afternoon. Maybe he talked some sense into all of the kids.

"By the way Katie, I know it's not a whole lot of help, but we're not the only parents going through this. Today, at the plant, at least a dozen other drivers told me they're having the same kind of talk from their sons. They want to help out in this fight, and as much as all of us parents worry about the dangers, you still have to be proud of these boys for being ready—even raring, like most of them seem to be—to risk themselves for their country. If our sons were 20 or more years old, I couldn't make myself argue against them going to the military. It's terrible, I know, but our young men must step up if we're gonna survive this war. I just want ours to wait 'til they are *men,* not *boys.*"

It was another silent meal at dinner. The girls were at choir practice, and the boys were unusually quiet again this night. After the apple cobbler was finished, Noah broke the silence: "Fellows, as you might figure, Mama and I are anxious to hear about Sgt. Mac's meeting. Who wants to start ?"

Bill looked at his twin, waiting to see if he was going to speak up. When he didn't, Bill outlined what had happened at the meeting, emphasizing that Sgt. Macdonald had urged all the boys to stay and finish their schooling, and why he thought they should. Noah thanked him and asked both simply: "Do you two agree with what he recommended?"

"It made sense to me," Bill replied.

"O.K.—wonderful! And what about you, Will?" Mama half-whispered her question.

"Honest, Mama, I just don't know; I know how you—you *and* Dad—feel, but I just look at it a different way. But as long as both of you feel so strong on this, I'm not plannin' to buck you," he said, staring down at his plate.

Mama got up, went around the table and embraced her son, tears now streaming down her cheeks. "Thank God for that! I've been half-crazy over this. You're doing the right thing—not just for me, but for you too, son. Oh, thank the Lord for this! Maybe I can sleep tonight. Now let's stop talking about these sad things—let's enjoy our supper and be thankful tonight."

Will felt the steady, and accusing, stare of his brother—even before they made eye contact. The stare silently, but clearly, cried out: "Liar—Liar!"

Mama slept well that night, but not so for Will.

It was 10 days later when Gary told Will that his "papers" (birth certificate, parental consent, high school transcript and diploma) were finished and ready at the Kelly home, whenever Will wanted to pick his up. He also said he had learned that the Aviation Cadet recruiting office was now open at the "new" post office in downtown Atlanta every Saturday, and that they could file their papers on one Saturday and probably take their tests the next. Gary suggested that they do it together and at the same time. Will sort of winced and hesitated, but then said he would go in with Gary on Saturday.

When the two arrived at the recruiting office the anteroom was packed, even at 7:30 A.M. on a rainy Saturday in Atlanta. A young staff sergeant was checking the paperwork of the applicants, then passing them to one of several even younger lieutenants who were interviewing and administering tests. To the surprise of both Gary and Will, the sergeant made each produce a picture I.D. To their great relief, each had a school I.D. with picture, home address, and telephone number on it, but nothing regarding age.

During the interview, the officer explained succinctly the then-schedule for training in the Army Aviation Cadet Corps. To Will, he said:

"Mr. Johnson, listen very carefully to me. I want you to be absolutely certain about what you are about to undertake if you are accepted into the Corps of Aviation Cadets, where every man is a volunteer. This is an elite group and we do not *want* anyone who has the slightest hesitancy about complying completely with the many standards expected from a flying officer in our Air Corps. So listen very carefully to me:

"1.  First, no college is now required, as of the effective date of Army Regulation No. 86734 6, dated 14 December 1941; otherwise you would not be eligible.
"2.  If accepted, you will be required to take the admission oath immediately, and await call to active duty at any time thereafter, with no more than ten days advance notice assured.
"3.  Under the present timetables, you will go first to Pre-Flight School, most probably at Maxwell Field at Montgomery, Alabama. Assuming that you successfully complete your eight weeks there, you will be classified for further training as a Pilot, Navigator, or Bombardier.
"4.  After pre-flight, all pilot-trainees go first through Primary flight school, training, normally, in the Stearman PT-17, a single-engine, open-cockpit, bi-plane; then to Basic flight school for further single-engine training in a Vultee BT-13. After finishing Basic you would then be classified for Advanced flight school training in either single-engine—probably an AT-6 for single-engine—*or* in multi-engine aircraft, depending on several factors, including your body-size.
"5.  After successful completion of Advanced you would receive your commission as a Second Lieutenant along with your "wings" as a pilot in the U.S. Army Air Corps. From there you will be sent to transition for training in the aircraft you will be flying later in combat—-single-engine trained people go into fighters, and the others to bombers or transports

"6. If, in preflight, you are classified as a bombardier or as a navigator, you will first be trained as an aerial-gunner at one of our gunnery schools. The reason for this is that all of our navigators and bombardiers are required to double as gunners, either in a gun-turret or on a waist-gun, when they are not occupied with their primary duties.

"For example, in a B-24, one of our four-engine bombers, the bombardier must be fully qualified to operate the Emerson electrically-operated nose turret which is equipped with twin 50–calibre machine guns, since it is located in the nose of the aircraft, just above the spot for the Norden bomb-sight, his main work station. Both before and after the bomb-run itself, the Bombardier is inside the nose-turret in his role as a gunner.

"Both bombardier and navigator cadets will be training at the same gunnery-school. (As an aside, I am a bombardier, as you can tell from my wings—temporarily assigned to this desk job—*very* temporarily, I hope. If you should go through gunnery as a bombardier, you may have to put up with some wise-ass songs from the navigators (the 'book-worms,' we call them) about "coming in with a dead bombardier." That's because they usually fire the "pop-guns" from the relative safety of the *side* of the aircraft, while we do the hard stuff against a 'bandit' coming at us from 12 o'clock high at a 'rate of closure' of 500 to 600 m.p.h., if you add the speed of the bomber to the speed of the incoming fighter. O.K, excuse my little 'detour,' and now, back to your briefing.)

"7. After gunnery, the navigators go to navigation school and the bombardiers to bombardier school. The schools are at many separate locations, usually in the warmer climates of the country, like from Georgia to Texas where there is better flying weather for much of the year. In my case, I went through bombardier school at Big Spring in west Texas. On successfully finishing their last schools, all bombardiers and navigators are also commissioned as Second Lieutenants and receive their wings as flying officers. Most are soon then off to their combat assignments.

"8. After a total of about 10 to 12 months, including transition training, all graduates will be assigned either to combat units or, in some cases, to work as instructors.

"9 Last, but certainly not *least*, I want to apprise you of the honor code we have in the Aviation Cadet Corps. It is extremely important to us, and it is expected that each and every member of the corps will, at all times, honor both the spirit as well as the letter of the code. A violation of the code is a mandatory cause for immediate dismissal from the corps, regardless of any other skills one may have. Violations include, but are not limited to, false statements of any kind, which may be reasonably construed to relate to your status as a member of the corps, as well as any other acts of dishonesty or deceit of virtually any nature.

"If you have any reason that you cannot see fit to observe this vital part of our program, it would be in your best interests, as well as in our best interests, for you not to proceed further with your application for admission. The reason I make this admittedly strong statement is that when a cadet is "drummed out" of the corps for a violation of the honor code, it is carried out publicly in the presence of his fellow cadets and his name is never thereafter mentioned in the corps. In short, it is a disgraceful experience for the individual involved and one which no one would want on their record.

"O.K., I must also inform you of what typically happens when a cadet is "washed out" of the training program (a term we use for elimination from the program for failure to meet our requirements for a reason *other than* a violation of the honor code). If you had already been trained as a gunner, you would be offered an opportunity to continue serving as a part of an air crew in that capacity. Most aerial-gunners are non-commissioned officers, ranging from a "buck" sergeant (a '3–striper') to a tech or master sergeant. The master sergeants usually are also trained in aircraft maintenance and double as the Top-Turret Gunner, as well as the Crew Chief on the heavy bombers. Likewise, the Radio Operator/Gunner is usually a staff sergeant (a '4-striper)

"Only volunteers are used as gunners. If you didn't wish to be a gunner, then the army would re-assign you, either to a ground job within the air corps, or to another part of the army; understand that could be *anywhere* in the army, with the exception of other purely volunteer units, such as the airborne units.

"O.K., Mr Johnson, that's it. Do you have any questions?"

Will had listened intently, mesmerized by most of the briefing by this articulate and "gung-ho" young officer. He quickly said, "No sir—no questions."

The interviews lasted exactly 15 minutes, then Will and his friend were fingerprinted and told to report for testing and a physical at 7:00 A.M. the following Saturday. They left in a mood that could only be described as "gleeful." But the following week was both the longest and the most frustrating of their young lives—longest, because they wanted so badly for Saturday to come before it's time and frustrating because they couldn't share with anyone their delight about what they viewed as a great adventure.

But Saturday did arrive finally, and all went well for them; both aced their tests and then passed their physicals. Will was told that his depth perception was not great but was "acceptable." A First Lieutenant Marshall, wearing pilot's wings, administered the oath to them and six other youngsters, congratulated them, and instructed all that they would be notified regarding a date to report to active duty, reminding them that they might have no more than ten days notice.

The boys were gushing with self-congratulations for being so clever. They thought they had covered every corner.

And they *had*—almost.

Several long weeks went by with no news from the army. Then one Tuesday, around 11:00 A.M., Gary's father showed up at school with his son's Orders to report to active duty for preflight school at Maxwell Field, Alabama. The Orders had arrived in the morning mail, and Harry Kelly knew his son wanted to know.

Gary was ecstatic, and ran to find Will, who had just left him in the hallway.

The first reaction from Will was a mirror image of Gary's—but suddenly he felt as if he had been hit in the gut with a sledge hammer. He was trying to say something, but couldn't. Finally he managed to get out, "My God, Gary! Did they send those papers to your *home?*" When Gary nodded, Will fought hard not to throw up, and suddenly started pounding the wall with both fists, as passing students stared aghast.

"Damn, Gary! Don't you know what this means? I probably got one at my house, too. I've got to get out of here—now! I gotta try to find out before Mama checks the mail. If she has seen this, I'm dead meat when she tells my dad!"

"Hey look, pal—just 'cause I got this, it doesn't mean you did too, at least not today. Damn! It never dawned on me that they would get in touch with us by mail. We sure dropped the ball on this."

"Look, Gare, I've got to get home—and *now*—*right* now! Next period is military; cover for me. Tell Sgt. Mac I got sick and had to go home. Tell him anything. I think I'm gonna *puke.*"

When he arrived home, it got worse. His father's truck was already in the drive, and his parents were both standing in the front door. They had called the school and were waiting for him. Noah Johnson had one arm around his wife, and a large manila envelope in his other hand. Even from a distance he could tell that Mama had been crying again.

He braced himself for his father's anger.

# Chapter Six

Anger was not what Noah felt towards this man-child he had loved and nurtured for nearly two decades. Perhaps this was because—he later thought—he was also not truly surprised. In his heart of hearts he had expected something like this from this son who, since infancy, had always seemed driven to walk on the edge.

Because he had half-anticipated it, Noah had also tried to prepare Katie for this event. So now they spoke with one voice to their Will.

"All right, son, sit down; we'll not beat around the bush. Mama and I have already talked—and cried—about this. There's nothing to gain by talking all day about it. The cover letter on these 'orders' says that you have already been sworn into the Army Air Corps. And that can only mean that you have flat *lied* about your age, and done God knows what-all else deceitful to back up the lies to get sworn in.

"Here's what we're gonna do. Tomorrow morning—early—you and I are going to see this Lieutenant Marshall, so you can tell him the *truth,* and we'll get you 'unsworn.' I had half-expected some stunt like this, and asked my boss to have the company lawyer check into a few things. He did, and told me that if you got in the army fraudulently, and if we could show that, then any enlistment in that way would be what he called 'a nullity'and would have to be be canceled by the army."

"O.K., what can I say? But why do I have to go with you, Dad? I'll look like a fool if I do that."

"Now listen to me, Will—and listen *good;* it's not a matter of *if.* You're goin' in with me—feet-first or head-first—but you're goin! I'm tryin' hard not to lose my temper with you, so it's best you don't push me. You want to play being a man? Why not actually be one? You're going to be one in this. You're going in, and you're gonna look that officer straight in the eye, and you're gonna tell him that you *lied* ! You caused this, and *you're* gonna set it straight—like a real man would do. Understand? Now leave us, and be here at 6:30 in the morning."

His son nodded, and as he reached over to hug his mother goodnight, he noticed from the corner of his eye a sight he had never known before; his father was wiping a tear from his own face. Will suddenly felt a sense of shame that was also a new experience for him.

But by the time he fell asleep, he was back to thinking hard about how to overcome this latest obstacle to chasing his dream.

$$\star \qquad \star \qquad \star$$

They were waiting at the door of the Army Recruiting office when it opened at 7:30, but Lt. Marshall was late.

Noah told the sergeant they would wait for "whoever signed this paper," while waving the cover letter under the non-com's nose. The sergeant could tell quickly that there was no point in arguing with this irate father of the red-faced youngster whom he recognized from a few weeks back. As soon as Lt. Marshall arrived, his sergeant closed the door to the small private office for a short time before the officer came out, shook hands with Will, and introduced himself to Noah, before inviting both into his office.

Noah passed the orders and cover letter across the desk and spoke first, "Lieutenant, I'm Will's father, and my son has something he wants to say to you. Will?"

Will spoke up, but very softly. He said he had lied about his age, as well as having filed a falsified birth certificate and parental consent form. He said he was sorry—not too convincingly.

The lieutenant said he too was sorry, but that the only recourse was revocation of the orders and official nullification of the enlistment. He said he had the authority to revoke the orders and that such would be effected that day, but that the nullification of enlistment would come from higher headquarters, although it was only a matter of time and a formality. He asked both Will and his father if they had any questions.

Will again stumbled through an apology of sorts, and said that he would try again when he reached age 18, if his parents would consent.

Before Noah could respond, the lieutenant addressed Will, somewhat bluntly, "This is not quite that simple, Mr. Johnson. I assume that you recall having the Cadet Honor Code explained during the recruitment process. That isn't merely 'lip service' by us, Mr. Johnson; we are dead serious about our honor system.

"If someone had done what you did, while an aviation cadet, there is no doubt but that they would have been 'drummed out' of the corps forthwith. I intend to request that the question of your future eligibility for enlistment as a cadet be considered at the appropriate level of command, and in the light of your past misconduct. If my request is granted, I will inform you of the resulting decision and/or recommendation, if any. Please understand—we are being deluged daily with applications from the cream of American youth. We have much more important things to do than waste time dealing with lies and deceit.

"In short, we expect more—*a great deal more*—of our aviation cadets, than is expected of most young men.

"Thank you, gentlemen, and please excuse me now."

Will was so shaken by the officer's closing comments, he didn't utter a word on the way home; not because he didn't want to do so—he was simply speechless. He had never dreamed that he might be disqualified for the reasons he had just heard.

Over and over, he asked himself: *Can this actually be true?*

Ten days later, he got his answer.

The letter came from: Headquarters, Recruitment, USAAC, Andrews Field, Washington, D.C. After reciting the background facts, it concluded by informing Will that: "You are advised that under current policies of the U.S. Army Air Corps, your misconduct, recited above, disqualifies you from future acceptance as an aviation cadet. While all policies of the army are subject to possible change because of exigencies of war, we do not anticipate a change in this policy, and you are advised to act accordingly."

At that moment, Will thought his devastation was complete. But 30 minutes later he was at the corner telephone booth, trying to reach Joe Hearn's sister, whom he had dated a few times. He knew she had stayed in close touch with her brother even after he had left to join the RCAF. Maybe she could help him in some way. Luck was with him; Polly was at home and sounded delighted to hear his voice again. "About time I heard from you again, Will Johnson. Where have you been the past year?" her voice smiled at him.

"I dunno, Polly, but I tried to call you a bunch of times; either your line was busy, or you were always gone somewhere," he fibbed. "Anyhow, we finally connected, so how about a movie tomorrow night—or better still, a walk in the Park tomorrow afternoon? We could talk and catch up that way."

"I vote for the park. We'd drive folks nuts gabbing away at the movie. Come by tomorrow at 4:00; I'll pack a couple of sandwiches—you bring some Cokes. But bring a jacket—it may be cool after dark."

"Sounds great, Pol. See you at four tomorrow."

As Will stepped from the booth, his brother spotted him from across the street. He crossed over and walked beside him for a block, then broke the silence, "Will, I've deliberately left you alone the last few weeks because I know how disappointed and down you've been about what's happened. But you're my brother, and I love you, Will. If there's anything I can do to help, I want to do it."

"Thanks—I believe you mean that, but there's nothing you or anyone can do. I screwed up big time, but I'll get over it. I'll work it out. Somehow, I'm gonna fly, Bill. If hell freezes over solid as a rock, I *am* gonna fly. And it's best—for us both—if I just leave it there. *Someday,* maybe you and the rest of our family will understand—this is something I just *have* to do, even if it hurts some people I love. Don't ask me any more about it, please!"

"Fine, my brother. Just don't do something you'll live to regret—and that's all *I'm* going to say."

They walked the rest of the way home without another word.

It was one of those late-winter/early-spring twilights you learn to love in Atlanta. A slight chill was in the air, flavored with a hint of spring—a perfect night for a young couple to stroll in a park, hand-in-hand. After what he figured was a proper interval, Will asked about Polly's brother Joe. She said she heard from him about every two months, though he had promised her to write more often; that his letters couldn't mention many things he did, since all were scrutinized by military censors. One had said that writing his girlfriend was like "dating in a fishbowl" since he knew "some #@$&###@@ censor" would "slobber" over every word of a really *great* love letter.

Will told Polly about trying to join a U.S. air unit, but only that they had said he was too young, and he wondered if the Canadians would consider him, like they had her brother Joe.

She said that she and her folks had received a visit of nearly a week from a friend of Joe, who had come home on emergency leave from England for his father's funeral in Lafayette, Louisiana. He had been one of the first American volunteers in one of the original Eagle Squadrons that had flown in combat as part of the RAF and RCAF since early on in the war.

She recalled his telling her dad during his visit that, although the official Canadian policy since Pearl Harbor was that they no longer accepted American volunteers, the fact was that they still desperately needed new trainees. It seemed they were sort of "looking the other way," given the slightest excuse. She also recalled—vaguely—his discussing an independent group, a mixture of maverick and secretive French Canadians and Free-French from North Africa, who were operating what he said many *Québécois* called *un métro français-canadien* (a French-Canadian underground). They were using as their front an all-night bistro/auberge in the Lower Town of old Quebec City.

He said that rumor had it that they were smuggling in volunteers from not only the United States, but other countries as well, for all sorts of schemes, all of which were in support of military or para-military actions against the Germans.

Will's heart skipped a beat at this and, trying to stay calm, he asked if the flyer had mentioned a way to contact that group. Polly replied that she hadn't heard of that, but she remembered that her father had been fascinated by the rumors of their clandestine activities, and that perhaps he had some more information. She said she could find out but, at Will's request, she promised not to mention his name to her father. Polly told him she would call if she learned more.

After he walked her to her door, and they had gently kissed goodnight, he walked on air the entire half-mile home. Feeling just a slight twinge of conscience at having used this truly delightful girl and friend, he promised himself that he would somehow repay her some day.

After a couple of weeks without hearing from her, Will was concerned and ready to give up on Polly as a source of information on the Quebec group. Then on a Saturday morning, he heard the telephone ring. Bill answered, "Oh, hi, Polly, how are you? Yeah, he's here somewhere; I'll find him." Then, loudly, "Will, get the phone—It's Polly Hearn for you!"

Will stumbled and almost fell rushing to grab the phone. "Oh Boy, I never saw you so excited, little brother! May I listen?" quipped his sibling. He got nothing but a glare for his answer.

Bill flopped in a chair about six feet away—grinning big. His twin whispered to Polly, "I'm glad you called, but can I call you right back? We need some privacy—do you understand? Can I call you in five minutes? Are you at home?"

She hesitated—then, "Sure, Will; I may have some good news for you. And maybe you can also tell me what's going on there; I'll wait."

As he bolted from the house and approached the telephone booth, he spotted someone in the booth, so he sprinted past it and ran on straight to the Hearn home; Polly saw him through the parlor window and had the door open when he hit the front stoop.

"Why all the mystery, Will? I never have seen you like this before."

"Look, Polly, my brother means well, but he has a big mouth sometimes. I don't want him—or anybody else—to know about what we've been discussing. Please promise me you'll keep this just between us."

"No problem. Actually I don't have much, but maybe it will help. My dad dug out this address our friend gave him—along with one name, a *Monsieur Jean-Paul Le Blanc.*" She handed a slip of paper to him. "Dad said he had written twice to this Mr. LeBlanc at that address, but never received any reply.

"Oh, Dad also said that our friend told him that these people in the Quebec group are extremely secretive about everything; that even his girlfriend, who apparently is part of the same group, won't tell him exactly what they do. So, Will, *please* be careful in whatever you are thinking of doing with them. I want that promise from you!"

Will was staring at the address in Quebec, but talking to her, "Sure, Pol—O.K. I really appreciate this. Excuse me now—I've gotta go. Thanks again, Polly. call ya tomorrow. Bye now." He was beside himself, and couldn't wait to get alone so he could think about his next step.

On his way home he caught the streetcar up to the small branch library, and asked if they had a map of Canada—also, if they had a map of Quebec City. He studied the maps, made some notes, thanked the teenaged girl at the desk, then stopped by the Greyhound Bus Station and asked for a bus schedule with Canadian destinations.

Meanwhile, Polly was deep in thought, agonizing over whether she should have made that promise to him.

### Québec City, in the Lower Town

Two nights later, Jean-Paul LeBlanc was upset. To describe him as *upset* about the conversation he had just had at dinner with his RCAF contact, Nigel Sturgell, was to seriously understate his Latin furor. Sturgell had called late in the afternoon to inform LeBlanc, "I must meet with you this evening, without fail. I have urgent directives that we must discuss."

Jean-Paul had never cared for this stiff-necked young anglophone—all of whom LeBlanc detested. But "*this fool,*" thought LeBlanc, not only didn't speak French but, worse, did not *know* a word of it; yet he thought,

"He is my only liaison I have, at this moment, with the air forces of Canada. And for that reason—and only for that reason—he is a person I am required to tolerate—even if my preference is to strangle him."

At dinner in the bistro, behind which Jean-Paul and his colleagues did most of their deeds, Sturgell had told him curtly that the Canadian government, and specifically the RCAF, was now ordering that Jean-Paul cease and desist from any and all of future activities in support of any Communist elements of the French resistance in France proper. And that, if he refused, the RCAF would neither continue to provide him it's secret, but substantial, financial support, nor would it accept any more volunteers via his group.

"*Mon Dieu,*" Leblanc had snorted, "do those imbeciles in Ottawa realize what a great disaster it will mean to abandon all *résistance* units who have communist members? You—or *someone*—must tell those fools that this would mean that aid would be terminated to all units who are indeed *seriously* killing Germans simply because all—each one—of the serious units have within their midst *some* communists. This is true since 22 June, last year, when the pig, Hitler, turned on and attacked their Russian 'friends.'

"Monsieur Sturgell, I too detest well the communists, as you must surely know, but I support their resistance units for the same reason that Canada now supports the Russians—because we NEED them to assist us to destroy Hitler! In many of the *maquis* units, perhaps in most, they are the only fighters with true combat experience—experience which they had gained during the Spanish *guerre civile.* After the swine Hitler is finished— but not before—*then* is when we must deal with *les rouges, au Canada,* in the States, *en France,* and—most probably—around this world entire!"

Sturgell had calmly continued puffing on his pipe, and had never changed expression during the tirade. At the first pause for breath taken by Jean-Paul, he responded quietly, "I sympathize, a bit, with your position, Le Blanc; but these are my orders, and I have no choice but to inform you as I have done.

"This policy is mandated from the very highest political levels of the Commonwealth, and *must* be adhered to, sir. Bear in mind that all financial support from the Canadian federal government may be terminated— *instanter*—if we find that you are continuing support, of any nature, to these chaps.

"And, by the way, if you are contemplating the seeking of subsistence in the form of provincial funds from any of your *Quebecois* friends, forget it *now.* Under the war emergency powers granted to the federal government, that too can be decreed unlawful—and no doubt shall be—if we should learn that you are seeking such aid. Is that clearly understood?"

*"Ah oui, Monsieur Sturgell,* I do understand and very well, but that does not mean that I also agree, and I am curious to learn if our new comrades-in-arms, *les américains,* are in agreement with your *imbéciles* in Ottawa. I shall be most surprised if they are equally foolish! *Merci et au revoir, Monsieur!"*

The door of the bistro had not fully closed behind the Canadian counter-intelligence agent, before Jean-Paul was dialing his colleague Angieline, a 21-year-old French-American.

Her attorney-father, Louis Hebert, had just closed down his lucrative law practice in Baton Rouge and moved to Washington, D.C., not because he wanted to, but because he had been requested to do it by his old law school classmate at Columbia, General William J. Donovan, the designated head of the newly formed Office of Strategic Services (OSS). His old and closest friend during his law school years, who was called "Wild Bill" by those really close to him, had told Louis that he badly needed some very able people whom he could trust beyond question if the wartime mission of OSS was to be fulfilled.

It was a request that Louis could not refuse, especially since his "baby girl" had already been "up to her sweet little neck, for about a year now, in 'some kind of spy business' up in Quebec," as Louis had described it to his new boss during their limo ride in from Washington National airport on the night Louis arrived.

Jean-Paul was pleased to find Angie at home. He said—in rapid-fire French—that it was important they talk, no later than the next day. They agreed to breakfast at 7:00 the next morning, away from the bistro at a tiny cafe close by, but not on, the *Grande-Allée.* Angieline was curious about the reason, but Jean-Paul said it was best to explain tomorrow and abruptly bid her, *"Bonsoir Angie, et merci."*

In Atlanta, Will was stepping into the phone booth once more, trying again to reach his friend Polly. He was excited about another idea that had just occurred to him,"Hi Polly. it's Will. Need to see ya. O.K. for me to come over?"

"Well, I guess. When?"

"Right now, if that's O.K."

"Give me an hour; my parents and I are just sitting down to supper."

"Great, Pol. Thanks a million. See you around eight."

"Fine. There's something I need to talk to *you* about, too—remember that."

"What's that?"

"I'll tell you when you get here, Will."

# Chapter Seven

Polly, with her mother and dad, were still doing the dishes when the doorbell rang. They told Polly to go ahead and be with her guest, that they would finish the dishes and see them later.

She led Will to the screened porch in back, so they could have some privacy. Before either sat, she said, "Look, Will—before you say anything, there's something I've got to talk about. I'm worried—about you—not me. Every hour since you were here last, I've wondered if I wasn't being part of getting you into trouble. I really like you, Will—I always have—and the last thing I would want to do is get you in trouble."

"Er . . . er . . . what . . . what do you mean, Pol?"

"I mean that a *fool*—who knew what I know—could figure out what you're up to, Will. You're thinking of trying to contact that group in Canada—the one I told you about. Now don't lie to me—I'm sure that's true.

*"You—are—playing—with—fire,* Will Johnson. And I don't want to help you get burned.

"After we talked last, I sat down with my dad again and sort of fished around for more on that group in Canada. Don't worry, I didn't mention your name or the conversation you and I have had on this, and he told me some more—stuff that scares me for your safety.

"It turns out that the only reason my brother Joe's friend even brought up the subject with Dad is that he remembered that Dad is a policeofficer, and he thinks the group is very dangerous. Mainly he's worried about the safety of his fiancee who works with them. She is American but refuses to quit because many of her father's family still live in France. Her paternal grandfather was born there, and she used to spend every summer with relatives who still live in the south of France, and she believes that her group— although rather rough—is doing some very effective work in helping those in France who are still fighting any way they can to help win this terrible war.

43

"Will, the rumor around Quebec is that these people have already killed two or three of their own group whom they accused of spying for the 'enemy.' No legal charges first, no trial, no nothing—just sort of an execution. But the local authorities won't charge the group because not only the rumor is that the Canadian government is secretly giving them money for their work, but it's also well known that the authorities who could bring charges against them are in control of Quebec province and are what— in Canada—they call 'separatists.' Also the leader of the group, this Mr. LeBlanc, has been a long-time and powerful figure within their same political faction that wants to eventually separate the province of Quebec from the rest of Canada; in the end, it seems that the group controlled by this LeBlanc just pretty much does what it pleases, including killing folks when it suits their purposes."

It really pained Polly to talk that way to this young man she really *had* always liked—maybe more than *liked,* she had sometimes admitted to herself—so she had turned her face away from him as she spoke so bluntly to him. She finished and waited for his response, but heard nothing. As she looked back toward him, she was surprised to see he was bent over, with his head face-down in his hands, and he was slightly shaking. She stepped over and touched him gently on the cheek.

He managed to look up and blurted, "My God, Polly! Don't *do* this to me! Right now you're the only hope I have to try to get the only thing I've really wanted in my entire life. Please, don't take that away from me! I came here to ask for some more help. The only thing that interests me about the Quebec group is that they seem to help people get into the RCAF. How they do it, I don't know—-and I don't care! I'm goin' there, Polly—and I'm *going* to seek out their help; if necessary, I'm going to *beg* them for help!"

"Will, please; listen to reason. These people don't even speak our language; how could you even communicate with them, much less explain your situation or justify their helping you?"

"I'm not sure, but I'll find a way. But I need some help in getting 'in the door,' so to speak—and that's why I called to pass an idea by you. Now, listen to it, Polly, and remember this before you say 'No'; I've *got* Mr. LeBlanc's address, and I'm going to try to see him—with your help or *without* it. My chances of success are better if you will try to help, so I hope you will.

"The first time we talked about this group, you said that Joe's RCAF friend had mentioned that his girlfriend was with them. Then, tonight you said she was his 'fiancee,' and that she is American, so she must speak English, too. If, somehow, I could get an introduction to her—say by a letter or something from Joe's friend—this would get me in the door; you follow me? What do you think? C'mon, Polly—please help me. If you are seriously worried about me, you can truly help me this way——'cause I'm going, come Hell or highwater!"

"I wish I didn't believe what you just said——but I do. I don't know what to do; if I help you I may be helping you get hurt—maybe killed. But if I don't, you're even more likely to get hurt, maybe for sure. If I agree to try what you just mentioned, you must understand that getting in touch with a combat pilot takes some time—sometimes we don't get an answer from Joe for weeks. And if the pilot is somewhere other than England, on some assignment, it could take *months* to make contact.

"Even then, I'd have to tell him the truth about your plan and he may not want to get mixed up in this. Do you understand?"

"Sure; I understand that. Will you do this for me, Polly? I'll never forget it if you will only do this for me. Please?"

"Do I really have a choice? I don't think so——I guess I have to; but I'll try only if you promise me that you won't go anywhere until I hear back from Joe's friend. And if you don't keep that promise, I'm through with you, Will. And I mean that too. Is that a deal?"

As Will leaped up and was and swinging her around in a happy frenzy, he heard the voice of her father, "What is this—some kind of celebration or a new dance step I somehow missed?" as he stood in the doorway to the porch.

His daughter smiled at him, "Just a little silly teenager stuff, Dad; you know how kooky we get sometimes."

Her dad grinned, then looked at Will, "I hear through the grapevine that you're trying to organize your own flying squadron, Will. Joe would be proud of you; I know I am. But don't you think you should wait a year or so, son? This war's gonna last a while—that's for sure."

Trying to avoid looking him straight in the eye, he replied, "Naw, Mr. Hearn, I tried to get in the air corps, but they said I was too young. Gotta wait; no choice."

He patted Will on the back as he opened the screen door to leave, "Good; your time will come——don't rush it. I've got to run down to the precinct for a few minutes, Pol. Don't ever be a cop, Will. See you later, kids."

As the door closed behind her father, Pol turned toward her friend, "He didn't get that 'organize your own squadron' from me; every dad in this neighborhood has heard about your 'pep' talk back of the school in December.

"O.K., I'm going to write to Joe tonight and ask him to talk to his friend, but I have no idea as to when I'll have an answer. Think you can muster a little patience for a change, Mr. Johnson?"

"You betcha, Pol, you *are* a sweetheart!! And a *real* friend! And I promise not to nag you 'til I hear from you."

### Stanmore, England; RAF Fighter Command

Joe Hearn had received his sister's letter the previous week, but had not been able to get over sooner from his airfield at Southampton.

He wasn't certain where his friend was currently based. He had last seen André Moreau in London, during a three-day R&R pass. They had done an appropriate celebration of André's recent promotion to *Squadron Leader* Moreau, not bad for a 23-year-old American from deep in *Cajun country*. The problem was that they had such an "appropriate" celebration that neither had felt like updating their addresses on the morning after.

The saucy little WAAF at the front desk almost cracked up when she heard the slow drawl coming from this handsome young flight sergeant in RCAF blue. She decided instantly that she liked this rather soft version of her native language, and gave Joe her most winning smile. "Most certainly, Sergeant, I *can* assist in the location of your squadron leader, but I am a bit concerned about how you managed to *lose* him."

Joe had been through this before, and was ready, so he affected, "Honey, I sure can understand how it sounds sorta dumb that *anybody* could lose *anything* on y'all's little bitty island, but it *did* happen, *sweetie-pie*—so let's get on it, *yuh heah?*"

That turned her serious, so she started flipping through a loose-leaf directory, and finally said. "You're in luck, lovey, he's based here at HQ now. He lives in BOQ No. 63; it's a couple hundred meters from where we are sitting. If you don't spot him there, try the Officers' Club next door to his quarters.

"Annnnd, if they won't let you in, try *me* again. I *luvvvvve* Canadians who talk like they're *chewing* their lovely words."

"Thanks *dahlin*. If I don't find him, you'll do fine—pro'bly *better*—but *bye* for now."

Joe found his buddy at the O-Club, and explained—over a few pints—why he was there. André told Joe, for the first time, that he had gone through family problems somewhat similar to Will's when he had first wanted to get in the RCAF, so he could sympathize with him.

He agreed to give Joe what he described as a "letter of introduction" for Will to take to his fiancee, to include a request that she aid him in any way she could. He emphasized that he had no idea about whether she could help, but he himself would welcome having a friend of Joe in Quebec and near Angie, because he was still deeply concerned about her being active with what he described as "that bunch of fanatics" in Quebec City.

He told Joe also that the over-riding objective—long-range—of the group was the separation of Quebec from Canada, and that everything else was subordinated to that. He said, "They are convinced that France will be ruled by the Reds after the war, and that they can then get help in their separation crusade by currying favor with the communists now, since they are now active within the French *résistance.*

"They aren't communists," he said, "but—right or wrong—they simply don't trust General de Gaulle, whom they have tabbed as simply a politician, pure and simple."

Just before midnight, the two left the club, and André walked Joe to the train station, promising he would write the letter that night and try to send it the next day in the daily courier pouch to Joe's Southampton base.

As the English countryside flashed by his coach window, in the light of a full moon, Joe reflected on how amazingly his life—and those of his boyhood friends, like Will Johnson—had changed in only a couple of years.

Angie had not been shocked to hear that there were official objections from the present Canadian government regarding her group's aid to communists in France. She was not too keen about it herself, but she had kept reminding herself that the résistants *had* been clearly strengthened by having the Reds with them. She had understood—but often deplored—the lack of direction of these freedom-fighters, most of whom were very young. It was a fact that the communists had provided the invaluable experience of many combat veterans of the Spanish Civil War, as Jean-Paul reminded her several times each day.

At their breakfast, though, she had seen her leader truly worried for the first time during their work together. LeBlanc knew that her father held some high position of authority within the American OSS, and was soliciting her to provide him with an entree to her dad. He thought that Louis Hebert could be the channel for him to ascertain (1) whether the U.S. concurred with Ottawa and (2) whether the Americans might become his source of aid if the Canadians carried out their threat.

She had told him that she didn't have *the foggiest idea* about that, and was reluctant to put her father in the awkward position of his daughter soliciting help for her work. At that, Jean-Paul exploded, "*Merde, mon amie!* Thousands—no, *millions*—of good human persons are suffering and dying each day—Frenchmen, *anglais,* now *Americans,* too—at the hands of these *Huns.* And you are worrying yourself about someone feeling awkward?

"*Think,* my dear Angie—think about what you have now said at this last moment."

"Peace, Jean-Paul. Perhaps you are right, but I must think about this one. One thing I know for certain: something this big will have to go to the General's level anyhow before a decision is made. Canada *is* my country's ally—remember?"


### E-Street Complex; Washington, D.C.

The headquarters building of the OSS, the first true central intelligence organization in U.S. history, gave no clue to it's complex mission, perhaps the most complex quasi-military mission in the country's history. From this address, it's wartime complement would grow to more than 20,000 volunteers who were willing—and eager—to fight a clandestine and mysterious war throughout the world, one that often posed, for it's combatants, singular dangers that rarely faced the strictly military soldier.

The unquestioned commander of this unique force was General William J. (Bill) Donovan, a blue-eyed holder of the Medal of Honor for his service during World War I; room 122 was his Command Post.

On this Monday morning his Deputy Commander, Colonel Piedro Recinello, was waiting there to meet with Lt. Colonel Louis Hebert, after his colleague had called him at home late on Sunday evening. Louis had said he was not calling from a *safe phone;* thus his boss hadn't pressed him for the reason he wanted to meet.

After Colonel Recinello had poured a cup of hot coffee for both, Louis spoke first. "Pete, I don't know if you are acquainted yet with a sort of free-lance French-Canadian group in Quebec, headed by a guy named Jean-Paul LeBlanc. It's the one my daughter Angie has been working with for some time."

When Recinello didn't respond, Col. Hebert continued, "Their main activity is doing various work for the French resistance, stuff like training forgers, preparing false identity papers, teaching some French to those who need it, and training recruits from the French colonies in Africa and elsewhere. This includes, since Pearl Harbor Day, some Americans who, for whatever reasons—usually criminal records for counterfeiting, safe-cracking, and other offenses—want to, but are not allowed to, serve in our military."

At this last comment, Recinello half-grinned and said, "Hold on Louis; we know LeBlanc's group. Lots of people—including the Nazis—know Le Blanc well. He's one more tough cookie. He is a serious student of our own

Revolution, and I'm told that his hero is Patrick Henry; even calls his group *"LOM."* Stands for *Liberté ou Mort,* in French; 'Liberty or Death' in English, right? I'm not sure which government he worries the most, the German or the *Canadian.*

"But I certainly didn't know your daughter Angie was with the LOM; she's traveling in mighty fast company, Louis."

"Damned right; I know that! I tried to talk her out of going up there, but she was hell-bent to go. Said that it was a way she could help our kin who still live in France. Anyway, she called me on Saturday. She first apologized about calling, but the more she talked, the more I felt it was something important enough to discuss with you or Bill."

After relating what his daughter had told him about the Canadian threat to withhold funding, and of the suggestion that the U.S. might step in, Louis paused for the other's reaction.

He said to Hebert, "This has got to be some politician showboating in Ottawa. All of us know that we must work with Stalin's crowd for now, not because we agree with the Soviet system, but because we have a common enemy who must—absolutely *must*—be defeated.

"Of course the Brits don't actually need the help of someone like LeBlanc as much as we do. They are way ahead of us in the intelligence business, having been fighting for their lives since September of '39, and they already have their trainers, too. In New York City, for example, they have a Canadian, a guy named William Stephenson, running their BSC under the cover *United Kingdom Commercial Corporation.* We have established a relationship with him and hope to utilize their 250-acre training camp on Lake Ontario for training in clandestine operations and unconventional warfare.

"But Louis, you know politicians are still politicians, even during wars, so who knows if it will be worked out. I think we need to be able to count on our own resources, and at some time—*soon* I hope—we must have the capacity to develop our operatives who will be qualified to work with any and all *partisans* or *resistants,* and that certainly includes the French.

"When the time comes for our guys to hit the beaches in Europe, for sure the French beaches will be key; it doesn't take a military genius to see that. Before that day, we want to have Americans on the ground, directing at least some of the activities of the local resistance, be it French or otherwise.

"The bottom line is that we're willing to help this guy LeBlanc, as long as he understands absolutely clearly that we expect—no, that we will *insist*—on his help in return.

"But Louis, this is very delicate from a political standpoint, so somebody from here has got to sit down, personally, with LeBlanc and lay this on the line with him, and to emphasize to him that he is to keep his yap shut about our helping him. If he breaks any one of these commitments, we want him to believe that the deal is over—*dead*—at that minute.

"Lastly, we not only need someone we can trust absolutely for this assignment, but also he has to be able to speak this guy's language. In fact, Bill has been giving a lot of thought to designating someone here at OSS as our liaison regarding all our dealings with the French. He has already told me he can't think of anyone better qualified than you, Louis.

"So you're 'it,' and the trip to see LeBlanc can be your first task in that job, agreed?"

"Thanks, Pete; and thank the boss for me. But I'd like for the research people to put together for me any and every thing they have about the Quebec group. If they can do it today, I'll call Angie and plan to leave tomorrow morning."

"Done. Check with me when you get back and, while there, you should dig up what you can too. And Louis—take a few hours to enjoy some time with your little girl; that's what we're fighting for, you know."

Louis, like many of his fellow Cajuns, knew French Canada well from visiting there from time to time. He also knew that whatever the temperature might be in Washington, they were still deep into winter in Quebec, so he opted for the train through Boston. Angie had booked him a small suite at the Vieux Quebéc, on the rue St. Jean, where he and his family had spent so many wonderful vacations when she had actually been a *little* girl.

As the afternoon took life, and his train moved north from Boston, the New England landscape flying by his window gradually turned into a pleasing snow shower, reminding him of other winter days on this same journey. For a while, Louis actually forgot this war that had engaged his every thought—night and day—for the last few weeks; instead he indulged himself in nostalgic memories of happier days. Then, grudgingly, he forced himself to think of the realities of the here and now, and wonder if the world could ever return to that more pleasant past.

The snow was almost blinding as Colonel Hebert stepped off the train in Quebec City. He was shivering after seconds in the sharp wind, when he heard a gleeful, *"Papa, Papa—over here, Papa!"* as his youngest daughter greeted him from across a low fence where she waited amongst a small crowd.

Suddenly *Papa* felt warm again.

As he used the key to the small suite, he was telling Angie that he had wanted the suite so they could dine there the second evening with M.

LeBlanc; he didn't want to risk someone seeing him with LeBlanc at a public restaurant.

She looked around the tiny kitchen, and volunteered to shop the next day at *La Epicérie Evangeline,* a little grocery just outside the wall of the city that specialized in Cajun foods, even to crayfish. "Not straight from the bayou, Papa, like at home—but crayfish, nevertheless—and I believe Jean-Paul will enjoy them also. We'll have something of a Cajun dinner, right here, tomorrow night; is that O.K.?" she asked.

"Perfect, *chérie.* Now, let me shower off the travel-grime real quick; and while I'm doing that, you call our old restaurant, *Cafe Maman*—if it's still here—for a table for two. Tonight we'll have ourselves a dinner from our past."

"Oh yeah, it's here—it was the first place I checked on when I got here last year. This will be great if we can get a table."

Her dad yelled from the bathroom, "Do they still operate with only the one main dish, the one *Maman* is serving that night?"

"Not exactly. Maman's gone modern; now she gives a choice—one meat dish and one fish. People still pack the place—there are only eight tables, remember? So I'm calling this very minute. Thank Heaven it's not a weekend—we'd never get in."

Madame Nathalie Bidault, *Maman* to most in her world, served dinner only, and always answered the phone herself until two hours before dinner time, because she insisted on making her guests feel as if they were guests in her home. In spite of that, she somehow remembered most of the regulars who had dined with her over the 32-year-life of *Café Maman.* Even more astounding, she seemed to forever remember their favorite table also. But Angie was still surprised when she remembered the Hebert family from faraway Baton Rouge.

She told Angie that the cafe was full that night, but because Angie's *papa* was in town for only two days she would make an exception and pull in another table for two, but only for the early seating.

As she was hanging up the telephone, she yelled above the shower noise, "Hurry *Papa;* we have a table—but we need to be there in a half hour."

# Chapter Eight

In the summer of 1908, *Maman's* family had left—with heavy hearts—their ancestral home near the ancient village of *Les Baux,* deep in the south of France.

Since Roman times, her forebears had been *chefs de cuisine.* It was the only profession she knew or desired, and surely her greatest love, an enduring love that had never dimmed over the ensuing 30-plus years in her adopted country. The only employees of *Café Maman* were Nathalie, her two sons and, on weekends, her cousin Monique. All understood clearly that their guests were to be considered—and *treated*—as guests in their home.

As Angie and Louis entered Maman's *"Bienvenue chez moi, Mademoiselle et Monsieur"*—in her warm Provençal accent—made them feel as if it had been the night before—rather than five years—since they had dined in this wondrous place.

A great log was burning in the hearth just beyond where her son Jacque—silhouetted against it's glow—was busily grilling several meats and three whole fish on an open grill within inches of two guest-tables. All the while he carried on a staccato and jovial conversation with two of the guests at the third table beyond.

They settled at their table while a beaming *Maman* was quietly placing a basket of hot bread, a bottle of olive oil, and two small pitchers of wine—a *vin blanc maison* and a *vin rouge maison*—in preparation for the parade of starters about to begin.

At Maman's there was no written menu; her guests need make only two decisions: (1) *viande ou poisson* (meat or fish), for the main dish, and (2) select a wine from her simple but superb cellar, which she had somehow maintained in spite of the war. The other four courses—two starters before the main dish, with a cheese course and a following dessert—were solely *Maman's* decisions; and they varied with each new evening, to the delight of her many regulars who dined there often.

Their small table that Jacque had tucked into a corner was perfect for the Heberts. Louis told his daughter that he felt almost guilty worrying about security in that, of all places, but, "In a world gone mad—and in my present business—I can't take any chances."

Three hours later, they kissed Maman, shook hands vigorously with each of her sons. Then, Maman kissed each of them again and they stepped into the Canadian night and a waiting taxi.

Back at the suite, they talked business for a few minutes.

Louis told her that he wanted the meeting with LeBlanc to include only the three of them—no one else; and that he was going to tell Jean-Paul in no uncertain terms that none of what OSS had to offer was negotiable, and that he would lay out the rest of the deal directly to LeBlanc.

He told Angie that the report OSS research had given him in D.C. on the day before had listed three former colleagues of LeBlanc that he had allegedly liquidated, and asked her for her opinion. Angie said that she had no direct knowledge of this, but it was true that Jean-Paul told everyone who commenced working with the group that he insisted on absolute loyalty to his mission, and that anyone who violated his trust and confidence would be dealt with, and "effectively." She told her father that she had been told the exact same thing when she asked to join in his work.

Her belief—with admittedly no hard evidence to support it—was that Jean-Paul had discovered "plants" in the group, put there by either the Germans or the Vichy regime, and that he may well have had them disposed of.

She said there was no doubt but that her boss was a fanatic zealot in the cause of eventual Québecois *separatism* and that he would stop at little or nothing to achieve it.

As she rose to leave she added that, in her opinion, this did not diminish what she perceived as the extremely valuable work they in LOM were doing to support the Allied war effort, and she hoped that could continue unabated.

At the door, she gazed back at her father for a long moment before adding, "Papa, if what I surmise is true, and if it had happened within OSS, would there have been a different result? In a way, this is *our* little secret war and as brutal as it is so often, is there another effective way to deal with such problems?"

"*Touché,* sweetheart; you're probably right. But then, my favorite person on this planet is not exposed to that danger there. *Here,* you are."

The next morning, when Louis stepped out of the hotel for his regular morning walk, he started toward the *Terrasse Dufferin,* leaning into the teeth of an arctic-like wind from across the St. Lawrence river. After a bone chilling quarter hour he retreated to the warmth of his room.

As he tossed his jacket across the bed he wondered, as he had so often in the past, "Why would anyone with Latin blood coursing through their veins want to endure these frigid winters?" Minutes later as he stood at his window—a mug of coffee warming his hands—watching the sun rise in the only walled city north of Mexico City—he had his answer. Without doubt, framed in his window was one of the most beautiful—and fascinating—towns in the entire world.

At breakfast alone in the hotel, Louis enjoyed the chatter around him, but couldn't resist smiling at how different was the French spoken here, compared to that in the Louisiana bayou country where he was born and raised. His father had owned a pepper farm a short distance from the town of Lafayette; zero English was heard on the farm, simply because none of the farmhands understood it. Yet no one from Quebec—and most certainly no one in Paris—would have understood a word of their version of *la langue française.*

As he turned the key to his room, the phone was ringing, "Mornin' Papa. We're all set for Jean-Paul to meet us there at seven tonight. He will be alone—no problem—he understands and said he would do the same. I'll stop by the grocer and pick up what I need to make dinner. It won't be Maman's, but should be pretty good. Expect me at around 5:00 or 5:30; that sound O.K.?"

"Just right, honey. Can you also pick up a notebook for me? I may want to make some notes after LeBlanc leaves."

"Got it, Dad. See you later."

At 5:40, Angie was rapping on the door with her elbow, her arms full of groceries. As Louis opened the door and reached to help, she said, "Bad news and good news; they didn't have crayfish today, but did have the makings for some terrific crabcakes and for jambalaya, and I got plenty of both. I know Jean-Paul loves the crabcakes—one night I saw him put them away in *bunches*—and you and I like both. I called him from the store. He offered to bring a couple of wines he thinks will go with both. And don't worry, Papa; he knows wines pretty well—for a Canadian."

As dinner was concluding, it was obvious that their guest enjoyed his meal—his spotless plate told the story well. Plus, the wines he brought had married well with both dishes. He vowed that both bottles were from Washington state, and volunteered that he had been shocked to learn that good wines could actually be made in the United States. But then hastened to emphasize that they were made there by a French-Canadian friend from his boyhood.

"The dinner was super, *Mademoiselle la Chef*—and *Monsieur,* the wine was perfect—wherever made!" Louis said, as he pushed back from the small table and reached to the counter for a file folder.

"Now, let's talk business.

"Monsieur LeBlanc, we in the Office of Special Services know of, and admire, the work you have been doing here, and we are hopeful that it can continue. We Americans are in need of your type of services as they relate to the training and other support to certain internal European resistance groups—especially the *French* resistance. I have just been designated by General Donovan as Liaison Officer of OSS to all our contacts in all French speaking countries around the world—and you are my first assignment in that job.

"Of course I know about your potential fiscal problems with your Canadian government, and I'm sure that you can understand the delicate political problems that poses for my government if we subsidize you.

"We are willing to risk those problems, but only if you are fully—and *unconditionally*—agreeable to the provisions I have stated in this memorandum that I will be handing to you momentarily. Before I met you tonight, I was not aware of your excellent command of English; that is why I did the memo in French—our common language.

"Please take your time and read it very thoroughly, enough so that you can retain it in your memory; then sign it—if you are in complete accord—and hand it back to me. You will *not* retain a copy, for obvious security and political reasons; instead, the original will be placed by me in the vault at OSS Headquarters in Washington, marked as: '*TOP SECRET*—FOR THE EYES OF GENERAL WILLIAM J. DONOVAN *or* COLONEL PIEDRO RECINELLO *or* LT. COL. LOUIS HEBERT, *ONLY*'

"If you are *not* in total accord with the terms of the memo, we will be disappointed but, notwithstanding that, I can only thank you for your time and bid you farewell.

"Here is the document; please take all the time your require. If you have questions as to the meaning or intent of any part, I will be glad to discuss that with you."

Jean-Paul LeBlanc was a proud man, totally unaccustomed to quietly accepting ultimatums, however politely phrased; but he was also, above all, a pragmatist, especially when he sensed that his life's mission was at risk.

Thus he resisted the urge to respond, and started reading studiously the single-page document. After what appeared to be his third reading, he stared at Col. Hebert for what seemed an eternity, reached for the pen, signed his name with a flourish, and handed the paper to Louis, all without a single spoken word.

He then turned abruptly, reached for his glass, and smiled at Angie, "I have yet a bit of wine, and I want to raise my glass to *you,* Angie. It is a rare day, in this life, that I meet a truly honorable man—I believe surely that tonight is such a day. That is why I have pledged my honor on that paper. And this could not have happened ever, without you, my most dear Angie—*à votre santé, mon amie!*"

Reaching for his greatcoat, the small Canadian extended his arm to shake Louis's hand, then left.

In Atlanta, Will was getting antsy, not having heard from Polly in more than six weeks. Bill had noticed this, but the two had not been close since Pearl Harbor Day.

Will felt that his twin had deserted him, while Bill thought *his* twin had caused his family much more misery than such great parents deserved. About the only time Will had said much to him recently was a few days before when Will had mentioned receiving a letter from Gary Kelly who said he had just finished pre-flight school and was headed to Ontario, California, for primary flight school in the Stearman PT-17.

Will had not stood still. He had begged Harry Kelly for the name of his counterfeiter friend until Harry had relented. He had gotten what he wanted: a fake driver's license in the new name of *Wade Johns,* with an address in Birmingham, Alabama—a town he knew from visiting his cousins there—and showing him at a new age of 22 years, figuring he would need that when he got to Canada.

Bill knew, better than anyone, how determined his brother had always been, and sensed that something was going on, but he couldn't figure out exactly what. His parents had confided in him about their intervention with the Army Air Corps, and they had made it clear to him again that they were counting heavily on him to keep Will from doing something foolish. For his part, he felt a deep sense of helplessness, and had gone to Sgt. Macdonald's office to seek his counsel.

Sgt. Mac listened patiently to the details, then asked, "What do you think he might try? He's made it plain that he wants to fly, so he has only one other choice left—the navy, right? Even if he managed to get on active duty by lying about his age again, I think your family is going to learn about it pretty quick, and—BINGO—he's back out. Bill, there's plenty of kids—I've known a bunch, personally, during my career—who get in the military while under age. Frankly, most recruiters sort of look the other way if a kid is otherwise qualified. Nine times out of ten, their parents signed the papers knowing full well what was going on, so their enlistment sticks.

"But when the parents really care about it, and are smart like yours are, it's next to impossible for somebody to get away with it in any of our services. So *hey;* it may not be as much of a problem as you and your folks think."

"I wish I could believe that, Sarge, but there's one thing I haven't mentioned yet—to you *or* my parents—mainly because I feel a little sorta like a rat in scheming about Will. But also because I hate to worry my parents even more.

"Back in December of last year; in fact, on the very night Pearl Harbor was bombed, Will and I were so keyed up we stayed up half the night talking about it. He was already raring to go fly; I told him then that we weren't old enough to be accepted. He brought up the idea of going to Canada, like Joe Hearn did a year or so ago. You remember Joe, don't you? He had even gotten a letter or two from Joe; they were always good friends—though Joe is older—and Will has dated Polly Hearn a few times. I've a hunch that he might be thinking of doing the same as Joe."

"No way, Bill. The Canadian policy—since the day we got into this scrap—is flat-out *not* to take any more Americans—period! So I think you can forget that."

"That's good to hear, but it still bothers me some. What if *their* recruiters decide to 'look the other way' too?"

"I'm not going to bet the farm that could not happen, Bill, but messing around like that with the rights of your country's *ally* is dynamite, and could—most probably *would*—get somebody court-martialed. A Canadian guy would be nuts to take such a chance."

Sgt. Mac, for all his military experience, was seriously underestimating the ingenuity of young Will Johnson, who was busily developing his own game plan.

Before obtaining his new driver's license he had grown a mustache (much to the dismay of his father, but to the poorly-concealed delight of his sisters), reasoning that neither he nor *Wade Johns* would look quite twenty-two without it.

But, to him, far and away his greatest problem was how to keep his whereabouts unknown to Noah Johnson after leaving for Quebec, while somehow still keeping his parents assured that he was alive and well. Contrary to the apparent belief of his brother and some others, Will's only serious regret about leaving was that his parents would be worried and hurt by it.

Since presumably the only person in Atlanta who might know where he was going was Polly, he searched his mind about how he could insure that she not be tempted to tell others. He knew already that she was concerned as to whether she was doing the right thing by helping him, and he feared that she might decide to tell his folks at some point. His best bet, he decided, was to convince her somehow that Quebec was to be only a temporary stop for him. Now he had to decide how to carry that off.

He thought he had the answer, but he needed some help.

In Quebec, Jean-Paul LeBlanc was continuing, each day, to thank profusely his colleague Angie for the help promised him by her father. He still hoped that his Canadian financial support would not stop, but now he did not feel compelled to, as he put it, "kneel at the feet of some idiot in Ottawa" in order for his work to continue, and he gave his young friend all the credit for that good fortune.

He had described to her one of the conditions contained in the memorandum he had signed that night at the hotel, asking her to think about how they could handle it. It specified that any and all communications between Col. Hebert and Jean-Paul, regarding U.S. financial assistance through OSS, must be transmitted by courier only, preferably by an American without any "derogatory history" (meaning "criminal record"). This provision created a serious problem for LeBlanc, inasmuch as his only American co-worker who had no *history* as a forger, counterfeiter, or safe-cracker, was Angie.

While pondering that one, Angie received something new that puzzled her. A couple of weeks after her father returned to Washington, a letter arrived from her fiancee, André, telling her to expect a letter or telephone call from a young man in Atlanta named Will Johnson, whom he described as "the friend of a very good friend and comrade of mine."

André had deliberately left out the details because he knew his letter would be read by a censor before it left the U.K., and he was concerned that the details might trigger a nosy censor into an inquiry that a new Squadron Leader could certainly do without. Instead he simply told Angie that this Will Johnson would give her the details, and urged her to do what she could to assist the young man.

Her curiosity was aroused, but she and André had discussed—when he had been there on leave—the problems of censorship , and she understood why some of his letters sounded sort of unfinished.

Down south, another month passed, and Will still had no word from Polly. He had seen her several times at school, but had bit his tongue each time and managed to stay true to his promise not to pester her about word from Joe.

Then, one Monday morning he walked into the school building a little late and was stunned by the news everybody was discussing, as if in shock.

All the bulletin boards had the information posted, and a huge black wreath was hanging in the entry hall.

*Gary Kelly had been killed!*

The handwritten note, from Harry Kelly to the school Principal, stated that on the previous Wednesday there had been a training accident at an airfield at Ontario, California.

Gary had been at the controls of the Stearman PT-17 on the down-wind leg of a landing approach, with his civilian instructor talking him in from the rear seat of the open cockpit aircraft, when the instructor called him on the intercom to say he felt like he was about to pass out.

There was a severe cross-wind on Gary's final approach, and the tower was urging him to pull up and go around, but he yelled back that a delay could be fatal for his instructor, and insisted that he could get it down safely.

The PT-17, a great airplane in every other way, was notoriously difficult to land, especially in a cross-wind—even by experienced pilots—because of it's narrow landing gear. It ground-looped instantly on touch-down, throwing Gary from the cockpit and a good 20 feet away onto the runway. Later the medics reported that the condition of his skull indicated that his head had struck the top wing of the bi-plane aircraft and most probably had also hit the concrete runway first as his body came down.

Gary had unfastened his seat belt in order to try to turn to see his instructor and, in his excitement, forgot to re-fasten it.

He died on the way to the base infirmary.

During the war, many of the flight instructors in the primary flight schools were civilians, and not required to pass the strict physical exams given to military air crews, but they were invaluable in training the aviation cadets. Gary's instructor had suffered a heart attack but survived. The Army Chaplain who visited Harry Kelly said that the few minutes saved by Gary not going around had almost surely saved the life of his instructor.

Will couldn't control his anguish, but did manage to hold back the tears until he found a private corner away from the others. Then he too sobbed aloud for his friend. After gathering himself, he left school immediately and stopped by Gary's home to see Mr. Kelly.

What he found was a broken-hearted and guilt-ridden father, who blamed himself for the loss of his youngest son.

He had obviously been drinking, but thanked Will for coming by, and started pleading with him to forget flying until he was a couple of years older. Harry said that he was ashamed now that he had helped his son get in the army so young, and apologized to Will for assisting him, too. He kept repeating that he was going to "burn in hell" for what he had done and that, "I damned sure deserve it."

Will tried in vain to assure him that it was not any fault of his, but soon saw that nothing he could say was going to stop this, and he finally decided to say goodbye as tactfully as he knew how.

He almost cried again as he deliberately walked the long way home , but the longer he walked and thought, the more his sorrow began to subside in favor of a growing determination that he must finish what he and his friend Gary had started together.

He kept telling himself that he owed it to Gary.

By the time he reached his house all he could think was, "When—oh, *when*—will I hear back from Polly?"

The telephone was ringing as he opened the front door.

It was Polly. She had gone home early, too. But she was crying hysterically.

"I know, Polly. We're all upset about Gary, nobody more than me. But I know Gary—he was my best friend. He was doing what he wanted to do, and he would want all of us to be *proud* of him; I know I am."

"Me too, Will. But it's such a waste, and he was so young. But something else happened today, Will. I need to see you; can you meet me at the park pavilion now?"

"Sure—in 20 minutes—O.K.?"

"See you then, Will; bye."

# Chapter Nine

Polly wasn't yet at the pavilion when he arrived. Neither was anyone else. Fortunately, Will thought, because she might still be upset, and it wouldn't help her to have others gawking at her.

He felt guilty that he had not offered to go by and walk her down, but he assumed she must have had a reason for suggesting the meeting in the park. He had wracked his brain about it coming down, but couldn't think of what might be the "something else" that she said had happened. He hoped that nothing bad had happened to her brother Joe.

He didn't see her come up, and it startled him to hear the voice behind him—not quite like her normal one—call his name, almost in a whisper. She was standing close behind him, and as he turned he could see that her eyes were still red; obviously she had been crying and she was trembling.

Without thinking, he embraced her, and held her for a full minute before either spoke.

Still holding her softly, he broke the silence, " My God, Polly; what has happened to make you so broken up? All of us feel sick about Gary. But I know Gary, and I know he would want us to keep going; let's try to do that, as a way to honor his memory."

She kept her face on his shoulder and, after a very deep breath, replied, "The news about Gary was terrible, but, as my dad said this afternoon, we'd best brace ourselves for that kind of bad news as more of our friends go off to this horrible war. But he was the first person that our neighborhood—and our school—has lost, and he was so very young, Will; that makes it worse."

Then she gently pushed back from him, and stared straight into his face, "What makes this so much more tragic though—-for me, that is—is I can see the same kind of thing happening to you, Will. And, if it does, I'm going to be partly to blame. Maybe that sounds selfish to you but, selfish or not, that's how I feel.

"I know I promised to help you, and I've tried to do that; but now I'm asking you Will, here and now, to let me out of that dumb promise. Because that's what it was: *dumb, dumb, dumb! If you don't—and you wind up like Gary—all my life I'll feel like it was my fault.*"

He tried to interrupt her, but she screamed at him, *"No! Don't interrupt me, 'cause I'm not finished! You said to me once, 'Don't do this to me!' Now I'm saying to you the same, 'Don't you do this to me!'* If you want to be a fool—and go kill yourself—go ahead, but do it by yourself, not with me helping. Don't make me hate myself for life."

"Please, Pol, try to calm down. I know how you feel, and I don't want to argue about this with you, 'specially when you're already feeling so down.

"This has been a real bad day for me too—maybe the worst I ever had. Let's just get a couple of Cokes and walk around the lake for a while. It would do us both good to just relax for a few minutes; one turn around the lake, and then we talk about it; that O.K. with you?"

"I guess—let's do that. And I'm sorry I yelled at you, but you're important to me Will. That's probably never *dawned* on you before, so now I'm telling you. Let's go."

As they strolled, hand in hand and in silence, he searched his mind for what he should say to her. He wanted to find the right words—for his own selfish reasons, to be sure—but also because he had finally realized that Polly was the only person around who had actually tried to help him much, and he didn't want to hurt her more than apparently he had already.

Nearing the pavilion again, he led her toward a bench at the edge of the lake, where the two had—together—fed the ducks back during their kindergarten years, with both their fathers standing by.

She was totally serene by now, and he asked, "Pol, are you sure that you've told me everything that's been bothering you today? I don't mean that what you've said isn't *enough* to worry you—it most certainly is—but I've got a gut feeling that there's something else. If so, we ought to talk about it too."

He heard her sigh, and then, "I guess you are right. There is something else that came with this dreadful day, and we've *got* to discuss it sooner or later.

"I was already a wreck when I got home today, and it got worse when I checked the mailbox. There was a letter from Joe."

She paused and sighed again as if it were painful for her to continue, "In the envelope was another letter that Joe described as one from André Moreau to his fiancee, Angie Hebert; she's the woman who works with the Canadian group. The letter from André was still sealed, but your name was on the outside, and Joe said it was to be given to you; that it had in it all tho information you would need to contact this Angie. Also, he said André had told him you should, by all means, call or write to her before assuming she can help you, and that her home address and telephone number are in the envelope.

"There! I've told you. But now I'm asking you—*pleading* with you—to let me burn that letter."

Will stood up and stared across the lake, trying to find the right words. His heart had skipped more than a beat—it had *leaped*—at the mention of the letter for him.

It was what he had waited for, dreamed of, and prayed about, almost every hour of every day for two months. *How could I now agree that it be destroyed, even for this wonderful person who has become my best friend in this world?* he thought to himself.

But he knew that he owed her an answer, so he turned back toward her, "Polly, you really have been patient with me—and wonderful in trying to help me. And you are certainly the last person I want to hurt. But this is all I've thought of for months. I just can't bring myself to toss it all away now. Maybe everybody else believes I'm crazy; but you know, I read a book for school last year where a fellow like me was doing something folks thought was really screwy, but he believed that was what he was born to do. And I've come to think the same thing about this. It's the only thing I think about, night and day. Can you possibly appreciate that?"

Polly didn't respond, and he continued.

"And believe me, Pol, while I appreciate the help you've given me, somehow, some way, I would have done this anyhow. If it turns out bad for me, it's nobody's fault but mine. Please believe that, Polly, 'cause it's a fact. I just can't make myself tell you that I don't want that letter."

She cried a little, again, but only for a moment, then wiped her eyes and said, "I knew you'd say that, or something like it, and, down deep, I knew you never would agree with me. I guess I shouldn't have even tried. Let's go by my house; I'll give you the letter, and just pray every night that you'll be safe, like I do for my brother Joe anyhow."

It was three days later, and well into the spring of 1942. The Dogwoods were already in bloom when he left the note for his parents—with a separate one for his brother—on the small table in the entrance hall of their home.

Fighting back the tears, he paused for only a moment, then quietly slipped out the front door, at around four o'clock that Monday morning. He figured that by the time the Greyhound bus got him to Chattanooga, it would be full daylight, and he would hitch-hike north from there. With some luck he hoped to get a ride with a long haul trucker, maybe all the way to the Canadian border.

He had some money—not a lot but enough for bus fare all the way to Quebec if necessary—but hoped to save most of it by "thumbing it" from Chattanooga. Will had decided not to call Angie Hebert before showing up at her apartment, figuring it is harder for anyone to say *no* face to face. Yet, if she should say that, he knew he would need what cash he could save for food and shelter until he found some paying work.

He had agonized over what to say in the note to his parents, tearing up four versions before the final effort. Mainly, he tried to assure them that he would try to contact them from time to time, to let them know he was all right, but plainly said that he was not going to let them know where he was, because he knew they would try to force him to return. He said, more than once, that he understood they were acting out of love for him, but that this was something he just had to do, and hoped that someday they would understand it and forgive him for the worries he was causing them by leaving.

To his brother, his note was a little on the light side. It said that if the war lasted very long he knew that he and Bill would eventually be standing side by side like they always had, but, as usual, they approached it in different ways.

The bus wasn't crowded. A handful of bleary-eyed civilians boarded ahead of him, and the rest were kids in uniforms that didn't fit, mostly army recruits headed to Fort Oglethorpe just south of Chattanooga. Will managed to sleep most of the way, until he was startled by the bus driver standing over him, shaking him awake. He had asked to get off where the bus left the main highway to avoid having to backtrack from the bus station to start the hitch-hiking part of his journey.

It was just after 8:00 on a bright and sunny morning, and he was glad to see that many 18-wheelers were already rolling north. He opened his small suitcase and removed two large McGill University logos, and attached one to each side of the well-worn suitcase. He reasoned that some drivers would be more apt to risk picking up a college student, and that a *McGill* student should have a distinct advantage if he were to be lucky enough for some Canadian to come along, headed toward Montreal or Quebec City.

The *McGill* idea didn't work out too well for his first ride. It turned out to be a north Georgia farmer whose kid brother had been among the 2,800 Americans killed during the two-hour attack on Pearl Harbor.

Before they had gone no more than a mile, he asked, "Just where is this *McGill University,* boy?"

When Will explained that it was a Canadian university in Montreal, he snorted, "How come you're goin' there? Ain't you an *American,* and don't you know there's a war goin' on, and you're needed right here?"

Will was shocked, but sensed at once that this fellow was looking for an argument, and that was the last thing he needed. So he told what his mother had always called a "white" lie, "Oh, I'm not going there; I just found this old empty suitcase outside the bus station in Chattanooga. I'd heard of McGill though—figured it would help me get a lift up to my home in Cleveland—er, er—'at's Cleveland, *Tennessee,* you know; it's just up the road from here.

"I'm already signed up to go in the navy. Cain't wait to get in there and kick some butt!"

This seemed to appease the driver, and he went on, "Sorry I talked to ya that way, son; I jumped the gun on ya just 'en. But I lost my only brother—ten years younger'n me, and my only kin—in 'at damned sneak attack by 'em Japs back in December. He was more like my son than a brother. I just ain't got no use for draft dodgers, and we've already seen a few croppin' up around here—not many, thank God. Just seems like tryin' to git in a *college* is one way they use, ya know."

"No problem, sir. I thought that most likely you had some reason for saying that. I'd probably feel the same way if I were in your shoes. Hey, you wouldn't have given me a ride unless you had a big heart, so don't worry about it. How old was your brother?"

From there, the conversation was friendly enough during the half hour-ride to Cleveland, but Will decided not to push his luck, so when he saw the first sign of the town he asked to be let out, saying his thanks and again expressing his regrets about the man's brother.

After the truck was out of sight, he stepped back to the side of the highway to be in view of the northbound traffic, thinking to himself that while that ride was short, at least he had learned something from it. In Lakewood—his real home—there was no such thing as a draft dodger, as far as he had heard. In spite of the experience, he left the logos on his battered suitcase, hoping for better results the next time.

He was pretty discouraged after watching cars and trucks breeze by for nearly an hour, not even slowing down. Finally a huge rig with a sleeper cab hit its airbrakes and stopped about a hundred yards past him. Someone leaned out the window on the driver's side and waved to him, hollering "Come on, kid! I ain't got all day!"

As he was pulling himself up into the cab he noticed that the sign on the door read "Anthony Trucking—Syracuse, N.Y." The driver stuck out a huge hand with, "Toss your bag behind the seat, kid. My name's Tony; and yours?"

"Wade Johns, sir. Thanks a million for stopping."

"Glad to do it; I could use some company. Usually we drive 'double,' my partner Jimbo and me. I drive, he sleeps; or he drives, I sleep——in the sleeper back there, ya know. We can cover lots of road in a big hurry that way, ya know. But lots of the time, one of us will be driving, and the other's sittin' there—right where you're sittin'—so we keep each other company.

"This trip—not so. Jimbo got sick as a dog the night before we were to leave on this trip—so I had to take it all by my lonesome.

"Had to do it though. We're in business for ourselves—these rigs cost a small fortune, ya know. They don't roll, we don't pay the note; next thing we know, we don't eat either! Just ran a load to Fort Myers, Florida. Headed now for Akron, but I'm gonna stop for the night at a great truck stop near Dayton. They've got terrific grub—got an Italian doing the cooking, that's *why*—and good sleeping rooms—little rooms, but clean as a whistle. Where you headed?"

"Well, I hope to get up to Quebec—the city of Quebec—in Canada. How far could I ride with you?"

"This may be your lucky day, kid—mine too, 'cause I think you'll be good company. Tonight, like I said, I'm staying the night near Dayton; then, tomorrow, into Akron, drop the load there, then home sweet home. Home is Syracuse, not that far from where you're goin'. If you want, you can ride all the way to Syracuse; and if you wouldn't mind helping me unload at Akron, I could pay you a few bucks for that, plus staking you to your eats all the way in. Maybe you would want to sleep here in the cab tonight—it's pretty comfortable, believe it or not—and save yourself a buck or so that way. That a deal?"

"You bet, sir; that's a super deal for me! Couldn't be better."

"For both of us Wade; but don't keep calling me 'sir'—my name's Tony; O.K.?"

"Fine, Tony. Thanks again."

They got to Hannah's Truck Stop, just east of Dayton, at almost 8:00, washed up in Tony's room, then went straight to the restaurant. It was packed, and not all were truck drivers. Many looked like bankers, lawyers, and the like. Tony said it was always packed for one reason—it was always great, and famous around Dayton. He said he had talked with people who had driven all the way from Columbus, and further, just to eat there.

Most everybody who came there seemed to be aware of—and accepted—one policy that might be unique to Hannah's: Truck drivers were seated first, no matter how many were waiting, or *who*. Legend had it that a famous—and powerful, he *thought*—mid-western Senator had taken a loud and boisterous exception to her policy one night, and Hannah had simply told him to "get the hell out of here."

Hannah's husband was the chef—-both he and she called him "the cook"—and he was Italian; *very* Italian, Tony proudly reported. A casual look at the menu certainly verified that.

Will knew little of Italian cuisine outside of spaghetti and pizza, and jumped to agree when Tony offered to order for him. Although the trucker was somewhat appalled when Will declined to have any of the red *vino,* it wasn't hard to see that the young man was enjoying immensely his meal, devouring, with gusto, dishes he had never heard of, all to the undisguised and very vocal delight of Tony.

Both were stuffed but happy when Tony left Will at the truck, after showing him how to make up the bed in the sleeper cab.

It was clear and cold when the two pulled out of Hannah's at seven o'clock sharp the next morning. Tony said he had called his wife the night before, at about 11:00, and she had said some snow was still flying in Syracuse, but the forecast was for it to melt off rapidly. Tony said, "Every year, spring fights hard to come back to Syracuse, but makes it sooner or later."

They made quick work of the unloading at Akron, with some help from the guys on the receiving dock there, and soon were running empty toward Syracuse. Tony asked Will if he had ever been to Quebec. When Will said *no,* Tony said, "Well, Wade, I hope you know a little of the French lingo, 'cause that's the main language there, and some of 'em won't speak anything else, even though most know some English, too. I've had a few runs there, and I get along O.K., mainly 'cause I learned Italian from my Mom and Pop—it's pretty close to French, you know."

Will said, "I had some French in high school—two years of it—but I'm not sure that'll help; I hope so, but I thought all Canadians used English, too."

"Well, I think they know it, but that don't mean they're gonna *use* it; that's the problem. But I'm sure you'll get along, Wade. You smile a lot, and that helps a guy anywhere; that's for sure.

"Hey, I'm changing the subject, but why don't you stay at our house tonight. It's gonna be a little late when we get in—no use in your starting out at night; then you and me can look at a map tonight and I'll drive you out east of town tomorrow morning and get you started toward Quebec; I can show you the best way to go. How about it?"

"That's nice of you Tony, but you've already done a lot for me; I hate to impose—"

"You ain't imposing pal; I want my Missus to meet you; it'll prove to her that I run into some actually nice guys on the road.

"O.K, that's settled. Hang on tight, pal! We're gonna move this rig down the road home. Hannah's was fine, but now I'm ready for some *home* cooking!"

"Thanks again, Tony; it really *was* my lucky day to run into you."

As he and Tony were finishing breakfast the next morning, his wife Tania came back in from getting the morning paper. "Ye Gods, it's still cold out there. Wade, have you got a heavy sweater or jacket? You're gonna need one, I think; it's even colder, usually, across the border. Has he got one, Tony? He's gonna need one, for sure."

"Don't know; haven't asked. Do you, Wade?"

"Well, naw; it was almost hot weather where I started from, but I'm going to be fine; I'll just bundle up with what I've got—it'll be enough."

"Like hell it's *enough*—you don't know how cold it can get here, Wade; it can be a killer here when the roses are bloomin' elsewhere. The calendar don't mean much this time of year. I'll get you one of my old jackets; you can send it back once the weather gets O.K. where you're at. And don't argue about it, 'cause I ain't listenin'. Now, get your gear and let's go; gotta get you way up and across the St. Lawrence River before dark."

"Bye, sweetie; see ya in 'bout an hour."

*Thank God for Tony and Tania,* he thought as his teeth chattered in the icy wind beside the highway headed north toward Watertown and the border. He was sure he would have been frozen stiff by now but for Tony's old fleece-lined jacket, along with the pair of his old thermal long-johns he had insisted Will put on at the last minute.

Tony had said that the temperature usually wasn't too bad this time of year, but that the wind out of the north was still a killer some days. This was one of those days.

In spite of the bone-chilling wind that felt as if it was straight out of the arctic circle, he felt extremely fortunate, and far beyond his expectations, to have gotten this close to the border in only two rides. Maybe that was a good sign for the future, he said to himself.

After a full hour, and no sign of another ride—and a beginning fear of possible frostbite—he built a small fire on the shoulder of the road. He could actually begin to feel his hands again, when he heard the unmistakable squeal of automobile brakes on the highway. A bright red 1940 Ford V-8 four-door sedan, with Canadian plates, was backing up—a tad too fast, he thought. The driver slammed on the brakes again, and stopped abruptly, abreast of where he stood staring at the car.

The right side front window rolled down and a young woman, with the most jet-black hair he had ever seen, looked out and shouted, over the wind and traffic noise, *"Bonjour, mon cher McGilly; il fait froid, oui?"*

Will knew it was French, but was dead lost after the *bonjour;* thus he simply stood in place and kept his stare alive like a deer caught in the headlights.

It must have seemed the same to her, because she was quick to say—slowly this time—in such a beautiful accent that in spite of the cold almost mesmerized him, *"Ooooh—pahdawn moh Cheri; you are able to speak solely l'ánglais, yes? And also, eet ees verrry cold, yes?"*

All Will could muster in reply was a mute nod of his head.

Mercifully, the right rear door now opened a crack and another lovely head—a strawberry blonde, this one—emerged, cooing—but in a language Will understood, "Oh, you poor pitiful boy; you must be frozen through and through. Whoever put you out in this crazy weather ought to be hosswhipped; that's what we'd do to 'em in Texas. Get in here *now,* fella—so we can *wahm* you up!"

He didn't wait for another invitation. In he went; more accurately, in he *squeezed,* with the two girls already in a backseat that was never designed for three adults to fit in, with comfort.

But, it *was* warm. And it did feel good to be close to a pretty girl for a change. He liked girls as much as—maybe *more* than—most normal 17 year olds, but since December he hadn't thought much about that subject. Of course he had been with Polly some, but he had always looked on her like a sister, so that didn't count, he mused.

This was different—these certainly were not his sisters—and he suddenly felt the twinge that any other young man with normal hormones would feel, especially when the blond starting gently massaging his back.

The girls said that the four of them went to a girls' school down near Hartford, Conneticut; *Miss Adams' Reform School for Girls,* they called it. The driver, a Canadian who spoke English with no accent, said that the only available males near their "prison" attended *Queerfield Academy,* and that was why they had "flipped" when they had spotted what looked like a "real-man type"—even if he had been "shaking like a leaf"at the first sighting.

Although he was enjoying immensely his massage, Will forced himself to remove—slowly—the deft hand, and explain that he wasn't a student at McGill, but simply someone named Wade Johns, trying to get to Quebec City, and asked how far he might ride with them in that direction. Nichola, the driver, replied that they were on spring break "from the prison," and that Marie-Helene had invited her and the other two to share it at her home near Quebec City. "Again, what is your city, Marie-Helene? And how far is it from Quebec City?"

"Loretteville; that is my home. It is a smaller town a bit north of the city of Quebec, but we will pass very close; it would require no more than a small *deviation*—a 'detour' you would say—to drop him off.

"But, my good and dear friends," she addressed the other girls, "I must ask you this question: we have only now found this great prize—one rarely

found in my dear country of Canada since the commencement of this foolish game of men—the game they call *'war.'* Are we to be so foolish that we
are to release him this quickly?"

An answer came from the strawberry blonde next to Will, "I got an
idea——let's vote on it; I vote NO! 'Cause not only is our 'prize' 'bout six
feet two and just plain *gawwwjous*—he's also got an East Texas accent like
I haven't heard since Lord knows *when!* We're not likely to be this lucky
'til this durned old wah is plain over and done with. I say: Let's keep him!
And *nevvver* let him go!"

Will had assumed that all this banter was teen-aged joking, but the
more it went on, the more he had begun to wonder, when the driver—who
apparently was their de facto leader—relieved him by, "Great idea girls,
but the sad part is that the adults in our lives don't understand our problem
like they should. Sadly, I think we have to release him, or risk having our
sentences at the prison extended."

Then, smiling at Will through her rear-view mirror, she added, with a
twinkle in her eye, "That is, when we have *finished* with him!"

After letting that settle in for a minute, Nichola said, "Don't mind us
Wade; we're just some healthy girls dreaming out loud a little. Seriously,
exactly *where* in the city are you going? We'll try to get you close."

Will called out the street and number of Angie's apartment, and said he
understood that it was in a four-story building just outside the walls of the
old town. Marie-Helene responded, *"Ah oui,* not a problem; I know well
that street. On many occasions, my *papa,* my *mere* and me, we enjoyed a
stay in a nearby *auberge* on that very street. It is a short one, and it is true
that it is just outside the ancient walls."

They found Angie's apartment building. All four girls got out of the
car to kiss him goodbye, a peck on each cheek by three, but differently—
somewhat more than convention required—by the blonde. When she finally disengaged, she sighed and said, "Well dahlin', I hope your friend
here retires late; do you realize it's 2:00 A.M.? But, whatever the time,
you're here—at your destination."

"No—*not* my 'destination'—just the first stop on the way."

# Chapter Ten

The minute the girls' car pulled away, he glanced at his watch, as he recalled doing about an hour earlier. It read 10:00—but then he realized that was *exactly* what it had shown an hour before. When he put it to his ear, he heard no ticking. His mind raced, *Ye Gods; the thing has stopped, so maybe it is two in the morning, like she said.* Then, *If so, I'll really shoot myself in both feet, if I knock on Angies's door this late.*

He had noticed a small park on the other side of the street as they had driven up. Amazingly to him, he had been happily surprised to find that the weather in Quebec was not nearly as cold—at least on this night—as it had been by the highway in upstate New York that morning.

By the moonlight, he searched the park for someplace out of the wind. There wasn't much there, except a small structure housing bathrooms and a bandstand shell, together with a small childrens' playground area off to one side. The kids' area had a short above-ground metal tunnel that had a serpentine-shaped section.

Will hid his suitcase in some bushes back of the bandstand, then managed to squirm his body, feet first, into the tunnel as far as the curved portion. *Maybe I won't sleep much in here, but at least I won't freeze,* he thought.

He was right on both counts. At best he dozed a few times during the night but welcomed the first glimmer of daylight, sliding his way out of the tunnel into his first Canadian dawn.

Will had rewound his watch the night before, and hoped that the 6:30 then showing on it's face was indeed correct. Regardless, he intended to find out if Angie was an early riser.

After retrieving his bag, he went to the men's room and looked in the mirror to see if he looked human. His verdict was *no,* so he fished out his razor and managed a cold water shave, finding it painful but effective.

At a little before 7:00, he was tapping on the door to *Appartement Numero 43,* as stated in the letter from André. He also was wondering if he had the right place. In the entry hall to the building he had noticed that the mailbox for *Numero 43* had the name "Angieline *Colbert*" on it—not *Hebert*. But he had double checked the letter from André before climbing the three flights of stairs, and 43 was the number specified.

It was only after the fourth time he knocked that a lovely voice responded, *"Oui, qui est la?"* ; then, hearing no answer, said, "Yes, who is there?"

"Excuse me, ma'am, but my name is Will Johnson—from Atlanta—in Georgia—the United States. I'm the fella' your friend André wrote you about."

"Will *who?* André? Oh yeah; I remember now. You have a friend who's also a friend of André's, right? If so, tell me your friend's name."

"Sure; it's Joe—Joe Hearn, from my home town. We used to go to school together. Then he left last year and joined the RCAF."

At that, the door opened, with a curt, "Since you're here, you may as well come on in."

"Ma'am, first let me apologize for coming here so early in the morning, but I got here at *2:00* this morning; and I slept over in the little park last night, and didn't know where else to go after I got up . . . "

"Don't worry about that," she interrupted. "What I want to know is *why* you're here at all; Andrè said you were going to call me—not just *pop in* like this. I'll make some coffee, and fix us a little breakfast, because we need to talk—a lot, it seems. By the way, how did you get here? You look pretty beat."

"Oh, I'm O.K., ma'am; just a little tired, mainly from tryin' to sleep in the park last night. I hitch-hiked from Chattanooga—took me three days—but it wasn't bad. Met some nice folks who helped me a lot.

"I'm real sorry if I've upset you by just showin' up. I'm gonna be flat-out honest with you about it all. The reason I came on, without calling first, is that I'd made up my mind to come on anyhow, even if you had told me not to. I plan to get in the Canadian air force here come hell or high-water, and whatever it takes, so I didn't see much point in calling first. I sure hope you're not gonna hold that against me, ma'am—'cause, believe me—I *need* your help."

Angie had to chuckle just a little. For a fleeting moment, she had found herself a little homesick from listening to his accent, but then said, without turning toward him from the stove, "First, I'm more likely to *help* you, if you will quit calling me 'ma'am.' I don't think I'm quite old enough for that honor from you. How old are you anyhow, Will?"

"Well, 'Will' is 17—goin' on 18—but I'm using a new name now, and *Wade Johns* is 22. I'll explain that, if you give me a chance to."

That turned her around. She looked straight at him, with an involuntary smile, "Oh kaaaaaaaaaah, Will—or Wade—whatever it is; looks like you and I have got lots to talk about. But don't worry about your *alias;* you would fit in real good around here. I use two names myself—and *I'll* explain later too.

"But, right now, I think we'd best arm ourselves by eating something. How you like your eggs?"

He almost breathed in his breakfast; for the first time that day he remembered that he and the girls had eaten nothing after their brief stop for lunch about 20 hours prior. As he pushed back from the table, he said, "Angie, if you'll let me take the time, I'd like to tell you everything about my situation—and I mean *everything*. I'm here begging for your help, but I think it's only fair for you and your boss to know the whole deal, with nothing held back. Of course, I hope that nothing I tell will screw me up in getting y'all's help but, if it does, I'll just have *to deal with it,* as my dad says."

He then told her his entire story, leaving out nothing. She was impressed by his fervor for his objective, as well as his unabashed and refreshing frankness about his shortcomings and qualms of conscience about hurting his family by his actions. It sounded so similar to André's experiences of 2 1/2 years before, that she found herself on the verge of tears at times.

Angie had been especially moved when he told her that one reason he wanted to use a new name was to protect Polly, the only person other than Joe and André who might know that he was coming to Quebec. He reasoned that he could soon make Polly believe that he was somewhere other than Canada if this "Wade" was the one here instead of "Will."

They were emptying their second full pot of coffee when Angie finished her own story of how and why she had started working with the LOM, leaving out some of the more sensitive security facts.

At around 9:00, she had called Jean-Paul and said she'd be a little late coming in. Now, at 10:30, she started to put on her coat and turned to Will, with "Wade—we may as well start getting used to that name. by the way— I'm still not comfortable with my *nom de guerre* of *Colbert* rather than Hebert. I don't know if my boss will agree to help you with this or not. If anyone can help, it's Jean-Paul, but there are potential down-sides here that even I can visualize; he may see more. I'll talk to him today, and maybe I'll have a feel for it by tonight. Where can I get you this evening, say after 8:00?"

"Er, I'm not sure; I'm gonna look for a youth hostel—or maybe a YMCA—something cheap. You know of one?"

"Nope, but I can call around today.

"Look; I know you must be exhausted; if you want, you can stay here today, get some sleep; then tonight—after we talk—I'll drive you to whatever we find for you. Just make yourself at home, use the fridge, and you can sleep on the couch if you wish. I'll try to be back by seven or so.

"See you later."

She took her time on the way to work, trying to fix in her mind just how to present this to Jean-Paul. It wasn't going to sit well with him, she knew. There were so many risks, without any substantial benefit to his cause; that was her foremost concern. Angie had already become sold on helping this bright and bold youngster—the word *intrepid* kept coming to mind. *A younger clone of André,* she kept thinking, as she strode briskly up the last incline toward the LOM's office behind the old bistro.

He had listened to her for nearly an hour; with uncommon patience, she felt. When she stopped he sat, slowly stroking his mustache and looking pensive, but without speaking a word. Finally, "Angie, you must know that this is a bizarre situation, with many possible problems if we are found out. In my head I can see it: angry parents, possibly angry governments, both in Ottawa and—more important to us, at this moment—Washington also.

"Then also, *where*—I must ask—is there a benefit to LOM? This, er—*boy,* he has no skills of which we have a need. *Maybe* he could fly with the Canadians, but that can be a reality only with much work—new identity, new name, most probably also a new *accent;* have you thought of that? Mon Dieu, even his *English* accent must be changed. I have stayed some days in your American South; *no* Canadian—even in B.C.—talks that way."

"Oh yes, Jean-Paul, I am aware of all you said, but this young man— he is *more* than a *boy,* I assure you—has shown great courage by coming here, a virtue that you and I treasure above all else for our work.

"And also, remember that he's here at the request of my André; how do I tell him that you refused to see this friend of his very best friend? Tell me that. Just *talk* to him before you say no. That's all I ask. Will you do that?"

"O.K.—O.K. Bring him down tomorrow. We talk—that is the end of what I will say—no more! We talk—no more. Now go; we have work to do."

*"Merci, mon patron,"* she cooed, and leaned over and kissed him on both cheeks.

During sandwiches and tea at her place, and on the way to the YMCA, she filled him in on her meeting with Jean-Paul.

She said she believed it to be a good sign that he had agreed to speak with him, and urged him to be as frank with her boss as he had with her. "And call him *Monsieur* LeBlanc. Never call him *Mister* LeBlanc," she counseled.

Further, she went on, "If he acts like he won't help, offer to do some work for him while you're here—*any* work—so he will *have* to get to know you; then, maybe later, who knows?"

Wade was quiet throughout the short drive, but hanging onto her every word. At the Y, she went in to make sure he was all set there, then told him she'd be back to get him at 7:30 the next morning.

At the check-in desk, he had opened his wallet; it wasn't hard for her to see that it was nearly flat.

Wade had enjoyed the hot shower, managed to get an iron from the desk, washed and ironed a shirt and his best pants, and felt good again. While trying to manipulate the iron, he kept repeating Mama's old saying, "When you *look* crummy, you *feel* crummy." He was determined not to *look*—or *feel*—like a bum when he met *Monsieur* LeBlanc.

It was 7:45 A.M. and crisp and cold when they arrived at the all night bistro that housed LOM's operations headquarters. Since the bistro was almost always a beehive of activity. 24 hours a day, the activities of LOM, in the rear of the building, went unnoticed by the public. Only the few who worked there were aware of the many activities being conducted in the cave-type spaces burrowed from the cliffside behind the noisy front.

As soon as Angie and Will entered, Jean-Paul quickly ushered them past the curious glances of two of his self-styled document authors—forgers who had been preparing a number of emergency passports during the night—into a tiny private room that doubled as his office. After shaking Will's hand vigorously, he invited both to share with him some still-steaming coffee, along with three crisp baguettes, a bit of butter, and some jams, at the side table.

When they had eaten, he flicked a few stray crumbs of a baguette from his unruly mustache, turned, and glared at Will for a full minute or more—slowly narrowing his piercing dark eyes until they seemed likely to disappear under a vast canopy of abundant graying eyebrows. It was a favorite tactic of *le patron* of LOM, and one that he believed gave him some immediate sense for the mettle of men he wished to test. He adhered to an adage he had once heard that "the eyes are the windows to the soul," to which he had added his own "and often a measure of the heart."

Some wilted a bit under this test; others would recognize the challenge and meet it with their own.

Will met it well; the older man blinked first.

Jean-Paul broke the impasse. "So, my young friend—you have this grand idea that you think you want to fly, eh?" he spat at the young man whose eyes—as sky blue as LeBlanc's were dungeon dark—were still locked on him like a laser.

"No, Monsieur LeBlanc. I don't *think* I want to fly! I *know* I'm *going* to fly. The only question is *when* and *where*.

"I *hope* it will be for Canada, sir; that's why I'm here."

Angie had positioned herself in the corner of the room, observing intently. She smiled slightly at Will's response; she had witnessed before these *tests* by her *patron,* and she knew that Will had passed the first one with flying colors.

Jean-Paul suggested that Angie leave them for a while, indicating that they would be finished soon. Two hours later she began to wonder how long was "soon," since Jean-Paul was the only Frenchman she had ever met who concerned himself in the slightest about the subject of time. After another hour, he called Angie back in.

"Wade—we use his *nom de guerre* only, starting now—and I have reached an accord. I have promised him *nothing*—nothing at all—about the RCAF. But I have told him also that, if he wishes, he can work here, cleaning the bistro, doing errands, dump the garbage. Whatever we wish him to do, he is willing to do that. Then, perhaps—and only *perhaps*—there will be a time when we can find a way to help his ambition. But there are *no* promises—that is the clear understanding—*d' áccord,* Wade? That is agreed, yes?"

Wade nodded, and Jean-Paul continued, "He will be paid a little, but not much, because his meals will be provided from the bistro, and he can sleep there, in the hammock in the store-room. If he proves to be worthy from a security view, then he can also act as—what do you Americans call it—our 'night watchman.' If he does not prove worthy for security well, I have explained the possible consequences. At the minimum, he is *gone,* like *pffft!*

"Tonight, Angie, I am asking that you explain, in more detail, the severe risks to him for serious breaches of security. And, please, explain that in great clarity.

"And, oh yes—and listen closely to me, Wade, as this is very, very, important; tonight also, Angie will prepare for you the background cover information that is required for you in using your new name. You are to memorize it *before* you come here tomorrow so that you are able to use it *tomorrow,* including with all other colleagues, as well as the *students* of LOM. Only two persons—Angie and myself—are to know you as anyone but *Wade Johns;* is that absolutely understood?"

The two worked late that night. While Wade was trying to familiarize himself with his duties, she prepared a background file, after some discussion with him. The file was then summarized to him, thusly:

Mr. Wade L. Johns, age 22, was Canadian by birth, having been born in the city of Victoria, British Columbia, on October 7, 1919.

Both his parents were native-born Canadians. His father had been killed in a skiing accident when Wade was three years of age. A year later, his mother met an American, Donald Johns, who had been working as a high rise steel-worker on a construction project near Vancouver. They were married soon thereafter and they, along with Wade, had gone to reside in a suburb of Birmingham, Alabama. He had lived there since, and his name had been changed legally to Johns, but he had dual Canadian/U.S citizenship.

Angie had typed additional details for him, and told him to study them thoroughly that night but, by all means, commit the summary to perfect memory by eight the next morning just in case Jean-Paul decided to test him with a few questions. Two days hence, she said she would retrieve from him the other information sheet she had just handed him and, at that time, she herself would test him on his recollection of all the details she had designed. Afterwards, the written record would be destroyed, but certain documents, such as birth certificates, passports, driving permits, etc., would be prepared and provided him.

She asked if he had retained any papers, of whatever nature, that might give a clue regarding his true identity. He replied that he had thought of that, and had burned all such papers before leaving Atlanta.

Angie laughed, "Good! Mr. Johns, you may have been born to be *not* a flyer but a *spy!*"

Both chuckled, then she introduced him to his hammock, and left for her apartment.

The second week Wade was with the LOM, he met a young Frenchman from Algeria who was preparing to go back for a week, prior to joining a group of *résistants* somewhere in France. Will asked him if he would take two handwritten letters with him, for mailing from Algeria. One was addressed to his mother, the other to Polly.

In both, he assured them that he was fine, in good health, and happy to be doing some good work in the interest of his country and the rest of the decent people in the world, but declined to say just where he was. He told his mother to please believe him when he said that he loved her—and all of his family—very much, and hoped they could understand that he had been compelled, somehow, to leave and seek what he thought was his place in the world.

To Polly, he emphasized that he had decided not to go to Canada, after all, as indicated on the postmark on the envelope, but that he would never forget the way she had tried to assist him.

Simultaneously, he persuaded Angie to send André a long note—hand-carried to England by one of their "students," who had been assigned to British Intelligence. The note explained that their "little friend from Georgia" had arrived, but had a new name, and that it was imperative that no one—repeat, NO ONE—in Georgia should know that he was there. "Explanation later," Angie had promised her fiancee.

As Wades's days continued at LOM, it was obvious that Jean-Paul was more and more impressed by his work ethic and intelligence, and amazed by his judgment and maturity. Increasingly, Wade was assigned difficult and security-sensitive tasks, performing above and beyond LeBlanc's demanding expectations on each occasion.

Col. Hebert was now insisting on receiving semi-monthly reports from LOM, detailing the proposed projects that would be funded by American dollars. Jean-Paul had previously informed the colonel that he did not have available a courier who met the OSS specifications for hand-delivering the reports, i.e; American, with no prior criminal record, with the exception of the colonels's daughter Angie, whom he needed in Quebec at all times.

Col. Hebert had telephoned that morning, and his answer was, "Damn it, if you want the dough, you'd better *get* somebody, and like *yesterday!* No more excuses, Jean-Paul. This is not my call; our congressional oversight committee *requires* it, or I can't release the money.

"Remember, we've got a real *democracy* to deal with here; it requires a little more than having tea with the King once a week!!

"Bottom line—no reports *by courier*—no money. Sorry, but that's the way it is."

Distressed by the call, he mentioned it to Angie. She paused only momentarily, then asked, "What about Wade? Why not use him for the courier?"

"Wade? But Angie, he is only a *boy!*"

"But Jean-Paul, are you not the same person who has said many, many times that in war, boys must sometimes become men? And you well know that many have indeed become men already during this war, many of whom you have trained here at this place. Is that not true?"

"Yes, it is truly what I have said. But what would your father say if he knew the courier has only 17 years?"

"Who knows? But the courier will not be *Will;* the courier will be *Wade,* who is 22 years! Remember that.

"By now, my father understands these things. Do you believe that our new OSS has had only mature and experienced operatives? The answer is a loud 'no.' I say let's use Wade; and, if necessary, *I* will answer to Colonel Louis Hebert."

On the eve of his first trip to Washington, Wade was briefed by Jean-Paul in the presence of Angie.

He was told that it was best he not know the content of the report he was to take to the OSS twice each month—that way it would be impossible for him to be broken under interrogation. It was of the very highest security classification, and must be delivered personally into the hands of one of two persons only: Colonel Louis Hebert, or his personal assistant, Mary Doss, and *no one else.* The report was on the new micro-film, so that if he found it necessary to destroy it there were various means that could be used: burning, flushing down a toilet, cut into slivers, or by swallowing the film in one or more pieces. But in no event was it to fall into improper hands; it was expected that he would do his utmost to prevent this, by risking his very *life,* if necessary.

Unless directed otherwise, he would travel by train, in a private compartment when such was available, but he was not to sleep at any time he was in possession of the packet; thus, he would, normally, take the day train to Boston, with a change there to D.C., then by taxi to the E-Street Complex.

His initial password for entry to the OSS headquarters would be—subject to future change, of course—"I have the maple leaves."

Wade listened in silence, said he understood, and that he was ready to go.

On his way out of the room, Jean-Paul slapped Wade on the back with, *"Bonne chance!* Angie will now brief you regarding the details of your rail travel, along with one other detail."

After giving Wade the travel data and his train tickets, she said she had something rather unusual to tell him, something that she and Jean-Paul had decided—after no little discussion—that he should know. ''Colonel Louis Hebert, LOM's contact at OSS, is my father," she told him. "That's the only reason I now use the name 'Colbert' as a *nom de guerre.* It is highly unlikely that I will ever be in a combat situation, but it was a concern of my father, shared by Jean-Paul, that there are people who might consider abducting me in order to blackmail my father. Personally, I think it's absurd, but when one is in the business of my boss here, and my dad in Washington, you tend to see a spook in every corner. Anyhow, we figured that Papa may mention this to you when the two of you meet; so now you will not be surprised.

"O.K.—-do you think you are ready for this mission? It *is* a little delicate, you know."

He smiled, "Ready? Hey, I've been an errand boy before; it's not so tough."

His train into the District was two hours late, having been put on a side track before leaving Boston, then again in New York, both times to give troop trains priority. In the cab, Wade wondered if anyone would still be at OSS at 7:30 P.M. on a Thursday night. He wasn't aware that the E-Street Complex never closed, and less, he certainly didn't realize that his particular OSS Colonel often showed up on all three shifts.

He was taken in to Col. Hebert within minutes of announcing, "I have the maple leaves."

Two minutes after the handshake and the passing of the micro-film packet, Wade was feeling much at home with his host. Col. Hebert was wearing civilian clothes, in shirtsleeves with an open collar, and was—as he put it—"in a visitin mood." He invited Wade, "Sit down, son, and tell me about yourself—where you from in Canada, that sort of thing; and tell me how Angie is doin'. She's my baby daughter; I guess you know that."

Wade thought to himself, *Damn! Why didn't they brief me on how to tell him about myself? I'm just gonna keep talking about Angie.*

As he did, he was relieved to find that his daughter was who this father *really* wanted to discuss, and they did so until Wade reminded him that he needed to get the 11:30 train out of Washington, because Jean-Paul had work for him to do on Friday afternoon.

At one point it had come out that although he was Canadian, he had grown up in Birmingham; then the subject got back to Angie again, much to Wade's relief. After their first good-byes, Louis walked him out to the street and said, "I sure enjoyed our visit, son; maybe next time we can have supper together. Believe it or not, we have a few—not many—restaurants here in Washington that have some pretty good home cooking. We'll have to try one of ém."

"Thanks a lot, Colonel; I'd like that. See you next trip, sir."

Early the next morning, Louis Hebert was on the phone to LeBlanc, "Well, Jean-Paul, you hit pay-dirt when you got this young man, Johns. I liked him; we talked for nearly three hours last night—got great common sense. It's hard to believe he's only 22 years old!"

"*Merci beaucoup, Colonel;* I also have wondered at that about Wade; he is mature beyond his years, no doubt."

As he hung up, he turned and beamed at Angie, "*How* did I do without you before you came, my dear one?"

It had been the saddest of times at the Johnson home after their son had left; the house had been more like a morgue than a home.

His mother had almost fainted on the afternoon that Bill came screaming in from checking their mail. "Mama, there's a letter from Will! It's from Algiers!"

She was trembling too much to open the envelope, and asked her son to do it. Then, after Bill had taken it and opened the letter, she could not read it through her tears.

Bill read it aloud.

Both were relieved to hear that he was well and happy, and broke into tears again as he mentioned how he loved his family. The letter said that he was under strict orders not to reveal much of what he was doing—or where—for reasons of security, but that it was not dangerous, actually rather boring at times. It ended by saying that he would endeavor to write from time to time, but that he could not predict how long it might be between letters. He closed by:

> "No matter what you may think of my doing what I did, please try to accept the truth that my greatest love is that I feel for you, and while I am doing what I feel I must do at this time, it will be my happiest day when I am with all of you again.
> "My love to you, Dad, Bill, and the girls,
> Will"

The next day Bill told Sgt. Mac the news. The Sarge shook his head and, leaning across his desk, said, "I'm afraid the time has come to 'let it be' Bill. I heard it said once that it's hard to harness a wild wind; sometimes you just have to let it blow itself out, and pray for the best. Maybe that's the only thing for your family now."

"That may be right, Sarge, but I doubt my folks can accept that yet."

It had been four months since *Wade's* first courier trip to D.C. All had gone uneventfully, the only exciting part being a couple of dinners with Col. Hebert and some OSS operatives who were in D.C. between assignments. They had talked shop guardedly in his presence, but enough for him to learn that their secret war was equally exciting—if not more so—as the one the public read about in the daily news.

In between trips he had become involved deeply in almost every aspect of LOM activities, doing well each task given him, far beyond the expectations of LeBlanc and Angie.

She had, more than once, marveled to her boss at how quickly Wade had learned whatever they tossed at him, and especially how much of the French language he had picked up. "Granted," she said, "it is a weird combination of Canadian, North African, and French Indo-Chinese versions, but somehow he makes people understand him!"

Shortly after his eighth, and last, D.C. visit, Jean-Paul had been informed by Col. Hebert that they need not continue, since the codes were now secure enough for the reports to be made via military TWX. In less than ten minutes after hearing of this, Wade was outside Jean-Paul's door, requesting a meeting.

He said that he had been reluctant to mention it while he was needed for the courier duty, but now he was requesting some active help with his goal to join the RCAF. The *patron* promised to give it thought and would discuss it with Angie without delay. He felt that the youngster had given the LOM more than they had ever hoped for, and now it was time for payback.

That evening he told Angie that though there were risks, he was confident it could be done with some help from their friend Marcel, who was still in recruitment for the RCAF. "It would be more simple if he were either a French-Canadian, or even an Anglophone, except that his English accent—more of a *drawl,* actually—could *never* be passed off as that of *any* Canadian."

"But, have you forgotten the background cover I designed for him when he first arrived?" said Angie. "It was for that very reason—the accent—that we had our Wade Johns reside in Alabama—the deep South— since he was about four years of age. *Voila,* the reason for his accent! But, by reason of his birthplace and his parentage, he is Canadian, also."

"*Eh oui, cherie!* It is true; I did forget. Then it will be a—how do you say—*a piece of cake* for Marcel. I may see him this night. But it is a pity— and much so—that we cannot hold this talent for our own cause. But he has his own special dream—as we ours—so we must aid him in the chase!"

✫      ✫      ✫

Marcel was waiting, sipping a pastis at a corner table, when his old friend stepped into the small smoke-filled bar, their favorite meeting place since their teens.

"Only an old bush pilot" was what Marcel answered, when people asked about his profession. For decades before the war, he had made a living by flying a multitude of times into the frozen northland of Canada— *Canada du nord,* the francophones called it—transporting hunters, trappers, and plain adventurers, along with an assortment of bored but rich foreigners. For whatever reason, they wanted to see how life was in that sometimes beautiful—and always *cold,* often unbearably so—land. He frequently bragged that he was the only pilot alive who had landed more on skis than wheels.

He was a true *Québécois,* to be sure—tracing his ancestry directly back to the first 12,000 French men and women who settled the area in the late seventeenth century—but not a *separatist* like his old friend LeBlanc. They had argued this issue many times, but it had not diminished their friendship. Marcel's position was that it was a lovely dream, but for the *absolute certainty* that a separate nation of Quebec could not expect to *survive,* let alone prosper.

He delighted in setting off his friend with, "I can see it now, *mon ami;* we are our own nation, oh so proud and gallic, speaking our beloved language as we please, *but* there is no *bread* for our children! Then I hear a royal voice from the past of France, except this time that voice is from Buckingham Palace; the voice proclaims, 'Well, let them eat cake.'

"So, I say to you, 'no thank you, Monsieur.' *Moi,* I prefer *bread* for my infants."

Long before the war, Marcel had been viewed by many Canadian authorities in the central government as a bridge of reason to the more radical elements of the Quebecois.

Thus, shortly after the start of hostilities, they invited him to assist in recruitment of the cream of Canadian youth—in particular, those of French descent—into the Royal Canadian Air Force.

There had been a fear among some that the francophones might not fully support the war effort. While some francophone groups did demonstrate and protest against mandatory conscription into the armed forces, the youth of Canada, including those from francophone families, never gave any indication of shirking their duty; quite the contrary was true.

Nevertheless, the grave situation in the British Isles, in the days following the withdrawal from Dunkirk and the collapse of France, had made the building of the RCAF a foremost priority. It was vital that no stone be left unturned in that effort.

The aging pilot responded like the true patriot he was; not only was he invaluable with those of French blood, he was equally effective with every element of Canadians, of whatever ancestry and age. And it was now well known that he had unrestricted access to, and influence in, the highest levels of the RCAF.

The only condition he had attached to performing his present job was that he could continue to spend most of his time in Quebec City. And a great deal of that time was spent here, at the bar of *Chez Cecile.*

On sight of LeBlanc, he stood and embraced him with a loud, "*Bonsoir Jean-Paul, ça va?*" to the response of, "Oh yes, I am O.K., thank you, old friend. And you?" Then, "I see you are having our drink, so where is my own?"

"Waiter, another pastis, please; for my friend who is dry!"

# Chapter Eleven

As they were leaving Cecile's, Marcel gave Jean-Paul his card, with a name, a Montreal address, and a telephone number scribbled on it, and instructed that Wade call the number after five days, giving his name only. The person on the other end would give Wade further directions. If Marcel encountered any problems before then, he would contact Jean-Paul, but he anticipated none.

Eight days later, in Montreal, a Flight Lieutenant administered the oath to Wade, shook his hand, and told him to report back two weeks later for active duty assignment.

Dreaming of his future during the train ride back to Quebec City, he was filled with joyful anticipation; but it was tempered no little by knowing he had so few with whom he could share this moment.

The next day, Angie sensed this and suggested privately to their boss that they could make up for this in a small way. On the eve of his departure, Jean-Paul and Angie treated him to a farewell dinner at *Cafe Maman.*

Nathalie had been told that it was for Wade's birthday. Accordingly, this dinner to remember culminated with a huge birthday cake being brought to the table by Nathalie, while she and her sons did a stirring rendition of *Joyeux Anniversaire,* followed by the sharing of the cake with the other guests in the cafe.

A pilot's training in the RCAF followed somewhat the same plan as the RAF itself, with some necessary changes due to the severe Canadian winters.

In England, a would-be pilot would typically have eight weeks ground training at an Initial Training Wing (ITW), ten weeks of flying and ground lessons at an Elementary Flying Training School (EFTS), followed by up to sixteen weeks at a Service Flying Training School (SFTS) on *advanced* flying practice.

This was, of course, subject to modification at times, if conditions demanded it.

The Canadians liked very much the American-made Stearman bi-plane used as an initial training aircraft in the U.S. but—because of its open cockpit—they found it impractical for use during their long cold seasons. At almost the same time Wade was entering the RCAF—October, 1942—they had attempted to have it fitted with a canopy enclosing the cockpit, but soon abandoned that effort and continued to send many of their trainees to one of the seven British Flying Training Schools (BFTS) that were lo-cated in the American sunbelt.

It was still December—and still very frigid—when Wade finished ground-school at the RCAF facility near Toronto. The day after, he was handed Orders to report as soon as possible for flight training at No. 6 BFTS, Ponca City, Oklahoma, along with train tickets there, with one change of trains—at the Terminal Station in Atlanta.

When he examined his tickets there was an immediate flashback to his summer of '41. He wondered if Aunt Beth's friend was still the Postal Tele-graph manager there—or perhaps Aunt Beth herself.

The flashback turned to panic: *What if I'm recognized there?*

At the Toronto station, he was surprised to run into another cadet, Ger-ard Morais, who had been in his class in Toronto; he was also headed to the Ponca City BFTS.

On the way south—as he continued to fret to himself about being seen at the Atlanta station—he told Gerard that though he had been raised in Birmingham, a city near Atlanta, had attended prep school in Atlanta for a year or so, and knew quite a few people there, that he preferred not re-minding them that he had chosen to join the Canadian military rather than the U.S., and he expressed a fear of being recognized there.

He then asked Gerard to help him by taking his ticket to the ticket counter in Atlanta if that became necessary, so that he himself could simply go from one train platform to the next and see as few people as possible.

His comrade looked at him quizzically, smiled slyly, and said, "Do you have any idea how *weird* that tale sounds? I'm fairly certain a girl is in-volved here, but I refuse to interrogate a new friend! *Done!*

"I only hope she's a *beauty*, and worthy of such concern."

Wade thanked him, but felt ashamed as he thought, *Oh God, I'll be so thankful if the day ever comes when I can quit all this lying—piling more and more lies on top of all the others.*

He stood nervously on the station platform for an hour and a half that evening, pondering each minute if he should risk phoning his family.

Finally, he decided he had lied enough for one day, and boarded the train for Oklahoma.

It was just as well; he would not have reached them that evening.

A small crowd of relatives and friends—along with Master Sergeant Duncan Angus Macdonald, resplendent in his full dress uniform and decorations—were gathered in the offices of the Army Air Corps recruiters—only three short blocks from the Terminal Station—to witness proudly the swearing in of six graduates of Fulton High, Class of June, 1942, including Bill Johnson.

As they took their oaths as aviation cadets, Noah Johnson beamed with pride, but in the back of his mind he couldn't resist thinking how it *would* have been if his other son were there, also. His wife Katie was thinking of Will also, but her focus was the same as it had been each day and night for most of that year, *Pray God; let him be safe and well, wherever he may be.*

The first to shake Bill's hand was his father, closely followed by Sgt. Mac.

Polly Hearn was there too, with her father, who assured Bill's family that Bill would do well, and that he had already written his boy Joe about Bill going into the air corps.

He added that he wished Joe had waited, but that Joe was well and happy, adding, "Maybe it all works out for the best that my bull-headed kid ran off to Canada like he did," hoping that this might help Noah and Katie a little. On the way home, he told Polly, "I didn't know what to say to them; I know they were thinking about their own lunkhead, but I'm afraid I didn't help a darned bit, honey."

Polly turned away so as not to let him see her tears, "Please; don't call him a 'lunkhead,' Daddy."

It was on that night that Polly finally admitted to herself that she was in love with—and desperately worried about—Will. She had never believed the story in the one letter he had sent her, but had gotten no response to her letters to Angie or to Joe concerning Will's whereabouts. But Will's story about Algeria *had* given her an excuse for not telling her part in his disappearance.

There were 18 in the training class at Ponca City, most of whom were from the British Isles, including three Scots. Wade and Gerard were the only Canadians.

Their Chief Instructor was Jake Hardin, a civilian and a Floridian who had been training students in the Stearman PT-17 since the first group of RAF and Royal Navy Fleet Air Arm cadets had come to the Naval Air Station in Pensacola, Florida, on July 24, 1941—all of them dressed in civilian clothes, presumably to preserve the "neutrality" of the United States.

As Jake briefed his latest group, they sensed right away that he had a certain love for the airplane behind him that he was describing, occasionally patting it gently as he talked.

He ended his comments with, "Of course, like most things, she's not absolutely perfect." He added, "well, maybe perfect in the *air*—or as near so as any airplane yet made—but when you start to set her down, you gotta be damned careful not to screw up the landing.

"Look close at that gear there and you'll see it's real narrow, so much so that even a good *experienced* pilot can ground-loop her at the drop of a hat. 'Cept for that, I promise you this: if you fly a hundred different birds before you hang it up for good, you're never gonna have one better'n this baby right here. Any questions?"

Wade had planned to ask a question, but had forgotten it the minute Jake had mentioned ground-looping; all he could think of then was his friend—Gary Kelly.

But those thoughts vanished quickly as he heard Jake explaining that, starting the next day, half the group would be scheduled for flying each day—weather permitting—while the other half attended ground school, thus permitting the most efficient use of their instructors, including himself. The schedule would be posted on the cadet bulletin board within the hour. They were then dismissed for lunch.

As Wade listened to the chatter at lunch, and the cadets exchanged personal information, it occurred to him that if they really *believed* him to be 22, they must be viewing him as the old man of the class; none could be more than 18 or 19, and several looked younger. The common thread among them was their contagious enthusiasm and the absolute confidence each obviously had in himself.

He was bursting with pride in being one of them.

It didn't take long for Jake's new class to begin to share his romance with their remarkable machine, as they experienced the unique exuberance of flying with the wind in their faces, especially during aerobatics that few, if any, aircraft were capable of performing so gracefully.

"I've always wondered how the *Eagle* feels; and now I *know*!" exclaimed one of the young Englishmen, after his first ride through a breathtaking demonstration of loops, slow-rolls, snap-rolls and controlled spins, with his instructor at the stick.

About halfway through the class, Wade heard the news that three of the RAF men had been *washed out,* meaning elimination from flight training.

He had gotten to know one of the Scots—who had been nick-named "Stump" by reason of his stature—fairly well. As Wade knocked at his new friend's open door, he saw him packing to leave. He told Wade it was "just as well," since somehow he froze on the stick each time his instructor had let him try a landing. "Don't bother yourself about me, laddie. I'll do better as a tail-gunner in a Lancaster. A bloody fool can see I'm the right size for that job.

"But I'll be Hun-hunting right alongside ye; ye can count on that."

It was a good act, Wade thought, as he pretended not to notice the still-red eyes that gave away his friend's feeling of failure.

All was the opposite for Wade. After Jake rode with him on his final check-ride—and as they were walking in on the ramp—he turned to Wade with, "Son, you're a natural for this business if I ever saw one. You did great!

"Just remember though, after you leave here, your airplanes are gonna get bigger *and* hotter. So don't get cocky just 'cause this was a snap for you. No matter how good a pilot is, these birds can kill ya in a split second.

"It's smart to remember an old and true saying; it goes something like this: 'There are *old* pilots, and there are *bold* pilots, but there're not many old *and* bold pilots.' You got 'at?"

"Sure have, Mr. Hardin. But don't worry; flying is all I ever really yearned to do in my entire life. I promise you that now I've gotten my chance, I don't plan to blow it.

"You're a terrific teacher, Mr. Hardin, and I'll never forget you—or this airplane, either."

Since the Canadian winter was far from over in mid-February, his class from Ponca City was soon on their way to England for their next level of training.

The troop ship they were on certainly fell short of luxury living but the slow trip gave them plenty of time to write letters, and to fantasize a lot about their future. They talked together for hours on end.

Twelve of the remaining 15, including Wade, wanted to fly fighters, constantly needling the three quiet ones who admittedly preferred bombers.

One of the would-be bomber pilots finally retorted, "Yeah, and after this bloody war, you blokes will be pumping petrol for a living, 60 hours or more per week. And *us* three? We'll be flying our 80 hours a month for some grand airline—complete with lovely lasses waiting on us on the flight-deck as if we were bloody Royals—banking our loot, living like three Squires should.

"But, never fear—if we see you some day in rags, we may toss you a quid or so; it's called *noblesse oblige* you see!"

It became a sort of custom with their group that at the end of these bull-sessions most would catch up with letter-writing to family and friends. It didn't go totally unnoticed that Wade never seemed to write a letter. No one pried, but Wade thought of it each time he saw one of them happily scribbling away.

He began to wonder, at times, if the price he had paid was too high.

The only real excitement on the sea voyage was a couple of U-boat alerts as they approached the Irish coast. But these were quickly responded to by their Royal Navy escort that had grown visibly larger as their convoy sailed eastward.

The first half of the 16 week training, all trainees flew the same airplane. During the eighth week each was summoned to a battery of interviews, dealing with what type of aircraft—single or multi-engine—he should fly next. One important factor was the physical stature of the cadet; a six foot four inch man wasn't an ideal fit for most fighter aircraft of the time. Temperament was another factor; it was the belief of some in authority that the nature of combat for a fighter pilot called for a different mental attitude, as well as physical reflexes, compared to a bomber or transport pilot carrying out a pre-planned mission over or toward a specific target or destination.

Most of this SFTS class was no different than others before them; almost all dreamed of themselves as destined to fly a Spitfire or Hurricane, in the image of those who had earned the admiration of the free world in the skies over England during the Battle of Britain

Wade was no exception. When he was interviewed by his instructor, he was complimented again for his superior record thus far in SFTS. The flight lieutenant pointed out, however, that his height recommended him for multi-engine aircraft.

When Wade grimaced slightly at this, the officer smiled and quickly said, "Just a minute now, Mr. Johns; I have better—and quite exciting—news for you. Have you heard of our RAF aircraft we call the *Wooden Wonder,* officially called the *Mosquito?*

When Wade shook his head, he continued, "No, I shouldn't think so.

"It shall become, many believe, the most effective machine in the air, for many different purposes. It is light weight—extremely so—because it is all *wood;* therefore it is faster than the Spitfire *or* the Hurricane, and probably is *the* fastest military airplane in Europe—so fast that *none* of the current enemy fighters can stay with it, certainly not at lower altitudes.

"It can be configured for photo-reconnaissance, as a fighter, a bomber, or as a fighter-bomber, for rescue missions, or many other roles. In short, it is an absolutely amazing airplane, and I assure you that a good half our veteran pilots in the RAF want to fly it."

"That's fine sir, but why are you telling me about it?"

"Good question, Wade; forgive me for getting a bit carried away for a moment.

"All instructor pilots, such as I, have been directed to identify outstanding cadets whom we would recommend for entry into the Mosquito program after this level of their training. There is now a special force within the RAF that is dramatically expanding its operations, and it will utilize this astounding aircraft primarily, if not altogether, for most of its future missions.

"I am not at liberty to discuss this with you further at the present time, but I can assure you that the proposed missions—if successful—will be of utmost importance to our war effort. The Air Ministry is insisting on absolutely *top* of the line candidates—but *volunteers only*—for this program. With your assent, I would recommend you with enthusiasm. Are you game for such?"

"Could I ask a couple of questions, if I may?" he answered, and continued as the officer nodded, "How many engines does this 'Mosquito' have, and how many crew members?"

"Twin-engines with a two-man crew—a pilot and a navigator/radio-operator sitting side by side. Some models are un-armed, some have nose-guns, depending on how the particular model is to be used; but *blinding speed* is its primary weapon."

Wade thought for a moment, then said, "Lieutenant, I wanted to fly the fighter—but I'm here to try to do what I can do best, long as it's flying. If the Mosquito is what y'all think is that 'best'—well, yessir, I'm game. What's next?"

"Bravo, Wade; you've made a good decision—you'll see! In fact I envy you!

"Next is eight weeks in the Airspeed Oxford; it's like a fat old cow beside the Wooden Wonder, but an altogether necessary next step in that direction. You and I will have at it for the next eight weeks."

On the day Wade had departed Quebec City, Angie had given him André's address as well as the telephone number of his unit headquarters, but when Wade had tried to contact him earlier, he was informed that André was on a temporary assignment elsewhere, but that they would give Squadron Leader Moreau his message.

A couple of days after Wade's interview, André had telephoned, suggesting that they try to meet the following weekend. André said he realized that cadets had little free time, so he would come there, and also that he would find out if Joe Hearn could join them, if that was O.K. with Wade. André added that he had been confused by the name Wade on the message but had sensed that it was related to the mysterious note Angie sent him via "some spooky guy with British Intelligence" several months prior, and therefore actually Will who had called.

Wade was thankful that his embarrassment couldn't be seen over the phone, but gathered himself enough to blurt out, "Yes, sir, I 'er; I know that *is* confusing; but it's kind of a long story, and I do want to explain it—at least *try* to—to both you and Joe. But, sir, if you do talk to Joe, please ask him not to mention to anyone back home that I'm here. O.K.—that's weird too, I know, but I hope to explain it all when I see you."

By now, André was trying hard not to break out laughing on the other end, and tried to reassure Wade, "Look Will—excuse me, I meant *Wade;* it's O.K. We'll get it squared away when we meet. Believe me; I understand that these cloak and dagger types—like the LOM crowd in Quebec— get into some pretty screwy scenarios with ease. That's one reason I worry about Angie being with them—and also one reason I felt easier when I knew a normal human being like you was there with her for a few months.

"Looking forward to seeing you, pal. I'll be back to you with details, about this Saturday; I was relieved to find that you can leave the base that night; catch you later—Bye!"

Wade wondered if—after that conversation—André still thought of him as a normal human being.

André and Joe were at the bar of the Fish 'n Chips 'n More, the only real restaurant in the village, when Wade walked in. Joe grabbed him in a bear hug that almost floored him, shouting at the top of his lungs, "Will, my man! How you been? God, it's great to see you again, ya heah? You gotta' tell me quick—how's your Mama and Daddy? And everybody at Fulton and Lakewood? What's Bill doin'? Where's Sergeant Mac now?"

Finally Joe paused for breath. André took both by their sleeves and guided them over to their table, grinning all the way, "Geez, Joe, hold it down, will ya! Every limey in here is staring at us and wondering what part of Canada *those* birds are from. All I'd have to do is give 'em a little Cajun chatter, and that'd really drive 'em up the wall. Let's sit down and eat." Then, "I'm André, *Wade.*" And, "Did you hear the *'Wade',* Joe?"

Joe had calmed down, "Yeah, I heard it, and I want to hear *more* about it—but *after* I hear about the other folks. So start talkin' boy!"

Wade filled Joe in about everything he could think of, but saved to the end the part about Gary Kelly, who had been on the same football team with them.

Joe was shocked and saddened, but told Wade that he should try to steel himself to expect to lose friends because it was going to happen sooner or later, adding, "Too bad the public doesn't know how dangerous the training of airmen is, so that if being a so-called 'hero' can help a family handle it better, they'd know that fellows like Gary were 'heroes' too."

Wade then told everything about his situation, answering questions as he did, concluding by expressing two requests: that they use his new identity, and that *no-one else*—including anyone in Atlanta—be told of it. He added that he hoped this did not put either of them in a compromising position.

André spoke up first, "Let's face it; I believe *all* of us could have a problem if this came out to some of the ' guard-house lawyers' we've all known;

you, Wade, for obvious reasons, and Joe and I because we knew it and concealed it, since I'm sure that would violate some damned regulation.

"But this I know; when *I* went to Canada, it was before Pearl Harbor; the RCAF taking me, an American citizen, at *that* time was a clear violation of the Neutrality Act in the U.S. And yet it was open knowledge that hundreds of Americans were doing the same thing, especially from California where there were more unemployed civilian pilots left over from the depression than you could count. There were even ads in the newspapers, recruiting for the RCAF. Some rich dude—I think he lived somewhere in Ohio—was financing the ads and bragging about it publicly!

"So, what I'm getting at is this; I've got no qualms about going along with this—and I doubt that many others truly give a damn about it—if we don't pop off about it ourselves; O.K.? Wade, you've already proven you've got the stuff to fly with us, and I want you by our side."

"You got a big ditto from me, Skipper; let's *do* it!" Joe raised his mug, and the trio clinked their glasses. "Now, Cadet Johns, tell us about this *Mosquito* business you mentioned a couple of hours ago."

It was obvious that the youngest of the three had relaxed as he calmly exclaimed, "It will be my distinct honor to enlighten you airplane drivers from a primitive era. Listen carefully."

Joe and André did just that—in rapt attention—as Wade divulged the considerable store of facts he had learned already about the Mosquito. They had been hearing rumors for a year or so, but most of it was about the controversy that raged in high circles about the basic feasibility of a *wooden* airplane for any military purposes. They also knew that some of the experts had been quoted as being "aghast at the thought" of such.

Until this evening they had not learned that its manufacturer, Geoffrey de Havilland, had prevailed and demonstrated the abilities of the Mosquito in many different roles. Further, even though each had heard about a new force of the RAF, called *The Pathfinders,* they were surprised to learn that the Mosquito was now to be its primary aircraft.

And, of course, they were most impressed that their friend, Cadet Wade Johns, had been selected to fly it. Joe's last comment—as they said their good-byes a little past two a.m.—was, "What a shame that all the folks back home can't know about you!"

Then, he added a loud, "Yet!"

The Mosquito became known by many nick-names, but probably the most common were the *Wooden Wonder* and the *Mossie.* It is quite likely that German and Italian airmen had other names for it, probably unprintable.

Before the end of the war, it had become, without question, the most versatile military aircraft in history.

It was simple in design and construction, and one of the most cost-effective aircraft ever built. Included in its construction was Ecuador balsa for the plywood skin, Sitka spruce from Alaska and British Columbia in the wing spar, and Douglas fir stringers and birch and ash for the longitudinal members, all held together with glue and wood screws. It was easy to patch, flew higher than almost any other aircraft, and was capable of carrying tremendous fire power and a bomb load over tremendous distances.

The bomber version operated over Germany with relative impunity to the end of the war because the Luftwaffe never had a night-fighter fast enough to intercept it. It also excelled as a day and night fighter, intruder, fighter-bomber, dual-control trainer, airliner, and a transport aircraft for the Dutch and French resistance.

Of course, instructors loved it, because they could sit side-by-side with their students and thereby observe their every move. Thus, immediately after his completion of the SFTS level, Wade found himself in OTU and at the controls of a Mosquito that had been modified to be a dual-control trainer. His instructor—a battle-tested Aussie who had been one of the first to fly the Mossie when it had debuted as an unarmed bomber—was at his right elbow.

After a few days of conquering the not-so-slight language barrier between student and teacher, Wade began to fully appreciate his good fortune in having Flight Lt. Herbie Wilson, RAAF, to guide him in learning to handle this exciting, but "hot as a cheap pistol"—as Herbie put it—machine, that would be his alone after several weeks.

Herbie had seen it all. He had been amongst the *"few"* to whom Winston Churchill referred—following the Battle of Britain—when he said, "Never in the field of human conflict was so much owed by so many to so few."

Later, Herbie's Hurricane had been crippled over the continent, but he had made it back to the channel where he ditched and watched his aircraft blow to smithereens within seconds after he had paddled away from it.

Through it all, he had explained to Wade, his only wound had been "a bit of shrapnel" still embedded deep inside a delicate part of his anatomy that encouraged him to "favor standing when practicable".

He had flown combat in six different airplanes, but "never in one the equal of Mossie," he told Wade the first day they met.

After three intensive weeks of days and nights, with Herbie directing and correcting from the right-side seat, Wade took it up solo, without anyone beside him—not even a navigator that he knew would sit there later. Herbie had explained why he was going totally alone with his usual broad grin, " . . . to insure that we don't lose a Navigator as well—in case you bash it, you understand." To which his now rather cocky student grinned back with, "Suits me, Lieutenant. That means I won't feel ill at ease by *not* landing like a hopping 'roo, as my *teacher* seems so fond of doing!"

Herbie was on the ramp, determined to be first to shake his student's hand as he taxied in, "Nice job, Wade; now you and I need to sit a bit and talk about your remaining month here. You need some flying time with a navigator 'cause that's how it'll be later, in most sorties. You need some cross-country, mostly 'round and about the U.K."

At the weather shack, over tea, he explained in more detail. "For the next couple of weeks, a navigator and I will alternate riding with you. You and he will do some cross-country, but not over the continent yet. And remember that the chap who becomes your regular navigator will have an additional duty as your radio operator and, on some trips, as what we call a 'bomb-aimer'—the Americans call that last job a 'bombardier'—so let him toy a bit with those, as you ride.

"After three more weeks, you and I shall say our *tearful* farewells, and I'll hand you to No. 8 Group (PFF), probably No. 105-or 109-Squadron. The Pathfinders have already become a truly elite unit, Wade; it's a compliment to you to be selected to fly with them. I hope you know that, and I have no doubt that you will fit in quite well with such company. Any questions?"

"Thanks Herbie; you've been great and I'll miss you. I just hope that some day I can say I've done even half what you have. But can you tell me exactly what the Pathfinders do? I know a little—but *very* little."

Herbie scratched his head for a moment before, "I'll try to tell you what I know."

He then proceeded to explain that No. 8 Pathfinder Group was unique, in that it had come into existence during the war, unlike Bomber Command Group and others that were continuations of existing peacetime organizations. The need for it grew out of the difficulties of RAF bomber crews obtaining accurate navigation to, and pinpointing accurately the location of, intended targets by night during the period 1939–1941. Soon afterwards the idea of a special force to precede the bombers and find and mark the targets began to make sense. Debate ensued as to whether such a force should simply be a part of the Bomber Command or a separate one. The latter concept eventually prevailed; hence the birth of the Path Finder Force (PFF) on August 15, 1942.

In it's infancy, PFF had utilized aircraft other than the Mosquito; the Mossie came with the addition to the PFF of No. 109 Squadron, as the 5th. unit, and soon proved it's unquestionable value to the force's operations, with it's high speed entry to a target area, sometimes at rooftop levels until

close to the target area to be marked with colored 'TI's'. The TI's illumi-
nated and marked the targets for the main bomb force of heavies that followed the Mossies into the target area.

The beauty of the Mossie was that when the enemy scrambled its pursuit aircraft, they were no match for the speed of the Mosquito. While late
in the war the Germans managed to develop a version of their Messer-
schmitt 109 that had better speed at high altitude, the Mossie needed only
to drop to a lower altitude in order to leave the German in its dust.

There were many and varied other ways in which this machine could
be—and was—used from time to time, even by the units of the PFF, and
Herbie concluded by predicting to Wade that there would be others yet un-
thought of before the end of their war.

That night, he thought of the next day, when he would finally be
pinned with his wings and commissioned as an officer in the RCAF. It
bothered him that he only qualified for the commission by reason of his
fake college degree that Angie had given him in Quebec along with his
*nom de guerre,* but since there was nothing he could do about it, his mind
drifted to other matters. Tomorrow would be July 4, 1943, and his thoughts
shifted to home.

In Atlanta, William Johnson, 2nd. Lieutenant, USAAC, was home that
day on a five-day leave, having just finished transition into a Boeing B-17
four-engine bomber, along with the others of the ten-man crew. He was
their bombardier, and they were on orders to join promptly the Eighth Air
Force, U.S. Army Air Corps, in England. Bill was 19; his Airplane Commander, and immediate Commanding Officer, was a 1st. lieutenant, age 23,
from Scranton, PA, who then had less than 300 flying hours, and *none* over
water. Their orders directed that they fly the North Atlantic, as a single aircraft, to their base in England, with one stop at Goose Bay.

Amazingly, none of their crew was the slightest bit concerned about
the trip.

Bill was concerned that his father and mother seemed to be in a state
of deep depression over not having yet received any more news about his
brother since the letter from Algiers more than a year earlier. Bill tried to
console them by saying that if anything real bad had happened they probably would have heard something.

That hadn't seemed to help, but he added that he was certain of one
thing: that somewhere, somehow, Will must be flying—that was his obsession, for sure—and he hoped that it was on the island where his own
crew was going.

He told both of them that when he got to England he was going to try
to find some clue to his brother's whereabouts. He didn't say so to his par-

ents, but he felt that Joe Hearn might know something—he had never forgotten what Will had said about Joe on Pearl Harbor night, and he intended to see Joe in England. He had visited Polly Hearn that afternoon to get Joe's address.

Polly had given him an address—but not the correct one.

# Chapter Twelve

His first combat mission as part of No. 105 Squadron was simply as a follower of sorts, there to learn by watching a master craftsman at work—his squadron leader who had commanded a Flight of No. 105 before it even *had* a number.

He was another from down under, but a New Zealander, as he was quick to let you know. Kevin was his real name, but everyone in the squadron called him "Curly," though no-one knew why.

Curly loved to tell of his boyhood on the sheep ranch, when he and his brother would shoot coffee cans off a farm fence with a rifle, from horseback at full gallop. He used the story to convince his pilots that "kicking Jerry's fat arse is a piece of cake" compared to those days.

Wade soon became Curly's protege and, after being the kiwi's shadow on several sorties, the young American began to wonder why he had been so fortunate—*blessed* was how he thought of it—to draw a series of such outstanding teachers. Prior to the advent of PFF, Curly had flown almost all versions of the Mossie—photo-recon, night-fighter, un-armed bomber, fighter-bomber, transport—and had loved each with equal fervor.

He told Wade that he preferred the Night-Fighter Mk II, that had a maximum speed of 365 mph, a range of 1,671 miles, with four 0.303 machine guns in the nose as well as four 20-mm cannons *under* the nose in the forward bomb bay. He explained that while Mossie's great speed was rather nice, "it is of bloody little use when Jerry is closing on one head-on, you see".

Two months to the day after joining No. 105, Wade was summoned by Curly to the squadron briefing room, where he was introduced to a Wing Commander Greeley and a man in civilian clothes whom Curly introduced simply as "an agent with BI," which Wade assumed meant British Intelligence. Curly then turned to the wing commander, "If we actually do this mission, I would like Johns as my wingman."

"Done, Kevin; provided Johns is willing. As I have explained, this must be a 'volunteer only' affair. Perhaps Agent Malone will be good enough to outline the scheme to him."

"Very well, sir; I'll endeavor to get to the heart of it right off, in the interest of time."

He explained that there was an important Italian *partisan* leader who had been taken prisoner by the Nazis a few days prior; the Allies had been counting heavily on his assistance in the Italian campaign that had only recently gotten underway "on the boot proper." Three days ago, BI had learned that a handful of Nazi agents were holding him at a small town called Ventimiglia, on the coast very near the French border. He said, "There is a very well-organized and effective French *resistance* unit based at Eze Village, a medieval mountain-top village no further than 20 miles from Ventimiglia. We have been in contact with them; they say they are confidant they could get Signore Marconi out and across the border for us. The question is how to get him totally out of the region before the Germans swarm the region and possibly terminate him if they should manage to regain possession of him."

The agent continued, "There is a landing strip, down by the sea near *Eze Sur Mer,* that Sir Edward here says could handle a Mosquito, barring horrid weather conditions and assuming a pilot with outstanding expertise. That is where your squadron leader enters the picture.

"He believes he can get a Mossie, properly stripped of excess weight but set-up, to carry Marconi and one Commando out. But—and here *you* become part of the equation—he wants another Mossie, specifically the night-fighter version with its nose-guns, to fly cover for him while on the ground and after takeoff until he attains sufficient altitude for normal speed.

"It is only fair to emphasize that this will be—at best—a risky outing, and one we do not normally ask of military personnel. We have our own aircraft, to be sure, but none of our chaps are qualified in your Mossie, and there is complete unanimity that it is the only aircraft of choice for this venture. Once Kevin is at a decent cruising altitude, your Navigator will plot a course directly here, and you, with your weaponry, will fly Kevin's wing home.

"If you wish to think on it, we can give you a half hour."

"I don't need any time; if Curly wants me there, that's it. But what about the range? How far is it from the north shore of the Mediterranean to here?"

Kevin spoke up, "We should be well within our range, Wade. Perhaps we will fly from one of our new airfields we now have in Sicily, which would shorten the trip a bit. You need some margin for error; in the event I'm on the ground longer than planned, you would burn more petrol doing the cover.

"And listen well to this—don't feel you *must* do this mission; it is truly voluntary. If you decline it, no one else will ever know you were asked. Yes, *I* did request you, but there are others who could do it—and well."

"No problem, Skipper. I'm ready when you are. When do we start?"

Agent Malone answered with, "First we must contact our young friends in France. Today is Tuesday, so they are scheduled to be be tuned to their short-wave tonight at midnight, U.K. time, 1:00 A.M. in France; I'll talk to them. I suggest we meet here again at 0700 tomorrow."

As everyone nodded assent, he turned to Sir Edward, "Meanwhile, you chaps may wish to do your own planning, as needed. I already have a top-drawer Commando on standby, within an hour's drive from this station. I'm guessing a tad, but I believe *Les Amis* will want to nab Signor Marconi on a Saturday. Oh yes, I should explain that the code name for this resistance unit is *Les Amis de Liberté;* in English, 'The Friends of Liberty.'

"When we last were in contact, our man in that region indicated that they want to go in while the weekly Saturday market in the town is going full tilt. Marconi is being held in a building very near the market, so the section there will be the usual mob of noisy natives—and damned noisy, most assuredly—in the neighborhood. Now, *if* Saturday is the day they hit Ventimiglia, that probably means you should be doing your pick-up on Sunday or Monday, since they may not be able to stash our man safely for more than a day or so. Is that enough time for your preparations?"

Sir Edward looked at Kevin, who replied, "Don't think that's a problem. We need to decide on a flight plan in—from here *or* from Sicily—and bang around a bit on the interior of the two Mossies; the latter may take a day or so. Yes, we'll be set."

The small town of Eze Village, situated mid-way between Monaco and Nice, has been inhabited since the Bronze Age. Throughout the centuries, Ligurian, Greek, Roman, and Saracen tribes invaded Eze. In the tenth century Eze came under the control of the Earls of Nice and Provence and from 1388 it belonged to the Counts of Savoy. After several French invasions during the sixteenth, seventeenth, and eighteenth centuries, it became part of the district of Monaco and remained so after the creation of the province, Alpes-Maritimes in 1792. It was not until 1860 that the people of Eze voted to rejoin France.

It is one of a number of "perched villages" that were created in ancient times to withstand the frequent and perilous attacks that occurred frequently in the region. This was especially true during the era when corsairs sailed the Mediterranean coast constantly, in search of young men they could capture and keep—or sell—as slaves, and for young women for their harems.

With defense foremost in mind, Eze was laid out so that it could be defended easily. Sitting at the top of its rocky mountain, with a double-fortified gateway dating from the fourteenth century as the only entry, it has long been aptly called *Le Nid d'Aigle* (The Eagle's Nest) of the Cote d'Azure.

And Eze was the chosen—and secret—redoubt of *Les Amis de Liberté* as they persevered in their ongoing battle for freedom. Tonight, their leader and his interpreter were crouching low inside the old church bell-tower, speaking over their tiny short-wave radio. BI Agent Malone was listening, furiously making notes on his pad.

Les Amis had been only five when they first left the Maquis advanced-training camp near Grenoble in the spring of '42. They had gone there to learn to organize as a team rather than continue working as five well-meaning but under-skilled individuals. Jean-Pierre was still the leader, and Bridgette, Dominique, and David were waiting nearby to hear the message from London.

Isabelle had grown up in the Alsace region hearing German spoken almost as frequently as French, and had summered yearly in the Italian part of Switzerland while a child. Her fluency in Italian, German, and English, as well as her mother tongue, automatically made her the interpreter for the unit. In Grenoble, she had been trained also to be a radio operator.

David was an artist of sorts, not only skilled in the preparation of necessary documents from time to time, but equally so as a photographer and creator of ingenious disguises. Dominique was their resident writer, whose primary job was to prepare flyers and other printed matter, in an effort to keep the populace aware that hope for liberation lived, thereby preserving aid from some and—hopefully—neutralizing those who were tempted to believe the Vichy propaganda that *résistants* were criminals.

And Bridgette? Bridgette possessed certain charms—and the willingness to use them—that were extremely helpful to their cause at times. She freely admitted to having been *une grande horizontale* in her early youth, and had long since mastered the art of manipulating the male ego for her purposes. She saw no reason why she should not utilize those same skills in her more noble role as a patriot.

All of the original five were now proficient in the use of several weapons, not only handguns and shoulder weapons, but also grenades, as well as the knife and the garrotte. The same was true for the five they had added since their training at Grenoble. It was their policy that the entire ten rarely quartered together.

Thus all members of Les Amis were not in Eze when the call came from Agent Malone; instead, the others were staying the night near the grand mansion of their financial backer—and clandestine comrade—at nearby Cap Ferrat.

It was almost 2:00 A.M. when Jean-Pierre and Isabelle descended from the bell-tower and returned to the waiting three at their quarters near the summit.

He said simply, "It is *go* for Saturday. Tomorrow we plan; but now we rest."

They met in Monsieur Georges Blanchot's boathouse, situated at the water's edge 200 yards down and through the garden behind his huge chateau on *Pointe Malalonge.* The point was on the Villefranche side of *Cap Ferrat,* very near *la Phare,* the lighthouse that guided ships safely by the point or into the Bay of Villefranche, as had ancient versions of it for centuries past.

A grand mansion, such as that of M. Blanchot, was not uncommon on this famous peninsula, which had long been a home or retreat—and a quiet playground of sorts—for the rich and famous from around the world. These stately estates—almost all of which were walled—literally lined both sides of the beautiful road that wound its way along the rim of the southernmost part of the cape.

Since the fall of France in the spring of '40, some of the homes had stood vacant, while the ones owned by those deemed *enemies of the Reich* had been confiscated by the Nazis or their Vichy minions, primarily for the pleasures—often lustful—of their favored friends. Thus, while M. Blanchot detested his new neighbors, he was happy that their influence in the current power structure begat an important benefit: it was rare indeed that agents of the Gestapo—or their Vichy clones, the *Milice*—dared to inquire into, or question, the activities of those then residing on Cap Ferrat.

The Blanchot family had been among the elite of the banking and financial life of France since before the Revolution. Their power—financial skills and influence around the world—was legendary, particularly so in the board rooms of the great banks of Switzerland. The family, of which Georges was now the 52-year-old leader, was not only respected, but also feared, even by Hitler's bankers. In late 1940, Berlin and Vichy had decided it was wiser to tolerate Blanchot's obvious disdain than to challenge him.

For his part, Georges Blanchot did not openly provoke those then in political power, but for a single reason only: Since the French resistance movement had become his passion, he had organized—and was providing the primary financial support for—*Les Amis.*

Prior to the war, the boathouse had been a larger-than-life building, utilized to house his equally large yacht, as well as elements of a small export-import business he had in Beaulieu, a small town nearby. Some of his exports were difficult-to-find electronic parts that were essential for heavy sea-going ships—including military vessels—with requirements for deep draughts.

The site of his boathouse was ideal, inasmuch as the deep-water Bay of Villefranche was one of the few on the Mediterranean coast that could accommodate such vessels, as it does to this day.

While Les Amis had been in training near Grenoble, he had slowly but methodically converted a part of the building into a concealed, but rather large and comfortable, safehouse, for the protection of his comrades as well as a refuge for downed Allied airmen awaiting safe passage back to duty. He called it his "halfway" house. He had visualized—and it had become a reality of late—that pick-ups of aircrew personnel could be made, on occasion, by British or American submarines entering the deep water of the Bay while submerged, then later surfacing—under cover of darkness—near his boathouse and dock.

The frequent coming and going of workmen, servants, and the like, was routine in the care, repair, and maintenance of these Cap Ferrat showplaces; accordingly each member of Les Amis had been provided two sets of appropriate garments to wear when arriving or departing the premises. Today, six of the group had gathered for their strategy session.

Five had cycled over from Eze, and were joined by Juan, a French Communist who had fought in the Spanish Civil War. Jean-Pierre sometimes referred to him as "our token assassin," which usually brought a rare semblance of a smile to Juan's normally unhappy countenance.

Juan had spent his childhood near the city of Nimes, where his father had been a common laborer at the *aréne* there, one of the few active bullrings left in France. The father's grand dream had been for Juan to become a matador, but he had died seeing his son still trapped in the same drudgery he himself had endured for a lifetime. Two days after his father's funeral, Juan left for Spain.

It was no secret to the others that their dark-eyed and somber comrade-in-arms had a different political agenda than they. He had refused to join any resistance group while he thought Stalinist Russia was an ally of Nazi Germany, but changed overnight when Hitler turned on and attacked the Soviets. Juan's longterm—and openly expressed—hope was that, after the war, France would be ruled by his Communist party. He was tolerated by his colleagues only because he had actual and varied combat experience that the unit needed from time to time—and Jean-Pierre believed that Saturday, in Ventimiglia, might well be one of those times.

Jean-Pierre opened the meeting by relating the information given him by BI.

Signore Marconi had been a political opponent of Benito Mussolini for years, and had continued to have a substantial following throughout Italy even after he had been forced to go into hiding to survive.

Throughout the war to date he had been leading many partisan activities from his base he had established in the Tuscan hill town of Cortona, roughly midway between Rome and Florence. After the U.S. Fifth Army had invaded Italy proper at Salerno a few weeks before, its Commander, General Mark Clark, had requested that Signore Marconi join his staff as a civilian advisor as his army moved northward toward the capture of Rome, and eventual 'liberation'—as Marconi described it in his pamphlets— of all the Italian people.

Marconi had been willing, but wanted first to take his wife to Ventimiglia, where she had lived in her youth and where she had family with whom he felt she could live safely. Apparently, German intelligence had somehow learned of his plans, and had abducted Marconi on his arrival at Ventimiglia.

According to an Italian informant, three Nazi agents were holding him in a house, awaiting instructions from their superiors. BI believed that they intended to try to force Marconi to act as a double-agent, and failing that, they would liquidate him.

Jean-Pierre then outlined his tentative plan for Phase One of *"Blue Waters,"* the code-name BI had given this operation.

By 11:00 on Saturday, the market would be having it's biggest—and usually it's noisiest—crowds. Also, it was the time the band would be starting to play in the small piazza. Fortunately, the one-story home where Marconi was being held was situated between the piazza and the massive shed that housed most of the vast Market. "With the Italians' market *bruit* on the right, and their brass band blasting on the left, there will be sufficient noise to cover a major battle; we can be sure of that!" he exclaimed.

The tradition in the town, especially true since the beginning of the war, was that the band would start with a few marches, then settle into music composed for dancing—*fast* and *joyful* dancing. Most of the Italian people had always opposed this war, and they had come to enjoy immensely their Saturday markets as a weekly emotional release from the trauma of the conflict.

The plan was that as soon as the band went into its dance music, Bridgette, dressed in her most seductive Italian attire, would grab a man and induce the dancing. If that didn't create a chain reaction of dance by the crowd, Jean-Pierre was certain that at least every male eye on the piazza would be locked in on the swaying hips of Bridgette.

The ideal scenario would have the Nazi agent-in-charge as one of those being mesmerized. BI's informant had noted that on the previous Saturday he had come out of the house and had seemed to enjoy his dancing with a young Italian woman, while a second agent leered lecherously from the front doorway.

In the meantime, Jean-Pierre and Juan would enter a window in the rear of the house where Marconi was confined. If they met resistance from two or more, they would have to use their pistols, in spite of the resulting noise. If there was only one, Juan was to use the garrote or stiletto only, if practicable. "The less noise, the better, obviously," commented Jean-Pierre.

Isabelle would be watching through the back window of the house. If all went well, she would go to the front, wait three minutes, then get Bridgette, and dash into and through the market shed to lose themselves in the crowd, before heading for the boat.

If Juan and Jean-Pierre were in trouble, Isa had several options from which she must select, depending on the exact nature of their trouble: (1) enter the room and assist with her small handgun, or (2) use the one grenade she had in her purse, or (3) retreat at once, get Bridgette, and hurry to the boat.

David would be waiting with the motorboat at the dock near the seaside restaurant owned by an Italian partisan friend of Marconi. He had agreed to hide the group in the cellar of his restaurant if that became necessary because of any unanticipated developments; in such event David would move offshore with the boat, and return after dark.

"What do we do with the fascist who may be still out front with Bridgette? What if he tries to prevent her from leaving?" asked Isabelle.

"Use your own stiletto on the pig!" volunteered Juan.

"No!" corrected Jean-Pierre. "First, I think Bridgette can get away O.K., because it should be rather chaotic. If not, Bridgette, try your 'karate to the crotch' act first, the one you almost disabled me with during our class at Grenoble," he groaned as he recalled. "If that does not work, then either of you should use the blade *or* your Derringer, whichever is more convenient at the moment. Remember, we want to attract as little attention as possible, to reduce the chances of a successful pursuit."

"After we are underway in the boat, we will have two options: to the boathouse on the Cap, or to the dock near Eze Sur Mer. I believe—and hope—that the authorities will assume we would withdraw by automobile and will set up roadblocks. If I am wrong we may have to abandon the boat near Eze Sur Mer, rather than compromise the operations of Monsieur Blanchot by leading the enemy here to the boathouse. Questions?"

"Yes; what about my role in this?" asked Dominique.

"Yes. Originally I had planned on you for back-up, but when I arrived this morning and saw the boat, it simply is not designed for more than six passengers. So you stay home this trip—maybe next time? You might use the time to plan on assisting Signore Marconi with some pamphlets; I'm sure he will be in the mood to tell his supporters about his latest 'adventure' with the Nazis."

David then spoke up, "We need to think about *dress* sometime today. The Italian police seem to have an uncanny ability to spot a non-Italian, and I'm sure it's by our attire. Again, we don't want to draw any more attention than necessary."

"Absolutely correct David; it's true even in the Italian part of Switzerland. Why don't you and I write up some suggestions for all," said Isabelle.

"Do it," Jean-Pierre ordered. "Now Juan and I need to check our weapons and ammunition. Ready, amigo?"

"Si, Senor," grunted Juan.

As he and Juan were leaving the room, he turned back to the group, "Oh yes, we must talk also about the pick-up by the RAF, Phase Two of *Blue Waters,* tentatively scheduled for Sunday at the airstrip. Be back here at 2:30, please."

At 2:30 sharp, the six had reconvened, joined by the remaining members of Les Amis: Marie-Françoise, Claude, Frederic, and Eugenio. Their leader outlined his plan for delivering the Signore to the RAF.

It would be done on Sunday, at 11:00 A.M. sharp, while most of the few residents of Eze Sur Mer would be either traveling to or attending Mass at *L'Eglise des Palmiers*—on the highway along the coast, called the *Basse Corniche*—six kilometers to the east of their village. On Sunday the small rail station was never staffed—another advantage, inasmuch as the landing strip was less than 200 meters west of the station.

The strip itself had never been used a great deal, and even less since the start of the war. Originally, it had been financed and constructed by the *Office de Tourisme* of the nearby principality of Monaco, for the convenience of wealthy visitors who preferred to travel there by their private— and usually light—airplanes. The terrain in the region did not offer many acceptable sites for an airfield, so they had selected the one reasonably flat surface they found near the rail station.

No expense had been spared in the construction, the sponsors keeping ever in mind that the clientele who would be using it were not accustomed to anything less than the best. Prior to the war, a white Mercedes stretch-limo—complete with liveried chauffeur—stood by during all daylight hours, on the possibility of an unexpected arrival.

Much had changed since the war. "A damned nuisance, this conflict," was how one of the Monaco casino-owners described it.

The customers never flew in anymore; the strip was covered in spots with moss and practically never used by any type of aircraft. It was too short for most military types.

The small but elegant building on the knoll just above the strip—that had once doubled as an odd combination of weather-shack to the pilots, but as a well stocked bar for their passengers—had long been locked and boarded up.

Based on their earlier check of the area, at exactly 11:00 A.M. on the previous Sunday, the likelihood of anyone being close by when the Mosquitos arrived was either (1) the man—or his wife—who ran the small combination grocery/tobacco shop just across the *corniche* from the rail station, or (2) one or more passengers waiting outside the station for an SNCF train. Both contingencies would be handled by having Marie-Françoise dawdle over a coffee at the grocer's while Dominique would be posing as a waiting passenger. They could then detain—at gunpoint if necessary—anyone who appeared inclined to intervene or alert the police.

Late on the Friday night before the delivery, Eugenio and Frederic were to open the former weather-shack to re-stock the bar with a few grenades, some Molotov Cocktails, the 50-calibre machine gun and its tripod, an abundance of ammunition and such other items as they might need on Sunday, but which would be difficult to transport undetected by day. While inside, he intended for them to also leave one of the new short-wave radios that M. Blanchot had received just that morning. These were capable of ground-to-air contact with the Mosquitos once they were within 100 kilometers of the strip. On Sunday, Isabelle would be continuously at the radio from 10:30 until both aircraft were fully airborne following the pickup of Marconi.

Four of the five men—each armed with an American-made Thompson sub-machine gun, would be posted at each corner of the strip. Jean-Pierre would position himself, along with Signore Marconi, just inside the palm trees near where he estimated the Mosquito would roll to a stop after touchdown.

Instantly after that stop, the British Commando would leap onto the runway, assist in lifting Marconi into the aircraft, re-board himself, and set up his automatic weapon in position to fire through the open hatch as the Mosquito taxies to prepare for immediate takeoff. If there is no significant wind, the RAF pilot may decide to take-off in the opposite direction from that of his landing; however, if there is wind of any degree, he would undoubtedly taxi back to the other end in order to lift off *into* the wind, given the short length of the strip. It was *vital* that the Mosquito be on the ground for the minimum time possible. On the ground it was very vulnerable; once airborne it was normally the master of its fate.

As far as Jean-Pierre or BI knew, there were no German or Italian military units close enough to be sent into the region on short notice, but he wanted to be prepared for a firefight at the strip, if necessary. His contingency plan, for the worst scenario, would be to try to get Signore Marconi back to the boathouse. This would be done by Jean-Pierre and Isabelle, in her old Citreon that she would have left in the station carpark on Friday afternoon. The rest would withdraw on their bicycles, as they had arrived; three would return to Eze Village, the others to Cap Ferrat.

Lastly, he told them that if he should go down, Isabelle would be in command, and in her absence they were to follow the orders of David.

He then asked for questions.

Dominique asked what she should do if the platform of the station was totally deserted. "Should I join the men in defense of the strip?"

"Not until the Mosquito has taken off, unless I send up a flare; so, if you are alone there, look in the direction of the strip from time to time. You will not see a flare unless the situation becomes grave."

"You mentioned *five* men a moment ago. Where is our *sixth* one to be?" asked Frederic.

"Of course; I should have covered that. Signore Marconi and David will stay at the boathouse Saturday night. He and David will come in the boat on Sunday morning, both having been disguised by David as if they were going to Mass. They will walk to the railway platform after docking; if all appears normal at that time, Dominigue will signal them to continue to the strip. If trouble has erupted, she will direct them to Isabelle's Citreon in the station's carpark."

"When do we regroup and withdraw?" asked David.

"As soon as the two aircraft are out of sight, assuming all goes well. Now, before we leave for the day—who needs further instruction on our new 'Tommy-Guns'? *No one?* O.K.—but just remember that the fire-pattern is from 8 o'clock diagonally across your target to 1 o'clock; don't *waste* your rounds by aiming at the exact center of your target; got it?

*"Tres bon!* Let's go home."

The first thing Jean-Pierre checked on Saturday was the weather. He knew that good weather would draw the desired large crowd to the market just across the border. It was a typical day in Provence; the sky was as blue as the sea as he looked first up, then down, from his window high above the Mediterranean.

All except David would take the 9:00 SNCF train to Ventimiglia from the tiny station down by the sea at Eze Sur Mer; the station was about a mile down from Eze Village via a narrow and winding road. David would bring the boat along the coastline from Cap Ferrat to Ventimiglia, appearing to be simply one of many other weekend boaters who were forgetting the war by enjoying a few hours on the sea on such a beautiful weekend.

## Sicily

The Allies had taken Messina on August 17, thereby effectively ending the Sicily campaign. Even prior to the fall of Messina they had been using well the captured airfields, including the one Kevin had decided to use as their departure point. He had estimated that this would reduce their flying time by nearly an hour, as compared to departing from any base in England. An hour saved could be critical, especially if they should be slowed by anything unforeseen—bad weather or otherwise.

He and Wade had brought their Mossies in on Friday, after the needed work on each airplane had been finished the previous day. Agent BI Malone had ridden down with Kevin and the Scottish Commando, Sgt. Andrew Bruce, Malone riding in the space that had been created for Signore Marconi to occupy on the return trip. At dinner, after landing in Sicily, Bruce suggested that they should let Marconi use the more comfortable navigator's seat on the way home. Malone—still rubbing his back because of the embryo position he had been required to assume for so long in the air—agreed, adding, "Otherwise our guest may prefer to have remained subject to the tender mercies of Jerry."

After dinner, Malone had raised Jean-Pierre on the short-wave. They had re-confirmed that the pick-up would be on Sunday at 11:00 sharp, French time. The Frenchman told him they now had the new radios that would enable them to talk with the aircraft when they got within 100 KM, and asked that one or the other of the RAF pilots call them when they were that close to Eze Sur Mer. He told Malone that they were all set to free the Italian, and suggested that he call again on Saturday around 5:00 P.M., and that the message would be either, "We have the package for delivery," or "The deal is off."

Malone said he understood, and ended with *bonne chance,* to which Jean-Pierre replied in English, *"Good luck* also to you and the Mosquito crews!"

The next morning, Kevin and Wade studied the aerial photo*s* of the landing strip, which had been made the day before by a photo-recon Mosquito. The pilot who had flown the recon Mossie also met with them and pointed out that the structure housing the rail station had appeared to be about the same height as the patch of trees at the other end of the strip. He then pointed to the wind sock in the photos and said that on both days they had flown over the strip it had indicated "zero" wind, so perhaps they may want to land *from* the station end of the strip, and take-off in the opposite direction in order to save the ground time that would be consumed by taxiing back toward the station in order to start their take-off roll.

The main concern of all three pilots was the short length of the strip; it was going to require a landing at close to stall speed, and the take-off was going to be, in the words of Kevin, "one of the most bloody exciting thrills of my life." But he thought it could be done, adding, "Christ, I hope this Italian chap is one of their *small* ones!"

Wade and Kevin told Malone that in view of the *résistants'* new radio capability, it might attract less attention in the community if, while Kevin was on the ground, Wade didn't simply fly in circles directly over the strip while providing cover. Instead, perhaps he could fly wider circles and the radio operator of Les Amis could alert him if they needed him to come in closer. After some discussion, they decided it was better to simply take the chances that might come with attention, and that Wade would cover in tight circles and "to hell with the community."

# Chapter Thirteen

All seemed to be going according to plan at Ventimiglio.

Bridgette had danced the crowd into quite a frenzy, with a line of cheering men awaiting—not too patiently—their opportunity to be her partner, when the blonde giant jerked the slender young Italian away from her, shoved him to the cobblestone floor of the piazza, and swept her off the ground with one arm around her waist. The panting breath in her face stunk of stale beer and the guttural voice was obviously not Italian or French. As he continued to nearly *crush* her waist—now with *both* arms—she realized that he was trying to pull her into the house where Marconi was being held—and she recognized his slurred words as clearly German.

Bridgette knew she needed to dissuade him from the house for at least a few more minutes. So, she finally squirmed sufficiently to stand on her toes and whisper directly and warmly into his ear, in her best imitation of English, "Oh, my oh so *wonderful* Nordic knight, I *desire* you much more than you could *possibly* want me, but dance more closely with me for only a *few* moments more—it will make the weaving of the magic I have for you to be even *more* wonderful!"

He murmured a delighted, "Yah! But only for a minute am I able to wait!" and continued his vise-like grip about her waist.

Then she heard the unmistakable sound of a grenade exploding—and it was from the house.

Jean-Pierre and Juan had gotten into the back room as planned, and had found Signore Marconi, bound and gagged. But as they removed his gag, he started screaming, in Italian, apparently not knowing who they were. They had not yet untied him completely when two men broke through the door that Juan had managed to lock.

One of the men slashed Jean-Pierre's right arm with his knife, causing him to drop his pistol, but Juan drove his stiletto into the man's throat and instantly turned to fire at the other one with his 45-calibre semi-automatic.

The first shot found the right shoulder of its target and the impact felled him as he dropped behind an old stuffed couch in the corner of the room. Hearing the commotion, Isa was now peering into the room screaming, "GET OUT—GET OUT! *Drag* the man if you must, but *get out!* My grenade is armed, but you must get *out* for me to use it!"

Jean-Pierre was bleeding badly, but dragged Marconi through the window with his good arm, with Juan pushing from the rear. Just as all three were clear of the window, Isa saw one of the Germans stagger to his feet with a Luger in hand. She shoved hard on the back of Juan, trying to push him down, shouting, "DOWN—DOWN—-NOW!!!!"

As he stumbled forward, Juan instinctively grabbed the belt of Jean-Pierre and dragged him and the Italian to the ground with him. The blast from Isa's grenade slammed her down behind the men. After lying flat and breathing audibly for a moment, she then started—-almost in a whisper—explaining to Marconi in Italian what she and her comrades were about. Then she sat straight up, as if startled; she had suddenly remembered *Bridgette!* She told the men to head for the boat, with, "I must find Bridgette!"

As she dashed around the corner of the building, she ran head-on into the object of her concern; Bridgette had come searching for *them,* but only after having first re-arranged her disheveled hairdo. She quickly but calmly told Isa that she had been forced to "do the karate on the drunken Hun" and then, concerned about the explosion, she had run back to his still moaning torso and put a shot from her Derringer directly into his crotch, "just to discourage his following me."

She added—laughing heartily as they jogged around the now nearly deserted market shed and toward the boat—that many of the Italians on the piazza had given her a quick round of applause before they scattered from the blast.

Signore Sergio Marconi spent most of the boat ride to Cap Ferrat in tears, pleading for them to forgive him for the problem he had caused his liberators.

Jean-Pierre tried to console him and, with Isabelle interpreting, explained the next steps that were planned for him. Meanwhile, Juan tended the tourniquet he had improvised for the slashed arm, and glared silently at the frail little Italian each time he begged for forgiveness.

At 5:30 p.m. on Saturday, Malone telephoned Kevin, "They have the package. Phase Two is *go!* Good hunting tomorrow!"

Before he retired, Wade wrote two short letters under his real name. He told his mother that he was temporarily in Sicily, well and feeling proud that he was doing his duty, but growing more unhappy each day about his feeling of estrangement from her and the rest of his family. He expressed hope that the war would not last much longer, and that the day would soon come when they could be reunited.

To Polly he said that he was missing her more than any of his other friends, and said again that he would never forget the way she had helped him before he left. He urged both not to be concerned if they didn't hear from him frequently because, "It is difficult to send letters, except on rare occasions." He asked Malone to mail them from Sicily after he and Kevin were gone.

Wade and Kevin were at the flight line early that Sunday morning, checking off items they had never concerned themselves with before. Both Mossies had been modified for *Blue Waters,* Wade's only slightly, but Kevin's had been drastically lightened—as much as they dared; he had even had Sgt. Bruce *weighed*—after dinner and in full gear—the night before they departed England.

They wanted to time their departure to give them an ETA over Eze between 10:55 and 11:05 A.M. The U.S. weather officer at the base was projecting that winds aloft at their planned altitude of 30,000 to 35,000 feet for most of the flight would be a mild head-wind of only 25 to 40 knots. The plan was to drop to very low level—to avoid detection by enemy radar—about 100 miles from the destination. All reports were that the seas were calm and no wind of consequence at that level had been detected.

Previously, it had been explained to both pilots that the seacoast cities along that part of the Cote d'Azure enjoyed a delightful—almost unique—micro-climate, partially because of the virtual windshield created by the nearby mountains to their north.

At 6:30 in the morning on Sunday, Jean-Pierre was discussing some details about the defense of the strip with Eugenio, the member who had most recently joined Les Amis; he had been recruited for his special skill as a sharpshooter. Eugenio was French by birth and by virtue of his French father, but his mother had been born in the Po Valley of Italy. His family resided in a rural village near Avignon, but he himself had been living with and assisting his elderly Italian grandparents in the spring of 1940 when Mussolini attacked France.

An attempt was made to force him into the Italian army, but he had fled into the mountains and lived off the land for months before making his way to France and the *résistance* training camp near Grenoble. Almost all his life his passion had been hunting and, before he was in his teens, his grandfather had taught him well how to use a rifle, in particular those with telescopic sights they had used so often in the high mountains.

At Grenoble, those who were charged with training snipers had spent only one afternoon observing Eugenio firing a rifle before declaring him *graduated*, laughingly adding that it was *with highest* honors.

This was why Jean-Pierre had decided to have Eugenio armed with a sniper's rifle, as well as his Tommy-Gun, and situated on the corner of the strip nearest the point where they expected to place Signore Marconi aboard the Mossie the moment it stopped.

Jean-Pierre had thought long and hard at how he would have approached the question of dealing with this situation, if he were the enemy and had somehow learned of the British plan to pick up the Italian at the strip. In the absence of a much superior military force at the enemy's disposal, the most effective way would be to silence Marconi so that he would be of no use to the Allies.

What could be more simple than to conceal a couple of riflemen on the roof of the rail station, to kill him when he showed himself in the open prior to boarding the aircraft?

The four *résistants* at the corners of the strip would be armed with Thompson sub-machine guns, and those weapons were useful—and *devastating*—at short range, but not very accurate at long range.

Eugenio—unlike most French-Italians—was a huge man, standing six feet, four inches tall, and weighing possibly 240 pounds. So, Jean-Pierre said, at the end of the session, "My friend, you yourself are a *large* target; therefore, I want you to be crouched inside the grove a few feet, out of easy sight from the rail station roof. Take these binoculars with you, and use them to pan the roof of the building constantly. If you see movement of any person there—*any* movement whatever—without regard to *who* it might be during the time from touchdown to takeoff of the aircraft, you are to *fire!* Do you understand?"

His young listener had admired the legendary Sergio Marconi from afar for nearly three years. He felt it was a high honor to protect this true Italian patriot.

"Yes!" was his reply.

Adding to his concern, the leader of *Les Amis* had received an urgent message during the night—hand delivered to him from M. Blanchot. He had learned that the raid at Ventimiglio had caused the Vichy government to call in for duty the entire Nice detachment of the detested Vichy version of the Gestapo, *la Milice*. By sunset on Saturday it had been confirmed that they were already picking up individuals for interrogation in the town of St. Jean on Cap Ferrat, as well as in Villefranche sur mer and Beaulieu, both of which were uncomfortably close to Eze Sur Mer. More troublesome, the Milice was also randomly searching dwellings and shops in the same venues.

The good news was that the Milice seemed to have no pattern to their actions and Blanchot hoped that its primary aim was, as he phrased it, "to pacify their Nazi masters," but he added, "We cannot assume that; the Nice detachment has had a military capability, however incompetent, in the past.

"Continue with Phase Two of *Blue Waters* as planned, but be alert to this intelligence."

Everyone was in position. Isabelle had just signaled that she had received a second message from *Blue Waters I,* advising he was estimating five minutes until touchdown. She had responded, "All is *go* here!"

At almost that precise moment, a mid-sized truck with camouflaged paint pulled off the highway and parked directly in front of the small grocer where Marie-Françoise was at a sidewalk table, sipping her coffee and pretending to read the morning newspaper.

She counted eight men and knew instantly that the uniform was that of the Milice; worse, each was heavily armed, with not only a sidearm but also some type of semi-automatic slung over the shoulder.

Two climbed out of the truck's cab, glanced at her, then entered the building demanding loudly to see the proprietor, while the others leered at her from beside the vehicle. She grimaced, knowing well that her Derringer would never suffice to detain them for long, if at all. She said a silent prayer that they would move on soon, before the Mosquitos arrived over the strip only a few hundred meters away.

She heard the ranting of one of the Milice, as he demanded to know if anyone with a bleeding or bandaged arm had been seen there during the past 24 hours. As she was straining to hear the reply of the owner she shuddered as, *instead,* she heard the roar of a low-flying airplane. As she looked up she saw it—as well as the clear RAF markings on it's wings and fuselage—as it flashed by.

It had also been seen by the six Milice at the truck, because they were now bellowing in concert to their comrades.

Kevin had made a quick low-level pass over the strip to take a peek at it before what he knew was going to be a delicate landing, with zero margin for error.

As the other two Milice exited the grocer's building, gazing up at the sky, there was a second and similar roar, as Wade commenced the first of a series of tight figure-eights at an altitude of only 1,000 feet, intended to locate the center of the "8" directly over the strip itself.

The commander of the Milice group looked up, saw the RAF markings, and dashed back to the door of the building, where the owner also was gazing curiously. He grabbed the owner by his shoulders, shook him violently, and demanded to know if there was an airfield nearby. The terrified man mentioned the strip next to the rail station, but quickly added that it was closed and never used anymore.

The commander barked an order to his men to board the truck just as the second Mosquito streaked overhead again. The truck's spinning tires threw a small cloud of gravel as it roared onto the highway and toward the rail station.

Kevin had already throttled back to beyond the danger point—and was almost in full flaps mode—long before he only slightly cleared the roof of the station, ticking a radio aerial with his landing gear on the descent.

Immediately after clearing the building, he cut both engines and deliberately stalled at three or so feet above the surface of the strip, slamming down on one end of the concrete runway with a loud *thud,* followed by two additional bounces, before the Mossie recovered and started rolling smoothly.

Kevin flashed a mischievous grin at Sgt. Bruce and cracked, "They'd charge you extra for that at a British amusement park!"

Bruce replied without smiling, "Do you think we damaged our gear back there?"

Kevin ignored that as he brought both engines back to low RPMs to control the taxi to the exact point of the strip where he had seen Jean-Pierre emerge—waving—from behind a large palm tree with a smaller man at his side.

As they neared the two men, Kevin cut his starboard engine while making a slow left turn, then stopped abruptly. Sgt. Bruce was halfway out of the plane while it was still moving, and now leaped to the ground and moved quickly to a position on the other side of Signore Marconi.

Jean-Pierre's right arm was heavily bandaged from the knife slash at Ventimiglio, so he turned Marconi over to the Commando and pulled his .38 pistol from his belt with his left hand, walking a few paces behind Bruce and Marconi as they approached the idling aircraft. A minute later a volley of gunfire erupted from the direction of the station, as the truck, loaded with Milice, rolled straight down the strip toward the Mossie.

Jean-Pierre recognized instantly the sound of his Tommy-Guns as their .45 slugs tore the left front wheel from the truck and brought it to a stop as it reached the middle of the strip; but then he heard weapons being fired from the truck.

He felt a burning sensation as something struck his already damaged right arm, just before he saw Sgt. Bruce get hit. The Commando spun around as if he had pirouetted, and staggered a few steps before another shot found the left side of his temple and took away half his skull. He collapsed face first on the runway, leaving Signore Marconi standing alone no more than two feet in front of the sergeant's body.

Jean-Pierre leaped ahead instinctively and jerked Marconi to the ground as he saw three of the Milice training their weapons on the Italian from a kneeling position at the nearside of the truck. A volley followed, and both men could hear the bullets ricocheting off the concrete.

Jean-Pierre was crouched over the body of Signore Marconi, when he felt a huge hand firmly but slowly removing him from the Italian he was trying to protect.

Eugenio then lifted Marconi from the ground and carried him in his arms—as one would a small child—toward the waiting aircraft where Kevin had been waving for them to hurry. Eugenio slowed for just a moment as two shots struck him in the small of his back, then continued a few feet before a third found his hip. He stumbled forward under the weight he was carrying until he was within a yard or two of the airplane; then he gave up his effort to walk, but managed to lower Marconi gently to the ground and cover him with his mammoth body as if to provide a human shield for the man he admired so much.

The great body shook several times as it lay there and suffered a score or more additional wounds as the infuriated Milice continued to fire into it.

As soon as Isabelle had seen the Milice truck become disabled on the strip, she had radioed Wade, who was then in the midst of a steep turn back toward the strip. As he passed over the scene the first time he strafed the vehicle with his .303 machine guns, hitting all five of the men crouching in the back of the truck, who had been protected from the ground fire by the armor-like metal on the high sides of their military vehicle. However, as he pulled up from his first pass, his navigator had noticed that the three kneeling at the side of the truck closest to Kevin's Mossie were un-harmed.

Wade made a tight turn back toward the strip, simultaneously arming his 20-mm cannon. Toward the end of a shallow dive he fired all the cannon and felt the airplane shudder as the truck exploded and burst into flames. As he pulled up through the flying debris he saw one of the Milice staggering across the runway aflame, until he was dropped by a short burst from the Thompson of Frederic.

The other two had been killed instantly by the cannon shells.

During their second pass Wade and his navigator had noticed—and wondered about—the huge body that lay motionless near Kevin's aircraft.

After Wade's second pass, a strange quiet settled on the scene. Frederic ran to Jean-Pierre and, together, they rolled Eugenio over and lifted Marconi up and into the aircraft.

Kevin asked if Sgt. Bruce was alive. Frederic replied that he had been wounded gravely and most probably was dead, but most certainly he was unable to board the aircraft. Jean-Pierre added that they would take the Commando with them and if he were alive they would endeavor to get medical care for him at once.

Kevin shook both their hands, closed the canopy, and prepared for immediate departure. He jockeyed the Mosquito as far back on the end of the strip as possible, glanced over to see if his passenger was buckled up, revved the twin engines up to absolute full throttle, released the brakes, roared back down the strip just past the still burning truck, and lifted off over the rail station, ticking the same aerial again even though the gear was in process of being raised.

As soon as he knew he had cleared the station roof, Kevin leveled off over the sea to gain airspeed, then did a 180-degree turn, and streaked directly over the strip, dipping each of his wings in salute to *Les Amis* below.

Wade followed closely behind his squadron leader, performing a climbing slow-roll above the strip for his lustily-cheering French comrades-at-arms.

Before leaving Sicily, Wade's navigator had plotted a course home that would take them northwesterly across France, southwest of Paris. After passing between Tours and Orleans in the Loire Valley, they would alter their course slightly to the north and then over Le Havre to the Channel and from there to an RAF base at Brighton in southern England. A U.S. B-24 would be waiting there to take Sergio Marconi at once to General Mark Clark's headquarters in Italy.

While there was a slightly shorter way, it had seemed more sensible to the navigator to take a safer route home, in order to try to avoid flak and enemy fighters; both Kevin and Wade had concurred.

During the entire flight, Wade could not get his mind off the image of the *résistant* Eugenio sacrificing his very life to shield the body of Signore Marconi. He had never before witnessed such an unselfish act of bravery.

The feeling was bittersweet as Les Amis placed the bodies of Eugenio and the British commando in the old Citreon and departed the site of their successful and important—but costly—mission.

Each was in awe of the selfless deed of Eugenio in sacrificing his life to protect that of Signore Marconi, and they were convinced that—but for Eugenio—Marconi would also have been among the corpses of the day.

Jean-Pierre was already thinking of how best to communicate the heroic circumstances of his death to his family. This was one of the more difficult tasks for all French *résistance* leaders, in light of the security risks involved for them as well as for the families of the deceased.

Kevin and Wade had been debriefed on Sunday evening at the Brighton base and stayed the night there. Early on Monday morning, they did the short flight to their own base.

Wing Commander Greeley was waiting on the ramp as the two aircraft taxied in. Late on Sunday evening, he had spoken to the debriefing officer at Brighton, who had summarized for him the events at the air strip.

He congratulated both and said that he was recommending that both pilots, as well as Wade's navigator—and Sgt. Bruce, posthumously—be decorated for valor during Operation *Blue Waters*. He advised them also that he was recommending that the young *résistant* who had died on the strip be considered for the Victoria Cross, the supreme British award for gallantry against an enemy in war.

The still weary airmen were most pleased by his words regarding Eugenio, and expressed that to him in the strongest of terms.

They also were pleased when Sir Edward informed them that they had been granted seven days leave, to be taken within the next two weeks.

When Wade arrived at his quarters, he saw a note taped to his door that Joe Hearn had telephoned him, and it had asked that Wade call him back as soon as he returned. He was still exhausted and dropped onto his bunk fully clothed and slept for a good two hours, despite the fact it was only 9:00 A.M.

He dreamed of nothing except the dead Eugenio lying on the strip.

He showered, then went directly to the phone in the hall and dialed the number Joe had left. Joe told him he had a few days off, was going to London for five or six days of relaxation, and André was due to join him on the weekend at the Hotel Lancaster. Both had hoped Wade could come up for a day or so; maybe be there for dinner on Saturday.

Joe said, "We plan to live it up at this great—but damned expensive—restaurant where some rich Cajun friend of André's is gonna take us for supper and stand for the check. André and I have reserved a small suite at the same hotel where this Cajun dude is staying, and you can sack out on the couch if you like."

Wade didn't pause a bit, "Sounds terrific to me; I'll be there! Maybe I can gloat over you two a little about how *great* life is in the PFF. Just tell me when and where."

**London**

In the late summer of 1943, the OSS had been directed to find and develop agents to enter France, as well as other occupied countries in Hitler's *Fortress Europe,* in preparation for future Allied landings.

Though the personnel of the various resistance units were often fearless—and always well intentioned—many of them sorely lacked trained leadership, and hardly any were adequately equipped to provide the assistance the Allies would need when the time came for the massive undertaking to liberate the continent.

In France, although the number of those active in resistance activities had steadily grown since the dark days of 1940 and 1941, there was no meaningful centralized command or coordination of their activities in any region of the country.

And France was far and away the key country in this problem; it didn't require a genius to see that the initial assault areas would be somewhere in France. The rumor mill was alive about whether the first landing beaches would be on the Atlantic/English Channel side of the French coast, or in the French Riviera region on the Mediterranean.

Thus, as the OSS liaison chief for all things French, Col. Louis Hebert now found himself in London to attend several joint planning conferences to be held over a period of two weeks with high level officials of SOE, the British version of the Secret Operations (SO) section of OSS.

The priority subject on their agenda was how to provide the best-qualified talent available to the resistants, especially in France.

On arrival at the Lancaster Hotel, he had telephoned his daughter's fiancee to see if he could come to London for dinner on the weekend. André had explained that he had previously planned to be in the city, but with two of his RCAF comrades.

Col. Hebert laughed, and said, "No problem; bring 'em along. It would be an honor to meet 'em. I know a really great restaurant that all of us will enjoy. But remember—this is *my* treat."

As André hung up the telephone, he thought to himself, *Angie knows the whole story about Wade, but there's no way the Colonel would know that too.*

Wade knocked at the door of the suite at three in the afternoon, only a half hour after his friends had checked in. André let him in, and yelled to Joe, "Your buddy from Atlanta is here! Maybe I could get *my* turn to soak in a real bath tub now!?"

André had just popped the champagne when Joe strolled into the parlor, barefoot and still dripping a bit, wrapped in a huge terrycloth bathrobe. He said, "Damn, this robe is so thick you could use it for an overcoat in winter at home."

"Hey, my cracker friend, that goes with the deal when you're blowin' a whole month's pay for a room. Just *enjoy!*" laughed André. "But if they were *really* first-class here, we'd have a coupla' dozen crawfish to munch on too."

"For the quid *I* am paying, all appears to be well within my *expectations,* my Lords," Wade clowned, as he bowed to his hosts and made a dismal attempt to imitate a British accent.

André started pouring into the three flutes, "O.K., enough B.S.; let's enjoy the bubbly some good fairy left here." Then, "Here's to us, my friends!"

André then told them that dinner was at the *Victoria Inn* at 7:00, but that they had been invited to join their host, Angie's father, in the hotel bar at 6:00, for a drink or two before taking a taxi to the restaurant.

He noticed that Wade had looked a little startled at the mention of Angie's father, so he asked him if she had ever spoken of her father while he was in Quebec.

Wade told them of his trips to Washington as a courier for the *Liberté ou Mort* group, and assured them that Col. Hebert knew nothing about his real identity, adding that, "He's a terrific guy; I'll be really glad to see him again."

Joe and André asked Wade about his experiences in the Mosquito—the aircraft that was fast becoming a living legend throughout the RAF—and were glued to his every word about the rescue mission he had just completed. He told them that he wasn't permitted to give names of people or places, but even absent that it was a fascinating story to them. Wade had dwelled a great deal about Eugenio's heroism, and how impressed he had been with the raw courage of the entire group of French *résistants* with whom he and Kevin had worked.

André asked if either had an interest in transferring from the RCAF to the U.S. Army Air Corps, as many American pilots of the RAF and RCAF had been allowed to do during the last few months. He mentioned that they could do this but still stay with their British units if they preferred; and he told Joe that he would be given a U.S. commissioned officer status— probably as a 1st. Lieutenant—even though he was now a sergeant in the RCAF.

Wade said he would dearly love to do it, because then he would be able to quit living like some fugitive and—more important—could probably renew his life as a real member of his family. But he added that he was afraid that the process might uncover what he had done and even eventually cause him to be "booted" out of the RCAF. He urged them to do what they wanted, but said he just couldn't take the chance of being discovered.

At 5:30, Joe glanced at his watch, "Geez, fellows, we're due in the bar in a half hour. We'd better kick it in gear if we're gonna' get dressed and go. It's not too smart to keep a *colonel* waiting, even if he *is* a nice guy!"

# Chapter Fourteen

During the war, most American military personnel were required to wear their uniforms at all times while in public. But that didn't apply to OSS people for obvious reasons.

It was dark in the bar, and when the airmen went in, neither André nor Wade recognized the distinguished looking, but graying, gentleman in the charcoal gray pinstripe suit, who was leaning against the bar and chatting quietly with the bartender as if they were old friends.

As they scanned the room for him, they heard a voice—a *Cajun* voice— call out, "Hey *boy;* you looking for someone—or you just *plain lost?*"

André recognized both the voice and the question. It was the exact question that Angie's Dad had enjoyed terrifying him with when he and Angie had started dating as teenagers in Baton Rouge, except that this time he was delighted to hear it. He embraced his future father-in-law for a long moment before remembering to introduce his friends, first Joe, then Wade.

Louis Hebert shook Wade's hand, and stared curiously into the younger man's face; after a long pause he asked, "Son, haven't we met somewhere before?"

Wade smiled, "We sure have Colonel; when I was working with your daughter Angie, in Quebec—my courier trips to Washington—for Monsieur LeBlanc and the LOM. Remember those?"

"OH YEAH! Sure! But I didn't know you had gone into the RCAF. Why didn't Angie tell me? Damn—it's good to see you again. What a great surprise! This is gonna be a great night for me; you guys wanna drink now or at the Victoria? Let's have one now! Champagne, or the hard stuff?"

André answered, "We just finished a magnum of the bubbly, Louis; the bellman hinted that you sent it to our room—and we thank you—but now I'll have a bourbon and branch -water, and we can dream we're at our old drinking hole on the bayou outside Lafayette."

"Sounds like a perfect dream to me," added Joe. "How 'bout you Will—er—*Wade?*"

Wade shot a half-frown at Joe, "Whatever suits y'all, suits me."

The old Victoria Inn was, Colonel Hebert told them in the cab, the best kept secret in London.

He said he had always agreed with the joke about the reason young Englishmen had been willing—even *eager*—to go to the far ends of the earth to colonize for the British Empire; they wanted something fit to eat. That is, he *had* agreed until he discovered the Victoria a few years back during a Bar Association meeting in London. Since, he had seized upon any excuse to return to London, in order to dine there again.

It was, he said, "Sort of continental French, with a hint of Creole in many of the dishes." in a word, it was superb.

The dinner lasted more than three hours, and each of the five courses seemed even better than the ones that had come before. The young pilots had wondered if any meal could possibly be as good as their host had predicted; it was better.

During dinner André asked the Colonel some questions about the U.S. government policy on granting transfers from the RAF or RCAF to the U.S. Army Air Corps. André knew that Hebert was aware that he had gone through some family objections and turmoil—as well as fear of legal problems—when he had left Baton Rouge for Canada as a teenager, in clear violation of the U.S. neutrality laws prior to Pearl Harbor.

Hebert waved his arm and said, "Forget that! That is absolutely no problem. A federal amnesty is absolutely in place for that and related so-called 'offenses.' Believe me; any politician or prosecuting attorney in America who tried to nit-pick about those things would probably get hung—and *fast*. But this is up to you fellows, and only you.

"But I do have a selfish interest in something I'd like to explore with all three of you, so let me throw that out now, if I may."

He told them why he was in London, and described the plan of OSS to recruit young American officers to go into Europe, behind enemy lines, especially France, to work with the various resistance groups before and after the future invasion of the continent.

He said that the British counterparts of OSS were worlds ahead of the U.S. because they had been deeply into "this secret war business" since 1939, but that OSS was determined to catch up "*before* our guys hit the beaches, whenever that time comes, as it surely will."

He added that while it was not an absolute requirement, ideally many of the U.S. agents would be qualified pilots. "A near-perfect profile would be a young officer who is a pilot, speaks some French, Italian, or German—

especially *French*— who has been through, or is willing to go to—the Army's Jump School at Fort Benning at Columbus, Georgia for a few weeks, and is willing to fly in some rather weird situations for us *spooks,* as we are sometimes lovingly referred to by the rest of the world."

"Why is being a pilot important?" asked Joe.

"Let me answer that by telling you of a recent *British* mission that was described in our conference this morning. By the way, the mission was performed to help an American general, simply because *we* don't yet have the capability to do such a job ourselves.

"An RAF wing commander described this operation that occurred a few days ago, and it was *a lulu.* Two RCAF pilots flying *Mosquitos*—like you do, Wade—went into German-occupied territory in France and picked up a famous, and badly needed, Italian resistance leader that a French *résistance* unit had taken from the Gestapo *just the day before* the pickup.

"They flew him back to England, where he boarded an American B-24 and—within 24 hours of the pickup—he was sittin' with our General Mark Clark's staff in Italy, feeding 'em vital intelligence that could well shorten the Italian campaign by weeks *and*—more important—save the lives of thousands of Allied soldiers.

"The two pilots are going to be decorated, as well they should be. It was a classic case of great, and *daring,* flying, combined with exceptional co-ordination with a very good resistance unit."

Col. Hebert had noticed that, about halfway through his description, Joe and André had started glancing oddly at Wade from time to time. When he had finished the story, André turned to Wade, "Why don't you tell the Colonel about *your* most recent flight, Wade?"

Wade went through a brief description of *Blue Waters,* playing down, intermittently, his own role, but praising highly the flying skills of his squadron leader, as well as the courage and commitment of the *résistant* group. He ended with a few comments—and some show of emotion— about the heroic actions of the *résistant* who had died on the strip.

Col. Hebert had hung on Wade's every word, mouth agape. At the end he almost shouted, "MY GOD, Wade; this is *absolutely* amazing! That's *got* to be the exact operation the Brit described this morning. Did you deal with a British agent named Malone?"

Wade nodded.

"Well, you did a great job, and a damned dangerous one too; it took plenty of moxie to pull that off. I'd like . . . "

"No, Colonel," Wade interrupted, almost in a whisper, " it wasn't *us* who had the moxie. It was the ten French resistance people who were in the *real* danger, both at the strip and before that, when they went into Italy and took the Italian from the Gestapo. Believe me—they're a gutsy bunch, and absolutely dedicated to their cause. Actually, I'm sure they are *still* in danger, for their part in this.

"I don't think I can *ever*—if I live to be a hundred—forget the sight of that man who made his body a shield that day; he knew he was probably gonna *die,* but didn't hesitate to do what he believed he had to do. *He's* the guy who deserves all the medals."

"You're too modest, son, but I'm glad to hear you were impressed by the resistance unit there. We know it well and have big plans for it soon. It's an unusually good one because it has some fine local financial support that I can't discuss in detail at this time. Many other units are not so fortunate.

"Now, back to my point in discussing this with you three. I'm reluctant to try to proselyte a squadron leader like André here—don't want to tick off our Allies too much, you see. But I'd hope that you—Wade and Joe—would consider being in our program. Wade, sounds like you have *exactly* the skills we're looking for, 'cept we would want you to go back to Benning for a coupla weeks at the Jump School.

"Joe, in your case we'd need you to have the jump training too, plus a cram-course for a few weeks to teach you a few words of French—with that you'd pick it up fast later, usin' it everyday. I'm certain you could be transferred over into our air arm as a 1st Lieutenant, and Wade as possibly a Captain. Either of you interested?"

Joe and Wade looked at each other, but neither spoke up. He added, "I know it's a big decision. Think on it, and let's talk again at breakfast tomorrow.

"O.K. who wants dessert? They make some great ones here."

At the hotel, the three younger men talked for a while after the Colonel had gone to his room. Wade told them that he had been so impressed by his experience with Les Amis that he would really like to go into the program—knowing that he would still be flying—but feared the worst because of his unusual situation.

Joe wasn't too excited about it all, and said he was going to explain to the colonel that he was happy with his work. "Besides," he said, "knowing me, I'd play hell learnin' French or any other language; let's face it—that's one reason I went to Canada—to get out of school. If they want to give me some silver bars anyhow, I'll take 'em but, if not, I'm happy with my old sergeant's stripes."

Hearing that, André told the others, "A suggestion. Why don't I call Louis tonight and tell him that Joe's gonna pass, but Wade will be down to see him at breakfast, but just to talk a little more about it. Then, in the morning, Wade, you ask him if you can talk to him 'in confidence'; I'm certain he'll say O.K. Then you sorta *hint* that you might have done a little lyin' to get in the RCAF, without telling him exactly *what;* he knows I did, so he's used to that. Then just see what he says.

"And look; I know this man; when he says you can talk in confidence, you can believe him—100 percent."

When Wade shrugged, André continued, "If the conversation gets sticky, you can always say you don't want to leave your squadron, and he'll accept that. Try it Wade; what's to lose?"

It was only 7:00 and the dining room was almost vacant when Wade walked in. The colonel—in uniform for his later visit to his conference—waved to him from a corner table that was off by itself.

They shook hands and Wade sat on his right so they could chat freely without anyone overhearing. After both had finished their food, Wade spoke first. "I don't want you to think I'm not interested in your program, Colonel. After my one experience with the resistance people, I would consider it a great honor to work with them.

"They are what I would call true patriots for their country, even though they are being hunted day and night, not only by the Germans but also their own government. I don't know if they mentioned it in your meeting, but we were told in the debriefing at Brighton that the eight-man group that attacked us at the strip—and tried to kill the man we were to bring home—was part of the Milice, a French para-military group that is constantly hounding the French resistance movement all over France.

"But I have a problem that you don't know about; may I discuss it with you very confidentially?

"Of course Wade, and you have my word that whatever that may be, it will go no further without your prior express consent."

"Colonel, I did some things that were against the law in order to get in the RCAF—before and after I went to Quebec—and, although I must tell you that I am glad I did, it has caused me a lot of worry, mainly because I have not even felt like I could let my family know where I am.

"My father and mother were very much opposed to my going in the service when I first tried and . . . "

"Hold on son, " Hebert leaned across and raised a hand, palm up toward Wade. "Since this is 'confession time' I've got to stop you and do mine. I think I know what you are about to tell me; and it's *not* necessary.

"You know, in the OSS we figure it's better to be *way* too careful, than to be even a *little* sorry. We take very few things for granted, especially regarding security. I hope you will understand *why* we did this.

"When you came to D.C. the first time, you may recall that you and I sat and talked for awhile, and I had Mary, my assistant, bring us a couple of glasses of Coke—glasses with perfectly *smooth* sides. She came back for your empty glass that night, and was extremely careful not to accidentally smudge your fingerprints with her own.

"The next morning, a nice set of your prints were sent across town to the FBI for a check.

"That was back in the very early days of OSS, when we were the new boy on the block and about as welcome in the Washington 'security community' as the blacksheep child at the family reunion. So the Bureau sometimes—make that *always*—tended to take its sweet time in anything it did for us.

"I'm sure they didn't *intend* it as a favor when they screwed around for about five weeks before sending us back the report on your prints. The report showed them to be the prints of a "Willard Johnson, age 18," who had been printed at the aviation cadet recruiting office in Atlanta in early 1942.

"Apparently some wise-ass in the bureau thought it might embarrass us, so he had also run down the fact that this kid Johnson was actually only 17 and had used fake papers to get sworn in, and that the enlistment had later been revoked because of his 'fraud.'

"Fortunately, by the time I received their report, you had been back a second time and I had gotten to know you well enough that I didn't give a damn about a so-called 'fraud' you may have used to try to go out and put your life on the line for your country. I would describe that—at worst—as a very '*well-intentioned* fraud' that many American kids have had guts enough to commit in order to serve their country; that includes André, who is as fine a young man as ever drew a breath."

He paused, then smiled and said, "My *other* reason for not admitting to anyone that I knew about your 'horrid' deception was that I had bragged so much, to Angie and LeBlanc, about how *mature* you were for a *22-year-old* that I knew they must have been cracking up privately. I didn't want them to realize they could then have the pleasure of doing it to my face! Come to think of it, that may have been the most important reason for me to keep quiet about it."

Wade felt like he was in shock, he didn't know what to say.

Louis again broke the silence. "What I *didn't* know until last night was that you had gone into the RCAF. Knowing my daughter and her boss—as well as what some of my *own* staff do from time to time—I think I can guess what happened.

"You don't need to comment on this next, so *don't,* but here's my theory: They gave you a *nom de guerre,* complete with new identity papers and all necessary and supporting biographical data. Then you made them look brilliant by becoming a superstar in the RCAF under your new name."

Wade finally spoke up, "Well, now you can see why I can't reveal all of this."

"Wrong! You're a first-class pilot, son, but a novice as a guard-house lawyer, and dead-lost in the strange world of the cloak and dagger.

"We're in a *war,* son! And it's one to try to save the world from a second dark age. *Pragmatism* should rule all our decisions, in my opinion, and there are people in the highest levels of our government who agree. The program I've been discussing is vital and an absolute priority. You fit the exact profile to fill our needs, including some excellent practical experience that few candidates would have.

"If you tell me you will accept an assignment to OSS, I can flat guarantee you that we will take care of any of the legal problems you are visualizing— with Canada *and* the U.S. You could use your *present* identity as your *nom de guerre,* be commissioned in the Army Air Corps under your *true* identity, get back in touch with your family and friends under your real name— even go see them while you are at Jump School at Benning; it's only 90 or 100 miles from Atlanta.

"Whatta you say?"

"I think I will do it, but could I think about it for a few hours? Joe and André are checking out this afternoon, but I have a couple of days leave left, and I can find another place to stay tonight. If you will still be here tonight, I'll call you then."

"That sounds good, but look; I'll take care of their room for another night. You can stay in it and we'll have dinner tonight, if you like; but not a five course one, 'cause I have to fly over to a morning meeting in Scotland tomorrow. Meet me in the main dining room at 7:00 tonight."

"Will do, sir; see you then."

Wade waited until it was noon in London, then telephoned from a booth in a quiet little park near the hotel.

It was 7:00 A.M. in Atlanta when his father answered the phone, and was so overwhelmed with emotion that he couldn't speak. "Dad, are you still there?" his son asked. Then he heard his mother's voice , "Will, is that *really* you?" she asked, trying to hold back her own tears of joy.

After all had cried a while, he said that he was safe and well and serving as an officer in an Allied military force, but that he might soon have an offer of a commission in the U.S. Army. He wanted to be sure that his parents would not object to his continuing to serve, if he accepted the offer. He added that he thought he would be able to visit soon if this went through, that he thought of them each and every day, and wanted badly to see them.

His father had been able to gather himself, and told him that the only reason they had objected before was because he was under age at the time.

His mother mentioned that Bill had gone into the cadet program soon after he had turned 18—with their blessings—and that he was now a bombardier, flying with the Eighth Air Force in England.

At the end of the conversation his parents were bubbling with anticipation of seeing him after almost two of the longest years of their lives. He said he hoped it would work out, and he would know soon. Before they said their goodbyes, he asked his mother to call Polly and tell her he hoped to see her soon.

At dinner, Col. Hebert was delighted to hear the news. He told Wade that he could expect to receive the necessary orders within two to three weeks, and hoped to have him on the way to Benning soon after that.

Wade asked if it were possible that OSS could use him in a region of France near where he and Kevin had picked up Signore Marconi. Col. Hebert said yes and that it was even conceivable that he might be working with the Les Amis unit itself, since it was key to some of their planning for improvement in the retrieving and rapid return of downed Allied airmen, as well as for a massive operation that was under consideration for the Riviera region. If so, they would want to send an explosive expert and a sniper in with Wade; and the person or persons selected for those roles would probably go through Jump School with him.

Kevin was surprised—and disappointed—to hear the news, and asked him, "Why this decision?"

Wade told him there were several reasons, and that one was a direct result of their *Blue Waters* experience.

He went on to say that the picture of Eugenio lying across the body of Signore Marconi—absorbing hit after hit from the infuriated Milice—seemed to be etched indelibly in his mind's eye. It had made him realize that this war was being fought by some for much more than simply a selfish thrill, as had always been his own motivation prior to that day at the strip.

Wade added that since that experience he had promised himself to try to be less self-centered. Colonel Hebert had convinced him that he had a combination of talent and experience that would enable him to fill a an important role in OSS. He said also that he saw it as a serious need of not only the United States and its Allies, but also as a crying need for the *résistants* who were in an almost "David and Goliath" situation unless the Allies could give them more effective assistance.

He then added that there was another important, and extremely personal, reason for his decision, but he couldn't talk about it yet.

Kevin slapped him on the back and assured him that he understood, but would sorely miss "the best wingman I ever had."

It was a Monday afternoon when Wade received a note to check in promptly with the Wing Headquarters.

The Administrative Officer gave him two sets of orders. One was a joint order from the RAF and The United States Army Air Corps, transferring him to the USAAC in the grade of captain; the second was from the USAAC, directing him to report immediately to HQ, Eighth Air Force, near London, to proceed via U.S. military aircraft to OSS HQ, Washington D.C., for two days of orientation prior to continuing to Fort Benning, Georgia, to attend the United States Army Jump School.

At the lobby desk of E-Street Complex the OSS receptionist gave him a message from Colonel Hebert. It said, in longhand, "Welcome to Washington, Captain Johns. Ask the receptionist to ring Mary Doss, and she will come out to show you to my office; we need to talk about a few items." It was signed, "Louis Hebert."

"First," said Louis, "let me explain the paper work done on you. *Legally,* you have been commissioned in your real name, 'Willard Johnson,' and you will be provided ID credentials in that name. All your *army* records will be the same, and you will use it in all your contacts with the army itself, *other than* with OSS people.

"Use *Johnson* with your family and others close to you, but do *not* give them your *nom de guerre,* 'Wade Johns,' which you will use, along with separate ID and other credentials in that name, in all your dealings with OSS and all other personnel, Allied people included. For example, you will be enrolled in the jump school as Johnson, but our records here will show that 'Captain Wade Johns' went through the school.

"Yeah, I know; it's more than a little confusing, but you'll get used to it. With the *résistants,* they use these false identities mainly to protect their families from retaliation or intimidation; we do it for various other reasons, good or bad.

"When you go to France, you will go as Captain Wade Johns, and you will take two sets of lightweight khaki army uniforms, complete with captain's bars attached. Obviously you wouldn't last long walking around in enemy-occupied territory in uniform, so you will have to wear civvies while there, hopefully the same kind as a Frenchman of your age would normally wear. The only problem with this is that if you are captured in civvies, you might be shot as a 'spy,' but if you are in military uniform, the German military would, normally, treat you as a POW—a *big* difference, believe me.

"We recommend that, where feasible, you always wear at least your army shirt, insignia attached, *under* your civvies. In this way, if you found that capture was imminent, you could possibly strip to the shirt before capture and claim the protections provided to captured military personnel by the Geneva Convention.

"When you arrive at Benning, you will have another new OSS agent who will be going through jump training with you. His name is Sergeant Luke Hatfield, who has served in combat as a sharpshooter/sniper in North Africa as well as with Patton's army in Sicily. We sent him to the army's school in Colorado for extensive training in the use of explosives, and he completed that course just a week ago. Get to know him well, because you and he will go as a team into France after jump school.

"The last I want to mention is something I think you will like; I know you asked about the possibility of working with *Les Amis*. I can't absolutely guarantee it, but it is quite likely that you and Luke *will* be working with that unit, the one you already admire so much.

"We in OSS, along with our British counterparts, are counting heavily on them for some truly important missions in the months ahead. They are almost unique in one respect; that is, they have continuing financial and other aid from a wealthy—and still influential—Frenchman in their region; *and* they have a strong need for exactly the skills you possess, as well as those of Sergeant Hatfield. For example, Hatfield is an outstanding sharpshooter, and would fill a void for Les Amis created by the death of the man you knew as Eugenio. So keep your fingers crossed, and *maybe* you'll see your French friends soon."

"That's great news, Colonel. Actually, I only 'saw' them from the air, but I saw enough to know it would be a great honor to be at their side."

"Oh yeah, Wade; after I got back from seeing you in London, I called Angie and Jean-Paul LeBlanc and pretended to raise hell with them about holding out information about you when you were our courier. I think I had ém worried for awhile before I couldn't help but bust out laughing.

"Both of them said to give you a big 'hello and thumbs up' from *LOM*. They're doing a great job for us—pouring out more well trained agents than any other *five* sources we have."

That night he called his family to say he would have to report to Fort Benning by noon on Monday, but would be home on Saturday and Sunday. They were still choked up with joy, but his dad managed to say he would drive him to Benning on Monday morning, and that it was less than 100 miles from their home. They wanted to have some friends over on Saturday evening if that was all right with him, because everybody in Lakewood now knew he was coming and wanted to at least say hi to him.

"Great; er—do you think Polly might be there, too?"

"I'll say!" Noah said, "It would probably take an *army* to keep her away!"

Will found himself wiping both his eyes as he replaced the telephone. And he felt a different—and very pleasant—surge of emotion at the thought of seeing Polly again.

By late 1943, there were too many Gold Stars hanging in homes in the little community of Lakewood. Consequently, it was always time to celebrate when one of theirs was home on leave, and *unharmed*. The neighborhood was abuzz with the news that one of the Johnson boys was coming in, if only for a weekend.

This one was of special interest, since no one, not even his own family, was quite sure what he had been doing. But just up the street from the Johnson house, at Kelly's corner store, the word was, "He's one of Noah and Katie Johnson's boys; so whatever he's been doing, he's doing his part—and doing it *right*—you can count on that."

He arrived at the old Terminal Station at 10:20 A.M., and his parents and all three sisters were on the platform when he stepped off the train, handsome in his army officer's green winter uniform and new captain's bars. The Johnsons weren't the only families enjoying a reunion on the platform that Saturday morning, but they felt they had to be the happiest.

During the ride home he told them he had been flying with the RCAF, and in Mosquitos, but hoped they would understand that he was not permitted to go into detail regarding some of his work. One of his sisters asked about the ribbon on his jacket representing his RAF decoration; he explained that it signified the Distinguished Flying Cross (DFC) he had received for helping in a mission flown out of Sicily, but offered no details.

When they arrived home, his mother finished cooking and then served a lunch of several of his favorite dishes during what he described as, "My best lunch in nearly two years."

At the end of the long lunch, he asked the family to let him tell them a little about the duty he was about to undertake, because he would again be doing work wherein sometimes he could not be in contact with them for periods of time; but *this* time it was solely because of the security-sensitive nature of the work, and not because he chose not to contact them.

He assured them he would be performing U.S. Army duties, but beyond that it would be better for them, as well as for him, that he say no more.

The first guest to arrive that night was Master Sergeant Duncan Angus Macdonald, in full dress uniform with a chest covered with ribbons. As Will strode smiling toward him to shake his hand, Sgt. Mac shouted, in his booming voice, "STOP where you are—Captain Johnson—SIR!" then stood at ramrod attention, and snapped a salute to Will. Stunned for a moment, Will weakly returned the salute, then quickly stepped forward to embrace his old Sarge.

The next people there were the Hearns, with their daughter Polly. She was a picture—and a beautiful one—of serenity on this evening. Since he went away, there had not been a day that she had not thought of Will, and there were many days when she had been convinced she would never see him again.

They embraced for a long time without a word being passed.

It was almost midnight before the last guests left and Will walked Polly home. They sat very close in the swing on the Hearn's front porch for almost an hour and chatted about their school days. He was grateful that she never asked a question about what he had been doing while away.

When he heard the Hearn's grandfather clock chime 1:00 A.M., he kissed her again and asked if he could come by in the morning for a walk in the park. She nodded and said, "Come down about 7:30, and I'll fix you a quick breakfast first."

On his way home, he wondered if he was finally in love.

There was still a morning mist over the lake when he and Polly arrived, arm in arm, at the park pavilion. On Sunday morning, it was rare for anyone to be there, so they had it to themselves.

They sat in a swing at the lake's edge and enjoyed the quiet. Then they smiled knowingly at each other as the ducks started to gather, noisily looking for a handout; it was a scene they had experienced often when they were small and had gone there with their fathers.

Polly turned to him and said, "Being here, like this, makes this terrible war seem very far away—almost like it's just a bad dream. Do you ever feel that way too?"

"Maybe sometimes. When you are a flyer, most of the real horrible parts of a war are sort of distant, and not too personal. Up until recently it was just a way to enjoy what I always wanted to do—fly an airplane. Sure, I had seen some of the sad part a few times, like losing a friend whose plane had been shot down , or didn't come back; but most of this was not 'up close' like for a ground soldier.

"Then, only a few weeks ago, I did see one of the real gory parts up close and this shook me pretty bad. It made me want to do more to help end the war."

"Well Will, I haven't said this to you , but I do hope you can stay in touch more often than before. I understand why you didn't write much while you were away, but I hope it won't be the same now.

"I know it will sound *forward* for me to say this, but I—Will,—I truly love you—and every day since you have been gone, my first hope for each day was to hear something to make me know you were alive and well."

"Don't apologize, Polly. I feel the same, but I don't express myself too well on things like that. And yes, I'll try to do better, but I can't promise how long it will be between letters. Some of my work in this new outfit may be—probably *will be*—in foreign countries—some of which are not too friendly with us—and in places where I won't be able to contact you, or anybody else, for long periods of time. I've already explained this to my family, and you're the only other one I'm going to discuss it with. Do you understand?"

"No, I actually don't understand, but I get the notion that it's something I'm not *supposed* to understand. But what worries me more is that it sounds like dangerous work."

He laughed, "Most work in war is 90 to 98 percent boredom—and two percent danger, like falling in the shower—this'll probably be the same.

"But—*enough* of that gruesome stuff! Let's enjoy this time while we have it! You game to race me around the lake, like we used to?"

She elbowed him hard, in the ribs, then, "You're on. Last one back to the pavilion has to wash the dishes left from breakfast!"

When he got home, Noah said, "You just missed a call from Bill; he tries to call us every Sunday. He was surprised—and absolutely beside-himself happy—to learn you were here.

"He left for England a few weeks ago with his crew, and was convinced that you were also there somewhere; but said that finding an American serviceman on that island was like finding the proverbial 'needle in the haystack.' Today he said he had finally found Joe Hearn just a day or so ago, but Joe was no help. He went on his first combat mission, an 'easy one' he said, but said he couldn't get into any details.

"He wants you to write him, Will. I hope you will. I think he some-times worried more about you than we did; kept saying that he hadn't 'kept his promises' to talk you into waiting."

"Sure, I'll write him—today, for sure. I understand, but what I did was no fault of his. He always did worry for us both. I guess that will never change."

# Chapter Fifteen

It was a two-hour drive to Fort Benning, just outside Columbus, Georgia, on the Chattahoochee River. Katie Johnson sat in the back seat while Noah drove. They didn't talk much on the way, but Will felt at home again as he gazed thoughtfully at the rolling red-clay countryside. It was the only land he had known before his recent adventures in Canada and England.

Almost to Columbus, they passed through the village of Warm Springs, and his dad pointed out the side road that led to President Roosevelt's Little White House. Katie mentioned that the president still came there frequently; and that he nearly drove his Secret Service detail crazy by insisting on personally driving his convertible—with the top down and *fast*—not only in and about Warm Springs, but also over the narrow mountain road to nearby Pine Mountain.

Will knew that FDR had grown to love Warm Springs during his younger years, while receiving therapy there for his Polio condition, but it was almost surreal to realize that decisions of world shaking proportions were being made in this sleepy little community in rural Georgia.

They let their son out at the main gate of the historic and imposing Fort Benning. He promised he would try to stop back by home when he finished his training there, hugged and kissed both, then stepped into the Jeep that was to take him to the Orderly Room of the jump school.

His driver was a corporal who pointed out some of the sites on the drive over. "Sir, everywhere you go here, you can almost *see* the ghosts of most of the great generals we've had in this man's army. Right over there is where General Patton lived when he was here. Two blocks further over is the polo field where they say he liked to play each Saturday he was stationed here. Some of the old-timers swear that he'd stand outside his quarters and stare up at the sky, wavin' his ridin' crop and cussin' like a mad man, whenever bad weather would screw up his Saturday for ridin' in a polo match.

"Ike spent some time here. I'm not sure about MacArthur, but most all the older West Pointers were here at one time or the other. The Rangers train here for some of their doings, if not all, and I think this is the only jump school in the army right now; if not, it's the oldest and biggest.

"The ones who come out of here as paratroopers are real fightin' men—I promise you that. Those birds the Germans think are their 'Supermen' are in for a helluva surprise when they meet up with the fellas who've gone through this base. They're trained to fight with every weapon in the book, including the bayonet and the knife; and I ain't met one yet who's scared of the Devil himself.

"Well here we are, sir; good luck to you. Hope I didn't talk your ears off."

"Not a bit, Corporal. That was very interesting; thanks. And the best of luck to you, too."

The next morning he reported to the assembly room at 7:00 A.M. as instructed, and found himself with 29 other army personnel. Most of them were privates from infantry units who had volunteered for paratrooper units.There were two other commissioned officers there—both were 2nd. lieutenants—along with one slightly-built tech sergeant who was talking non-stop to a couple of young soldiers while all were standing and having coffee prior to the start of the meeting.

As Will walked in, the sergeant spotted him, suddenly stopped talking in mid-sentence, strode briskly toward Will with a distinct swagger, and extended his hand, "S'cuse me, sir, but you must be Cap'n Johnson—since you're the only Cap'n here. My name's Luke Hatfield." Then he added, but in a *whisper,* "I hear we're gonna be workin' together soon." Will shook his hand, and replied, smiling, "Great to meet you, Luke; and I've heard the same thing, but maybe we should talk later about our work together, like after we finish here today."

"Yessir, at's just what I wuz about to say. Maybe I can buy ya a beer afterwards."

"Sounds good to me, Luke. Oh, it looks like our meeting is about to get underway. Let's grab a place where we can sit together."

A master sergeant, wearing the wings of a paratrooper, approached Will and Luke just as they had seated themselves, and handed Will a note, saying, "Sir, Major Kennedy—who will be conducting this session—told me to give you this." As he walked away, Will opened the sealed envelope; it said:

Captain Johnson:
    Please stay a few minutes, after the others are dismissed; I need a few private minutes with you and Sgt. Hatfield.
Bill Kennedy"

Major Kennedy, also a paratrooper, welcomed all to the Fort Benning Jump School, and summarized the course:

"First of all, this is a course for volunteers only, from the beginning to the end. If, at any time, you should decide, for any reason, that you do not want to continue in the course, simply notify me—privately if you prefer—and you will be relieved from continuing and sent back to the unit from whence you came.

"The course consists of four stages:

"Stage A: This will be (1) a physical-fitness stage, with (2) some lesser time spent teaching you to pack properly your parachute. Why do we do this? We believe that no one should be jumping from an airplane, especially from altitudes of 800 feet—or less—unless that person is physically fit; *and* I doubt that I need explain *why* you would prefer that the 'chute you use is properly packed; that is why we teach you to do it *yourself.*

"Stage B: In this stage, you do jumps from a 34-foot tower, attached to a cable that will slow your descent as you approach the ground, giving you a feel for the landing, but not as rough a landing as the real thing.

"We also continue with the physical fitness bit during this stage.

"Stage C: In stage C you will be jumping from another tower, except that this one is not 34 feet high—it is *300* feet high. This time you will have a 'chute; it will be already open above you, but your landing will be much more like the real thing.

"Stage D is the last stage. During this last stage you will do five jumps from a C-47 aircraft, from different altitudes: the first jump will be from 1,500 feet, the second from 1,200 feet, the third and fourth will each be from 1,000 feet, and the fifth and final training jump will be from 800 feet.

"If, for whatever reason, you miss any one of the five scheduled jumps, you must start over again with the *first* one, in order to receive your paratrooper's wings.

"If you finish the program I just outlined, you will receive the wings of a paratrooper in the U.S. Army, and will have become a member of a small group of proud and elite soldiers. I can also assure you that on that day you will feel a sense of accomplishment that will be with you for the rest of your days."

After another half-hour of covering housekeeping and other items, he told the group, "With that, this meeting is adjourned, but please report next door for your introduction to taking care of the paratrooper's best friend—his parachute. Thank you for your attention, and good luck to all."

As the rest were filing out, the major motioned to Will and Luke and led them into a small private office adjacent to the meeting room. He told them that he was one of only two people on the base who knew that they were in OSS, and he wanted to mention that (1) they could be excused from the rather severe physical fitness part of the first two phases if they wished, and that (2) after they had finished the basic jump training he had outlined, the air corps people on the base would have them do two additional jumps from altitudes of 5,000 to 8,000 feet, since they may be jumping from those altitudes in their OSS work, rather than the low "combat" altitudes used by airborne units, which were sometimes as low as 300 feet.

Will thanked him for the offer to be excused from the phys-ed work, but said he would like to have it since he would be there anyhow. Luke agreed, saying. "And we shore don't want your guys thinking we're a coupla goof-offs. Besides, if I'm gonna have the right to *wear* them wings, I wanta *earn* 'em."

Luke was born and raised in the mountainous coal-mining county of Pike County, Kentucky, in that part of the state that is shaped like a slice of pie, bounded by western Virginia on the East, east Tennessee to the South, and West Virginia to the North. His Daddy had owned and worked a tiny parcel of a coal-hill, and the tipple for his single mine shaft stared out from the side of the hill just above the small two bedroom cabin where Luke and his nine siblings lived until Luke left to join the army at 15. His father had worked the mine almost to its death by that time, while managing to eke out only a meager existence for his family, and he felt it best to aid and abet Luke's lies about age in order give his son a chance at a better life as a soldier.

Though Luke had very little formal education, he had accumulated more than his share of *savoir faire* on the art of survival in a harsh and unforgiving environment. Each summer, since his tenth year, his job had been to find and bring home meat to the family table from the abundant supply of game in the mountains. He had soon become an expert tracker of the large animals, and "the best shot in Eastern Kentucky" with a rifle, according to not only his daddy but also by every serious hunter in and around Pike County. It was said—admiringly—that Luke was the only one in the county who could tell from a distance of more than 100 yards the exact amount of rabbit stew a hare would make, and thus decide if it was worth a shot to bring it home.

His other area of expertise lay in the use of dynamite. Dynamite was used in the mining business all over that part of Kentucky, and sometimes was even used as a defensive weapon. More than once, in the '30s, when his father had insisted on operating his mine during the coal miners' frequent strikes—thereby causing the so-called "flying squads" to threaten attack on the Hatfield tipple and mineshaft—Luke and his daddy had used lighted sticks of dynamite quite effectively in order to persuade the intruders to depart.

When he had entered the army back in 1938, Luke's skills as a sharp-shooter were immediately recognized and honed by the army. And it wasn't long before they also recognized his talents with explosives. After he had built quite a reputation by his exploits in North Africa and Sicily—both as a sniper as well as in some rather ingenious assistance to the army's combat engineers in two separate instances—he had been discovered by the OSS and sent to the army's school on explosives in Colorado. It was shortly thereafter that he learned that in OSS he would be teamed with a Captain Johnson, an American pilot who had flown with the RCAF.

They spent most of the rest of the first day in the equipment room, learning to pack a parachute, both the type designed to be opened by the static line, as well as another type called the reserve chute. They each packed and repacked both types until all had done them right at least two times.

The same master sergeant who had given the note to Will was in charge of the inspecting, assisted by three other non-coms, all of whom wore paratrooper wings and the shoulder patches of the *Screaming Eagles,* the 101st Airborne Division. A captain had spoken briefly after each trainee was handed two chutes and assigned to one of the long work tables in the huge room: "Today we will start learning how to pack properly each type of parachute; at the end of this week you will be able to pack each while blindfolded. The reason for this is to enable you to pack it in the dark if the occasion ever requires that.

"The first chute we passed to you is the one a paratrooper uses in a combat jump, and is opened—if you have packed it right—by a static line as you jump from the aircraft. You do nothing to open it—except, of course, *jump* from the aircraft. One end of the line is attached to the release apparatus in your chute, and the other end is attached to a horizontal line which is in turn attached to the interior of the aircraft.

"The entire group of soldiers who are to jump are referred to as 'the stick.' Just prior to the time to jump the 'Jump Master'—usually a senior non-com—will give the order to 'stand up and hook up.' When he does, the entire stick should do just that—stand up and hook up to the static line. Next the jump master will order 'GO!' and the first man will go, followed as promptly as possible by the others—the faster the better.

"It is sort of like a *stampede* once the 'GO' is given, so don't dawdle around; you get the hell out the door as fast as you can. Otherwise your stick will be spread all over hell's half acre when all of you get on the ground. In a real combat situation this can be disastrous, because you can find yourself in a hostile environment without any help.

"The second chute is called a 'reserve chute,' to be used in the unlikely event that the first chute doesn't open, or fails to 'blossom,' for some reason.

"Depending on the altitude from which the jump is made, the reserve chute can be handy to have. Of course, if the jump is to be made from an altitude of 500 feet or less—which is not at all unusual—there's not much point in carrying the reserve chute, simply because you don't have time enough to use it if the first chute fails. When you *are* carrying the reserve chute, it buckles onto your harness in the front, and therefore is called a 'chest pack.'

"Any questions?"

"Yeah; what happens if the man in front of me decides not to jump?"

"Not likely to happen. When the jump master gives the command 'GO' it really is like a pure stampede; the only man who might succeed in balking would be the last one in the stick. If a man does have any doubt about leaving when that command is given, he'd best not board the aircraft to begin with. I know I'd hate to be the only guy who didn't 'go' and have to ride back alone with the typical jump master. I'm proud to say that there have been damned few troopers to finish this school and refuse to jump later. Some of us may have been so nervous we heard our knees knocking sometimes—but that's O.K—we still went out the door."

They were released at four o'clock and Luke and Will walked down to the Post Exchange together. Will suggested that they have dinner together that night but somewhere in town, so they could talk privately. Luke mentioned that he knew Columbus fairly well because he had been stationed at Benning for a while shortly after he had finished Infantry Basic Training in 1938. He suggested a steakhouse on the highway to Columbus that was only a mile or so from the main gate to the base.

When they arrived at the restaurant, Will was pleased to see that very few customers were there on a Tuesday evening, and he asked for a table in the corner, so they could talk OSS in privacy.

Luke mentioned that it sounded like they would be learning to jump from much lower altitudes than he had heard about from some OSS veterans he had met in his Colorado class.

"Maybe so, Luke; but it's also possible that we may have occasion to go in at such low altitudes, perhaps even *with* an Allied airborne drop. Things are still sort of fuzzy about future plans or—at least—very few people really *know* what the definite plans are for going back onto the continent, except that sooner or later we *are* going back. It's probably best that you and I are trained for whatever we're asked to do."

"You're right, Cap'n. I like it better 'at way anyhow. I plan to stay in the army to retirement, so the more trainin' I get the better, 'at's for sure. I'd like to go back home, but there's not much decent payin' work there anymore, 'cept for the mines, and my daddy made me swear I'd never go in the mines like he's had to do all his life. It's a rough life, Cap'n."

"By the way, Luke, I know we have to use this 'Captain and Sergeant' stuff on the base, but do me a favor—when we're in private, make it 'Will', O.K.? Another good reason is that when we go in to work with the resistance people we shouldn't be using army terms anyhow; it would be a dead giveaway, and might get us captured—or shot. We need to get used to the other way—agreed?"

"At's fine with me Cap—er, I mean 'Will.' But it's gonna take some gittin' used to, after five years of the other—so gimmie a little time. But I wanta say this—I can tell right now you're gonna be great to work with, sir."

They talked throughout dinner, and later that evening, about what their work in OSS might be like. Will told him some about *Blue Waters* and the young French *résistants* he had come to admire so much, and how that experience had changed his personal reasons for serving in the army.

He said to Luke that, as a result of that experience, he had made promises to himself that he was determined to keep.

During the evening, Luke told him he had been asked to think about OSS in Sicily, shortly after he had made a suggestion that "turned out good" to a combat engineers officer who was trying to determine how to blow away a three-foot-thick wall of an ancient prison holding some Sicilians that the OSS wanted freed. Luke said it really "wasn't no big deal— just sumpin I learned while I wuz a kid in the hills." Apparently the OSS agent had been impressed, since he tried to recruit him on the spot.

The second day at jump school was a day to remember. For a long time after he finished jump school, Will would say frequently that it was the most difficult day of his life—unless it was the third day. He had thought he was fairly fit until the first and second days of the physical fitness part of the course. By the end of the first he was about to collapse; and to make his embarrassment complete, the others, to a man, seemed to be hardly winded by the six continuous hours of exertion. This was especially true of Luke, who laughed and cracked jokes the entire day as if he were playing some parlor game that delighted him.

The next day Will woke up so stiff he could hardly get out of bed, and when he finally managed to do so he could hardly walk for the first ten minutes.

But, blessedly, by the end of the second week, he was doing all that was asked of him without visibly hurting, and Luke had finally quit grinning at him every other minute.

From a fear standpoint, Stage B was—surprisingly—the most difficult part of the course to most in the class. Somehow the 34-foot tower, from where one could see the ground—so near, yet so far—was more intimidating than the *300-foot* tower in the next stage.

Time passed rapidly at the jump school, and soon Luke and Will found themselves part of a stick of ten, airborne in a C-47, ready for their first real jump. By this time, there was no doubt that Luke Hatfield had performed far and away as the best in the class; so much so that an impartial bystander would have thought that Luke could have taught the class.

On the day before their first jump was scheduled, Major Kennedy had spoken to Will privately, "Captain Johnson, I know you're not infantry, so please decline this if you wish, but we in infantry are proud to claim that our most effective command is '*Follow me!*'; so, normally, the trainee who is senior in rank is the first man in the stick on this first jump—and therefore the first man out the door on 'GO!'

"Do you have any problem with doing that, since you will be the only officer on the aircraft tomorrow? No problem if you do; I think all the men know, by now, that you are not infantry, and Sergeant Hatfield—who would be next in rank—has already volunteered to do it."

Will laughed, "Of course I'll do it. You know, in the air corps we also know how to lead a little, sir.

"Besides, there's *no way* I'm gonna give Luke Hatfield another excuse to grin at me for the rest of the war! Put me down as the first man out the door, and he can come right behind me if he wants, but *behind* me only!"

The final stage was uneventful, except that the final jump was a bit exciting, mainly because they were not issued reserve chutes, given that the jump was to be made from only 800 feet.

On the Saturday of the last week there was a short graduation ceremony when 29 of the original 30 trainees received their paratrooper wings; the 30th one had broken an ankle on his second jump.

The instructors had unanimously designated Luke Hatfield as the outstanding graduate of the class; thus he was the first to be called forward to have his wings pinned on him by the commandant of the jump school and presented with a certificate commemorating his achievement.

Will and Luke spent the next week working with the small complement of army air corps personnel based at Benning.

They learned to pack and repack the larger back-type parachutes used by most airmen, as well as the standard chest-type used by crewmen such as bombardiers. They also made two additional jumps from a C-47, one from 5,000 feet and the second from 8,000 feet. Luke asked why they weren't making more jumps, and the air corps instructor quipped, "In the army air corps, we don't believe in practicing something that has to be perfect every time."

On the last day of jump school, they received sealed orders from Colonel Hebert's office, granting them three days leave after finishing at

Fort Benning and directing them to proceed afterward to OSS Headquarters in Washington for further assignment.

Will told Luke he planned to spend his three days with his family in Atlanta, and invited him to come along as his guest. Luke thanked him but decided to go by Pikeville for a quick visit on his way to Washington.

The train from Columbus stopped at Warm Springs and Fayetteville before reaching Atlanta. The day-coach was packed with soldiers leaving Benning; many of them were airborne, not long out of jump school themselves. Some were headed for a whooping weekend at the old Owl Room—a favorite Atlanta watering hole for soldiers from Benning, especially the airborne types.

A couple of the younger ones had obviously gotten a headstart on their weekend, and were vocally curious about why an air corps captain had been to *their* jump school. Will laughed it off, "You know the army; they're forever trying to put square pegs into round holes; it's 'SNAFU'—so what's new? Who knows why they sent me? Probably just something to keep me busy while you guys do all the fightin', right?"

He was met again at the station by his family; but this time Polly was there too, at Will's request.

After dinner, he suggested to Polly a walk to the park, that he wanted to talk about something special. As they sat on the bench—one that Polly had come to call "our bench"—Will said, "I'm not good at expressing some things, Pol, so bear with me in this, please.

"You know, I've been gone from here for a pretty long time. And I've met a good many girls—in Canada, in England, and some in Oklahoma, and a couple in Columbus the last few weeks. But the funny thing is—I just haven't been interested in them, except for a laugh or two. The truth is—every time I'm around them, I find myself comparing them to you. Isn't that strange?"

"Yes, I guess so, Will, but what are you getting at?"

"Well—what I'm getting at . . . is . . . this. . . . Someday, after the war, I want to get married—and *you* are the girl I want to marry. What do you think?"

Polly didn't say a word; but she leaned over and pulled him close to her for a very long time, finally saying, "What I *think* is—this is the most wonderful news I have heard in my entire life! And something I have dreamed about for about three years."

"Boy; what a relief! I was afraid you'd tell me I was nuts. Two years ago, *I* would have thought it was nutty, but things look different to me now, and I really want to do this, as soon as I get back home, at the end of the war."

They walked back to the Johnson home and told his parents and sisters the news, to the delight of all. One of his sisters blurted out, "Well,

Will—my brother—this is certainly the smartest idea *you* ever had; Polly Hearn is the sweetest girl in the world—and maybe the *prettiest* too!"

It was late when he got back home that evening, but his mother was still up and waiting to see him. She told him again how happy she was at the evening's news, and so relieved that he was back in contact with his family again.

Will apologized again for all the worry and anxiety he had caused her, saying that while he still believed he had done the right thing, he knew now that he had not done it the right way. As he described it, "The truth is that I've been a selfish ingrate, and I promise you now that I'm gonna try to make it up from now on."

"You've already done that, Will. Don't give it another thought.

"Oh yes, son, I almost forgot; Sergeant Mac called tonight. He asked if he could see you for a few minutes before you go back."

"Good. I had planned to drop by the school to see him before leaving. He's on my 'apology list' too. I'll go by on Monday; I'm not leaving 'til Wednesday. Also, I want to try to see Gary Kelly's Dad. Have you heard anything about him lately?"

"Yes, and it's not good. He'd never been the same after his wife died; then the terrible loss of Gary just about killed him. Thank God his older son is still alive, even though he's in a German POW camp."

"Gosh, Mom; I didn't know that. Was he shot down?"

"I'm sorry; I guess we just forgot to tell you. As I understand it, he was on only his second flight—'mission' I think y'all call it—over northern France, near the German border. Another pilot—the air corps letter said 'his wingman'—saw him parachute from his airplane after it was hit by anti-aircraft fire. They say he was first picked up by some friendly French group, but was later captured by the Germans.

"Actually, Harry has gotten several letters from him, and he says he is being treated well. But, naturally, Harry is real worried about him anyhow. It would really make him feel good if you went by. Right now—bless his heart—he just feels like he's lost everything he ever cared about.

"I thank God *every* single night that you and Bill are still O.K. I just pray to God I can always say that."

"We're gonna be *fine*, Mama—just you wait and see!"

"I pray the Lord you're right, son. Goodnight now; see you at breakfast. I'm fixing all your favorite things, pancakes and all the rest."

On Monday morning, Will knocked on the door of the Kelly home at nine o'clock sharp. After he had knocked a third time, and was ready to walk away, he heard a man say, in sort of a sleepy groan, "Who's there?" and it sounded like Harry Kelly.

"It's Will Johnson, Mr. Kelly; I'm home on leave. Could I see you a minute?"

"Will Johnson!!" the voice shouted this time, "Just a second son; I'll be right there."

A full five minutes later the door opened, but Will could hardly recognize the man he had known just two years before. He was a skeleton of his former self, looked as if he hadn't shaved for a week, and smelled like stale gin. But he broke into a huge smile at the sight of Will, then embraced him with tears streaming down over his cheekbones, muttering over and over, "God, am I glad to see you, *boy!* then, "Come on in here; let me feast these old eyes on you!"

Harry put on a pot of coffee, and they talked for a full hour in his kitchen, first about Gary and Charlie, then about what Will had been doing.

He told Will, "You are the only boy from the neighborhood who's been to see me since Gary died, but I understand that; it's not easy to talk about such things. Anyhow, as I always told your Daddy, you and Bill always were the cream of the crop, and I was always proud that a boy like you was Gary's best friend; still am."

As Will said his good-byes, he felt that he had seen a change in this sad man, in only an hour's time. And he also felt good that he had gone to the Kelly home.

When he entered the tiny waiting room to Sgt. Macdonald's offices, he could hear the booming voice on the telephone in his private office. The longtime civilian clerk, "Miss Alice"—she had been called that for 20 years—looked up from her typewriter and said, "Good morning, Captain." Then she screamed, "Good heavens! Is that *you,* Will—or is it *Bill*—Johnson?"

Will almost cracked up laughing, "It's Will—not *Bill,* Miss Alice! I thought you always said you were the one person at Fulton who could tell us apart!"

They next heard the booming voice, "Hey, what's all the commotion about out here?" as the Sarge stepped from his office, then stopped abruptly with, "I'll be damned; it's Wi—er—it's *Cap'n* Will Johnson!" snapping a delayed salute as he corrected himself.

"Yes, Master Sergeant Macdonald; and I've got *one* order for you! Unless some four-star general is in the room, I don't wantta hear you call me 'captain' again *and* I don't want any more *salutes* from you. I don't care *what* the army rules are—I feel silly being saluted by a man whose rifle I'm not fit to carry, so *don't* embarrass me again! IS—THAT—UNDERSTOOD, Sergeant?"

"Yes sir, *Will!* Come on in and sit down; I *really* appreciate your coming by."

"Sarge, I had planned to come see you, even before Mama said you had called. I feel I owe you an apology for not heeding the advice you gave us kids over in the gym a day or so after Pearl Harbor.

"As I told my mother this weekend, I still believe I did the right thing—for me—but the *way* I did it caused some good people a lot of misery. And if I had been patient, I could have gotten the same results in about the same time.

"I like to believe I've changed some since I left here. For the better, I hope."

"Forget it, son. Whatever you've done, you must have done it well. The Brits don't give out what you're wearing on your chest without a damned good reason. Were you flying with us, or with the RAF, at the time?"

Will went on to tell him a little about *Blue Waters,* as well as more about his flying while based in England.

Sarge was enthralled by it all and couldn't stop asking questions. But when the questions turned to his next duty assignment, Will tactfully changed the subject. "Mama said you wanted to see me about something, Sarge. Maybe we should discuss that before I have to go."

"Yeah, and I hope you won't think I'm sticking my nose where it don't belong, Will, but it concerns you and your twin. I've received probably 20 letters from Bill since he's been in the air corps, and no matter what else he talks about, he *always*—in each and every letter—mentions how much he has missed you, and how he wants to be in touch with you again.

"Last week, I received the last one from him. He knows you were here more than a month ago—and that your folks gave you his APO address—but says he hasn't heard a word from you. Based on his letters, Will, he has spent every free day since he has been in England trying to find you.

"You've got a lovin' brother, son; lots of folks cain't say the same. Why don't you get in touch with him?

"Hey, I realize you may be fixing to tell me to go straight to hell, but I cain't help it. You two boys are about the finest I've ever been around, and I'm not gonna sit here on my duff and say nothin' if I can help get you back together.

"So there it is; let me have it, if you wanta."

There was a long silence before Will responded.

"I guess I'm not saying anything because I really don't have a make-sense reason for not having contacted him *now*. I guess I just didn't want to have to try to explain it to Bill. I can't go into detail, Sarge, but there *was* a reason—no fault of Bill's—why I couldn't contact him or my parents for a long time.

"And, in my new job, that may be true again, and soon, but for different reasons. You've done me a favor today, Sarge, and *this* time I'm gonna follow your advice; you can count on it.

"But remember this: I may have to sort of *disappear* again in my new job, so don't worry if it should happen again. That's all I can say, without bustin' the hell out of security; as a professional soldier, I know you can appreciate that. If it comes up later, help my folks—Bill included—with it, please."

As he stood to leave, Miss Alice called him from the door, "Will, your mother is on the phone; says she has an urgent message for you."

Mama told him that Mary Doss had called from Washington, and said that Will needed to call a Colonel Hebert ASAP, and it was *urgent.*

Will asked Sgt. Mac if he could call from there. The number was the colonel's direct—and secure—line, and he answered the call. "Will, glad I found you. Sorry to do this to you, but I need you and Sergeant Hatfield here *toute de suite,* like *yesterday.* Hatfield is already on his way, and I can have an OSS aircraft pick you up at the Atlanta Municipal Airport at 4:30 today; can you make that?"

"I'll be there. But how will I find the aircraft?"

"Go to the private aircraft hangar on the Virginia Avenue side of the field. The airplane is a converted AT-11 and is blue with 'Arlington Farms, Inc.' in bright red letters on the fuselage as well as the wings. You can't miss it. The pilots will be in civvies, but will have OSS credentials. Just to be on the safe side, ask to see their credentials. I'll have a car waiting for you at Andrews; he'll bring you straight here. Again, sorry, but *c'est la guerre!* I'll have some chow sent up from our cafeteria, so we can eat here in the office. See you this evening."

# Chapter Sixteen

The flying weather in the southeast was not good that afternoon, and the "Arlington Farms" flight was late leaving Atlanta, arriving at Andrews Field, just outside of D.C., at 7:50 that evening.

An unmarked government staff car was waiting on the ramp—motor running—as Will left the airplane. At first he didn't quite pick up on it when the driver asked if he were Captain Wade Johns. But it quickly dawned on him that he was now back in his *nom de guerre* mode, and answered "Right!" just as a familiar voice from inside the vehicle yelled through a window, grinning, "Hop in Cap'n—we're late already!"

On the ride in to the E-Street Complex, Luke asked him what was going on. "I haven't the foggiest, Luke, but we should know soon. The boss is waiting for us, so it sounds hot to me."

Luke mentioned that he had been told to select "one of them *nom de guerres*" and he had chosen "Ethan Delfrey," and wanted to be called "Duck."

Wade guffawed at that, so Luke laughed too, then explained that in Pike County he had known a man named Ethan Delfrey, and that people had always called him "Duck." The poor fellow had been an orphan, and had died—hit by a coal-hauling truck one foggy night on U.S. 23—just before Luke had joined the army. Luke had figured that since the real Delfrey had no living kin, it would be "mighty hard for the Krauts" to intimidate his family.

"Besides," he continued, "before I went in the army, some people said I kinda walked like a duck, and they called me by the same nickname, so 'Duck' stuck. Course, that kind of walkin' changed in a helluva hurry under the tender care of my drill sergeant during basic training—in the middle of July—at Camp Croft, South Carolina, way back in '38. Anyhow, I sorta got attached to the name 'Duck,' and wanta keep it if 'at's O.K. with you."

"Suits me if it suits you, 'Duck.' Let's go with it."

At E-Street reception, they were met by Mary Doss and escorted to a large conference room just beyond Col. Hebert's office. The colonel was there, accompanied by a graying civilian who spoke with a heavy French accent. Two of the walls were covered with maps of the south of France, including its Mediterranean coastline, with one map of the French Alps region.

The colonel shook hands heartily with both, then, "I'm sure you boys are hungry, so why don't you go ahead and eat while Jacque and I tell you why we jerked you in so fast. By the way, Jacque here is our resident expert on the part of France you see on the wall over there, so any questions about that should be directed to him."

He then told them, "You may have read that the president just finished a conference in Tehran with Churchill and Stalin. Two days after the end of that meeting—that was day before yesterday—we were informed that we needed to expedite—dramatically—our plans for work with the French *résistance,* in preparation for a possible major action by the Allies in the south of France.

"We still don't know precisely what it's gonna be, but all signs are that it's gonna be big—real big. We have heard—remember I said *heard*—that it will be called *Operation Anvil,* and its objective will be to tie up a *bunch* of German divisions while we try to cream them with our main attack somewhere on the Atlantic coast of France. When and if it pops, we're gonna need all the help we can get from the French résistance units.

"Plus, regardless, we need to step up *Operation Rapid Recovery* anyhow; that's the code name for our intensified effort to recover our downed airmen more rapidly, in order to get those experienced airmen back to duty ASAP; in view of the increase in flown sorties and missions in Italy, southeastern France, and surrounding areas, we need their expertise more than ever.

"O.K., this is where you two—and others—come in. We need to get you to France pronto. You need a few weeks of training at the French Maquis's training facility near Grenoble—it's where Jacque is pointing now on the map—in the foothills of the French Alps. That's where you will learn something about the martial arts, among other useful skills. The Germans have moved practically all of their military units out of the French Alpine region and sent them over to help their forces in Italy. This has permitted the *résistance* training camp to operate full blast of late.

"And, Wade, I want you to start working hard to improve your French the *minute* you guys get to Grenoble; that's one reason we're sending you there instead of to the Canadian place. I realize you learned some at Quebec, but that was *Canadian* French, and you'll find the real stuff quite different. I know my Cajun version never fooled anybody in Paris.

"Nobody expects you to be fluent, or not have an accent, but you do need to learn a good many common phrases, and for doing that there's no substitute for getting to practice them every day. As for you, Duck, we just want you to learn a few words, like *good morning, thanks, please* etc. Otherwise, you're gonna have to play the role of a deaf-mute—and I've never seen a Kentucky mountain boy yet who could keep quiet long enough to do a good job at *that.*

"To assist you two with the language part, we're 'borrowing' a young lady—an active member of the résistance—to come to Grenoble to tutor you two during your time there.

"Her name's Dominique, and I hear she's a *beauty* too, so that part shouldn't be hard to take.

"Then—and you're gonna love this, Wade—you're gonna go straight from Grenoble to Eze Village, that ancient little mountain town near the Italian border, to work as our liaison with the French resistance unit called *Les Amis de Liberté.* Duck, in English that's *'The Friends of Liberty.'*

"Wade has already dealt with them in his other life; he knows they're a first-class outfit. Oh yeah; your tutor—the one I just mentioned—is from the *Les Amis* unit. Monsieur Blanchot—the original organizer of the Les Amis unit—told us that they have another woman in the unit who knows more languages, but they need her to stay with the unit for interpreting, and that this Dominique is well qualified to tutor you.

"Your first job—after Grenoble—will be to improve the speed and volume of *Rapid Recovery.* At the moment, it is taking too much time—sometimes six months or longer—to get our pilots and other experienced airmen back to duty, even when the enemy doesn't capture them. We're fast getting to the point in this war that this simply is not going to do us any good. We are hoping to start bringing some back on our own aircraft, at least in the Italian/French regions where we expect to be able to use local airstrips soon. That's why we need one of our pilots to be in the area, Wade—to evaluate the airstrips available, among other things.

"Also, in the neighborhood near Eze—specifically near Cap Ferrat and the deepwater Bay of Villefranche—we hope to bring some home by submarine with the help of the facilities of Monsieur Blanchot at Cap Ferrat.

"Soon, we should be getting more information regarding the *rumored Operation Anvil.* If it comes off, we plan on big things from *Les Amis.* That's one of the main reasons we put you in this unit, Duck; we're gonna supply you and *Les Amis* with enough of the new and improved plastic explosives to blow half the Wermacht to hell and back *if* you can make the opportunities.

"Also, Duck—on the sad side—another reason we wanted you in this group is that they are still without a true sharpshooter to replace the gentleman they lost not long ago during *Operation Blue Waters;* that was an operation in which Wade was involved while he was flying with the RCAF."

The Colonel said he wanted them to stay in Washington for the day or so it would take to prepare false identity papers and supporting background information on "Ethan Delfrey." Then he wanted them to go ASAP to Tempsford, England, where they would prepare to be parachuted into France, probably fairly close to Grenoble, *if* the early winter weather didn't dictate a drop further south.


**Tempsford**

Inasmuch as the flight from England to the drop zone situated on an Alpine meadow was a long one, the plan was to fly them over on one of the converted B-24 Liberator Bombers. This was an American four-engine, long-range aircraft, in the belly of which had been installed a large round hatch to provide an easier exit for the parachutist.

The U.S. airmen referred to this 'hole' through which agents jumped, as the "Joe Hole." By using the Joe Hole, it also enabled the chutists to use a static line for opening their chutes. A number of other modifications had been made to this B-24 to allow the effective night drops that were commonly performed.

The plan was that a specially trained Maquis team, from their Grenoble camp, would light the drop zone with five lanterns, one on each corner of the meadow—and one near the dead center of it—immediately after they had received the agreed code signal from the aircraft that it was within twenty minutes of its ETA over the meadow.

Wade and Duck waited three days at Tempsford before the weather cleared sufficiently over the Grenoble region for a safe flight. The meteorologist finally cleared the flight, but still forecast a light snowfall for the night of their arrival. In view of this the OSS agent-in-charge at Tempsford recommended that Wade and Duck wear white jumpsuits for the jump. He explained that their *résistance* comrades would most likely be dressed in their ski-troop whites if it were snowing, since it provided better camouflage under those conditions.

At Grenoble, five veterans of the Maquis were ready and waiting at the same meadow where they had so frequently received both supplies and people for the past half year since the German military units had practically vacated the region. And there was a slight dusting of snow as they awaited the signal. The five were in ski-troop white and hardly visible as they crouched by their short-wave set.

The signal came at 10:30, *"L'heure est prés, Monsieur"* ("The hour is near, sir"), then was repeated two more times. It took exactly four minutes for the five lanterns to be set and lit; then Emile, the group leader, radioed his reply, *"Votre table est prêt, Monsieur"* ("Your table is ready, sir"), also repeated twice.

It was risky—being so near the mountains—to come in as low as 6,000 feet, but it was a clear night except for the very light snow, and the American crew had dropped supplies and agents there before. Consequently, shortly after take-off, the pilot cracked to his two passengers, "We're plannin' to drop you from 6,000, 'cause if we drop you from much higher, you're gonna freeze your butts off before you hit the ground."

Then he continued, "Even going from that low, you may want to forego using the static lines so you can free-fall a couple thousand feet before pulling your cords; that'd get you down quicker. It's up to you, Cap'n Johns."

Wade looked quizzically at Duck, who simply shrugged. Then he told the pilot, "Thanks, but since this is our first night jump, I think we'd better take the cold; it won't kill us, especially with these ski-masks on."

"O.K., but if you change your mind, let me know before we transmit the code for the actual drop to our friends on the ground; after that it would probably be too late to make a change. I'll holler at ya about ten minutes before we transmit."

By the time the airplane commander had transmitted his signal the snow had stopped completely, and a full moon was making it seem like daylight over the beautiful snowscape below them. He called back to the crew on the intercom, "Heads up guys! We've got better weather than they forecast—that's a *change*—so let's thank God for small miracles. From now on in, just keep your eyes peeled for any peaks—'cause we know there're some around here—and some are a damned sight higher than 6,000 feet.

"If you spot one—no matter how far away or in what direction—I wanta' hear 'PEAK!' loud and clear, and I wanta know *where* it is on the clock—like one o'clock high or three o'clock low—whatever. Everybody understand? If not, tell me *now*—not after we bash one."

Within minutes, Wade and Duck were hooked up to their static lines, each with 60 pounds of pack on his back and a reserve chest chute hooked on in front. Just before they saw the five lights below, the huge B-24's airspeed had already been slowed close to its stall levels in order not to 'slingshot' them beyond the drop zone.

The crew chief, doubling as what he called "your temporary jump master", counted down, "Five, four , three, two, GO!", and Wade was through the Joe Hole in a flash, with Duck a split second behind.

Before he had finished pulling both static lines back up through the hole, the chief felt the plane go to full throttle and simultaneously into a sharp and climbing right turn away from the peaks that could now be seen silhouetted against the horizon; and—through the waist window that was still open on the starboard side—he could hear the now familiar sound of the Davis wings of the B-24 slightly creaking from the strain.

Both their landings were *"Parfait!"* exclaimed Emile as he dashed over, "Welcome to France, my friends; my name is Emile," to which Wade replied, " *Enchanté Monsieur; je m'appelle Wade, et mon ami ici s'appelle Duck."*

"Well, Wade; it's certainly nice to hear your speaking well the French. That is always a great help with many here, you know. *Bien*—but let us leave this place now, before someone gets too curious. We have a lorry hidden just a way from here. It is not too comfortable, but will accommodate the seven of us well enough. We have a one to two hour drive to our camp, depending on snow conditions along the way.

"I'm sure you chaps are a bit hungry; in the back of the lorry we have some bread, fruit, and some good French cheese we brought along for you to munch on. I hope you enjoy a red wine; it is one of the local ones. We call them *vins de pays*—'country wines' in English.

"Up you go; Guy will bring along your packs and 'chutes. *Guy! Apportez tous les choses, s'il vous plait!"*

It was a rough ride—and cold. Emile explained that no road repairs had been made on that road surface for three or more years, but added that it was one reason they had been able to use that particular drop zone fairly safely, because "No sane person would drive this road if they had any other option."

Wade complimented him on his excellent English, saying that it sounded British. "Well, it should be better than it is. First, my father spent enough money sending me to English schools in my early teens. Also, I taught English for three years to French-speaking Swiss kids near Lausanne, until the war began. Then, I was in London from May of 1940 until a year and a half ago, as an interpreter for DeGaulle's people there.

"I finally decided that there must be more I could do for our side than sip gin in a London pub every other night while trying to please some fat and boring politician. So your OSS slipped me back in here—nearly 17 months ago—to assist in training our youngsters—as well as chaps like you and Duck who are *truly* fighting for France, as well as your own country.

"Actually, I needed quite a lot of training myself—and I received it in a crash mode.So here I am, an old bird at 32 years, but I actually feel as if I am helping now; and it's a bloody *good* feeling, too."

It was well past midnight when they reached the training camp. Emile took them to a room with two bunks and told them he would show them their less-private barracks the next day.

At breakfast their first morning in camp, she had quietly entered the small meal tent and seated herself opposite the two Americans, smiling shyly at them as she moved with the grace of a gentle deer. She was tall and slender, with jet black hair, and wore a sky-blue turtleneck, which accentuated crystal-blue eyes unlike any that either man had ever seen.

For the remainder of their days, Wade and Duck would say to all in their worlds that she was the most beautiful woman they had ever had the pleasure to see—before or since.

Both men realized they were staring, but neither could resist doing so. Mercifully, Emile soon seated himself next to her, and broke the spell, smiling broadly, "Wade and Duck, I would like to present *Dominique*. She will be tutoring both of you in your French during your stay here. She speaks English rather fluently, but it would be better if you will make your best effort to improve your command of the language while here by using it when you can, and use English only when you panic.

"Dominique, my dear, this is Wade, on your left, and Duck, on your right."

She smiled, "It is my grand pleasure to meet both of you. But tell me quickly; are those truly your *noms de guerre* that you plan to use while in France? I offer my sincere apology for being *negatif* at this first moment of our meeting, but you must—for your own safety—use a name that has a sound that is French. The alternative shall cause you and your comrades at arms to be compromised at an early moment if you are working in France. Am I not correct, Emile?"

"Yes, *ma chérie.*

"Gentlemen, I do agree, exactly. I thought of this when we first met last night, but knew you two were fatigued, and I felt it could wait until today. In any event, it has now been expressed to you in an immensely more charming manner than would have been possible from me; I am certain that we are in total agreement on *that.*"

Wade seemed to break out of his trance, "That does make sense, but if do use other names, it must be *only* in our oral communications here in France; otherwise our new identities on file with OSS are rendered useless. Additionally, we must advise OSS promptly, at least in the London office. Can you do that by a coded message on your radio?"

"No problem, Wade. Why don't you two and Dominique chat later today. She knows all the *Les Amis* personnel, and can therefore assist in avoiding a duplication of any names used in that group."

"*Tres bien,*" offered Dominique, "I think we will be able to locate names that are—how do you say—*related* to 'Wade' and to 'Duck.' That will make it more easy to remember the new name. *Par exemple,* 'Duck' could be changed to 'Duc,' but 'Wade' is a bit more difficult; I must give more thought to that one."

"In the meantime, gentlemen, we need to get you settled in the place you will be sleeping, so come with me," Emile motioned to the men to come with him. When they were outside the tent, he asked them to walk a while with him, because he had something delicate he needed to discuss. "As you are undoubtedly aware, we have many French—and some Spanish—Communists with us in our resistance movement. I don't like it, but it is a fact of life that we *do* need them; early on they had talents and experience that were desperately needed by our rank amateurs, and we *still* need them, albeit to a lesser extent than, say, a year ago.

"At this time there are five *rouges* amongst the 30 or so trainees now in this camp. Most of them are no trouble, but we do have two who seem to have "*a chip on their shoulders*" as you Americans might put it. Worse, both have been very vocal in complaining because we are now working closely with, and largely dependent on, your OSS. And knowing that you two were to join us, they have uttered some poorly-veiled threats against you personally.

"My security people—who work here undercover because we sometimes have infiltrators from the enemy—are going to keep both of them under close scrutiny while you are here, but I felt it my duty to warn you of this potential problem.

"It is likely that both will be at lunch today; please sit with me, and I will identify them for you. One is a Frenchman from Marseille who has a long black beard, and the other is Spanish—a huge man—with a very conspicuous red star tattooed on his left forearm; the former calls himself MoJo—don't ask me why—and the Spaniard is Roberto.

"Lastly, if either should presume to trouble you, please feel perfectly free to show them no mercy, their being '*résistants*' notwithstanding; I would not be unhappy if they became a sad statistic.

"Now, on a more pleasant note, I learned just this morning that the room I put you in last evening—temporarily, I thought—will be available for you during your entire stay. So, you may want to take an hour or so to settle in, and we can get started on your training schedule a bit later."

Duck snorted, "I'll be damned! You know, I saw two sum'bitches like you just described, when we first went in to the eatin' tent this mornin'; I thought they wuz givin' me and Wade some mighty dirty looks. I hope they don't jump me or my Cap'n, sir; but if they do, I ain't makin' any promises about 'em livin' very long. We're here to do sumpin' more important than havin' to keep lookin' over our shoulders for some backstabbin' sum'bitch."

"No argument from me, Duck. I learned long ago that these kind aren't worth the trouble they cause; but I hope you understand that I can't evict them from the camp for simply talking. But an *overt* action—that's quite different."

"Don't be concerned," added Wade, "we can handle it—and *will,* if necessary."

They put away their gear, dressed in their civilian clothes that the OSS had purchased from French Algeria, and reported back to Emile, where Dominique was waiting with him.

Emile said, "I thought that it would be nice for your first 'class' here to be an enjoyable one; therefore it will be the opening language class with your most lovely 'professor.' Dominique?"

She smiled, stood, did a graceful curtsy to the three men, and replied, "*Merci Monsieur;* I shall do my very best.

"But first we settle the issue of *un nom de guerre français* for each of our new friends. Duck, from this moment on, in all verbal conversation while you are in France, you should use the name *Duc*—spelled D-U-C. It is perfect for you, because it is *very* close to the proper pronunciation in *French* of 'Duck.' It is pronounced here as you Americans would pronounce *Duke.* I suggest you practice—repeatedly—that way to say your new name, until it becomes natural for you.

"For you, *Wad*—pardon me—I should say it as 'Wade'; I suggest we give to you a name used by millions of French men; it is spelled *J-E-A-N.* You hear it constantly, in every part of France." She then frowned slightly as she heard a loud snicker from 'Duc,' quickly adding, "It is not like you think, Duc; here the name is pronounced similarly—but not exactly—to 'Jon' in English; but remember that the last letter *n* is not *emphasized.* It will require some practice for both of you, but I will help you by constantly calling you by your new names. I suggest *Jean* for Wade, because it is so similar to his *nom de famille,* his family name, and therefore more easy to remember. Do these seem O.K.?"

Wade replied, "They sound fine to me, *Mademoiselle;* how 'bout you, Mr. *Duc?*"

Duck flashed his best grin again, "Hey, your'n ain't so hot ; but mine sounds great! Wait'll we finish up 'is damned war, and I tell 'em back in Pike County that I was a *Duke* in France!"

"Fine, gentlemen, I'll leave you now until lunch." Emile stood up to go. "*Bonne chance* with your first lesson."

Dominique had just celebrated her twentieth birthday when she left her home and family in Aix-en-Provence—in early 1943—determined to assist the growing number of young French men and women who were risking their lives to help liberate their country from the yoke of it's Nazi masters.

Her father was a professor of ancient history at her university in Aix, where she was majoring in Romance Languages, with a minor in English and American literature. As a child she had accompanied him frequently on Saturdays when he enjoyed lunching with his friends at *Le Café des Deux Garcons.*

The sidewalk cafe is on the beautiful *Cours Mirabeau,* the main street of Aix, and reputedly had been a favorite gathering place for their planning by intellectuals prior to the French Revolution.

Dominique could recall hearing—when she had been very young— her father and his friends speaking with enormous pride of the independence and glory of their France. But in the year or so prior to the Autumn of '39, their conversations had shifted more to the threat of Bolshevism to French liberty.

Then came the awful spring of 1940.

Since that spring she had endured the not infrequent agony of seeing an arrogant German officer laughing at the side of a visiting Vichy lackey, as they strutted beneath the branches of the great Plane trees shading the ancient boulevard.

By the early winter of 1942, she could stand it no longer. On Christmas night, she went to her parents and begged them to understand why she must—as a matter of conscience and self-respect—leave to join the *Résistance.*

She had recently met a young woman who was the daughter of Georges Blanchot. He had sent his daughter to live in Aix—where he himself had attended university many years prior—in order to protect her from the potential dangers inherent in his wartime activities on Cap Ferrat. Unbeknown to her father, she herself had enlisted with a Lyons unit of the Maquis, and had confided in Dominigue in general terms regarding the nature of her father's connection with *Les Amis de Liberté.* She had known Dominique was already considered by the University as something of a prodigy as a writer, as well as a linguist, and told her that there was a definite need for such talents by her father's group.

It had been an emotional and tearful meeting with her father and mother that evening. Dominique was their only child, but they lived constantly under the fear that, ultimately, she might be conscripted and sent to a forced labor camp or factory far away, probably Germany. This had happened to a number of their friends' young sons, and many had speculated as to when the young women might meet the same fate.

In the end, they gave her their blessing, and by mid-January she was in Eze Village.

As the door closed, Dominique laid out her lesson plan. "Inasmuch as Duc knows no French, it will be necessary to have separate sessions with him. Any other method would be too slow for you, Jean; actually, it would also be very *detrimental* to your progress since, with Duc, I *must* speak a good deal of English, but, with *you,* I will speak only *en français,* with some rare exceptions.

"However, I want Duc to sit in on each and every session with you, Jean, so he, along with you, can—at a minimum—begin to develop an ear for the language—*la musique*—the *music*—of the language, as we French call it. This is very, very important in learning a new language. In the beginning, Duc, you will *listen* only, saying *nothing,* during Jean's sessions; later, if you seem to be progressing, you will be allowed to participate a bit more.

"Now, listen to me, and listen *well!* There will be *no notes* taken in this class—not a single one! Most students are surprised to hear that said, but here we take no notes. We are going to learn the basic parts of a new language as you learned our mother-tongue. Trust me—taking notes will *not* help you do that—taking notes will *hinder* your doing that. *Are* we together so far? If not, speak up!"

"Yes, ma'am!" came their answer, in unison. Actually, both were thinking more of the *beautiful music* to which they had just been treated, simply by listening to her.

As they walked to the meal tent without her, Duck turned to Wade, "Well, *'Jean,'* we shore know now that *all* war ain't hell! At's the first time I ever *enjoyed* a sort of tongue lashin' frum a teacher."

The minute Emile entered the tent, he quickly scanned the room and spotted the two Communists sitting at the third table from his own. He watched them closely for any reaction as the Americans entered and sat at his table; the two Reds commenced to whisper together immediately after Wade and Duck had seated themselves, while casting nervous glances in the direction of Emile.

Emile deliberately pointed toward the Reds' table, and leaned over to say in Wade's ear, "It won't hurt for them to think that I already suspect them; they are fully aware that our code of conduct commands serious action—including possible *execution*—for betrayal of or seriously attacking a comrade.

"Now, further to your training here. Starting tomorrow, each afternoon for the first week, we will follow lunch by Dominique giving you about an hour orientation concerning the history, structure, and personnel complement of *Les Amis*. I am aware that you, Jean, have some knowledge of that outstanding unit, but Duc needs the information also, and you can use some updating.

"In any event, it will be nice for both of you to have a bit of a break after lunch and prior to the martial arts training that normally follows the meal.

"Quite honestly, the martial arts activities can be rather difficult for most; you two appear to be fit enough, but I must confess that my old body found it to be a miserable experience, particularly during the first week. Yet, as you endure it, be assured that it may be your most valuable training while amongst us. Someday, it may well save your life.

"Later in the afternoon, you will be given instruction in the use of the typical weaponry used by *Les Amis,* including the knife, handgun, carbine, automatic weapons—including your U.S.-made Thompson sub-machine gun—and the garrote.

"During your last few days with us, we will go to some nearby cliffs for a short course in ascending and descending in mountainous terrain, with emphasis on the use of the rope for such activities. This is not a customary part of our course, but was specifically requested for the two of you by your OSS superiors.

"Last, each night from eight until nine, Dominique will continue her language classes with you, except for a couple of nights when both of you will be given instruction in the operation of three different types of radios normally used by the typical résistance unit, including *Les Amis*.

"So that's it. How does it sound to you?"

"It sounds terrific, Emile," responded Wade. "I had no idea that it was so comprehensive. No offense, but I figured that your camp would be on the run and, at best, we'd get very little help in the subjects you have covered."

"A year or so ago, you would have been absolutely correct; although this area was patrolled mostly by the Italians—most of whom weren't truly enthused about Mussolini's war; yet, old Fritz had his own patrols roaming around. But, thankfully, all that changed dramatically once your armies—and the Brits—got into Italy proper. Almost all the German units have been sent there, giving us the freedom to do what we had always aspired to, by way of training; I think you will find it extremely helpful."

That evening they had their first serious lesson with Dominique. For an hour she spoke in French only, gracefully gesturing occasionally to herself, one of them, the door, window, and other objects, as she spoke, in soft and melodious tones—except when she would ask that Duc or Jean repeat the last phrase or so that she had uttered.

Very little of it was new to Wade, but Duck felt totally lost for the entire hour, but was astounded at the end, as he suddenly discovered that he could—slowly, but accurately—tell Wade his new name, *en français.* He was still as excited as a child in toyland when, a quarter hour after the class, he insisted on saying to Emile, *"Bonsoir, Monsieur. Je m'appelle Duc!"*

After the two turned out their room light, Wade was still wide awake long after his roommate was sound asleep. As hard as he tried, he couldn't get off his mind the image of the beautiful and charming young woman who had just entered his life.

The afternoon language class quickly became the most pleasurable part of their day for the two Americans; unfortunately it was followed by their daily two "hours of torture" as Wade termed it. The term *martial arts* was something of a misnomer; a better name would have been "how to survive hand-to-hand combat-training—*if you are lucky."*

On the first day of it, Emile emphasized that—at least for the time being—*nothing* would be prohibited, other than use of a weapon, although certain tried and proven techniques would be demonstrated after the first two days of freelancing.

He placed 15 names in a helmet, then had those 15 stand on one side of the arena, while the other 15 were each ordered to draw a name for his opponent for the day. Duck drew Roberto, who was easily twice his weight and a good foot taller.

The Spaniard couldn't—or wouldn't—stop bellowing with laughter as they squared off, circling each other.Then, with a mighty roar, he charged the smaller man, grasped him by the neck with both his huge hands, swept him off the ground, swung him around twice in the air as if he were a lariat, then *slammed* his body to the ground.

Twenty feet away, Wade thought he heard Duck's bones shattering as he hit the ground, and prayed that he wouldn't try to get up, on the off chance that he was still conscious.

Roberto stood gloating over the now-still body like a predator over a dead prey, beating his chest with one hand and waving at the crowd with the other. Wade ignored him; instead he was gazing at Duck for some sign of life.

He was beginning to fear the worst, when Duck suddenly did spring to life. From his knees, he gripped the left foot of his tormentor and sank his teeth deep into the ankle. Roberto screamed from the pain and lifted his wounded leg by reflex. As he did, Duck raised to a crouch, grabbing the same foot again and, using his body for leverage, rolled and twisted the distorted ankle until it cracked with a sound not unlike that of a dead limb snapping.

The Spaniard howled in agony again and dropped to the ground momentarily, but managed to regain his feet, badly limping as he circled again—cautiously this time. His eyes were still wet from his pain as a voice from the crowd yelled, "Bravo, Duc!"

Roberto turned his head in that direction with a scowl. At that moment, Duck lurched forward and kicked him squarely in the groin with a steel-toed boot that felled him again. As the groaning giant lay holding himself, Duck delivered four vicious kicks directly to his face, before Emile stepped in to order, "Enough! That's *enough!*"

After the cheering of Duck had subsided, and before the next contest was announced, Emile told the group, "When I said 'anything goes' I assumed you understood that I meant *anything short of killing—or maiming—* one of our own. Please keep in mind that we need *all* of you for combat against the enemy, not *ourselves;* After the last exhibition, I expect to see more than a bit of caution and discretion from the rest of you."

The next morning, Emile called Roberto in for a private meeting, telling him, "Senor, we in France are grateful for your efforts on behalf of our cause, but I must caution you that your recent actions have brought you extremely close to expulsion from our work, or worse. Yesterday, in the afternoon, you willfully attempted to cause permanent injury to a comrade-in-arms, and one with skills that we have requested and badly need in our work.

"In addition, I am well aware of comments previously made by you— and your friend—which I interpret to be threats of harm to Duc and his colleague Jean, threats made well before either of you had laid eyes on either of them. I had hoped that those comments were simply idle nonsense, until I observed you in the arena yesterday; now I believe that you truly meant those remarks.

"For your own selfish interest, it is important that you listen carefully to—and that you *heed*—what I am now to say: I will not tolerate *any* further conduct that is even remotely similar to that I have mentioned here today. It will be dealt with summarily and effectively—probably much more *effectively* than you would believe . . . "

Roberto interrupted, "But Emile . . . "

"*Silence!* There will be no *buts.* Go now—but understand that you act at your peril *if* you choose to ignore my well-intended words! Now *go!*"

# Chapter Seventeen

## London

After their twelfth bombing mission, Bill Johnson's crew was halfway through the normal tour of 25 missions and had been allowed to take ten days leave—their first of any consequence since arriving in England.

He had spent most of his time trying to find and meet with Joe Hearn, after Polly had finally given in to his barrage of letters begging for Joe's RCAF mailing address. Once they had made contact, Joe readily agreed to meet with him, but had been very ambiguous when Bill asked about his brother's activities prior to the OSS transfer.

On this morning—his last day of leave—Bill had been waiting for an hour and a half, with growing impatience, in the anteroom of the OSS offices in London. He wanted only one thing—the mailing address of his twin brother.

Finally, a man, graying at the temples and dressed in civilian clothes, stepped from a side door and approached him. "Good morning, Lieutenant Johnson; I'm Jack Abbot. We received your letter. Won't you come in my office, please?"

As Bill seated himself, Abbot commented, "I hope I can assist you." Then—raising a blind at the window—added, smiling. "My, my; have you ever seen such weather as London's? It's a miracle that mildew doesn't conquer us all."

Bill recognized the distinct Boston brogue, and was encouraged by the broad smile but—after his long wait—he was in no mood for small talk. "You're damned right you can help me! I want to get in touch with my twin brother. Why in hell is something *that* simple so *difficult* for me and my family?

"We send letters to him at the address he gave my parents after becoming part of OSS, but it's always the same; they don't come *back,* and we never get an *answer* from him."

"Please, Lieutenant. I understand your concerns, but surely you must be aware of some of the work we do. Often, our people are in situations where it simply is impossible—*utterly* impossible—for them to correspond with, or otherwise contact, anyone, not even us at OSS.

"In the case of your brother, I honestly do not know where he is at this moment; and *if* I did, it is quite probable that security considerations would prohibit my giving you that information. But I can tell you this: it *is* probable that he is working in enemy territory as so many of our agents do.

"Often they do this for months—occasionally it may become *years*. In those circumstances, keep in mind that forwarding a letter to such an agent—were it possible—could likely be the equivalent of composing his death warrant. I would think that your brother would have previously advised his family of this—one of many peculiarities we must live with in our sometimes odd calling.

"You and your family may be assured that the mail you have sent to him will be kept safely until he is in a position to receive it. And, I assume that he will answer it when he is in a position to do so without creating a danger to himself or his colleagues. But that is his decision, not ours."

He then walked over to Bill and put his hand on his shoulder, saying softly, "Lieutenant, I know quite well that this is *not* the answer you came here to hear—but I hope you can accept *why* we can do no more."

Bill bent his head down momentarily, then looked up, "Sorry, Mr. Abbot; I shouldn't have popped off like that. My brother and I were extremely close as kids, but since the war things have changed some. I guess I was taking out my frustration on you. That's a raw deal; please forgive me. I'll pass this on to my family.

"Good day; and thank you."

In the Maquis camp it had been an interesting—sometimes difficult—few weeks. During the grueling martial arts sessions, Wade had been—more than once—consciously and vocally thankful for the fitness training he had gotten at Benning. Duck—on the other hand—grinned his way through it all once more, apparently none the worse for what he called his "little scrap" with Roberto.

Outwardly on his best behavior, Roberto was seething with fury within from his beating by the much smaller American. Dominique had cautioned both her students, "Be very careful of this man; his voice may be silent, but his eyes speak his hatred."

It was good advice.

Two nights prior to the day they were to leave, they had finished their last class with Dominique.

Duck had decided to turn in early, while Wade and Dominique took what had become their usual evening stroll down by the nearby stream. Wade walked her to her quarters, and as he entered his building and approached his room, he heard Duck yell, "*You dirty sum'bitch; whatcha think you're doin'?*"

Wade jerked open the door, but never saw the other figure until WoJo had struck him a glancing blow with the blackjack that all trainees had been issued. As he staggered across the room and fell, Wade caught the sight of Roberto astride Duck in his bunk. Roberto's right hand held a knife above Duck and a different hand—reaching from below—was grasping the Spaniard's wrist.

From the floor, Wade's vision was blurred from the blow, but he could make out the image of WoJo raising a hunting knife above him as Wade groped in his sock for his double-barreled Derringer.

The first shot found WoJo's left temple, and he collapsed over Wade.

As he struggled free, Wade could hear Duck yelling, "Git 'is mother, too! He's too strong fur me; I cain't handle 'em much longer!"

Wade struggled to his feet, jammed the other barrel of the tiny pistol directly into Roberto's left earhole, and squeezed the trigger.

The next morning the other three Communists offered to bury them.

Emile agreed, then commented to Wade, "Excellent! The sons of Mother Russia deserve that chore, even though they may not share my pleasure in the occasion."

After dinner on their last evening in camp, Emile invited the two Americans and Dominique to join him in his room for champagne.

He expressed again his appreciation for the assistance being given the French *résistance* movement by the British and Americans, and especially for the OSS program of rendering aide through agents such as Jean and Duc.

"We need badly the skills and expertise that people such as you can bring to us. You should be aware that—even now—there is no central coordination of *résistance* activities. On paper, yes—to a degree; in reality, no!

"Why not?

"Some of the reasons are purely political, the outgrowth of a struggle that is already underway for control of France after the war—the Communists on one side, the Gaullists and others on the other. Prior to Hitler turning on the Soviets, you could hardly find a French *rouge* who was active in a *résistance* unit anywhere in this nation, north, south, east or west. Since then, they have been crawling out from under every rock from Normandy to Marseille. And yes, I have accepted their help, but I have no illusions about their allegiance; and it is *not* to *my* country.

"You are truly fortunate to be going to *Les Amis*. I believe it to be one of our *creme de la creme* units, perhaps the best in all of France.

"Young Jean-Pierre is a born leader. He was enrolled and nearing the end of his first year at *l'Ecole Militaire*—our 'West Point'—when Pétain asked the Nazis for armistice terms in mid-June of 1940.

"That same evening, on the advice of his father, he took the night train to Nice, and from there he cycled to the home of Georges Blanchot on Cap Ferrat. Jean-Pierre's father is a graduate of *l'Ecole Militaire* and had a brilliant military career—going back to the first World War—until he openly and publicly opposed the concept of French dependence on the Maginot Line. He was eventually forced to resign from the army as a result of that dispute. Of course, history proved that he was absolutely correct, but by then the fate of France was sealed.

"The father and Blanchot had become close friends in their youth, and had always shared the same opinion regarding what both regarded as the dangerously chaotic conditions in French national politics during the late '30s. I am told that on each of their many social visits, the conversation inevitably drifted to that subject.

"It was only days after the Dunkirk debacle that Blanchot received a telephone call from Jean-Pierre's father, suggesting that both start preparing for the worst; and it was during that conversation that the phrase 'French Maquis' first passed between those two patriots of France."

Emile glanced at his watch, "Pardon me for getting a bit carried away—it is late and I know that you leave before dawn—but I felt you should know these things about the people with whom you will be working in the south of France. *Oh* that we had more patriots like Georges Blanchot, young Jean-Pierre, and his father!"

Wade smiled, "Well, *we* think we already know at least *one;* he calls himself *Emile*. I mean that very sincerely; I can only hope that some of the other *résistance* training facilities in France have similar leadership."

Duck added, slapping Emile on the back, "I can shore echo that, Emile; you're the greatest!" followed quickly by Dominique's soft, "*D'accord, Monsieur.*"

As they shook hands and embraced, Emile said, "I wish I were going with you; but perhaps someday we can work together again. I will be here if you ever need me. *Au revoir, et bonne chance!*"

It was cold and dark as the three quietly prepared to leave the camp before five o'clock the next morning.

Prior to departure, their guide, Guy, warned them that their progress would be painfully slow until they got further south, partly because of the lingering ice and snow, but more because he preferred using the back roads, which neither the Germans nor the Milice liked to patrol.

He assured them that he had used the same route many times, and that there were several reliable safe-houses where they could rest, and sleep overnight if they wished. Guy spoke only a few words of English, but was so animated that his body language spoke volumes, as during the moment his eyes had twinkled as he promised *un diner magnifique* at one—perhaps two—of the homes they would visit along the way.

On a map of southeastern France, he ran his finger slowly along the proposed route, pointing to the larger towns: first to Gap—possibly requiring two days—then to Sisteron—or, with luck, as far as Digne—on the next day; surely as far as Antibes on the following day.

Finally, following the coastline to the area around Nice, they would rendezvous with Jean-Pierre high on the Col de Villefranche, a few kilometers west of Eze Village.

Barring any unforeseen problems, the entire journey was to take five— maybe only four—days. As Guy explained, the time was not important, avoidance of capture *was*.

Late the previous evening, Guy and his younger brother had taken the lorry into Grenoble and conducted what Duck called a "moonlight requisition" of fuel for the truck, as well as filling six extra large containers which would fit in racks behind the cab. Guy said it was due to the courtesy of *les Nazis* in departing their storage facilities so hastily in an effort to save Rome. Upon Wade's inquiring, he was reassured by Guy that he had other contacts for re-fueling along the proposed route.

Wade also asked how Jean-Pierre would know when to meet them. Guy led him to the lorry and pointed to a small cage—covered by a cloth— in the space just behind the driver's seat. He lifted the cloth, revealing two cooing white pigeons and said in French, "Our little friends are most loyal and reliable; before we depart Antibes, they will carry faithfully that information to Jean-Pierre."

Guy showed them four bedrolls that he had stowed in the back of the lorry. He said that all four of them could ride in the cab if the weather became too severe, but in the interest of safety, he would suggest that— normally—one or two ride in back, using the blankets if necessary for comfort and perhaps rotate the riding up front. If they had to sleep in the lorry at night, all four could easily do so, and they could close the rear doors to shut out the wind and make it tolerable.

Duck offered to stay in back the entire trip and let Dominique and "the Cap'n" ride in the cab, but Wade rejected that with, "No deal *Duc!* And drop the Cap'n stuff; we left the '*rank*' malarkey in England—remember? Here we share and share alike."

The trip to the town of Gap indeed consumed two full days, and there were moments when all but Guy questioned whether they would get there at all.

The mountain roads were narrow and cold, and most still had snow falling almost every night. During the day the snow would turn to slush by mid-day, then freeze over shortly after sundown.

Thus they traveled only by day, sleeping in the back of the lorry both of the first two nights. There was barely room for the four and their bedrolls but—as Guy mentioned—each could benefit from the body heat of the others.

By chance or otherwise, on both nights Dominique and Wade slept side by side. During the first hour of the initial evening, Wade found sleep difficult while his emotions ranged between quiet pleasure and a twinge of guilt as he listened to and felt the rise and fall of her gentle breathing.

All were relieved when they embarked on the third day, along a good—and dry—road in bright sunlight. And there was a lusty cheer when Guy announced that he believed they could reach his favorite stopover by dinner time, "*le mas des freres Brosset*" (the farmhouse of the brothers Brosset), who ran a safehouse at their farm outside of Sisteron and—more importantly—set the best table in that region of France.

He added that perhaps they might even be able to have a hot bath—before or after dinner—and a real bed for the night.

The farm was tucked away in a small valley, reached only by traveling six kilometers on a dirt road that obviously had not been built for motor vehicles. The land had been in the Brosset family for twelve generations; it was now inhabited by the brothers, along with their sister Anne-Marie who had been widowed in the first World War. Both brothers had survived the trenches of that conflict and returned in 1919—with their sister—to tend the farm.

For income they depended on their herd of goats. For over 20 years they had sold locally all their production of milk and cheese, although they had been solicited many times to sell to several of the famous cheese shops in Paris and beyond. The revenue was modest, but sufficed for those few needs of the family, which could not be raised or made on the farm.

Their clothes, except for shoes, were sewn entirely by Anne-Marie, and their ample supply of grain, vegetables and fruits, beef, veal, pork, and fowl were produced from the eight hectares of rich land by the hands and backs of the brothers.

They were the epitome of a free and independent French farm family, and were amongst the first in France to vow that they would never heel to a German master. Thus their passion for the past three years had been the dedication of themselves—and their limited resources—to the *Résistance* movement.

On arrival at the gate to the farm at dusk, Guy commented that his fondest dream was that he was being hunted by the enemy and had been given permanent sanctuary at *"Chez Brosset"*—especially at mealtime.

The Americans and Dominique were soon to learn that their guide was probably serious.

Soon after Guy entered the farmhouse alone, he returned with the three Brossets close behind, beaming and excitedly welcoming the three *résistants* to their home, and announcing that a *diner spécial* would be prepared that night in celebration of their visit.

Anne-Marie showed them upstairs to four small, but whistle-clean and comfortable, bedrooms—each complete with two huge goose down pillows—and invited them to enjoy a hot bath and rest before dinner, which would commence two hours later at 8:00.

At 7:30, Anne-Marie rapped on each door with the message that dinner would be served soon.

As Wade maneuvered his way slowly down the ancient spiraled stairway, he followed the enticing scent of true country French cuisine to a large oaken table—ready for seven—in a massive kitchen that doubled as the dining hall. Anne-Marie was busy at the wood-burning stove and Dominique was tossing salad in one corner of the room, while one of the brothers was removing just-baked huge loaves of country French bread from the oven adjacent to an open hearth.

At the hearth the second brother was tending three spits simultaneously as he greeted Wade briskly with, *"Bonsoir Jean!"* then, in broken English, "I hope you have rested yourself well *and* are prepared for a dinner Brosset!"

Wade and Duck were famished. When the first course was served, each—thinking that was their entire dinner—piled his plate high and filled their ample wine cups to the brim with a hearty red wine from earthen pitchers that had been placed near each corner of the table. Guy noticed, and leaned over and whispered quietly to Wade, "Jean, enjoy, but be *very* careful. We have no idea of the number of courses the family Brosset will serve this night, but I do know they will want—and *expect*—us to consume and enjoy each and all."

Five more courses and multiple liters of wine later, Wade and his comrade more fully appreciated Guy's words. After all eventually—with great reluctance—vacated the table, and endeavored to ascend the stairway, Guy assisted Duck, and Dominique giggled like a schoolgirl as Wade leaned heavily on her while she guided his movements upward, step by careful step.

It was not quite first light when Guy woke the group—one by one—urging them to hurry if they expected to take breakfast before continuing their journey. Wade rolled over, yawned audibly and doubted that he would ever be hungry again after the sumptuous *Diner Brosset.*

His wonder turned into amazement after shaving, dressing, and approaching the kitchen where all three of the family were again busily preparing a breakfast described by Anne-Marie as a *petit déjeuner* that would "strengthen them properly for the road."

The aroma of the freshly-baked baguettes, croissants, and apple tarts, together with that of the cup of steaming coffee handed him by Guy as he entered the door, revived fully his appetite before he had settled at the table.

The Brosset brothers were standing near the door as they left, embracing them tearfully, and thanking all for their service to the *résistance.*

Anne-Marie handed each a large basket, explaining that it contained three *grands sandwiches* for their mid-day meal. Then she kissed them farewell and pressed a small hand-carved wooden *Fleur-de-lis* into each person's hand.

A few kilometers south of Sisteron, they saw a sign announcing that they had reached the region called *Haute-Provence,* and the weather confirmed the sign; though still a bit cold, it was bright and sunny. Guy accelerated the old lorry and it hummed along the narrow roadway like—in the words of Duck—"a good coon-dawg trackin' a big 'un."

They were now able to move at double their previous speed, and continued late that evening under a full moon. They didn't quite reach Antibes, but stopped on the outskirts of Grasse.

Guy pulled into a small wooded park that had been abandoned by the town since the start of the war, saying it would be safe to spend the night there. Next, he told them that, inasmuch as the weather was surprisingly mild—even for Provence that time of year—they could save time by sleeping in the lorry again. Then, in the morning, they would travel in a slightly northeasterly direction, passing south of the town of Vence and on to the Col de Villefranche and their rendezvous with Jean-Pierre. In this way, they could avoid the heavily traveled coastal road, thereby reducing the possibility of any confrontations.

Each had saved, for dinner, one or more of Anne-Marie's delicious—and large—sandwiches. As they were savoring the last morsels under the light of the moon, Guy released the two pigeons, carrying the message to Jean-Pierre.

On one of the main thoroughfares—called the *Moyenne Corniche*—that has long run from Nice through the Col de Villefranche and Eze Village to Monaco, there is an overlook that provides a magnificent view of Villefranche sur Mer, Cap Ferrat, and portions of Beaulieu. For centuries, it has been a place where strangers to the area have gone totally unnoticed, simply because they have always been there.

On this afternoon, two bicycles were leaned together in one space on the Villefranche end of the parking area. The young couple who had ridden them there had been immersed in an apparent lovers' quarrel for two hours, alternating between long periods of somewhat quiet conversation with their two bodies interlocked, and periodic outbursts of shouting and screaming accusations, which drew attention from all on the overlook.

Bridgette and David—even when screaming and cursing each other—were also watching closely for an old lorry. It would be blinking its headlights on and off as it came around the curve and approached the overlook from the west.

The moment they saw it approaching—very slowly—they started screaming at and threatening one another shrilly in high decibel levels and language that startled their already embarrassed listeners, but who, nevertheless, gave them their rapt attention.

So entertaining was the show, that no one noticed when, at the other end of the parking area, two men and a woman stepped quickly from the lorry with their packs and into an old and battered green Citreon that backed out quietly and headed east toward Eze Village.

As Guy turned the lorry around and drove back by the now-loving couple, he glanced their way with a knowing grin and signaled *thumbs-up*. They then pedaled away toward Eze, holding hands from their bikes, with Bridgette smiling ever so coyly at their still-staring audience.

As soon as the Citreon had passed through the first tunnel on the road to Eze, the young driver turned to Wade with, "Welcome very much to our world, Monsieur. And *merci* again to you; but for you and your Mosquito, my colleagues and I might not exist today."

From the back, Dominique said, "Remember, Jean-Pierre, that his *nom de guerre* is *Jean,* and here in this seat is his comrade in arms, who is called *Duc*. They both now speak some French—*Jean* rather well, while *Duc* is making some progress."

"Good; continue your tutoring with both. Jean, tomorrow we visit Monsieur Blanchot at Cap Ferrat. He is looking very much forward to meeting you both."

"And I him," replied Wade. "I am honored to be a part of your group, Jean-Pierre. I will never forget our day at the airstrip, especially Eugenio."

"*Ah oui,* that was an expensive victory, but such is often the price of war; but it could have been a disastrous defeat. Tell me, are you now part of the American military? I thought you were flying with the British."

Wade chuckled, "I can understand how you—or anyone else—would be confused. Yes, I *am* American—and an American OSS officer—and yes, I *did* fly with the Canadians. As we say in my country, 'It's a long story,' but some evening I will try to explain all of it to you."

"It is not of great importance to us, Jean. We believe that we are fortunate to have you and Duc at our side. I am of confidence that we can do great works together."

Of the ten members of Les Amis at the time of Blue Waters, nine of them were still active. After the OSS had offered to provide a sharpshooter and explosives expert to replace Eugenio, Jean-Pierre had decided not to add anyone. He held to the belief that that having too many people was as bad as too few. This was particularly true for a *résistance* unit conducting guerrilla warfare, yet requiring adequate, but near-secret, housing accommodations.

He and M. Blanchot had chosen the perched village of Eze Village as their base for several reasons: The range of their radio was extended dramatically by transmitting and receiving from the church steeple near the summit of the mountain; if discovered, their mountain-top redoubt could be defended for quite some time by a small rear-guard against a much superior number of attackers; if withdrawal did become necessary, they could do so by rappelling down the high wall behind the ancient ruins of the chateau of patrons from centuries past, and—from there—through the old cemetery that lay behind and below the ruins.

But the truly great advantage was that the permanent residents still in the village were as dedicated to their cause as the most committed member of *Les Amis;* while most were too aged or physically limited to be combatants, their provision of shelter, food, clothing and other assistance was absolutely invaluable. However, as an added safeguard against the worst case scenario—the death or capture of the entire group—Jean-Pierre had continued his policy of never permitting more than half of the unit to stay overnight in the same location.

On arrival at the flat area on the roadside below the town, Jean-Pierre concealed the Citreon in its usual spot and waited until David and Bridgette joined them a quarter-hour later for the walk up the trail.

In the expansive wine-cellar of the restaurant a few yards from the summit, all the others—including those who normally stayed at Cap Ferrat—were assembled to meet the two Americans. All had been informed that Jean was the *Blue Waters* RCAF pilot who had taken out the Milice at the airstrip, and they were eagerly awaiting their chance to know him better.

During the short meeting, Jean-Pierre told the group that it would be necessary for Jean, Duc, and him to meet and plan a great deal in the coming weeks. Because of this he wanted both to be housed at Eze for the time being, along with Isabelle, David, and Dominique. The remaining five would stay at M. Blanchot's facilities until further notice.

The room for Wade and Duck was small and Spartan, but clean, in a cottage situated next to a small and newly planted garden unlike any they had seen before. As they opened the shutters to their window, Wade commented that the little plot looked almost identical to scenes he had seen of the Arizona desert in the National Geographic magazines collected by his mother. Duck then pointed to a tiny sign at the edge of the garden:

> *Ce petit jardin exotique a planté*
> *en mémoire de notre ami*
> *Eugenio.*

The sign and garden honoring Eugenio recalled for Wade the reason he was there. He slept peacefully that night, knowing that he was where he belonged.

# Chapter Eighteen

By late March of '44, a good many of those who had once thought Hitler to be invincible had come to doubt their prior judgment. One result was that the number of Nazi sympathizers and Vichy collaborators on Cap Ferrat had diminished to the point that Monsieur Blanchot had few neighbors remaining.

Blanchot described it in a private meeting with Wade and Jean-Pierre, "That is a great blessing for us all, as well as for the success of two primary missions that have been entrusted to *Les Amis* by the Allies; we can now operate with more freedom and effectiveness."

He continued, "Three weeks ago, I had a visitor who is the chief deputy of the OSS commander for the European Theatre.

"He came to my home by American submarine—a good example of our enhanced freedom of movement here. Not only have the jackals largely fled the peninsula, but also the German military has moved nearly all of its units to Italy where General Clark's American 5th. Army is approaching Rome itself.

"Our first—and immediate—task is to improve our efficiency in the rescue and return to duty of downed Allied airmen; the operation *name* has now been changed by your OSS from *Rapid Recovery* to *Operation Rapid Return*. In recent months, we have *recovered* them rapidly enough and, in most cases, returned them eventually; but *eventually* is no longer acceptable.

"Our second mission has been named *Operation Cork the Bottle*. While I do not know precisely *what* is being planned—or *when*—it is obvious that some *very* important operation is forthcoming, demanding the availability of as many experienced aircrews as possible.

Apparently such an operation—or a portion of it—is scheduled for our part of the Mediterranean, since our second mission is to take an active role in preventing any effective return of German units from Italy back into France when any such Allied operation gets underway; simply put, we *keep* the cork in the *bottle*.

"I have some thoughts regarding how we can best accomplish both these efforts, but I prefer that the two of you study the issues, independently of any influence by me, and we shall then decide together the final plan.

"There are some pertinent facts that you should be aware of, and should consider, in your planning. A *good* fact is that the Allies now control the Mediterranean almost completely; so much so that the enemy has been forced to practically abandon use of the Bay of Villefranche, which I view daily from my balcony.

"The *bad* is that although the German military presence in this area is now slight on land, the Milice continue to be a very real threat. They are better armed than in the past; also, they are now desperate men, fearing that they may soon face their well-deserved fate as collaborators.

"The skies over our region also belong largely to the Allies; however, as of this moment we do not control the ground itself sufficiently to have use of the available airfields.

"Those fields which are not being actually used by enemy aircraft are being monitored heavily by the Milice. For example, the airstrip you used during *Blue Waters*—the one next to the rail station at Eze Sur Mer—is now constantly guarded by the Malice and some of their sympathizers amongst the local police."

M. Blanchot then stood, shook hands again with Wade, and invited him on a tour of the boathouse, chuckling, "Jean, this may be the only boathouse on our planet that can provide shelter, rather comfortably, for up to one dozen or more guests in the very shadow of one of the regional headquarters of 'the dreaded'—they *think*—Milice.

"The conversion of this structure was painfully slow, and was only possible because of the cover provided by my small export-import business—which was needed by a diverse group of nations—together with the studious application of that very accurate American expression: 'Money talks!'

"I will be interested in what you think of it."

A half hour later, Wade turned to his host, "What I think is that what you have done here is *amazing!* If someone had simply described it to me, I would have never believed them. Until you opened the doors to what you call your 'guest quarters' I would have sworn this was simply an elegant—but very private—'play and work' station of one of the world's rich and famous, nothing else.

"I deliberately did not converse with the two American airmen I saw. How did they get here, and how will they get back to duty?"

"They are the only two survivors from the crew—the co-pilot and the navigator/bombardier—of one of your B-25 medium bombers. It was necessary to ditch their aircraft off the coast of Italy, near the northern tip of the island of Corsica. After two days on their rubber raft, they were picked up by a Corsican fishing boat out of Bastia. The fishermen transport often their catch to the market at Nice; they stopped by here on their way.

"Actually, the two Americans could have been simply turned over to the Allied forces that now control effectively Corsica, and are busily repairing the bombed-out airfield at Bastia. The fishermen were aware of this, but preferred not to be 'discovered' as my allies by people whom they do not yet know and trust totally; therefore, they brought the airmen to me.

"You asked, 'How will they get back?' Slowly, to be sure. Probably by the usual method of passing them through possibly six or more safehouses across France. It will take many weeks, maybe *months*. That is our major problem—the snail's pace of the return. Occasionally, in the past, we have been allowed to use a submarine, but that is rarely available to us, and a system for such use has yet to be organized to any meaningful degree.

"There you have it; those are your most important tasks at the moment. I hope that we will be prepared to discuss your recommendations within a week; OSS is awaiting eagerly our conclusions."

The younger men promised to have a report within the week, and Wade suggested that they meet again exactly seven days later, at the boathouse.

That night at Eze, Jean-Pierre and Wade conferred again, to share their first impressions on how to proceed. Jean-Pierre said that the principal need for *Rapid Return* was faster transportation, by air and/or sea, and he would defer largely to Wade on that subject.

On the other hand, he continued, "It seems to me that the keyword in an effort to contain the enemy forces in Italy is *geography,* specifically the geography of *this* region of France, that slice of land between our beaches and the nearby mountains. Since the days of Julius Caesar it has been true; when his Roman legions first crossed into Gaul, it was by way of what is now called the *Grande Corniche.* For those discussions we will need the input of Isabelle and David, to be sure.

"Perhaps you, Jean, should draft—independently—some rough thoughts regarding *Rapid Return,* and I should do the same about *Cork the Bottle.* Then, the day after tomorrow, we meet and proceed further?"

"Makes sense to me. Let's do it!"


### E-Street Complex; Washington

"My God! Tell me you're kiddin' me, Pete!" Louis Hebert blurted out. Then, "Sorry' I didn't mean to yell, but that is *incredible!*"

He had just been told by Colonel Recinello that there was hard evidence that the Nazis had moved four key scientists from a location deep in Germany to a laboratory somewhere in Switzerland.

They were the brains behind the German research concerning which Albert Einstein had warned President Roosevelt by a personal letter dated August 2, 1939 that the Germans were working on a nuclear fusion project that could lead to the construction of extremely powerful bombs.

"But *in* Switzerland? Do the Swiss know this?" said Hebert.

"It's hard to believe they don't, Louis. Why would you risk putting such an important project in another sovereign nation's territory if they hadn't authorized it in some fashion?"

"Right. And we know already, Pete, that the assholes have been making and selling military equipment to the Nazis—and otherwise kissing their butts six ways from Sunday——from day one; so why not this, too? In my book, they're plain blood-sucking SOBs hiding behind the pretense of being a neutral."

"Whatever the reasons, the White House says it's gotta be stopped! If they get a working weapon like the one referred to in Einstein's letter, they could change the entire course of the war in one strike. We have known for some time that they were revving up their work on this project, and we knew *where,* until recently. We thought we were close to nailing it for good when it was suddenly moved, lock, stock and barrel; now we think we know *where* they took it.

"Of course we could probably take it out by bombing the hell out of it, then finishing off the details with a Ranger drop—exactly what was planned when it was located inside the Reich—-but some of the political brass are reluctant to hit it that way in Swiss territory, *if* there's any other effective way. Unfortunately, we still need the Swiss in some ways, they tell me.

"But first, we've got to pinpoint the location. The best guess is that it's somewhere near the French border; that's why I'm talking to you, Louis. Bottom line: It's now in our court. Think about it and give it your best shot. Let's find it; then let's figure a way to eliminate it.

"Needless to say, this one is a *must!*"

In Eze, Wade was saying, "O.K., Jean-Pierre, here are my thoughts. We need to set up a systematic way to get our guys—the airmen, that is—away from Cap Ferrat, and back to work fast. Considering that many—if not most—are going to have to travel as far as the U.K., all the way across Europe, there's only one way to do it—by *air.*

"The kicker—er, excuse me, I should say the *problem*—is that we don't have a nearby place to land and take-off, not here on the mainland. But how far is Corsica?

"As I recall, Monsieur Blanchot said that the fishing boats often come to Nice to market their fish. If they can do that, it must not be a long journey, especially for a modern military vessel. If we could get them to the airfield now being repaired at Bastia—I think that's the Corsican city mentioned by Monsieur Blanchot—they could be flown directly to Italy or England within hours."

Jean-Pierre frowned and said, "What kind of 'military vessels' do you speak of? Subs?"

"Probably, to begin the voyage. The sub could come in close to the boathouse—probably under cover of night—submerged, I presume. It would surface briefly to board the passengers, dive and go either directly to Bastia or rendezvous with a nearby destroyer that would take the passengers on to Bastia.

"Our army air people already have in being a program, using modified B-24 heavy bombers—exactly like the one that flew Duck and me to Grenoble—to drop agents and supplies to partisan and resistance groups all over occupied Europe. They certainly could be used to transport our downed guys back to the job, perhaps even on the 'return' trip occasionally. Their passenger capacity is huge, and their range is long. The only concern I have is whether the runways at Bastia are long enough to handle a B-24. If not, a modified Mosquito could be used, but the number of qualified Mosquito pilots is limited, plus they don't have the passenger space of a B-24.

"What do you think, Jean-Pierre?"

"The concept appears sound. We must discuss the distance to the island with Isabelle; I know that she has taken the ferry from Nice many times before the war. And David also; David is an avid private mariner and can help us with that.

"Also we must learn much regarding the airfield at Bastia; M. Blanchot should be helpful with that. A thought, Jean; perhaps we could find more aid from the fishermen—transporting *to* Bastia. If necessary, we could possibly provide their boats with engines that would decrease crossing time to the island?"

"Yes, if necessary. But I would prefer the armed military ships; also they would not be as vulnerable in bad weather."

"*D'accord mon ami!* I like your ideas. Now let us discuss how to keep the 'cork in the Italian bottle.'

"Look for a moment at this map of our area. If the enemy wishes to move large forces of troops from Italy into this region of France, there are only two ways.

"The first is by sea. The other is by land, using one or more of the three *corniches,* the *Grande Corniche,* up very high, or the *Moyenne Corniche,* the 'middle' one—it is just below where we are now sitting—or the *Basse Corniche,* the lower road by the sea. Those are the only main thoroughfares leading from the Italian border into this part of France.

"The sea is not a viable option; the Allies would destroy—at once—a fleet of troop-carrying surface vessels *if* the Germans had one. That leaves the corniches as their only choice.

"If we can disable or *block* the corniches, *VOILA!* The cork remains in the bottle! *Simple! Oui, Jean?"*

Wade smiled, "Maybe, but how do you plan to block or disable the corniches?"

"Yes, that could be a problem with one of the three. We need the advice of both Isabelle and Duc regarding that.

"I believe it quite possible to damage or destroy—by explosives—both the Grande and Moyenne Corniches to the extent that it would take weeks or months to repair either.

"The Grande is high and narrow, subject—I believe—to destruction through landslide, generated by a *nudge* from a bit of Duc's plastique. Duc will know after I take him there.

"And the *Moyenne?* Perhaps you remember the tunnels and the high bridge we passed through and over in the Citreon—just west of here—a few days ago? If the bridge were destroyed, or one of the tunnels blocked, no vehicles could pass in a westerly direction until they were repaired.

"This leaves the *Basse*—the lower road down by the sea. It presents a much greater problem. My present feeling is that we could create a massive landslide above the road-bed at a point near *Pont St. Jean*—the bridge over to Cap Ferrat—and block it temporarily, but it would require a substantial military or paramilitary force to prevent its repair by enemy combat engineers. We need some thoughts from M. Blanchot regarding resources that may be available for that.

"Also, we must be aware that if we destroy the bridge or block the tunnels on the *Moyenne,* we must also abandon Eze Village as our base, perhaps permanently, because we ourselves would no longer have easy access to this village.

"Before we meet with Monsieur Blanchot, I want to take Duc and Isa to view the three roads."

Wade nodded, "And I—if you and Monsieur Blanchot concur in my plan—need to go to Corsica to evaluate the Bastia airfield on the ground. If it is totally inadequate, my tentative plan is fatally flawed. The question is: How do I get there?"

"Monsieur can best answer that one, Jean. If you are in agreement, I will send a message asking for a meeting on Sunday—with Isa, David and Duc present also. Tomorrow we go to visit the road that Caesar made famous."

"O.K; let me know when."

On Sunday afternoon, Wade and Jean-Pierre arrived at the boathouse at two o'clock by bicycle, with Duck, Isabelle, and David close behind. Wade presented their plan regarding *Rapid Return* first, then asked for comments or questions.

Blanchot said, "It is a sound plan, subject, as you mentioned, to the condition of the airfield at Bastia. But, why do you believe that you yourself need to inspect the airfield?"

"For two reasons: first, Col. Hebert—my boss in OSS—wanted a pilot for this assignment for precisely this type of issue—determining the adequacy of airfields; second, if the Bastia strips are too short for the B-24s, the only other aircraft that I know of that can use short runways *and* have the range capabilities to fly from Corsica to England is the British Mosquito. And only a Mosquito pilot can determine that in a marginal case."

"Very well; then let us now discuss how to get you there and back," responded Georges Blanchot. "One way, as Jean-Pierre has suggested, is through one of our Corsican fisherman friends. David, do you remember Monsieur Antonio Cesari?"

"To be *sure*, Monsieur; all the fishing families in the region know that he has the largest and most seaworthy fishing boat afloat, complete with two cabins. It is a converted 'subchaser' from the first World War—all wood. Is he a friend?"

"Yes, and a good one too. He has served France faithfully—but quietly—and it is vital that the *quiet* part continues; this conversation is only for the ears in this room. Antonio can make the crossing rapidly when necessary, but he is careful; he often pretends to fish en route, for security purposes. Therefore it takes a few hours longer than a direct voyage. I think he is our man, Jean."

Isabelle added, "Jean, you will need an interpreter in Bastia. Corsica, while a part of France, is as much Italian as French in its language and culture, and the French one hears there is laced heavily with Italian."

"No problem," said Jean-Pierre. "Both Isabelle and Dominique speak good Italian, but we need Isa here. Dominique will accompany you."

"Settled. Now tell me; how are we to *keep the cork in the bottle*, Jean-Pierre?" asked Georges Blanchot.

Jean-Pierre explained his plan, then added, "Duc, Isa, and I examined well *les trois corniches* before coming here, and I want to ask Duc to tell you his opinion; Duc?"

"No problem, Mister Blanchot—least not the two high 'uns. Blowin' 'em two to hell and back would be like takin' candy from a baby, if you know what I mean.

"Now, the one down by the water—'at's a different story. We could go up a ways on that narrow little road that circles right above it and create a helluva landslide onto the road. That'd block the traffic for sure, but a really good combat engineers unit could rebuild it in nothin' flat if they weren't opposed. 'At's our only problem."

"Thank you, Duc; I understand. I think we can handle this. If the Allied operation takes place as anticipated, we hope—and expect—to have at our disposal, several thousand—perhaps as high as 20,000, but I doubt that—well-armed, and fairly well-trained Maquis whom we could use to secure the Basse Corniche. They would come from the areas of St. Paul de Vence, Grasse, and many smaller villages in the Haute-Provence region.

"We expect to first attack—and destroy—the Milice garrison now quartered in the ancient Citadelle at Villefranche Sur Mer. We could then use the arms we would capture there as well as then have our own formidable fort as a new base.

"Another possibility is for an Allied *quickstrike* unit—airborne, Ranger, or Commando—to assist us at the Basse Corniche. Perhaps I can soon learn if that is possible.

"But—either way—it shall be done. It *must* be done!

"The great unknown is *when* this needs to be done. Obviously, only a handful of people will know the exact date until a very short time prior to the commencement of such an Allied operation. We simply must be—and remain—prepared to move on a moment's notice.

"Duc, how much preparation time do you need for the disablement of the three corniches?"

Duck paused for a moment, then replied, "We're probably gonna' have to work the sites at night, right? I can have ever'thing set to go before we git the green light to blow 'em. I'd say two nights at the sites; *one,* if there's a nice bright moon."

"Excellent! Now, Jean; when do you want to leave for Corsica?"

"As soon as possible, sir."

Antonio Cesari had been a fisherman since his father had taken him to sea in the Spring of 1904, fourteen years after his birth in the Corsican seaport town of St. Florent, on the other side of Cap Corse from Bastia. His mother, Nicoletta, was born Italian, and had grown up on the nearby island of Sardinia, situated south of Corsica.

For ten years, father and son fished far and wide in Mediterranean waters, ranging from the southern tip of Sardinia to the coast of Marseilles, in their small boat, *La Nicoletta,* until shortly after the outbreak of hostilities in World War I.

One evening, they had brought in their nets at dusk, stowed them, and were underway back to Bastia, when a German U-Boat surfaced and fired a shot across their bow. Thinking it to be an order to stop, Antonio—who was at the wheel—brought the boat about toward the submarine while simultaneously shutting down his engine.

The second cannon shell was a direct hit. It shattered the tiny boat, and Antonio stared in terror as he suddenly realized that the bloody body he saw floating in the debris was that of his father.

He dove into the cold water, but before he could reach the body it had disappeared below the surface. As Antonio turned in the water to desperately beseech the submarine crew for help, he saw the U-Boat's conning tower slowly disappearing as it submerged.

During World War I, a class of ship called "subchaser" first came into being. As the German U-boats had become more and more aggressive, they came to be viewed by many as a threat to the then neutral United States. By the middle of that conflict, they had begun to roam our Atlantic coastlines and had actually sunk some ships along that coast.

A young Assistant Secretary of the Navy named Franklin D. Roosevelt drew the assignment of diminishing this threat. He worked diligently with naval architects to develop what was to be known as the subchaser: an all-wood vessel that could be built in small boatyards, not requiring the attention of the larger shipyards that were busy with the much-needed and larger steel ships.

The end result was a design inspired by those used for centuries in whaleboats and other types of extremely seaworthy vessels since the days of the Vikings. In addition it did not require the use of steel, a scarce commodity at the time.

Possibly the best of all, the small boats could be handled by most skilled amateur boatmen, with a minimum of training.

By the end of World War I, more than 400 subchasers had been constructed and put in service. One hundred or so were sold to France, and many were used in the Mediterranean. The most effective subchaser captain in the French navy was a Corsican named Antonio Cesari.

After that war, hundreds were converted and used in many other ways: for deep sea pleasure fishing, luxury yachts, a packer boat and tender in the Alaska fishing industry, a sightseeing boat on the Great Lakes, and myriad other uses.

In 1925, the French government placed its remaining subchasers up for sale to the public. Three were purchased by *La Maison des Poissons*—a large and expensive seafood restaurant in Nice—and then converted into state-of-the-art fishing vessels, complete with two lavishly furnished cabins for occasional use by their best clientele—at an *enormous* cost.

By the autumn of 1933 the Great Depression was beginning to take its toll worldwide; the stream of big spenders into Nice had dwindled to a trickle, and *La Maison des Poissons* was bankrupt. At the auction of its assets, Antonio Cesari—with the help of a generous loan from a banker named Blanchot—purchased one of the three, and immediately painted *La Nicoletta II* on its hull.

His business had boomed after that, and his boat was the talk of the industry around the entire Mediterranean rim.

After France had been over-run in 1940, Antonio had found it expedient to lead a double life. He spent a great deal of his time furnishing an abundance of delicious *fruits de mer* to the tables of Vichy collaborators and their masters in all the cities along the French Riviera, as well as Toulon and Marseilles. As repugnant as he found those activities to be, it had enabled him to operate somewhat freely—and extremely effectively—in his clandestine role as a major provider of transportation and intelligence information to the *résistance,* primarily through his old and good friend, Georges Blanchot.

Occasionally, he had been detained and boarded by a curious German U-boat commander since, despite substantial modifications to her hull, *La Nicoletta* II had retained, partially, the silhouette of a subchaser. Almost always the detentions were brief, although at times Antonio was forced to produce his *Letter of Free Passage,* signed and sealed by none other than Petain's Minister of the Interior.

This appearance of consorting with the enemy had made many of his old friends shun him. In turn, this created great grief for Antonio, but he was comforted by the knowledge that it was for a much greater cause—the eventual liberation of his beloved country.

The night Wade returned from his meeting at the boathouse, he wrote three short personal letters, thinking that he might meet some transient airman at Bastia who could later mail them from elsewhere.

One was to his brother. He apologized for not writing sooner, but quipped that "such is life as a *spook* in wartime." He went on, "As you well know, I jumped the gun for one selfish reason—so I could *fly.* But, at long last, I have learned that there are more important things involved—*much* more important things—in this war, and I feel that I am now doing what I was meant to do in my life. When we both get home, I'll be able to tell you of it all; and I think you may agree that it was intended by a higher power."

# Chapter Nineteen

The note from M. Blanchot had been hand carried to Wade by Juan, who said softly, "I am to await your written reply, Monsieur."

The note read:

Dear Jean:

The Corsican is prepared for your voyage. Can you and Dominique be at the west end of the marina, in St Jean, Cap Ferrat, in front of the restaurant called *Cafe de l'Homard,* at noon on Thursday? It is near the public carpark. If so, the *La Nicoletta II* will be in its slip and in plain view.

Have Dominique wave toward the boat with a red scarf; then someone will approach you and ask, "What time is it in Singapore?" If you reply, "Sorry, my watch is broken," he will escort you to the boat and the owner.

Please write your reply and return it to me by Juan.

Good luck and God speed,

*G. Blanchot*

Wade asked Juan to excuse him for a moment, and stepped across the pathway to speak to Dominique. She said she would be ready on Thursday, and added, smiling, "You will love Corsica, Jean. I visited there once with my University class, and it is truly beautiful."

Wade wrote a short note, asked for an envelope that could be sealed, then returned and handed it to Juan. Duck was waiting to go to lunch, and had invited Juan to join them.

It was a windy day at St. Jean, the only town on Cap Ferrat, and Antonio said that the sea had been very rough that morning. He showed them to one of the cabins that had come with the boat when he purchased it 11 years before. He had maintained the cabins well because—prior to the war—his wife and daughters had sometimes accompanied him to the mainland. Since that time he had used the second cabin often for the concealment of downed Allied airmen whom he had sometimes carried to Algeria before the Allies recaptured Corsica. He emphasized that he wanted them to remain in the cabin, in case he was boarded by a U-boat officer, and informed them that the two American airmen from the Blanchot boathouse were in the other cabin.

He said that if the boat were boarded by an enemy officer or agent *and* a search appeared imminent, he would signal them from the wheelhouse with three short rings; that would be their cue to vacate the cabin and go into a concealed closet situated five meters down the corridor from their cabin. He showed them the closet and how to enter and exit it. He emphasized that they should remain in the closet until he or one of his crewmen signaled them by rapping on the closet door five times, then saying loudly, *"les serpents sont parti"* ("the snakes have left").

Antonio also advised that he had decided not to depart until well after nightfall, as a security precaution and, "That means we must travel most of the night, but food—not wonderful, but not bad—will be brought to your cabin at 6:00; we dine early when at sea. For your lunch, there is a good bottle of Sardinian wine—a *rouge*—on the counter, as well as sandwiches, cheese, and fresh fruit in the cabinet above. We should arrive in Bastia well before dawn. Relax and enjoy."

After he left them, both were amazed as they examined their accommodations in more detail. Dominique exclaimed—sitting and bouncing gleefully on the side of the bed, "What a surprise! This is *elegant,* Jean; that is the only word to describe it. I had visualized sleeping in a dirty bedroll against a wet and cold bulkhead. Look at this bed; it would befit a Queen!"

"Quite true; and it shall *have* one this night, Mademoiselle. To me you *are* a Queen."

*"Merci;* you are *too kind,* Monsieur! But there is only one bed; we can rotate its use."

"No way. I will suffer on the couch; it looks to be large enough for the Queens's entire court.

"In the meantime, *your highness,* this bottle looks very lonesome," he clowned, "Let us give it the honor of our immediate attention. I am told by my *staff* of wine consultants that they pour an *acceptable* red on the Isle of Sardinia; I can only *hope* that it is fit for my *Queen.*"

She stood close beside him while he slowly poured the wine and, with her head on his shoulder, whispered, ever so quietly, "Oh how I wish this moment could be *forever."*

As he put down the bottle and turned to kiss her, he replied, his voice now quite husky, "And I also, Dominique. But in our present world, we must enjoy such magic *when* we have it. For *tomorrow,* who knows?"

Then he forced a laugh, "Hey! Let's stop the sad talk! I raise my glass to toast my beautiful Queen—*à votre santé, ma belle reine !*"

That returned her smile. Clinking her glass with his, she said "Yes, you are absolutely correct. I must continue to remember the image of the 'cold and wet bulkhead' that I had visualized for this voyage. That should make me thankful, as well as happy."

After lunch they sat together on the couch and chatted for hours, mainly about each other's childhood.

Due primarily to the urging of her father, and because he was close friends with a multitude of his former students throughout Europe, Dominique had visited in much of the continent as she grew up. And she had been encouraged—again by her father—to read widely about North America and the United States, saying that one of her favorite studies had been American literature.

Her experiences fascinated Wade, because, as he told her, "As terrible as this war has been for so many, it has opened up a completely new world for me.

"I was blessed by having wonderful parents—much better than I deserve—and the people where I live are as fine as anywhere on Earth; but none of us were well off, and few had an opportunity for a first-rate education. *Dummy* that *I* am, I left school early because I had always dreamed of flying, but I plan to make up for that once this war is done.

"Maybe I can return here someday and you could show me your land without the clouds of war surrounding us."

"Nothing would give me more pleasure; and I would like also to see your land, especially the place that produced a man as fine as *you*, Jean!"

Each then read quietly; he about the rugged terrain of Corsica, while she refreshed her Italian vocabulary.

By five that afternoon, their books had slid to the floor, as both had fallen sound asleep. She was still sitting upright; he was stretched out on the couch with his head in her lap.

At 6:00 sharp, there was a knock at the door, and the booming voice of Antonio, "*Bonsoir, mes amis.* I hope you are hungry because Mario and I have your dinner, and some of it must be enjoyed while still *hot!*"

They opened their door to the delicious aroma from a pot of very hot *soupe de poisson,* "The fish soup for which Mario is famous," said a beaming Antonio, as he placed the steaming pot on the table and set out two bowls beside it. He was followed by a darkhaired, dwarf-like, man with an infectious grin and bushy mustache, who was laboring with two huge bowls, one containing two dozen mussels—also steaming—and the other one overflowing with large steamed shrimp.

Mario stepped back into the corridor and returned with a huge loaf of country French bread, a bundle of small and flat crusty toasts, along with a container of soft and grated cheese, laced heavily with a pungent *aïoli* sauce.

Antonio had already pronounced *bon appétit,* and was nudging Mario toward the door, when Mario slapped himself in the face and screamed, "*Mon Dieu!* Did we forget the *rosé?*" To which Antonio snapped his fingers and answered, "*Ah non;* no problem; but I left it in the corridor." He strode to the doorway, reached outside, then plonked a bottle of chilled Bandol *rosé* on the table, with "*Voila la rosé! Bon appetit encore, et bonne nuit.* But remember—*sorrrry*—-but we arise before dawn."

When they left, the door did not shut completely; Dominique could hear the men snickering like teenage boys as they scurried down the corridor.

As she reached over to shut the door, Wade laughed and said, "If I'm dreaming, don't wake me! If I didn't know better, I'd swear we were in the honeymoon suite of a fancy cruise ship somewhere, instead of on a fishing boat in the middle of a war."

"Yes, and I believe that we have two friends who wish to encourage that impression. But you must remember that they *are* Frenchmen, though rather dear ones, I think. Shall we dine?"

As they ladled the soup into the bowls, Dominique said, "Now, I must demonstrate for you the proper manner to enjoy these small toasts—and the *cheese/aïoli* sauce—with your soup. Watch carefully: first I spread the cheese/*aïoli* sauce on the small toast; next I float the toast in the hot soup; then, I *splash* some of the soup over the floating toast; last, I *submerge* the toast in the soup; *then*—and *only* then—do you begin to eat the saturated toast.

"*Here;* try this one" she said as she reached her spoon over to his lips. "Is it not indeed *magnifigue?*"

"Wonderful! Now it's my turn to do one for you."

"Good! But not too much *aïoli;* this one is—how do you say it—'loaded' with garlic."

After the mussels and shrimp, they continued to sip the *rosé,* but Wade noticed the slight hint of a frown on her face; he asked why. "Oh, I was thinking of my cousin who lives in Paris, and feeling some guilt for having this grand meal tonight.

"As you have undoubtedly learned by now, Jean, mealtime in France has always meant more than mere sustenance or nutrition; indeed it is a major part of our lives in so many other ways, a *ritual* that feeds our souls as well as our bodies. Since the occupation, all in France—wherever they live—have, of course, had to make some adjustment in that 'ritual,' but we in the provinces have borne *nothing* to compare with the hardships of those in the large cities.

"For example, the last time I had a letter from my cousin, she said that she, my aunt, and uncle were living off practically nothing but *rutabagas,* a horrid tasting *root* that we would not have fed to our swine before the war. Most of the time she must eat it almost raw, inasmuch as they are allowed to turn on the heat in their apartment only two hours a day, one hour in the morning and another in the early evening. She has not had a hot bath in more than three years. And a meal, such as we enjoyed this evening, is unheard of there, except—of course—for those who have sold their souls to the enemy."

"Yes, it *is* terrible; but *you* should never feel even a scintilla of 'guilt.' You have chosen to risk your very life every day for what you believe in; what more can one do? And I am certain that your cousin would not disagree with that.

"Some day—soon, I hope—you and your cousin, with me if I'm *lucky,* will dine at the best three-star in Paris, while the *Krauts* will be eating the rutabagas. *Remember* who told you that; I guarantee it! Now, give me that smile that always lights up *any* room, and let's be happy tonight!"

An hour later she fell asleep again on the couch. He lifted her gently, carried her to the bed, kissed her on the cheek, and murmured "Goodnight, lovely Queen. I think I'm really in love this time." He paused at the bedside for almost a full minute—deep in thought—then wheeled abruptly, crossed the room, kicked off his shoes, curled up on the couch, and turned off the light.

It was almost sunrise when they heard the knock on the door, and Antonio's cheery, "*Bonjour, mes amis! Pardon,* but I must awaken you to welcome a Corsican sunrise, without doubt the most beautiful in the world.

"We are now in Corsican waters," he continued from the corridor, "controlled by the British navy; it is safe now for you to take breakfast with us from the ship's galley. We can sit on the starboard side, the better to watch the sun rise over the island."

Both had awakened more than an hour earlier, expecting to arrive at Bastia much sooner. Wade replied, "O.K., we are ready; wait a second, and we will go topside with you."

On the way down the corridor, Antonio explained. "Late last night I received a coded message from Georges that one of your Army Air Corps officers is planning to meet you in town—at *Place St-Nicolas*—after we dock at Bastia.

"I felt that it would be more convenient for you if I delayed our arrival for a few hours; therefore we changed course a bit, fished for awhile, and are now sailing north along this, the western coast of Cap Corse. Not only did we fill our nets again, but also *you* get to view our glorious sunrise, one of God's grand miracles."

As they entered the galley and were seating themselves, he gestured excitedly, "Look quickly! *There!* The sun is now beginning to peek up—slightly—over the Cap."

"Oh yes, Antonio! I've *never* seen one more beautiful. I certainly understand why you love this place so much. Is it always like this?" Dominique asked.

"*Ah oui,* to me it *is* always; yes, *always!*"

After breakfast, Wade returned to the cabin, while Dominique stayed on deck and savored the complete sunrise. When she returned, she was surprised—and quite impressed—to see him in his military uniform for the first time. "*Ah, la la!* You are so very, very handsome; *Captain* Johns, isn't it? But tell me; why the uniform today?"

"If I am dealing with a flier, it is best that he knows I am a pilot; this is the simplest way of telling him. Plus, it will cover my real role effectively, in case there are any curious types here."

"Tell me; are you a *real* captain? If so, are they all so young?'

"Yes," he laughed, "I *am real;* at least *I* think so. Many of our much higher ranking officers are not much older, if any; the term 'Boy-Colonel' is not uncommon in our air corps. Regardless, we're getting the job done."

"You surely are, and thank God for all of you. What do you think we will be doing today?"

"Inspecting the airfield, probably; above all, its runways. Most important is whether they are long enough for landing and takeoff of large and heavy aircraft. Apparently, Georges Blanchot has somehow gotten the word to the U.S. military that we were on the way here; he is quite an amazing person, your Monsieur Blanchot."

"Agreed. Would that there were more like him in France during these awful times. *Oh,* I can feel us turning. I think we are about to dock; let's go on deck."

"Go ahead, if you like; I'll wait until the last minute, then wear my civilian trench coat over my uniform until we are well away from the boat. Antonio says we are to meet a Major Henry Larsen in the lobby of the *Hotel de l'Ile.* Could you slip my cap into your handbag until we get near the hotel?"

"I will take it now and return for you after the boat is tied up."

When Wade reached the deck, he saw Antonio standing on the dock with three tearful women embracing him. He waved to Wade and Dominique, beckoning them to join him and his family.

His wife Lucia invited Wade and Dominique to stay at their home, but Antonio said that Major Larsen had requested that they stay at the hotel, the temporary HQ of the army air corps unit in charge of the airbase.

Antonio said he would check with Wade the next morning, regarding return plans.

It was a short and pleasant walk to the small hotel and to their surprise of finding that it was occupied totally by American army personnel, pending repair of the buildings at the airfield, most of which had been bombed out by the Allies while the island was in Axis hands.

The entire Corsican hotel staff had continued to operate the little inn, but only the Director and the two-person reception staff spoke any English, as Wade soon learned. The others used a melodious mixture of French and Italian, but heavy on the Italian side.

The sad part was that the army had taken over the food service operation at the hotel, much to the thinly-veiled displeasure of the Corsicans, as well as the American airmen staying there.

Wade had removed and folded his civilian trenchcoat as he and Dominique approached the *Place St-Nicolas,* and was in proper military dress as he entered the hotel and told the desk clerk that he was there to meet Major Larsen. She smiled brightly, "*Si, Capitano;* he is waiting for you in the *risteronte.* He wishes for you and your lady to join him for your morning *repas.* You will find him at the window table in the corner, next to the fountain."

As soon as they entered the restaurant, a man with very blond hair at the corner table pushed his chair back and, using a cane, walked across the room to greet them, smiling, "You must be Wade Johns? I'm Hank Larsen." When Wade nodded, he waved them to his table and motioned to a waiter, saying, "The food here isn't great, but it beats C-Rations, so order up if you're hungry. The Corsican in charge here is ticked because the army won't let him do our chow—and so am *I*—but *hey,* we can't have everything; right?"

"Thanks, but we ate on the boat. Everything here looks pretty nice to me, Major. By the way, this is Dominique. She came as my interpreter."

"My pleasure, ma'am; I could certainly use one myself. But the Corsicans have been great to us, so somehow we manage to communicate. My First Sergeant is from Newark, of Italian descent. He speaks some Italian, and that's been a godsend so far.

"They call me the 'Administrative Officer.' My job—right now—is to get the airfield here in shape for our aircraft to use it ASAP.

"I'm not too happy about it," he said, while tapping on his cane. " Of course I'd prefer to be back in the cockpit, but when this leg caught a piece of flak it grounded me for now, and it also got me this temporary assignment. But activating the local airbase *is* important; we need it. And I hear that's why you're here too, right?"

" That's *close,*" said Wade, "but this is pretty graveyard stuff, Major. I'd feel better discussing it somewhere more private; could we do that?"

"Sure; you're right. It's tempting to get a little lax around here. The people are so damned friendly, it's hard to make yourself observe good security procedures. Let's go up to my room; I'm using it for an office, too. Your rooms are just down the hall from mine, so you may want to bring along your gear."

Larsen asked about the wings worn by Wade. "They're *RCAF,* Major. I trained and flew with the Canadians until I transferred, like a lot of other guys. Normally I don't wear a uniform in OSS work, but we'd like to keep it quiet that any OSS are here, O.K.?"

"Sure; thanks for letting me know that. The only message I got yesterday was that I am to help you with whatever you need. By the way, call me Hank; I'm more comfortable with that.

"Here we are at 'my place.' Pull up a crate and have a seat; real chairs are a little scarce around here, since some moron in Army Supply decided to replace most of the beautiful old hotel furniture with this GI crap, even though we're s'posed to be staying here for only about another month. Now, what can I do for you?"

Wade explained his concept of channeling downed airmen into Corsica to be flown out of Bastia back to England or other Allied-controlled destinations, but deliberately avoided mentioning *how* they would be gotten to the island.

He asked if Larsen thought the field could handle a B-24; not the typical bomber version, but one modified to lighten its weight, similar to the one that had brought him and Duck to France.

Not surprisingly, Wade later thought, Major Larsen had never heard of the special unit of modified B-24s, a unit called *Carpetbaggers* that was doing drops all over most of occupied Europe. But he was familiar with the B-24 bomber edition.

"We'll take a drive out there this morning, and you can see the situation for yourself. It's a mess right this minute. Our own guys bombed the hell out of this place when the Luftwaffe had it. The engineers are working as close to night and day as is possible, but we've still got a way to go.

"But as to your question, I'd say 'maybe' so—a *big* maybe—*if* you stripped all the armor off a 24, and didn't have to take on a full load of fuel for the trip out. We could probably lengthen a couple of the runways, but only at one end of Number 2, cause the other end is too close to the water.

"But I'm doing a lot of guessing here, some of it not even the educated kind. Let's grab a Jeep and run out there and talk to the guy in charge of the engineers. You ready?"

As they approached the field, Wade saw two familiar looking airplanes parked near three Quonset huts the engineers had recently finished setting up. He tapped Larsen on the shoulder and asked, "How did those Lysander IIIs get in here?"

"Oh *those?* I hear that those birds can land damned near anywhere. The two you see are RAF planes that came in yesterday with some supplies for the British naval guys; they sat down on the grass strip on the other side of the field. They only need about 250–300 yards of runway. They look like hell, but they're said to be sturdy and reliable.

"The trouble is, if they should run into enemy fighters in the air, they're *helpless*. It'd be like shootin' fish in a barrel; they're slow, have no armor, and no weapons to shoot back with if attacked."

"Yeah, I know. I saw them once at a base in England, while I was flying with my Mosquito outfit; I think our Carpetbaggers unit have also used them at times."

They met with the Commanding Officer of the engineers unit. He said he'd have one runway operational within a week or ten days, but it would take a week or so longer to finish No. 2. He told Major Larsen, "The barracks will be ready sooner, but you'll need to use a field kitchen for a while; maybe you should keep your crowd working at the hotel a while longer, except for the maintenance guys and any other critical types."

Wade asked, "What do you think will be the useable length of the longer of the two runways, when you finish your work?"

The engineer thought for a second, then, "That's pretty hard to say, Captain, at least for *now*. There are some pretty formidable hills at one end, as you can see, and the terrain is a little 'iffy' toward the water side; we're gonna stretch 'em as much as we can."

"Thanks," Wade said as he shook hands. He then turned to Hank Larsen, "Could I take a look-see, up close, at one of those Lysanders?"

"Sure; no problem."

On the way back to the hotel, Wade asked if any other Allied aircraft had recently landed there, other than the Lysanders. Larsen told him that when the engineers had first come, they had patched up one of the strips in order that some essential cargo could be flown in before they started using their big machines. "A few days afterward, six of our *Gooney Birds* came in and had no trouble landing—*or* in taking off the next morning. Of course there was near perfect flying weather both days; that didn't hurt any."

Wade's eyes lit up at the news that some C-47s had been there. "That's *great* to hear. I had wondered if they could be used here. Some guys who fly them told me—when I was at Benning—that they had put them in and out of some pretty primitive airfields; and their range—about 1,500 miles—would be plenty adequate for what I have in mind. The big problem is that they too are slow, with *zero* armor."

As they crossed the small lobby toward the restaurant, Nadia, the desk clerk, called to Wade, almost musically, *"Capitano Johns,"* then added something in a fast combination of Italian/French. "She says that she has a message for you," said Dominique. *"I* will get it; you can stay here."

The note was from Antonio, in the same baffling mixture of languages.

Wade asked Dominique to translate it, aloud: "We are prepared to return you tomorrow, but only if you finish today. Let me know, please. You and Dominique are invited to dine with me and my family tonight, if you are free. If not for dinner, perhaps you will join us early for a glass of good Italian spumante. My home is only one kilometer from your hotel. Please advise."

Dominique paused for a moment, then continued slowly, " Nadia, at Reception, offered to tell you the way here. Actually, she offered to come *with* you, but I discouraged that—for reasons of *security,* of course. Sorry, *mon ami; c'est la guerre!"*

Dominique looked up, frowned sternly at Wade, and snapped, "Go in and find a table for us!" adding that she would get the directions from "this *Nadia."*

At the table, Wade asked, "Hank, could I interview some of your Operations people this afternoon and tonight, perhaps one-on-one with a few? Maybe they could shed some light on the questions I have in mind. For example, does anyone who is here *now* know what types of aircraft are expected to use this field? Also, I need to get a read on the typical weather conditions here; those high hills we saw do trouble me some, if there's much ground fog here."

"I doubt anyone can tell you much about the aircraft question. I know *I* can't, and you would think I would have been told if that had been decided. But certainly you can talk to anyone you want. I'll jot down some key job classifications, give you the names of who's in the job, and make them available. You tell me when.

"On the weather bit, I'll get Lieutenant Schmidt in; he's our weather guy, and I know he has already been working hard to get a handle on local conditions."

As Dominique sat down at the table, Wade said, "Good. After lunch, Dom and I will walk over to Antonio's and beg off on the dinner and vino. Maybe we could have a couple of sandwiches brought in while we work tonight. Also, I think we may as well get out of your hair tomorrow; I should be as ready as I'm gonna be by then."

Early the next morning, Wade and Dominique met Major Larsen for breakfast, and Wade told him he that he would like a few more minutes with Lt. Schmidt before leaving. He also asked for a personal favor, "Could you please mail these three letters for me, either from here or by having some transient do so from elsewhere? It's very risky for us to try to send mail out from where we are working; plus, our bosses in OSS *frown*—and that's putting it mildly—on us giving any real clues to our specific where-abouts, when on a duty assignment such as my present one."

"No sweat, Wade; they'll be on their way with our next packet out of here."

On the return, they departed late in the morning, but the *Nicoletta II* fished the waters off the northern tip of Cap Corse for several hours be-fore turning toward the mainland. Antonio explained that he did not wish to be in close proximity to Nice before darkness fell. "Also," he quipped, "if one pretends that he is traveling there to sell fish, it is wise to have some *fish*, no?"

The night before, Wade had made copious notes during the course of six interviews, as well as having been given a large sheaf of documents by Lieutenant Schmidt. He hoped to be ready to give a full report to M. Blan-chot and Jean-Pierre by the time they reached St. Jean.

Some of the weather related papers had apparently been abandoned by Schmidt's German predecessor eight weeks prior, in the Luftwaffe's rush to vacate the premises.

The rush had been triggered by an urgent radio alert that two Ameri-can regiments of airborne infantry—troopers whom German soldiers had come to call "devils in baggy pants"—had made a drop into a nearby val-ley, and were then on a forced march toward Bastia, closing rapidly on the airfield itself.

The Lieutenant had surmised that the records had been kept by Corsi-cans, inasmuch as all were written in the Corsican style of French/Italian.

Dominique spent most of her day translating them, first into English for Wade to read with ease, then in French for further use by others. Wade became intrigued as he read them. Although the information wasn't favor-able to all his tentative plans, he was grateful to have some authentic in-formation to provide a basis for decisions.

A few minutes before dusk, they took a break to admire a spectacular sunset through their small window. As they gazed quietly—cheek to cheek—she said in near inaudible tones, "Jean, this is almost like a dream; at this moment, we are witnessing God's world at its very *best,* a world of almost indescribable peace and beauty; yet, in a few hours we will re-enter one of turmoil and brutality. Why does it have to be so?"

He gently squeezed her hand, "I can't explain it. Perhaps some day we—or our grandchildren—will know the answer. But there is one truth I *do* know; we must never *ever* allow *brutality* to prevail."

Antonio appeared at their door soon afterward, carrying a basket that he said his wife had prepared for their dinner, "Bread she baked early this morning, some cheese, grapes, and smoked salmon. Not the meal that our Mario could have created in our galley—he is not with us this trip—but good, and healthy as well." Next he smiled broadly as he reached into a crimson velvet bag and said "*Voila!* We have also the bottle of spumante that was intended for you last night."

They invited Antonio to join them for the meal and the sparkling wine. "*Non merci;* I have eaten already, but I will lift a glass with you; the Italians are not famous for their *sparkling* wines, but you will find this one to be an exception."

While they sipped, Antonio advised, "An hour ago, we released a pigeon to fly to Cap Ferrat. I feel certain that Georges will dispatch one of *Les Amis* to meet the boat at the port of St. Jean."

The sea became somewhat rough for the hour or so before Antonio sighted the lights of Monaco dead ahead, and started a sweeping turn to port for their final run along the coast toward St. Jean.

As the boat tied up, Antonio called them to the deck and pointed to a short man on the dock, waving wildly to them with a snow-white scarf in grand and exaggerated motions. It was Duck, and Juan was standing at his side. Dominique exclaimed, "Look! It is Juan; and he is actually *smiling!*"

Wade shook his head and chuckled, "No one but Duck would dare to chance attracting attention like that, but he's so nonchalant who would dream that he is a *résistant?*"

# Chapter Twenty

"I think that our original plan for *Rapid Return* is largely sound," Wade said to Jean-Pierre and Georges Blanchot, as he stood before a map showing the area from Cap Ferrat southeast to Corsica, the lower two-thirds of the Italian boot, and Sicily. "However, as a result of my visit to the island, I want to suggest some modifications to it.

"First, we may not need submarines for the trip from here to Bastia, if Antonio is willing to transport the returning airmen on a reasonably frequent basis. For a so-called fishing vessel, the *Nicoletta II* is a quite remarkable craft. She is a modified subchaser from the First World War, but since she was reduced in size—and therefore in weight also—during the modifications, she has substantially greater speed than in her military days. My guess is that she can cruise at close to 20 knots with a flank speed of up to 28 or 30 knots.

"She has two large cabins that could be fitted to accommodate—comfortably—at least six passengers in each. She is completely seaworthy, probably much more so than many of the more modern military vessels designed in this era. Finally, Antonio has kept her in *mint* condition.

"I don't think we should totally forget the use of subs, but our primary carrier by sea should be Antonio's boat.

"So, what shall we do with them after we get them to Bastia? The repairs to the airfield should be finished soon, but I don't believe its runways can handle—safely—the B-24s I had visualized using for the flights to England or elsewhere. The Mosquito is one option; I know it could get in and out of Bastia; and it has the speed and range to fly—at high altitudes—to get them home safely, *but* it is very limited in its passenger capacity, and that is a long flight for such a small payload.

"Everything considered, I believe our best bet is to use one of two aircraft; the British Lysander III, *or* the American-made C-47 transport, called the *Dakota* in the RAF—and the *Gooney Bird* by Americans. With its crew of three, the C-47 could still carry 25 or so additional passengers, it has a range of 2,414 kilometers, and those who fly it claim it could land in a plowed field!

"The Lysander is a great little airplane, but has only a single engine—that's not good for overwater flying—and its passenger capacity is not much better than the Mosquito.

"Both the C-47 and the Lysander are very slow for military aircraft and neither performs well at higher—therefore safer—altitudes. If either is engaged—without escort—by an enemy fighter, it is probably doomed."

"Well then," asked Jean-Pierre, "what is our best option, regarding the use of aircraft?"

"My recommendation is that, for the time being, we use either the C-47 or the Lysander—or both—but that they take the airmen to some larger and closer base; let's say in Italy or Sicily, rather than all the way across occupied Europe. From there, the B-24s could be used for the final flight to the United Kingdom.

"Later, perhaps that can change, and we could revert to close to the original idea—with the exception of substituting the Gooney Bird for the B-24—but only when we have attained clear control of the air over continental France. For now, however, I believe we would be risking the loss of our airmen en route back to their duty stations, thereby defeating the primary purpose of operation *Rapid Return.*"

M. Blanchot posed a few more questions, stood and shook Wade's hand, "*Merci* Jean, for a task well done. I will meet with Antonio as soon as possible. In the interim, I will recommend strongly your plan to OSS in London. If Antonio cannot do this—for whatever reason—we will revisit the subject of submarines.

"Now, while you are here I would like to bring in Duc and Juan, for a different discussion. First, let us outline briefly the subject with you."

He said that his informants in Villefranche had reported recently that the Milice had been bringing in huge quantities of ammunition and weapons—including items such as howitzers and other weapons they had not possessed previously—and storing it in the magazine at the ancient Citadelle in Villefranche.

More serious, Blanchot's undercover agent in the Milice had reported that its new local commander had announced that his first order from Vichy was to find and liquidate *Les Amis,* immediately and completely, adding that, "The new cache of arms should make success much more attainable."

Blanchot explained that—during Wade's absence—Jean-Pierre had dispatched Juan and Duck to Villefranche to determine whether the magazine was vulnerable to being 'neutralized.'

At this point, Jean-Pierre spoke up, smiling, "Of course, *Duc* says '*of course,*' but we have learned already that the word *impossible* is not in his vocabulary, *oui?* That is why we need to discuss it again with him and Juan."

"Why Juan?" asked Wade.

"Because Juan had insisted on accompanying Duc to Villefranche. They have become quite good friends since Duc volunteered to make a sharpshooter of him. In fact, Juan is very protective of his new friend—as if he *needed* protection.

"Unbeknown to us previously, Juan has a personal contact in Villefranche—an old friend of his late father, who had worked the bull-rings at Nimes with the father; and he now works at cleaning various parts of the old Citadelle. He tells Juan that the Milice treat him like a 'swine.'

"And—this is the most important part—he claims to have access to the magazine!"

M. Blanchot looked at his watch, "Let us bring them in now; they have been waiting a long time."

When they walked in, Duck was carrying a detailed map of the town of Villefranche, which he proceeded to spread out on the table before them.

"O.K., look here; right over there is this big fort they call the Citadelle, and boy, is it a *big* 'un! This sucker's got walls about six feet thick and like solid *rock.* Then, right over *here,* you got a little underground street called the *Rue Obscure;* 'at's where Juan's buddy Carlos lives. That's his name; right, Juan?"

Juan nodded.

"O.K., so Carlos lives there on this *Rue Obscure*—the wierdest damn street I ever did see—in this little-bitty, sort of cavelike house that's been dug out of the side of this big tunnel. And he's not the only one on the street; he's got a coupla neighbors, but says they ain't nosey.

"But the *good* part is it's only about 100 or 150 yards from the front entrance to the big fort, and Carlos says he's got room for us to store stuff there 'til we're ready to use it. Now let's talk about the fort and this magazine.

"This *fort* has got walls that'd make Fort Knox look like your kids' playpen. Let's face it; I doubt a earthquake would dent it! *But* the magazine'*s* walls ain't near as thick; plus it's on the top deck of the fort and sort of toward the back side. Now, we could tell that the roof of this magazine has been replaced no tellin' how many times. We slipped in with Carlos one night, and I crawled all over it.

"If we can git some of my new stuff inside it—and we *can,* through that roof—we're gonna have the biggest and best fireworks ever seen this side of Hell itself! I doubt the wall's comin' down, but ever'thing inside's gonna either go up in smoke, or be as useless as a tit on a boar hawg if it don't!

"Any questions?" he finished, with a broad smile.

Wade couldn't refrain from smiling to himself at the various expressions on the faces of M. Blanchot and Jean-Pierre as they had strained to understand the accent and downhome expressions of this enthusiastic— and obviously very intelligent—colleague, one whom they had long since come to admire greatly for his never changing *can do* attitude.

Wade spoke up, "Yes, I have a question; it is for Juan. Are you confident that Carlos can be fully trusted? If not, we may be inviting a major disaster."

"Monsieur, I can only tell you that he was my father's best and trusted friend. I am certain that he works for the Vichy pigs only for the reason that he is a simple worker, and must have some way to live—the same reason my papa and his friend Carlos slaved in *les arénes* in Nimes. Even the poor must have bread. You . . . "

"Hold on, Juan. Lemme say sump'in else," Duck broke in. "Cap'n, I know what you're gittin' at. But if Carlos is tryin' to con us, why'd he let us in the fort at midnight, and why would his bosses have let us see the layout of the magazine and still get away alive? The las' night 'ere, we slept at Carlos's little house; he—or they—could have cut both our throats in our sleep, if they'd wanted."

"You may be right," Wade responded. "On the other hand, it could be that they are simply setting the bait to trap more than two *Les Amis,* if the intelligence about the new commander's priorities is accurate."

"I tend to agree with Duc's reasoning, Jean," said M. Blanchot, "but I want to hear his entire plan before deciding. Duc, please outline your plan; *all* of it."

Over the next seven days, Marie-Françoise and Juan made daily afternoon visits to the fishing pier at Villefranche, strolling each evening up the hillside via the *Rue Obscure.* No one seemed to notice that their old valise—labeled as if to hold fishing tackle—always disappeared before they exited the dark little street.

## Atlanta in April, 1944

It was a glorious spring day in Atlanta, the time of year everyone lived for. The Dogwoods had spread their annual cover of glorious white throughout and the city was smiling again.

As mail carrier Jay Robinson finished his work day and headed home, he was immensely pleased to know that he had given at least two women great joy that day. Two letters he had handed to Katie Johnson, and one to young Polly Hearn, both within a few blocks.

Almost every afternoon of every day, for months, each had been at her front door, hoping for a letter from young Will Johnson—whom Mr. Robinson had known as a toddler. He had felt the pain of disappointing them, until this day. When he had noticed the words "Captain Will Johnson" scribbled on the corner of the envelopes, Jay thought, "To hell with Post Office policy; I'm gonna give myself the pleasure of hand-carrying these to these fine ladies!"

The second letter for Mrs. Johnson had been sort of a bonus; it was from her other son, but she had been receiving letters from her son Bill with regularity. Jay handed her that one only after she had wiped away most of her tears and halfway composed herself.

Her letter from Bill said that his crew had almost completed its 25-mission tour of duty and that he would be rotating back to the States soon. He mentioned that he had still not located Will, nor heard from him, but hoped that someone would hear from him soon. He expected to have some leave before his next assignment, and would see her soon.

Blocks away, Polly Hearn was reading her letter for the sixth time. That night she slept with it under her pillow.

The next morning Polly read her letter one more time. She had thought it sounded a little aloof the day before, and it still seemed that way. But she also remembered her brother Joe's remarks about military censors "slobbering" over letters to girlfriends, and told herself that was the reason. She had been relieved that he had said it had been impossible for any mail to be forwarded to him since he had been home; that meant he hadn't simply ignored the many she had mailed.

She was finishing breakfast when the phone rang. Katie Johnson was on the line, and first apologized for not calling the night before, but said that her letter from Will had mentioned that he had also written her and Bill, and she hoped Polly had received hers. Katie also mentioned that she hoped to see Bill soon, that he was expecting to be home for a while.

"What about Will*?*" Polly blurted out, "He must be in a really dangerous job, Mrs. Johnson; why else all this secrecy? If he *must* go through whatever it is they're putting him through, he should be able to get away from it sometimes too!"

"I know; believe me, I do know. I pray every day and every night that he's all right. But Polly—*honey*—*all* the boys are in danger; it's just that Will *chose* to do this work. Nobody else *put* him in it. It's Will—bless his heart.

"As Noah says, he marches to a different drummer; those of us who love him just have to accept that."

"Aw, I know, Mrs. Johnson, I'm sorry. I shouldn't talk like that. I don't mean to worry you more. Thanks for calling me though. I'm sure we'll hear again soon."

The moment she put down the telephone, Katie leaned her head against the wall and sobbed aloud, looking up at the ceiling, "*Lord God!* What did we *do* to make our children suffer these terrible times?"

The massive *Citadelle* at Villefranche Sur Mer has stood for centuries.

One of the great fortresses of the Mediterranean coast, it was built to protect the local citizenry from the many marauders who had sailed that coast in ancient times. The main entrance to its interior faces to the east; it appears to have once had a protective moat and drawbridge, but by 1944 the front entrance was protected simply by a huge and forbidding gate of steel.

At the rear of the fort, another road had been created for access from the west. Exactly at the stroke of midnight of Good Friday, a small group had driven their dull green Citreon the few yards from the *Port de la Darse* up and onto that small service road, and waited until Carlos flashed the signal that he had begun the process of opening the main gate.

The plan was that, as soon as the signal came, the Citreon—driven by Dominique at her prior insistence—would pull around close to but not through the front entrance. At that point, Duck and Juan were to unload the explosives, wiring, and timing devices, and race to the roof of the magazine at the rear of the Citadelle. They would be followed by Wade, carrying two snipers' rifles, ropes, and other paraphernalia for their withdrawal.

During the quiet afternoon of this Holy holiday, Carlos had removed nine square feet from the roof of the magazine at its northwest corner, through which Duck would drop into its interior in order to, as he said, "do my magic." Juan's first task was to lower to Duck the tools of his trade, after which he would stand guard with a sniper's rifle until Duck climbed back out. Meantime, Wade was to secure the ropes and prepare for their rappelling down the outside of the steep wall to the place where Dominique would have by then moved the Citreon.

All went well until just prior to Duck finishing the setting of the plastique and the timing device. In fact, as Wade was doing his work at the wall, he smiled to himself as he heard Duck actually *humming* while he worked.

But then he heard a woman's scream from the Citreon below. He looked down the 80-foot wall to see Dominique struggling in the clutches of a large man in some kind of uniform, one arm around her neck, the other waving a pistol. Wade had a pistol in his belt, but didn't dare fire for fear of hitting Dominique. Without thinking, he leaned far out over the wall, shouting, "STOP! NOW!"

But the man didn't *stop;* instead he fired at Wade, hitting him in the left shoulder.

Hearing the shot, Juan sprang to the wall—cocking his rifle as he moved—and shouted to Dominique to try to drop to the ground. She dug her fingernails into the man's left eyelid, and squirmed quickly from his grasp and toward the surface of the street; before her entire body had reached it, Juan had squeezed off his first shot, shattering the right side of the man's skull.

As the body jerked convulsively on the cobblestones, Juan carefully placed his second shot into the other side of the skull, then calmly turned to Wade with, "He is finished. How bad are you hurt, Monsieur?"

Duck was emerging from the magazine as Juan fired the second round, "What the hell's goin' on up here?" Then he saw Wade bleeding. "Damn! We gotta' get outa' here in 15 minutes flat before she blows, Cap'n. We'll take care of you soon as we hit the ground. But can you rappel like 'at, Cap'n? "

"Maybe," said Wade. "If not, I'll have to slide down the rope; but it'll take longer. Let's just hope nobody heard those shots and gets curious."

"You're gonna be one-handed, Wade. If you slide that far, you're gonna *fry* your hand. Here; take my gloves I was using in the magazine just now. And let's put your rope right next to mine. If you git to feelin' like you ain't gonna make it, *holler* at me; if we hafta', you can git on my back. I ain't leavin' ya—'at's for damn sure!

"And Juan; *you* git on down 'ere with Dominique, *fast* as you can! Take my rifle too, just in case anybody shows up lookin' for trouble.

"Now let's all *move* it before we gitta be part of the fireworks!"

It required what seemed an eternity for Wade to slowly make his way down the rope, a foot or so at a time; but make it he did, thanks to Duck's gloves, as well as the fact that he discovered that he could make some use of his left hand.

Duck stayed at his side the entire way, glancing at his watch periodically. The second they touched the cobblestones he shouted, *"Ever'body in the car! In exactly three minutes she's gonna blow!"*

When Dominique started to run toward Wade in tears, Duck grabbed her by the arm, "No time for that now! *Git* in the car and *git* it started; you're drivin' and I'm gonna be in the back seat tryin' to stop 'is bleedin'. Juan, rip the belt off 'at dead sum'bitch, so I can make a tourniquet for Wade. And *move* it—*move* it—*move it!!* We gotta git out'a here, and *fast!"*

The old Citreon seemed to rocket off as Dominique jammed the accelerator to the floorboard and gunned it up the hill and away from the wall of the Citadelle. They had barely rounded the first curve, when they heard a thunderous explosion, and felt the little auto shake from the concussion. Duck had just tightened the tourniquet on Wade's arm for the first time, and let out a loud *whoopeeeee* at the blast, and another—even *louder*—when the sky lit up over the old fort behind them.

As they wound their way up the narrow winding road through a residential neighborhood of Villefranche and toward the Moyenne Corniche, people were already in the streets in their sleeping clothes, or calling questions from their windows, about the explosion that had rocked the entire town.

When they reached the Corniche, Duck told Dominique to pull over, so they could change places. He explained to her how, and how often, to loosen the tourniquet and—with a big wink at Wade—added, "I'm pretty sure our patient would ruther have you here than me."

Georges Blanchot had been standing on the balcony of his Cap Ferrat chateau since midnight listening for the blast, as had Jean-Pierre from the ancient ruins at the summit at Eze Village. Both breathed a sigh of relief when they heard it, and each shouted a loud, "*Bravo, Duc!*" into the clear night as they saw the promised *Fireworks by Duc* light the sky for miles around.

A quarter hour later, Jean-Pierre and Isabelle had walked down to the Corniche, and were anxiously watching for the green Citreon to cross the high bridge a few hundred yards away.

They slapped hands in celebration as it hurtled across the bridge; but their joy turned to deep concern as they caught their first glimpse of Wade gingerly emerging from the back seat. On the ride over, Dominique had removed her underslip, torn it into strips, and used them to bandage his entire left shoulder and upper arm. But by their arrival, his blood had soaked the bandages so completely that one would think the wound to be a grave one.

Jean-Pierre ordered Isabelle and Juan, "Take him—*at once*—to the home of old Doctor Champion. He will have retired hours ago, but he will understand our need. We cannot chance waiting the night; the bullet may still be in his body, possibly even near his heart!"

He then turned to the now near-hysterical Dominique, who was moving to assist with Wade. "*No,* Dominique! You *stay!* Your tears will not help our comrade, and may only distract the doctor in his work."

The old doctor answered the door in his nightshirt and cap, being careful to peer through the glass part of the door before opening it. He recognized Isabelle immediately, and waved them in. Without asking a question, he told them to take Wade to his basement where—in the summer of '41— he had converted his former wine cellar into a makeshift treatment room, and where he kept most of his surgical instruments. The room had proved adequate on several occasions, except for the less than bright lighting. Juan helped Wade onto the table, while the doctor stood on a stool and lit two large lanterns suspended above the table.

With Isabelle assisting, he cut away the makeshift bandages and Wade's shirt, then bathed clean the entire shoulder and arm.

Five minutes into his examination he stopped, washed his hands, slowly removed his spectacles, turned, smiled, and said very quietly, "He is a very fortunate young man. The missile entered his upper arm *here,*" pointing with one end of his glasses, "and it exited *there,* on the backside of the arm; no *bone* touched, nothing but *flesh,* as well as some relatively unimportant blood vessels—hence the bleeding. Barring an infection—which is unlikely, in my opinion—he will need some time for full use of the arm, but should be well able to perform most ordinary tasks within two to three weeks.

"I called him fortunate because if that missile had entered his chest only a few inches away, there is good possibility that he would now be a corpse! Take him home, Isabelle—and urge him to thank his God tonight."

After hearing the good news from Isabelle, Jean-Pierre embraced Wade, and asked to see him early the next morning, privately.

The sling Wade wore at breakfast prompted questions from David and others, but Dominique—sitting in her normal place beside Wade—appeared to be on the verge of weeping, until she stood and excused herself abruptly, with half her meal left on her plate.

When Wade walked into Jean-Pierre's room, he found him standing at the window, staring out into the usual morning mist. As the young Frenchman turned, he said, "Please sit down my good friend. I have something rather personal that I feel I must discuss with you; it involves Dominique, and an error in judgment that *I* made.

"Jean, we are fortunate indeed that we did not lose you last night. You could have easily been killed. Of course, that is a risk we assume in our work daily, but it is also one that can—and should—be minimized by sound and rational command decisions.

"Of course, you are certainly not under my command, but Dominique *is.*

"When she learned that you were to be on the mission in Villefranche, she came to me, and first demanded—then *pleaded*—to be there with you. Against my better judgment I relented and agreed for her to go—a terrible mistake on my part. Dominique is of great value to our group, but not as a combatant; she is not trained for it. There were at least three others of *Les Amis* available—and better qualified than she—whom I could have used; instead, I allowed her emotional appeals to over-rule my reason. I . . . "

"What did she do wrong?" Wade asked.

"Nothing! Absolutely nothing!" Jean-Pierre answered, "But hear me out now, my friend and valued comrade; and I trust that you will not be offended by what I am about to say.

"All of us have noticed—with much pleasure and pride—the growing affection between you and our dear Dominique. I have no problem with that—none whatever—*unless* it endangers one of our group, as I believe it did *you* last evening. Why do I say this?

"When she was attacked and called out—precisely as she *should* have done—you shouted, according to Juan, something such as '*STOP*' to her assailant, *oui?*"

"Something like that, yes; but only because I doubted the wisdom of using my pistol from that distance. "

"But—and please do not get angry with me, Jean—did you truly believe that *shout* would deter him?"

"No. But what else could I have done?"

"Where was Juan, with his sniper's rifle, Jean? A meter away?"

"O.K.—I see your point. But that kind of mistake could be made by anyone."

"Conceivably, yes. But in our work we are wise to—how do you say it—*reduce the odds* if we can. I believe that you would have been more likely to re-act logically and objectively if there had been one of us—*other than* Dominique—being threatened below that wall. And the same would apply to *me,* if I were in a similar situation and concerned about someone I love—that is only *human.*"

"I understand. You're probably right; but what do we do about it?"

"It is most important to me that you *do* understand; that is why I wanted this very private conversation with you. In the future, when the decision is mine, I am *not* going to allow her to persuade me to place the two of you in such a position again, and I wanted you to know my reasons.

"I think it best if we keep the reasons between ourselves, but only with your full concurrence."

Wade stood and smiled, "You have it, *mon ami.*"

As he opened the door to leave, Wade paused, then looked back over his shoulder at Jean-Pierre, "And I *do* thank you very much. You are very perceptive. The more I'm around you, the more I think that you were born to lead."

Following Dr. Champion's instructions, Wade stopped by his home a week after the injury. Dominique had asked to accompany him.

The doctor removed the bandage, examined and cleaned the wound. "Ah good; it is progressing satisfactorily. However, the bandage should be changed more frequently; the one concern I have is possible infection. Is there anyone who could do that for you? Perhaps daily?"

"*Yes;* I will do it Doctor, if you will show me how," answered Dominique.

"Good. Also, I would be less concerned, Jean, if you could avoid septic conditions for a minimum of—shall we say—two weeks. I know well the work of *Les Amis,* and the conditions under which you work are sometimes far from antiseptic."

"I understand, Doctor, but in war we cannot always choose our conditions."

"Oh yes, I know that to be true. But the reality is that you will be of little value for *war*—physically—for several days. Indeed, I can visualize some scenarios wherein your presence—in your condition—could be a hindrance to your comrades. I urge you to discuss this with Jean-Pierre; this would not be a first for *Les Amis,* I assure you."

Wade stood, "Sorry, Doctor Champion. I appreciate your concern and your advice, but I don't intend to do that. I feel quite certain that he will tell me if this becomes a problem. If you are finished with me, sir, we should go now."

Dominique tugged on his sleeve, "Not yet. Not until the doctor shows me the proper way to change the bandages."

Both were completely silent as they walked back up the path until they reached the door of Dominique's room. She stood on tip-toes to kiss him on the cheek, and said, "The doctor is right, you know. Even soldiers are given a rest at times. I have friends in Cassis; a few days in the sun there would do wonders for you—and for *me.*"

She smiled back at him—somewhat impishly, he thought—as she quickly closed the door behind her.

Georges Blanchot was in a mixed mood when the meeting opened on this first Monday in May. He had asked that only Wade, Duck Isabelle, and Jean-Pierre be present, because of the extremely sensitive nature of the matters to be discussed.

He was still savoring the destruction of the Milice's magazine at the Citadelle, and was pleased to report that Antonio had enthusiastically agreed to the increased usage of his boat in *Rapid Return.*

However, he said he was sad to say that he had been advised—over the weekend—that the major Allied military operation scheduled for the Riviera had been postponed. "Apparently *Operation Anvil*—that is what it is called—is still possible, but not as early as originally planned. Unfortunately, this means that we must wait to reclaim this part of our nation.

"OSS was greatly impressed with Jean's plan for *Rapid Return,* and the Americans are arranging—while we speak—for the aircraft and support systems necessary for its early implementation.

"And Duc, they were no less impressed with your innovative approach to our recent raid at the Citadelle. All of which brings me to the primary reason we are in this room today.

"Before I speak, please remember that what I am now about to tell you *must never* leave this room!

"The Allies are now preparing—and have been doing so for *months*—to assault Hitler's *Atlantic Wall*. The codename is *Operation Overlord*.

"Only a handful of high-level people know where the assault will take place. It could be anywhere from Denmark to the westernmost Atlantic coast of France; but the most likely location is somewhere in France on *la Manche*—the sleeve of water that the English call *the English Channel*—because of the shorter distance from the English coast.

"One possible area is in Normandy, one of many coastal areas where the Germans have heavily fortified their *Wall* by means of a massive construction program that has been underway for years.

"There, one of the most serious concerns of the Allies is a series of fortified bunkers—'small fortresses' would be a more apt description—which have been built to command the beaches where an Allied landing might take place. Most were built by the hands of Frenchmen who have been forced to labor on sites such as the one called *Pointe du Hoc* and similar places.

"OSS needs not only better intelligence regarding these sites, but also some innovative expertise—such as was devised and executed by Duc and others at the Citadelle—regarding how to best destroy or neutralize them—*if* Normandy should be selected as an assault site.

"Our immediate task is to form a select team to go to Normandy, gather intelligence, and possibly recommend a plan of action, for possible later execution by us or others. OSS has ordered that *Duc* and *Jean* are to be part of this team. I need your decision regarding the others, as soon as possible.

"Time is of the essence."

On the way back to Eze, Duck could hardly contain himself. "This has *gotta* be the big 'un, fellers! Ever'body an' their brother knows we been buildin' up a helluva army in England. Makes no damn sense if we ain't comin' the shortest way—'cross 'at channel and right *at* the bastards. Last I heard—befo' we left England—was it was gonna be at Calais where we'd land. They said Patton was directly across the water from there, cussin' and raisin' hell like always, buildin' up a new army, pawin' the ground and raring to git after the Krauts near their own backyard.

"Course, the Calais talk could be just a *feint*—*we* may be headed to where the *real* action's gonna be."

Wade and Jean-Pierre met as soon as they arrived at Eze, trying to decide what they could expect to be doing in Normandy, and thus who should go. Jean-Pierre expressed concern about Wade's arm, but Wade waved him off, "That's a moot question. Colonel Hebert's footprints are all over those orders from OSS. He expects me there, and there's no way I'm gonna let him down. Besides, it's much better since I dumped the sling two days ago. I'll be ready."

Jean-Pierre nodded, "Of course I expected that. I believe that we will need Isabelle, Juan, Frederic, and possibly Bridgette and David. Together with you, Duc and myself, that would be eight. Is that too many?"

"Depends on what we anticipate doing and *how*. For example, why did you name those five?"

"Because I think we will need to develop a great deal of rapport with the locals; getting to know some who actually did work on the enemy forts would surely be useful. Hence we need Isa, Frederic, and Bridgette; also, Isabelle can do our radio—in four languages if needed—and, in a *fight* she is not too bad either.

"And Frederic? He's French, also fluent in German, and handles a weapon almost as well as Juan. Perhaps we should leave David here to be in charge while we are gone?"

"You're a better judge than I; let's go with the seven."

"Be prepared, Jean; Dominique is not going to be happy with this. Help me with it if she complains to you."

"I don't relish it, but I'll do what I can. The *truth* is sometimes useful; she's simply not trained for combat. And, though I don't dare say it to her, to you I will confess that I'm glad she isn't going, because you were right about my emotions at the Citadelle."

# Chapter Twenty-One

On the morning the group was to depart, Georges Blanchot met with Wade and Jean-Pierre at Eze. He gave them contact information for local *résistance* leaders in Normandy, in the cities of Caen and Carentan, as well as the village of Ste-Mére-Eglise, all of which were fairly near potential landing beaches. He especially recommended that they contact Claude-Paul LeFevre at Ste-Mére-Eglise—another university classmate of his—who had been endeavoring to map and record the details of the German fortifications from their beginning.

Claude-Paul had interviewed dozens of Frenchmen who had labored in their construction, and many had related to him the most minute details of their work. Each had also expressed embarrassment at having aided in the construction, but explained that they had desperately needed the paltry wages for the survival of their families.

It was a sad farewell for Wade when Dominique walked slowly away. He had tried to reassure her that their mission was not dangerous, but her tears told him he had failed.

It was the sixteenth of May, 1944, when they reached quiet and beautiful Ste.-Mére-Eglise, which was destined to become the first French town to be liberated from the Nazis, following the Allied landings in Normandy.

Unknown to any except the very highest levels of Allied political and military leaders, the nearby beaches would become—exactly three weeks later—the most famous in the history of warfare. To an entire generation of Americans, beaches that were to be forever called *Omaha* and *Utah* would become sacred ground, consecrated by the blood of young men— many of whom were still *boys*—who would leave their youth and their lives there in order that the rest of us could live free.

But there were others who had planned a far different future for the world. And they were determined to resist and destroy any and all opposition to the grandiose scheme of their *Fuehrer* to be master of the world.

Along the entire coastline of western Europe, a multitude of fortresses built almost entirely by the sweat of forced—often slave—labor, stared westward at the sea in mute but menacing witness to that determination.

Claude-Paul LeFevre had lived and written in his adopted city of Ste-Mére- Eglise for more than a decade by the time France had fallen to the Nazis. He was a serious student of history, and had written two successful historical novels after his early retirement from his law practice in Paris. He had always claimed to be a realist in all things; thus he—along with many others—had retained little hope for regaining the blessings of freedom in his lifetime, after Hitler had conquered all of western Europe save for the British Isles.

However, on the evening of December 7, 1941, he had felt a sudden burst of hope for freedom in his time. While the Nazis celebrated their Axis friends' attack on Pearl Harbor, Claude-Paul had his personal and private celebration, but for a different reason.

Unlike many Europeans, he had studied American history thoroughly and objectively—and not only from books. During each summer of the three years he had spent at the University of Virginia as a law student, he had traveled, due to the urging—and the largess—of his well to do parents, in much of mainsteam America, from the industrial midwest to the Mexican border, to the mouth of the Columbia River, and back to the Shenandoah Valley each September.

He had come to know and admire the real people who made up the country's heart and soul. And he knew that the Japanese had just awakened a sleeping—but mighty—giant. Even better, the giant was now an ally of his beloved France.

Now convinced that the day would eventually come when it could be useful, on January 1, 1942, he made his first methodical entry in his journal, relating to various German activities in his region.

On the same date, he decided it would be useful to take up the hobby of birdwatching, with emphasis on photographing those he found along the local beaches. As the soldiers in the German garrisons manning the new forts grew in number, Claude-Paul LeFevre had become a familiar figure to them as the bookish-looking little man cycled daily amongst them.

By the date of the visit to him by *Les Amis,* there were 17 small volumes of his journal, indexed fully, complete with hand-drawn maps and recreations of floor plans of German military installations along a six-mile stretch of the coastline on either side of what was to become Omaha Beach.

The hundreds of photographs Claude-Paul had taken of the Wehrmacht sites were to prove quite useful. Oddly, each scene had some species of *bird* in the foreground.

Wade couldn't believe his eyes when the records were retrieved from behind Claude-Paul's bookcase and spread before him, Jean-Pierre, and Duck for their review.

With typical German efficiency, the forts had been well constructed. Most were dug in more than 20 feet below ground level and then covered by dirt and sod, with the aim of minimizing their vulnerability to seaborne artillery or aerial attack. There were tunnels and trenches for underground movement of men and some materials, as well as some limited living quarters underneath those which the Germans considered key to the defense of their *Fortress Europe.*

The amazing part was that the work had not been done by heavy machines; practically all was done purely by pick and shovel, in the hands of men only.

After hours of poring over Claude-Paul's records, he suggested that they might understand better the situation if they actually saw one or more of the forts. He said he would arrange it for the next morning, because it must be in daylight for them to appreciate what they would view.

Shortly before daybreak, an entourage of Jean-Pierre, Wade, and Duck, led by Claude-Paul, had entered an old bombed-out house on a knoll no more than 300 meters from the huge fort at *Pointe du Hoc.* The fort was where—thought the Allied High Command—the enemy was housing some of its most deadly and effective artillery—its 155-mm cannon. Its importance lay in the fact that it commanded ingress to the beach later to be designated by the Allies as *Omaha,* and that the only access from seaside was up a sheer cliff more than 100 feet high.

At first light, they climbed the rickety stairs to a second floor bedroom window through which they peered at the mighty fort.

All was quiet until there was a long, and low, whistle, followed by Duck's voice quietly murmuring, almost as if to himself only, "*Whooo—weee!* This is gonna be a *tough* nut to crack."

Wade took three photos, and they left.

By twilight that day and early morning the next, they viewed, from a distance, six other lesser but extremely formidable gun and radar positions in the same area. All seemed to verify the accuracy of the drawings made for Claude-Paul by the workers he had interviewed; and all, though not as elaborate, followed a construction pattern similar to the one at *Pointe du Hoc.*

During the three days of their visit, the other four *Les Amis* had been busily getting acquainted with their local counterparts—and, in turn, *their* friends throughout the community—as had been arranged by Claude-Paul. After dinner of the third evening, all met in Claude-Paul's home.

Jean-Pierre opened the meeting, "We came here for two purposes: first, to learn a great deal about the enemy's defensive fortifications; next, to endeavor to devise an effective plan to destroy or neutralize those positions.

"A secondary problem—yet crucial—is that we do not yet know *when* we would be permitted to execute such a plan, or how much prior notice we or others might receive if called upon to proceed with an attack on the enemy positions.

"Regardless, we first need to have a realistic *plan,* without which the amount of notice means nothing. I have asked Duc to give us his thoughts first; Duc?"

Duck swaggered to the front of the room and turned to his audience, "Thanks, Jean-Pierre. Folks, I'm gonna be flat honest about this. Ain't been many times I couldn't figger sumpin' out, but this un's got me stumped, and stumped *good.* Gotta give credit where credit's due; 'em Krauts have built some dandy little forts in these parts, and it's gonna take sumpin' special— *real* special—to wipe 'em out.

"I don't believe any air bombin's gonna do the job—artillery neither. If we're gonna rip 'em up, I think we gotta do it from the *inside.* Maybe— member now, I said *maybe*—'at's the answer. It's kinda like that old Citadelle we saw at Villefranche; ain't nothing gonna bust the *sides* of these places. And the Germans sure thought about *air* bombin, cause it looks like the *tops* are just as thick. So, it's most likely we git to it from the *inside* or nuthin'—at least 'at's the way *I* see it.

"But, ya know, Jean-Pierre, I'd be real in'trested in knowin' what our *scouts* over there have learned while pokin' around town for three days. Maybe they've learned sumpin' helpful."

"Absolutely, Duc," said Jean-Pierre, as he stood. "I think Isabelle is prepared for that."

"We do have some new intelligence. I hope it is credible." Isabelle unrolled one of the maps that Claude-Paul had provided her on arrival, and she and Frederic pinned it to the wall. "First, let's discuss *Pointe du Hoc,* here on the map. We were told something quite startling by a local gentleman who cleans the latrine ditches inside the fortress; he says that is a violation of Wehrmacht security regulations, but that the arrogant Nazi now in command says it is 'Frenchmens' work' and refuses to allow his men to do it."

"So?" said Juan.

"So," laughed Isabelle at Juan's characteristic bluntness. "This man says that there are *no big guns* installed inside the fort! At least, not at this time. Further, he believes that the artillery normally inside this fort—the 155-mm cannon—is now being kept in a building behind, but a bit inland from, the fort itself. He has a cousin who still lives nearby, and he swears that the rail tracks leading from the fort to the other building exist solely to enable rapid movement of the cannon when truly needed."

"Yes; that *is* startling news if true; but *why?*" asked Wade.

"Because of the recently intensified Allied bombings of the fort, according to our informant. The Germans believe that this fort is the *key* to repelling an assault at two important beaches. They are convinced that they would have sufficient knowledge of any serious impending invasion here in Normandy—so distant from the Allied troop buildups in southern England—to enable them to set up their 155s with time to spare. In the interim they do not want to risk even the *possibility* of damage to them from the almost daily aerial bombardments."

"Perhaps your sources know exactly where the artillery pieces are being kept," Jean-Pierre suggested.

"They tell me that they do. If so, why not simply destroy the pieces where they stand?"

"Not that simple, Isa," frowned Wade. "Assuming that could be accomplished, we don't know when *or* where the Allied landings are going to occur. I doubt that anyone—even Eisenhower—knows for certain on the *when;* something like a change in the weather could change the actual date. If we did it too early—and the landings turn out to be *here*—it may alert the enemy and give him ample time to shift his reserves; plus, if it were too early, they might have time to *replace* the guns. We could query London, but our present orders are to do nothing of that sort without express prior authorization."

"O.K.; gotcha!" spoke up Duck. "But how's about gettin some detail on the insides of one of these places. That might give us some help. My guess is if we ever gutted one of these suckers right, it'd take months fur em to fix it agin. Didja git any ideas on how to see the *insides* of one, Isabelle?"

"Perhaps, just *perhaps.* Bridgette and I spent the last two evenings at the bar of the only bistro left in this town. The only reason *it* is allowed to stay open is that it's where the Hun soldiers can always find a whore. And apparently this new commander at the *Pointe* is the best customer, except he refuses to *pay* for his pleasures, whether wine *or* women.

"He says that we French 'owe' him decent wine, and that French women *should be grateful to have a real man, without charge.* What a *pig,*" she spat in disgust, then turned to Bridgette. "Could you finish this, please?"

Bridgette chirped, "*Bien sûr!* I have a small plan to *finish* also this *pig.* Anne-Marie, the *serveuse* at the bistro, told to me, just last night, that *Le Porc*—all the women call him that—has taken some women to the fort to a room under the main level—a sleeping room that he alone uses—and that he has a very small cache of very bad wine there, of which this imbecile is very proud. But this cache is almost empty at this time.

"My plan is simple. I would approach him, pretending to be drawn irresistibly to him; he will certainly *believe* that one, this fool. Perhaps Claude-Paul will contribute a great bottle of wine, as additional bait for my trap.

"I will *purr* into his ear that I desire to see his celebrated *chambre d'amour* at the grand fortress, of which other women have boasted. I will tell him that there we would share a wondrous wine as we look into the very face of God and *create our world for only two.*

"Of course, once there, I will drug his glass. While he sleeps, I shall examine the quarters in detail—possibly with photos included. If you wish— and no soldiers are there to intervene—I will be pleased to garrote him before I depart in the name of all the women this pig has attempted to violate.

"*Voila!* That is my plan. Questions?"

Claude-Paul had listened intently, but with a distinct look of disbelief, to Bridgette's smiling and animated presentation, and was the first to speak. "My dear, are you actually *serious* about this? You could be killed, alone in such a viper pit."

"Make no mistake, sir; she is serious," answered Jean-Pierre, "but her cavalier manner *can* be rather astounding if one doesn't know well our Bridgette."

For another hour they discussed her plan. At the end, Jean-Pierre said he would like to think about it overnight but added, "My tentative feeling is that I would agree only if this could be done late at night, when the German cadre at *Pointe du Hoc* is normally light, and on condition that we have a minimum of ten armed *résistants* within hearing of Bridgette's Derringer and prepared to rescue her forcibly if need be.

"Obviously, such a skirmish *could* interfere with the primary mission of *Les Amis,* and that must be considered fully before a decision is reached. Wade and I will decide tonight.

"Oh yes, Isabelle; please stand by tonight. We may need to radio London."

After the others had gone, the discussion centered around the risk/reward questions raised by Bridgette's idea. "Bizarre as it is," Wade said to Jean-Pierre and Claude-Paul, "it might actually work. But is it worth possibly alerting the enemy if we are not going to be permitted to follow up at once?"

Jean-Pierre looked at Claude-Paul. "Yes; that is a most frustrating factor—not having a timetable to guide us. Do we dare ask London for a clue?"

"I have no problem with asking, but I already know the answer. All legitimate *résistance* units here—along the entire coast—have been informed that we can expect 48 or so hours notice—no more.

"It will be by code, of course, and the codewords are known only to a small number of very select leaders. Most of those are in command of units designated to disrupt German military transportation and communication lines immediately prior to, during, and after the landings. The element of surprise—relative to the exact time and place of the landings—is obviously vital. I certainly can understand why such information is not widely disseminated.

"I abhor being negative," the older man continued, "but I am certain that your call would be futile. We should settle on a plan and then execute or recommend it. Now, that said, allow me to offer my thoughts on the bold and very courageous one presented by your Bridgette.

"Unless *all* goes perfectly—and, as we know, it rarely does—you are going to be required to use your ten armed *résistants* to try to rescue her. Now, allow me to summarize the defenses in place for *Pointe du Hoc,* all of which are described in detail in Volume Fourteen of my journal. First, at its seaside, there is a sheer cliff 40 or so meters high, protecting it from assault from the beaches.

"Shortly after Field Marshal Erwin Rommel assumed command of this region, he made major additions to the defenses. Apparently assuming that the fort is not vulnerable from the seaside, the main perimeter defenses for the fort proper have been erected on the land-side, and they are quite formidable, manned night and day by well-trained troops, many of whom are battle-tested veterans of the Russian front. The slightest indication of gunfire from the bunker—certainly one at night—and one would be confronting a heavily armed force within minutes. And, remember; if you succeeded in reaching her, she would probably be a *corpse* by that time!

Then he smiled, but only slightly, "As you may have discerned, I am opposed to the plan."

"I must agree," Wade said. "Additionally, knowledge of alterations of the interior of *Pointe du Hoc* tells us nothing about that of the lesser forts. Though not as important, they cannot be ignored."

In the end, they settled on several decisions. The *Bridgette plan* would not be attempted, but they would remain in Normandy for another week or more, concentrating on locating more eye-witness sources regarding information similar to that they had obtained regarding the 155-mm cannons. Wade and Jean-Pierre felt that this type intelligence, combined with the detailed data contained in Claude-Paul's journal, should be invaluable to the Allied commanders if Normandy had been selected as the site of the invasion.

By noon on June 5, they had finished compiling their report—including a verbatim copy of Claude-Paul's journal, laboriously made by *Les Amis* at night over more than a week. By day's end on June 5, the voluminous report was delivered into the *résistance* courier system and on its two-day journey to London.

At ten o'clock that evening, the seven of *Les Amis* were making their way across the Loire Valley, returning to Eze.

Exactly two hours and fifteen minutes later, the first stick of young American paratroopers jumped into the night sky above the town of Ste-Mére Eglise.

The courier had gone to bed early at a safehouse in Le Havre.

# Chapter Twenty-Two

The thatched-roof cottage beside a small clear stream had been quiet when the seven had arrived after midnight the night before. They had been greeted by the elderly owner in his nightshirt and shown at once to the cellar where he said they could sleep as long as they wished the next day.

But now Wade had been awakened by excited chatter—a man and a woman, in rapid French—and a radio voice, laced with static. He glanced at his watch and it showed 7:00 A.M.

He thought the radio voice sounded like a BBC transmission, so he pulled on his trousers and climbed the stairs to his host's kitchen. M. Broussard and his wife were leaning over the table, listening intently to a tiny radio they had pulled from its hiding place in a large and battered coffee can.

Their wrinkled faces were beaming with obvious delight, and they burst into tears of joy when they saw him enter the room. Both rushed to embrace him, "*Merci, merci, Monsieur! Merci à Dieu et à vous! Les Americains sont ici! Dans Normandie ils sont arrivé!*"

By then, Jean-Pierre had also emerged from the stairs. Wade said to him, "They are talking so fast I can't understand them. Why are they so excited?"

Suddenly Jean-Pierre was also excited, "They were thanking you! *And* others! And are saying that the Americans have arrived—in *Normandy!!* It *must* be the landings. *Merde!* We must have just missed them!"

Soon, there were nine gathered around the radio, with Jean-Pierre ordering, "*Silence!* We need to hear this!" The voice at BBC was starting to repeat—in slow but clear French—what was apparently a pre-recorded message:

"Greetings to the people of the great French nation.
Your moment of liberation has commenced. Shortly after midnight last evening, airborne units of the United States of America and Great Britain led the greatest military force ever assembled into a crusade to liberate France— and *all* of Europe—from the yoke of Nazi oppression.

"At 6:30 this morning, the grandest armada of military vessels in history, representing free nations from the entire world—including Free French forces yearning to free their homeland—appeared off the shores of Normandy, from whence they are now dispatching onto the beaches the legions of dedicated young men who shall deliver the blessings of liberty to all of Europe.

"Take heart! Your freedom is near!

"VIVE la FRANCE!"

As it ended, everyone cheered lustily, except Wade, Jean-Pierre, and Duck, who stared silently and a bit sadly at each other.

Wade spoke first, "I know what you're both thinking. Our report was too late. We should have destroyed the 155s *without* the damned report!"

"Yep! Maybe, Cap'n. But ain't no use lookin' back. As my Daddy always said, 'Somebody might be gainin on ya.' Let's look straight ahead; it's still gonna be a long war. We got lots more butts 'at need kickin' 'fore we're done."

"You are correct, Duc," added Jean-Pierre. "We did our duty as the situation dictated. It is difficult to ask for more. We will have other opportunities."

### London—June 8th, 1944

It had been the most tense two days of his life, as Colonel Louis Hebert had anxiously awaited news about the landings. He, like all the others directly involved in the planning of *Operation Overlord,* had long ago faced the reality that D-Day might result in a disaster of immeasurable proportions; one that could literally impact dramatically on the whole of civilization.

Now, on D-Day plus Two, he was relieved by news of the expanding Allied foothold in Normandy, yet devastated at the price already paid for that success. As he strode down the hallway toward the main OSS conference room, he was handed a large packet—the report of *Les Amis.*

He knew he was early for this unusual evening conference, so he took it with him, planning to read at least the Summary pages before everyone else arrived.

When he finished the third paragraph of the second page, he *exploded.*

"*God-damn it!* Look at this damned report. Just *look* at it!" He was livid, and storming around the OSS conference room. "Wade Johns' boys *knew* the damned guns weren't in the damned fort more'n a week ago, and could have taken care of them. If we hadn't been so damned paranoid about security, we would have told *him*—one of our absolute *best* agents—the date we planned for D-Day. Then maybe we wouldn't have lost so many good men tryin' to climb that damned 100 foot cliff with some friggin' *fire department ladders* that some dumb-ass dreamed up."

One of the two others already in the room looked at him, disapprovingly. "Calm down, Louis; the Rangers found the guns anyhow, and wrecked 'em. Those 155s never fired a round at our guys. No damage was done."

"Like *hell* there wasn't! Are you *nuts?* Why the hell would we have sent the Second Rangers, one of our *best* units, straight up that damned cliff—with the god-damn Germans dropping grenades in their faces every foot of the way—if *Les Amis* had already wiped out the damned guns? And they *could've. WHY,* DAMN IT—*WHY?? We lose some damned good men—for no* good *reason*—and you say *'no damage?'*"

He paused a moment, glaring at his two colleagues, then picked up a water pitcher and hurled it against the far wall, with, "You call having 135 Rangers dead or wounded—out of 225—*'no damage'?* What the hell's *wrong* with you? How the hell can you *say* somethin' like that? If you cain't answer that, *shut up* and get the hell out of my sight! "

"Best that we leave him alone, Joe," whispered another agent. "I know you mean well, but we're only making him worse. Let's let him calm down some; then we can discuss the other—*bigger*—problem with him. Buzz the others and tell them to hold up for about an hour; *then* we'll start the meeting."

It had required longer than planned for the seven to reach Eze. But they had taken great pleasure in the changes they had observed in the French citizenry encountered by them during their return. Despite the enemy propaganda claims of their *victories* in the fighting at Normandy, even the Germans were now conceding that the Allied beach-head was expanding.

It seemed to Jean-Pierre—and the other four French *résistants*—that, in every village through which they passed, there was a distinct bounce in the step of their compatriots that had all but disappeared during the dark days that had passed since the spring of 1940.

For themselves, they sensed that victory was at last in sight, and were eager and impatient for their next opportunity to hasten its arrival. All felt they had failed in their Normandy mission, and the four French had barraged Jean-Pierre and Wade with questions, primarily questioning *why* they could not simply return to Normandy and join in the fighting for control of French soil.

After three days of that, Jean-Pierre's patience was exhausted, "Because we too are *soldiers!* We follow *orders.* That is *why* enough! Our orders will come soon; until then, save your energy for *fighting,* not *talk!* And I want to hear no more talk of failure! We did our *duty,* and we did our best. It is for others—not us—to judge our success or failure. "

It was the fourteenth of June when they finally walked wearily up the path toward the summit of Eze Village as the sun was lowering itself. On the way up from the corniche, Duck had noticed some flyers taped to nearly every utility pole along the way. He could tell, even from a distance, that all were red, white, and blue. He stepped over to pick one off the next post, and could then see that all four borders of the two pages consisted of a series of small *fleurs-de-lis.*

At the top of the first page, Duck saw the headline:

## *"L'heure est prés pour reconduire notre liberté!!!"*

*"Les Amis de Liberté"*

He flipped quickly to the bottom of the second page, and saw a bold facsimile signature:

*Dominique*
l'Historienne
Les Amis de Liberté

Duck yelled, "Hold up ever'body! Tell me what 'is paper's sayin'. Looks like sumpin' signed by *Dominique.*"

Jean-Pierre reached for the flyer, "It first says that '*the hour is near to take back our liberty,*' then it describes the Normandy landings, telling that American, British, and '*some of our own Free French,*' are now pushing the '*blood sucking*' Nazis across northern France. It is urging the entire populace to defy the Milice and sabotage the *other* enemy also, at each and every opportunity, stating that each blow—however slight—will bring nearer our '*moment of complete liberation.*'

"*Mon Dieu*—this is strong! I hope—and assume—that Monsieur Blanchot knew of it before it was distributed. Let's locate our *petite historienne,*" he smiled, "and find out."

They learned that Dominique had gone to Cassis with Monsieur Blanchot, but was expected back at any time. David told them that the flyer they had seen was the second written by Dominique, printed by some friends of hers in Cassis, and distributed by *Les Amis,* all since D-Day.

"And *yes,* the action had been approved by Monsieur, but only after much insistent urging by Dominique," he assured Jean-Pierre and the rest. However, the overwhelmingly favorable public reaction to the first paper had dictated the follow-up.

In it she had related chapter and verse of the Allied successes during their first two days on the Normandy shores—as well as the supreme sacrifice made by many young Americans who had never heard of France three months prior to the last day of their lives. She had also described the victorious entry into Rome by the American Fifth Army on the day prior to D-Day, with special attention to the details of the cheering residents of the Eternal City.

David continued, "Admittedly, some of it may have been motivated by no small feeling of shame but, whatever the reason, it seems that a new resolve for defiance has swept this region, attributable by many to Dominique's handbills.

"The Milice, in Nice as well as Villefranche, has been so vilified by the general population—often publicly—since the first distribution, that they have almost disappeared from sight. We hear that there have been massive desertions from their ranks, and Monsieur Blanchot seems convinced that their effective influence here on the Cote d'Azure is finished."

It was almost midnight when Wade answered the knock at his door, and received a long, warm embrace from Dominique. It only ended with an affected and loud *"Harrumph!"* from Duck's bunk, followed by "Y'all want me to take a moonlight stroll, or sumpin'?"

They broke the embrace and laughed; Wade said, "Go back to sleep *mon ami; we'll* take the stroll."

It was a clear summer night, with a beautiful full moon over the Mediterranean, as they walked up through the *jardin exotique* to the ruins of what had once been the ancient chateau of many of the Lords of Eze in centuries past.

They sat on one of the old ledges and silently enjoyed the incomparable view, until she finally broke the silence. "Thank God you have returned safely, Wade. Each night you were away, I prayed to the Virgin for your safe return. I missed you more than I can describe."

"And I you Dominique, but I hope you have not endangered yourself un-necessarily by signing the papers you have so eloquently prepared. Why did you think it was necessary to *sign* them?"

She smiled, "That is the exact question I was asked by Monsieur Blanchot; I will give to you the exact answer I gave to him. Until recent times, the majority of my people have seemed to be resigned to the fate of being vassals to the Germans. I say that not in a condemning sense; the Nazis are brutal adversaries, and it is not an easy matter to oppose them. But, whatever the reason, it is the truth.

"But now we have an opportunity to be brave, to be *bold,* to actually be *actors* in tearing the shackles of Nazi domination from ourselves. The German military presence is almost *nothing* in the south of France at this time; they are either busily opposing the relentless Allied march up the Italian boot, or they are rushing north to attempt to prevent the Allied breakout from the Normandy beachhead. If we—the people of France—step forth and do our bit, we can be of great assistance.

"It was my feeling that if a French *woman* actually signed the papers, perhaps it would cause many men—hopefully, some women also—to take heart and rise to action.

"And—judging from the reactions to my papers—I believe I was right."

"You may have been right, but it has probably marked you as a special target with the Milice as well as the Germans; and I think it was a risk you should not have taken."

"All of us are at risk; this adds nothing more for me. It is nothing indeed, compared to that of the thousands of young men, few of whom were Frenchmen, who were willing to die on the Normandy beaches last week. And many of them *did* die there in order that the enslavement of the French people can come to an end.

"And I must tell you something else. If you go out again, I intend to be there with you. I plan to see Jean-Pierre tomorrow to settle that. I know his reasons, but I expect to remind him that there are more ways to further our cause than simply physical combat. I did not come to *Les Amis* to be a shielded violet."

The next morning, Georges Blanchot was already in the boathouse meeting room when Wade and Jean-Pierre walked in. He congratulated them on a successful Normandy mission, saying that there had been a decoded message from Colonel Hebert waiting for him on his return the previous evening. The message praised the work of the seven, and added that the journals and maps of Claude-Paul the seven had sent to London had already proven invaluable to Allied Intelligence, since they had contained a great deal of detailed information on German military activities and installations reaching far beyond the Normandy beaches.

The last paragraph of the note said that he and several others wished to confer personally with Blanchot, Wade, and Jean-Pierre at the earliest possible time, concerning a matter of the utmost importance. He requested that they radio him the next day at 9:00 A.M. French time.

It was then 8:30 A.M.

Wade smiled broadly when he heard the booming voice with the Cajun accent, "First thing I wanna know is how ma boy Wade's doin'; you there, Wade?"

"Sure am, Colonel; and everything's fine. Sorry we didn't get the 155 information to you soon enough, sir."

"Forget it son; notcha fault. We have more'n three people in this out-fit now, so natcherly we got our own damn *bureaucracy.*

"O.K. folks, let's get down to business."

In flawless French, he then said, "Monsieur Blanchot and Jean-Pierre; do you prefer that we speak French during our conversation?"

Blanchot answered, "English is fine, Colonel. If we don't understand something, we will speak up *en français.*"

"Fine. Actually this will be short. I—along with two of my colleagues—would like to meet with the three of you at the earliest possible time, to discuss an extremely important—and equally sensitive—matter. I prefer not to discuss the nature of it in detail until we meet. Would it be possible for you to come to London within the next couple of weeks? We now control some good airfields south of Rome. We would arrange to get you there, then on to here on a Carpetbagger B-24 with fighter escort if needed. I don't want to discuss the other travel arrangements *or* dates without coding it. Just tell me *if,* and I'll follow it up with you on the other details. Is that O.K.?"

M. Blanchot glanced inquisitively at his two young colleagues, who nodded assent, and said, "Of course, Colonel. We will await your further contact."

"Good. I already have one message ready to send. You can expect it within the hour. Goodbye gentlemen, and thank you much. Hey, Wade; I'm really lookin' forward to seein' ya, boy!"

Within minutes they received the coded message. It gave two alternate dates, and said he could have them taken to Bastia by American submarine if they preferred, and from there to the airfield near Rome by C-47, with an American fighter escort.

After a short discussion, they decided to use *Nicoletta II,* and M. Blan-chot raised Antonio by radio. It was agreed that he would pick them up on the evening of June 24, inasmuch as June 25 was the date that had been suggested by Col. Hebert for them to be in Bastia.

Before they left, the two younger men asked M. Blanchot once more if there was anymore he could tell them about the purpose of the meeting.

"I assure you that you know as much as I on this one, gentlemen. Apparently it involves something immensely important, as well as very, very sensitive; otherwise, why go to London? We shall no doubt learn more after 25 June. Until then I suggest that we not tell anyone that we are having this meeting, including our local comrades in *Les Amis.* Simply tell anyone who might ask that we are going to review the condition of the airfield at Bastia. *D'accord?*"

"*D'accord,*" agreed both younger men.

In London that afternoon, Colonel Hebert opened the meeting by announcing to the two Agents that he had just received confirmation that he would be meeting on June 26 or 27 with the leaders of the *résistance* group he planned to use in *Operation Top Drawer.* He also stated that, "A high level representative of the U.S. Department of State and of the British Foreign Office will be here also, along with the two of you."

He then leaned over the small table and stared intently at OSS Agent Joe Cassidy and Agent Spencer Stuart of British Intelligence before saying, "So look at me, and listen up *good;* we gotta quit *screwin' around* and find out *exactly* where these birds are working! You keep telling me they're 'in Lausanne' but that's not good enough. We must know exactly—*e-x-a-c-t-l-y*—*where* the assholes are! And I need to know it soon; like *yesterday!* Is that *clear?*"

"We're on it night and day, Louis," Cassidy responded. "Hopefully we'll nail it any day now. Our informants say it's definitely Lausanne, but they don't have precisely the location."

"Well, if they *know* that they're in Lausanne, why cain't they find 'em? Lausanne's not exactly New York City. It's just a small town on the north shore of the lake. Tell 'em to get crackin' if they want the damn money. This ain't horseshoes; *close* ain't good enough. We could well be playing for all the marbles here, so let's start *actin'* like it."

"After today, I want a daily report on my desk every damned morning—*detailing* what we did the day before in this search—until we locate these guys."

As he stood to leave the room, he added, "Understand me?"

"Yeah, we do, Louis," said Cassidy.


## Atlanta, June 20, 1944

Sergeant Mac had searched his mind constantly for three days wondering why Bill Johnson wanted to meet him at the school at night. When Bill called him, he said he was in a "military facility" nearby, and would like to meet at the school when no one—not even Bob the janitor—would be around. The old soldier had asked why, but all Bill would say was, "Let's talk about it Tuesday night. And one other thing; please don't mention our meeting to anyone else—especially not to my folks, *please.*"

Sarge was relieved to hear the night bell ring at half past eight, but a little surprised that Bill was a half hour late. *Not like him,* he mused. As he neared the door he saw through the glass a figure in the familiar summer gabardine uniform, with blouse, worn frequently by Army officers. The figure seemed to be leaning forward in an unusual body position. As soon as Sarge opened the door he understood *why*.

Bill was using a crutch under each arm, and a black patch covered his right eye, and his face was gaunt and pale as a ghost.

It was a spontaneous reaction from Sergeant Mac, and one which he regretted the minute he said it, but he blurted out, "My God almighty, son! What the hell's *happened* to you?"

Bill managed a slight grin, "Just take it easy, Sarge. I'll explain it all, but I need your help with some of it. Where can we talk, *very* privately?"

"*O.K., O.K. son;* we can stop in the Principal's office; nobody's here 'cept us and it's just down the hall, lots closer than my place. Here, let me help you."

"Thanks Sarge, but *NO! No* help of *that* kind—that's rule *number one.* I can walk—it'll be *slow,* but I'll get there. Then I'll explain."

Bob had last oiled the beautiful wood floors of the old school building's hallways two weeks before, after school had let out for the summer. Knowing it would be the last and only oiling until September, he had used more than usual, and they were still slippery in spots. Halfway down the hall to the office, Bill suddenly slipped and fell sprawling. Sarge leaped over and went to one knee to help him up, but was waved off by Bill as he lay flat on his back. "NO, Sarge!" he yelled. "I can get up by myself. Just hand me those crutches, and give me a little time! Excuse my yelling—I know you mean well—but I've *got* to learn to do this myself."

Finally in the office, Bill, now sitting, took a very long breath, smiled for a moment, then said, "Look, old friend, please accept my apology for shocking you like this, but I couldn't figure any other way to do it. After I explain why I need your help—in something extremely important to me— I think you'll understand."

"Nobody in my family has seen—or even heard about—what shocked you so much a few minutes ago, and I don't know how to tell them without half killing my parents, 'specially Mama. I figured that if anyone could help me with this, it would be you. I remember your telling us once—back when we were kids here—about how you had to notify relatives of men who were casualties during *your* war, and I thought you might give me some ideas."

There was a long silence before Sergeant Mac could utter a word. He finally gathered himself enough to say, "Fine son, but first I'd like to know how you got hurt, and how bad. How bad *are* your legs—and is your eye gonna be O.K.?"

"It was supposed to be the next to the last mission for my crew, Sarge. I was the lead bombardier in a larger than normal formation. We were headed again to the German submarine pens not far from the channel. We caught flak like never before. It was when we were on the very last minute or so of the bomb run and almost directly over the target, so there was no way to take any evasive action and still expect to hit our target.

"I had just released our bombs and—of course—the rest of the formation toggled theirs on cue when I released. My pilot had gone into an immediate turning climb to evade the flak, and I had barely looked up from my bombsight, when a shell exploded just inside my nose gun turret no more than a yard from me.

"Ironically, the twin fifties of my gun turret took some of the flying metal and probably kept me from being killed outright. My legs—they're in pretty bad shape, Sarge—one is off just above the knee and the other just below. My left eye is gone—just waiting for a false eye to replace the patch.

"So there you have it. As bad as it seems, it could have been worse. Our co-pilot was killed instantly, about two minutes after I got hit; and we also lost our tail gunner when the German fighters came up to clean up what their ack-ack had missed. At least I'm alive, and thankful for it. They say I darned near bled to death as we limped back to base that day, and I probably would have if it had been a long flight back. But somehow I didn't. Makes you wonder, doesn't it? Why do two men die—within 30 feet of me—yet I survive?

"O.K., so I pouted for awhile. Well, more than just 'pouted'—I was bitter, *real* bitter. If I hadn't been taught in church that the only unforgivable sin is *suicide* I think I'd have killed myself when they told me they had to amputate *both* my legs. There were days when I wished I *were* dead. When I would wake up in a morning and realize again what had happened to me, I'd get sick at my stomach and want to run to the latrine and *puke*. Of course even that wasn't an option—I couldn't *run* anymore!

"Then a miracle happened for me, Sarge—literally a *miracle!* Actually, *two* miracles, The first one I didn't see that way; in fact it pissed me off so much I threw the Orders in the face of the Army Nurse when she first showed them to me at the hospital in England.

"The orders were transferring me to—of all places—the hospital at Fort McPherson, only about *three miles* from the house where I grew up! They thought I'd *love it* because it's close to home, but I *hated* the idea 'cause I'd not decided if, when, or *how* to tell my parents about all this But, like it or not, there I was taken. Have been out there for two months now, getting equipped with new legs and feet, and trying to learn how to walk with them.

"As you know lots of Lakewood people work at Fort Mac, and some used to be at the hospital there. The first week or so there, I'd hide my face whenever any new person showed up in my ward, 'cause I was afraid I'd see somebody who'd known me. I was still thinking seriously about killing myself, but was so screwed up I didn't really know what I wanted to do."

"Well what else happened, son? You said there were *two* miracles."

"Yeah, well, about the third week there, they told me I was gonna have a physical therapist assigned to work with me every day, that it was time to start using my new legs. My doc said I'd like her—that she was a good looking young gal. I guess he was trying to cheer me up, but my first thought was; *What good would that do a cripple like me?*

"That same afternoon I had just finished a short nap and was lying on my left side, just gazing out the window and wondering what to do next, when someone tapped me gently on the shoulder and called me by name, in sort of a whisper, "Excuse me, Bill, but are you awake?"

"I thought maybe I was dreaming but I thought I recognized that voice. I rolled over and there was—of all people—*Polly Hearn.* Do you remember her, Sarge? She went to school here and lived just down the street from my house."

"*Course* I know Polly! She and Will were sort of sweet on each other. I remember she was at your folks' house when they had a party for Will the time he came home. And she and her Dad came to your swearing-in ceremony at the Old Post Office too—'member that? That really *is* a coincidence; but what's she doing at the hospital?"

"*She*'s my second—and most *important* miracle, Sarge. She wheeled me out to the gazebo that afternoon and we talked for hours. About Will, about her, my folks and her folks. She told me that when Will first disappeared, she thought about nothing but him and the danger he must be in, then about me and the other guys we all knew.

"Then she decided to—as she put it—'do something more than just sit home and cry half the day.' She saw a piece in the paper about the crash courses being offered to get more therapists to work with the amputees who were being sent back from combat. She took the course and has been working at Fort Mac hospital ever since. Polly says she is not a fully qualified therapist, but knows enough to do some good with minimal supervision.

"That first day she also told me that she had almost fainted when she saw my name on a chart at the nurses' station on my ward. It had a note—in bold red—that I had requested that none of my relatives be advised that I was there and that all personnel were to respect my wishes until and unless directed otherwise. She promised me that she too would respect that.

"Toward the end of our talk, Polly gave me a real lecture. First, she said she wanted—and intended—to be my therapist. She also told me—in no uncertain terms—that she didn't want to hear any more talk of suicide 'from one of the Johnson boys!' She said, 'WE are going to whip this,' and that 'YOU, Bill Johnson, are going to lead a happy and useful life that will be an example to the world, but *especially* to those thousands of other boys who are going to be coming home with the same challenges before them. God gave you the stuff to do it—so you owe it to others, as well as yourself, to *do* it!'

"So help me Sarge, those are almost her very words, and it was the most uplifting moment of my life. Every day since that first day, Polly has spent not just her required time with me teaching me to walk again, each evening she comes back on her own time. She reads to me, and we play games together. We go outside, sometimes she wheels me out, sometimes we walk—*all* the time we *talk* about everything under the sun. She wants me to go to law school, says I was 'born to be a lawyer, and maybe some day a great Judge.' Last week she brought me the papers I need to apply for law school out at Emory—says she got them from the Dean, personally.

"She's an *angel,* Sarge—there's no other word to describe her. She's made me want to live again, Sarge.

"There's one big problem left though. How do I break this news to my folks—about my *condition,* I mean? Right now that's my biggest problem. They've had enough on them without this being piled on top of them, too. I'm convinced that this war has been harder on many parents than on us younger people. You saw how seeing me affected you—it's gonna be a lot worse for my folks."

"You mean they know absolutely nothing about your injuries, Bill? How can that be? It must have happened a while ago."

"Right, but I wrote them that I was on a desk job in England. I would send my letters to our Squadron Adjutant back there, and he'd mail the letters to them for me. I feel guilty about it, Sarge, but I just didn't have the heart to break the news to them. And my God, if you think I look bad *now*—you should've seen me two months ago."

"I think your parents can handle this, Bill. We've already lost five Fulton men from your neighborhood who are *never* coming home; two of them are somewhere on the bottom of the Pacific, but nobody knows exactly where. I'm pretty sure your folks knew all five, and must have dreaded—every day—that the same might happen to you or Will.

"I think I should go see them first, so the shock wont be quite as bad as just seeing you first. It might help if Polly could be with me; then we bring you to them a day or so later. Why don't I drive you back to the hospital? We can call Polly now, and see if she can meet us there.

"But remember, Bill, the way *you* appear to be handling this is gonna be the *most* important thing that's gonna affect how your parents react to it."

As they drove out from the school parking area, Bill asked, "What else is new around here, Sarge?"

"Very little, except the news we keep gettin' about all our men from Fulton. Your class is spread all over the world, and makin' us proud. Five days ago the Marines landed on Saipan in the Marianas; we got two Fulton men—both from your class—in one of the marine units there. Then there's Johnny Edge—who was always Will's sub on the football team—who has been in the Italian campaign all the way up the '*boot.*' Last Sunday's paper said he was awarded the Silver Star after the Allied breakthrough of the German line south of Cassino; had a picture of him with General Mark Clark himself pinning it on his shirt.

"*God,* you're *all* makin' me so proud, Bill! I just wish I could have been there by some of ya."

"You did your part—and more—Sarge, while all of us were still babes in our Mamas' arms. By the way, I finally got another letter from Will. I'm guessing a little, but I think he's off on some clandestine assignment—being a *spook,* as he calls it—where he can't send or receive any mail. He's probably in up to his ears in God only knows *what*—and lovin' every minute of it.

# Chapter Twenty-Three

The ride over to Bastia was another pleasant experience for Wade. After a few miles at sea, Antonio came down and invited them topside.

He pointed to the running lights of a ship a half mile or so off their stern on the starboard side, saying, "That's an American destroyer. Before I departed Bastia this morning I was told by the commanding officer of the airbase that it will stay near us the entire voyage—pretending to track us as a 'suspicious vessel'—in the unlikely event that an enemy sub should threaten us. It may disappear, then reappear, from time to time during the night, but we shall be always within range of its guns.

"I must confess that it is a comfortable feeling, but thought that you might wonder about it if you noticed it. Sleep well, *mes amis;* there are people in high places who are insisting upon your complete safety!"

Major Larsen met the *Nicoletta II* when it docked the next morning, and had a staff car waiting to take them to the airfield where a C-47 was sitting on the ramp with its crew of three standing by. A half hour later, they were airborne. Taking off in a westerly direction, the Gooney Bird gained some altitude, then did a climbing 180-degree turn and leveled off directly above the island, headed east.

As they looked down at Corsica, the pilot came on. "Welcome aboard, gentlemen; this is Major Jim Brooks, your pilot. As the crow flies, we are about 200 miles from our Italian destination, but our flight plan makes it a little further. Just to be extra careful not to run into any uninvited company, we're gonna cruise almost due south—over the beautiful Tyrrhenian Sea— until we get south of the city of Rome, then we'll turn east to our final destination a few miles south of the city.

"Oh yeah; if you will look out the window on either side of the airplane, you'll see we now have two of our buddies with us. Those two P-38 Lightnings will be ridin' shotgun on this trip, to make doubly certain we're not disturbed."

The pilot then laughed out loud, "*Uh-oh;* they *heard* me. *Wave* at 'em, please, so they'll quit waggling their wings at us, the *show-offs.*

"The crew chief, Sergeant Jack Rogers, has some hot coffee and some rather tasteless army-style rolls back there, if you'd like some. We should be on the ground in less than an hour and a half, so just relax and enjoy the view on this lovely June day."

When they were almost over the Allied airfield in Italy, the P-38s peeled off and landed first, and the two fighter pilots were waiting on the ramp when the C-47 taxied in. Each looked like 'the kid next door,' even to Wade, as they introduced themselves to him and the Frenchmen. While they walked together to the weather shack, they said that they would also provide escort for them and their B-24 across the continent that night as far as Tours in the Loire Valley, where the B-24 would rendezvous with two RAF night fighters for the remainder of the trip to London.

In the shack they met the airplane commander of the B-24, and he traced their planned route on a map of Europe. He said they could relax until a few minutes before 9:00 P.M. when they planned to depart under the cover of darkness, continuing that, "This is because there is still some—but not much—enemy air activity in French airspace, mainly to the east of Normandy where the fighting is still intense."

He traced the proposed flight path northwesterly from the Italian airfield, saying, "We will pass over Corsica, across the Mediterranean to Toulouse, France, near the Spanish border, then we will head north to Tours. From there we plan to sweep in a wide arc over the Brittany peninsula, cross the Channel, pass over Southampton, and on to London.

"This route should not only permit us to avoid running into enemy fighter aircraft, but also there should be few, if any, manned anti-aircraft batteries along our line of flight. Right now the Germans have more than they can handle in the Normandy area, considerably to the east of our route.

"After the rendezvous with the RAF guys at Tours, the P-38s will return to Italy, unless there should be some mix-up in the rendezvous, in which event the Lightnings would continue the escort to London. One great thing about the P-38 is its exceptionally long range, for a fighter; also, due to its twin engines and unusual twin-fuselage design, it carries some *serious* guns and cannon in its nose, which gives it more concentrated firepower than most fighters.

"Unless you have some questions, the driver will now take you to the VOQ—the Visiting Officers' Quarters—where we have a room set up for each of you to get some rest. One of us will check with you about lunch in a couple of hours."

The flight to London was uneventful, and they were met by Agent Joe Cassidy, as they deplaned well after midnight. He showed his credentials and led them to a waiting unmarked sedan. On the drive into the city, he told the three that Colonel Hebert had arranged rooms for them in a small hotel just around the corner from the OSS offices where the meetings would take place. The hotel was owned and operated by British Intelligence, and there would be no need for them to register further; Cassidy already had their keys. He also said that Colonel Hebert preferred that they not give their names—*nom de guerre* or otherwise—to anyone until the meeting.

When they entered the hotel, Cassidy nodded and spoke to the desk clerk by name, as they went directly to the tiny elevator. On leaving, Cassidy said, "Get some rest, Gentlemen; I know you've had a long day. I'll be here at 11:30 A.M. to pick you up. For your breakfast later, call the desk, give your room number, and he will have whatever you like sent to your room. You will have lunch later with Louis at the offices, prior to the meeting. Goodnight for now."

The day was a typical London day—foggy. By the time Joe Cassidy arrived, it had still not burned off. The four strolled the short distance to the inconspicuous old building that was occupied jointly by the OSS and BI.

Louis Hebert was waiting impatiently for them in the lobby, and charged over to embrace Wade before the door had closed behind them. The two Frenchmen smiled sympathetically, as they saw tears welling in the eyes of both Americans, and Georges Blanchot leaned over and whisperd to his countryman, "Now I know that we French are not the only emotional ones."

Wade made the introductions and Colonel Hebert said, walking them down the hall to his office, "It is my great *honor* to meet both of you! I have admired your work—and your exceptional patriotism—from afar. You and your *Les Amis* have been the model for all similar organizations on the continent since I came to my work."

Opening the door to his office, he waved them in, "Come in, please; we are going to have lunch here, so I can fill you in a bit prior to the conference with the others. Mr. Richard Hopkins, one of our Under-Secretaries of State, flew in from Washington last night, and will be joining us for the conference. He will be accompanied by Sir Jerome Alexander of the British Foreign Office.

"I will also have in the conference Joe Cassidy, whom you have already met, and BI Agent Spencer Stuart; both have been investigating—full time, for several months—the matter we will be discussing.

"I would prefer to brief you later, along with the two visiting diplomats, on all the details, but I do want to emphasize—*now*—several matters.

"First, the mission we're going to ask you to perform is extremely dangerous; secondly, it is of the utmost importance to the Allies, and, perhaps, to the future of the free world. Thirdly, it is a mission that must be kept absolutely secret, *forever,* not simply until it is *finished.*

"*Last,* but obviously of tremendous importance, there are two more unique items: *if* you should be captured on this one, you could be treated as spies, and subject to execution; ***plus,*** neither I nor the government of the United States or Great Britain would *admit* that you were working for us."

He paused for a long moment, trying to read the expressions on their faces, then continued, "If I were you, I am certain I would be wondering why—a *large why*—about the last item I mentioned, but I believe you will understand after our meeting; I can only request that you trust me on that for now. One of the reasons I brought you here was in order that you will understand, fully and completely, the special *oddities*—and that word is an *understatement*—of this mission *before* you decide whether to accept or reject it.

"If you do decide to accept it, it must be with full acceptance of the conditions I have mentioned already and perhaps some others.

"However—and this is the main reason for this private meeting between you and me in this room—if you decide *not* to accept it, no one other than those meeting with us today will ever know that you were offered the mission. But I must have your sworn commitment that in that event you will never breathe to *anyone* the purpose of the proposed mission that I will outline today."

He paused for a long moment, looking each man in the eye in turn, before asking, "I must ask each of you now, are you *willing* to make that sworn, and *unqualified,* commitment to me, at this time?"

Georges Blanchot answered first, "On my sacred honor, sir; I *do!*"

"And I swear that also, sir," said Jean-Pierre.

Wade said simply, "The same here, Colonel."

"Good! That's what I expected. Now; one more thing.

"After we have discussed the whole deal today, I do not want any one of you to say—today—whether you accept *or* reject the job. I'm keeping you over through tomorrow deliberately, because I want it to be a truly *considered* decision, after the three of you have had the chance to think about it, knowing what it entails.

"In sum, we *talk* this afternoon; but you guys *decide* tomorrow! Got it?"

The Frenchmen looked a little puzzled, until Wade explained, "'Got it?' means 'Do you understand'?"

At that, all chuckled, and Colonel Hebert said, "Great! Now, let's have a sandwich. And tonight, we're all gonna eat at the Victoria; 'member that place, Wade?"

After a few minutes, Joe Cassidy stuck his head in the door saying that Mr. Hopkins and Mr. Alexander had just arrived and he had taken them to the conference room on that floor. Louis stood and motioned to follow him.

Hebert opened the meeting by first introducing the American and British diplomats, then asking each of the others to introduce himself.

He said that he would try to summarize the reason for the meeting, adding, "I realize that some of what I will be discussing will be repetitious to some of you, but it is very important that everyone here is aware of those items.

"First of all, please believe me when I tell you that it is no exaggeration to say that this operation—which we are calling *Operation Top Drawer*—could be equally important as—possibly *more* than—*Operation Overlord* now underway in Normandy."

He signaled to Cassidy to pass out copies of a two-page letter, as Hebert continued. "Under date of August 2, 1939—almost exactly one month prior to the commencement of this war by the Nazi invasion of Poland on September 1—Albert Einstein wrote a personal letter to President Franklin Roosevelt; a copy of that letter is now before you.

He first states that he believed it to be his duty to bring certain matters to the president's attention. The letter goes on to discuss the work then being done by various scientists whereby uranium could be turned into a *'new and important source of energy in the immediate future.'* He continues by saying that *'The new phenomenon could lead to the construction of bombs,'* and that *'extremely powerful bombs of a new type may thus be constructed.'* He then refers to activities of the Germans, relative to uranium, after the Nazis had taken control of the uranium mines in Czechoslovakia.

"During the time since that 1939 letter, abundant evidence has continued to accumulate concerning the efforts of German scientists to develop a powerful bomb similar to that visualized by Dr. Einstein, and we have proof positive that they have made much progress to that end. Until a few months ago the site for the research was in Germany, and we were preparing to destroy the site—and liquidate the scientists if necessary—by military action, when it suddenly was *moved,* lock, stock, and barrel.

"Recently we learned that it was moved completely *out* of Germany, and—much to our surprise—to the supposedly neutral country of *Switzerland!* Our first information was that it probably was in the vicinity of the French border; later evidence indicated the vicinity of Lausanne; and the very latest intelligence—as of *yesterday*—assured that it is *in* Lausanne, somewhere on the lakeshore. Joe, let's see the map of the area."

After Joe rolled down a wall map, Hebert pointed a yardstick at the map,"Here we have Lake Geneva, called *Lac Léman* by many of the

French. Covering 220 or so square miles, it may be the largest lake in central Europe. A portion of its southern shore is in France, but all of the northern shoreline is in Switzerland, and *there* sits the town of Lausanne, almost exactly at the top of this crescent-shaped body of water. It is a good many miles away from France by land, but only about five miles by water to *Evian-les-Bains* on the French side.

"We must—absolutely *must*—prevent the Nazis from making a bomb that could change, overnight, the course of this war. Those are the Orders we have from the very highest levels of both the U.S. and British governments, as evidenced by the presence in this conference of Mr. Hopkins and Mr. Alexander.

"Unfortunately, as of this moment we have not learned the exact location of the laboratory, but our informants have some rather convincing evidence that it is located in an ancient but renovated religious priory near the lakeside.

"Once we locate it, we still have the problem of how to eliminate it. *Politically,* military action is a last resort. Apparently the Swiss charade of claiming to be a neutral still has substantial value to us and our Allies. That is why our friends Jean-Pierre, Georges Blanchot, and our own Captain Wade Johns, are here today. We need their help.

"We need them to do the job of eliminating this threat." Then, glancing in the direction of Cassidy and Stuart, "And we may need them to also find the exact location if our current sources don't produce that information immediately.

"I have already explained to them that none of them would be allowed to carry any military ID, and if captured, they'd have no protection under the Geneva Convention. Also unfortunately, that our governments would be compelled to disclaim any connection to this operation, be it a success or failure." He then glanced at Mr. Hopkins as he continued, "I've already gone on record to Washington as saying what a crock of *crap* I think that is, Mr. Hopkins, but I'm a soldier too, so we'll try to do this job. And if it's gonna get done, I know of no one to whom I would rather entrust it more than to these three men.

"I've already explained all the screwy downsides to them, and have told them emphatically that I don't want their answer until *tomorrow* . . . "

At this, Sir Jerome Alexander interrupted with a somewhat sarcastic tone, "I find that to be *quite* strange, Colonel."

Hebert's face turned a light crimson; he turned away for a long minute, then glared at the Englishman, "Pardon the expression, Mr. Alexander, but I don't give a rat's ass *how* strange you find it; that's the *way* it's gonna be! Those kinda details *I'm* gonna decide—*nobody* else!

"If these men accept this task, they're puttin' their lives on the line, much more so than normally—under *extremely* difficult conditions—and I have made it crystal clear to my bosses that I will *not* be involved if I have to clear every detail with *any* damned politician—of *any* nationality."

A slight grin slid across Hopkins' face; he had dealt with the independent Cajun's now famous temper before, and was happy not to be the target this time around. He said, "Fine Louis; just take it easy; that's no problem. Let's discuss a couple of other items about which the president himself has expressed a concern. One is about any Communist participation; it relates to concerns of security later, perhaps even extending until well *after* the war. Have you discussed that with these gentlemen?"

"No, Dick; not yet. We may as well do that now.

"Monsieur Blanchot, our President knows this present alignment with the Soviets may—probably *will*—fall apart once Hitler is finished and realizing that, he is concerned that Communist knowledge of this contemplated action would blow our security about it at some time in the future, if that should serve the Soviets' interests.

"Do you have any admitted Communists among *Les Amis?*"

Georges stood to respond. "As you are undoubtedly aware, gentlemen, many French *résistance* units have avowed Communists amongst them. We have only one, and Juan openly admits that he has a different political agenda than the others of us.

"However, I must hasten to add that he has been an important contributor to our work and a key one in several of our missions. At this point, I do not know enough to say that we would need his presence in this operation; but are you suggesting that we would not be *permitted* to use him?"

"No; I am not saying that as an absolute," answered Hebert, "but I have been instructed to explore that subject and, as Dick just mentioned, our president is personally concerned about it." He then turned to Hopkins. "Dick, correct me if I'm wrong, but my understanding is that, in the end, this issue is to be left to my discretion, understanding the preferences you have just indicated."

Hopkins nodded and Hebert continued. "I got no damn use for most Reds, but gentlemen, if there was ever an operation where we've gotta put first things first, it's this one. Plus, we may as well face the fact that anybody who winds up knowing the facts of this operation could go bananas on us some day and spill his guts to the whole damn world.

"Monsieur Blanchot, let's talk about Juan a little more later; we'll work sumpin' out."

Wade spoke up with a question. "Are we restricted in recruiting others whom we may feel we would need for this mission?"

"Not at all, but I would want to be consulted before you act on someone."

"Of course, Colonel. The reason I ask is that I know someone who might well be very valuable for an operation in Lausanne."

"Good. We need that kind of input. But first, let me go further now, in outlining my tentative thoughts, primarily to give you three a basis for deciding *if* you are willing to take on this mission."

The meeting continued for nearly another hour, with Hebert discussing his ideas, assuming that they find that the lab was in fact on the lakeshore. He seemed to be as much concerned with how *Les Amis* could execute a safe withdrawal as with how they could destroy the site and neutralize the scientists

He talked about how they might be able to withdraw by boat to the French side of the lake, and possibly by air from *Evians-les-Bains* to a safer region of France. In regard to that, he asked if Wade had been "checked out" on the British Lysander III. When Wade said, "No, but I know the aircraft and I think I could fly it with a minimum of instruction," the Colonel asked that Wade give some thought to that, suggesting that, if need be, he could arrange to send a Lysander and an instructor to Bastia for that purpose.

At one point Georges Blanchot referred to the *Les Amis* commitment to *Operation Cork the Bottle,* and questioned whether this mission would reduce the ability of *Les Amis* to perform adequately that prior obligation.

"That's a very appropriate question, sir.

"First, I can now tell you—confidentially, please—that *Operation Anvil* will not commence until August, at the very *earliest.* And that, to our surprise, the Germans have committed more forces to Italy that we ever dreamed they would. That factor, together with their obvious need to move forces to Normandy and its environs, has depleted dramatically their military strength in the south of France, the net result being that when *Anvil* commences we are almost positive that the enemy resistance will be light.

"I can understand well that the liberation of that area has a high priority in your heart, Monsieur; after all, it is your home. But I assure you that your group's proven skills and courage are much more needed in *Operation Top Drawer.*"

Colonel Hebert led his three visitors back to his office before they left the building. There he urged them to discuss their decision privately that afternoon, and be prepared to give him an answer the next day.

As he walked them to the door, he said he would pick them up for dinner at 7:30, slapping Wade on the back and laughing, "Boy! I'll never forget that dinner you and I had with Andre and Joe Hearn that night at the

Victoria Inn. This mornin' the boss there promised me he was gonna' make this one just as good or better."

He then grinned mischievously at Jean-Pierre and Georges. "Actually, I think I made him a little nervous when I told him two *real* Frenchmen were comin' with me tonight, so it *better* be right."

"See you at half past seven."

They were waiting in the lobby when Louis walked into the hotel. Georges asked him if they had time to chat a few minutes before leaving for dinner. Louis said, "Sure, but let me tell Joe to stay with the car; finding a parking place in this town is a nightmare."

The four stepped down the hall to Georges' room. He offered Louis the only chair as he and the two others sat on the side of the bed.

He told Louis that while he, Wade, and Jean-Pierre appreciated his gracious gesture of not pressing them for an answer until the next day, they had made their decision that afternoon and wanted him to know that they were eager to get started with planning the operation. He added that they regarded it a high honor to be asked to conduct it, and that they had every confidence that it would be a success.

Hebert said, "Thanks a million, fellows. I felt certain you'd accept, but I wouldn't have faulted you if you hadn't; this one's got some weird aspects to it, but it couldn't be more important.

"Now, let's go make this night a *celebration.* We can talk more over dinner."

Anticipating that there might be questions at dinner, Louis had reserved a small private room at the Victoria, telling his guests, "It's not as much fun as watching the crowd, but it gives us some privacy if we cain't resist talkin' shop. After awhile in our business you begin to imagine a snoop behind every flower pot."

The Chef apparently *did* want to impress the Frenchmen. The dinner was declared by them—with *feeling*—to be *un diner superb.*

Hebert asked Wade whom he had in mind when he had asked, during the afternoon, if they could recruit others for the operation.

He said he was thinking of Emile from the Grenoble training camp, and told of the years that Emile had lived and taught in Lausanne. He said, "I've never met a more competent individual and—knowing his penchant for detail—I'd bet he is a walking encyclopedia regarding Lausanne."

"I know him also, Colonel," said Jean-Pierre, "and I share—totally—Jean's opinion of his abilities, but I was not aware that he had lived in Lausanne."

"I know that name, but would he be able to leave the training camp to participate?" asked Hebert.

"That is not a large problem at this time; a year ago, *yes,* now, *no!*" commented Blanchot.

"Actually, there are very few trainees there presently; most Maquis field units are now staffed fully—*grace à Dieu*—for the first time in our existence. I know Emile also; if he knows Lausanne, he would be invaluable. And he is absolutely *fearless.* I am certain that he would welcome a role.

"But how do we discuss fully the unique delicacies of this mission with him? Surely not by *radio,* however coded."

Wade turned to Colonel Hebert. "One way would be for me or Jean-Pierre to go to the camp to discuss it with him personally and in detail. If that makes sense, it probably should be me, in view of Jean-Pierre's greater leadership duties with *Les Amis.* Possibly a drop could be made on the way back. If so, that would save valuable time."

"Our immediate need is to pinpoint precisely where the lab is. Assuming that it actually *is* in some sort of old religious monastery or whatever, would this Emile be any help in finding the place?" asked the Colonel.

"That's impossible to answer without discussing it with Emile, but I can tell you this, from my own recollections of European history," said Georges Blanchot, "there may be a number of such structures remaining on the shores of Lake Geneva, many dating from the sixteenth century and the Protestant Reformation.

"There were many bitter—*very* bitter—conflicts in Switzerland, particularly after John Calvin fled France and went to Geneva in 1536.

"Geneva and its environs became a strong center of the Protestant movement—many have called Geneva 'the *home* of the Reformation'—as well as something of a refuge for other dissident groups which were, for whatever reason, out of favor with Rome and/or their own monarch.

"In 1542, only six years after Calvin went to Geneva, Pope Paul III established in Rome the Congregation of the Inquisition, also known as the *Roman Inquisition.* During those times, many religious priories and the like came into being in that part of Switzerland, and most were built like *forts*—not churches—because their inhabitants were constantly fearful of violent reprisals. Of one thing we can be certain: should we find the laboratory in one of those structures, we will be dealing with a formidable *fort,* with walls not unlike those we have at the ancient Citadelle in Villefranche."

"Interesting," murmured Hebert. "O.K., let's talk priorities. First, we gotta *find* the damn place before we can develop a make-sense plan for attacking it. Emile could be the key to that, or at least a start; let's go from there.

"But since it looks like a definite that we will be using Emile in some capacity, my preference is to get him down to Eze right away so you can all be together in moving the project along with him there from the git-go.

"It may require some of you to go to Lausanne pretty soon, even if our guys should find the site independently, and it sounds as if you're gonna need to take Duck along for some explosives expertise."

A good hour later, Louis glanced at his watch, and pushed back his chair as he stood. "But one thing's for sure; the management needs for us to clear out of here; plus, we can't decide everything tonight anyhow. First thing tomorrow morning, I'm contacting Emile, and I hope to have him waiting for you at the airfield in Bastia when you get there. We'll move it on from there."

Before they got out of the car at the hotel, Colonel Hebert added, "Come by the office tomorrow around noon. We can talk more before you leave. I'll give you a check-list on security issues, etc. to cover with any others who may have a 'need to know.'

"And Wade, I *do* think you should plan to check out on the Lysander, so give that some thought, too. It's my guess that Emile will be flown to Bastia in one.

"See ya tomorrow, guys!" He yelled out the open window, as the auto drove off into the fog.

Standing on the sidewalk, watching the car disappear, Georges Blanchot said, "Quite an interesting individual, your Colonel Hebert."

Wade tried to hold back a grin, "It's probably his French blood, *Monsieur.*"

Their escort from London brought back fond memories to Wade when he saw the Mosquito FB VI flying abreast of the B-24 as darkness enveloped the English sky. Their pilot had told them there had been unconfirmed reports of sporadic anti-aircraft fire in parts of northwestern France during the last day or so; consequently the two Mosquito fighter-bombers had been assigned the escort duty as far as Tours, and he added that they would rendezvous with a pair of P-38s over Tours for the remainder of the trip to Italy.

Emile was standing on the ramp at Bastia and waving to the C-47 as it taxied in at noon the next day. As each man stepped from the aircraft, he embraced him with the same exclamation, *"Merci beaucoup mon ami,* for liberating me from Grenoble!"

Then, walking in he asked, "To what do I owe this delightful development? I was told only that I was to join *Les Amis de Liberté* without delay. After that I asked no questions. Ah, the Riviera in June! Who could ask for more?"

"Restrain yourself until you hear more, good friend," said Wade. "We'll explain in due time. There is Major Larsen now; I wonder if Antonio is ready to sail."

Larsen said that the plan was for *Nicoletta II* not to depart until midafternoon, with another destroyer on guard, and that VOQ rooms were ready for them to use again.

The hours before departure flew by as they briefed Emile on what they knew of *Operation Top Drawer.*

His first comment was "What a *signal* honor to be included in such a mission!" and his next was, "I know the person we need to see in Lausanne. He lives in Ouchy, the port of Lausanne, and knows every inch of the lakeshore there. He is a professor of religious history, and his specialty is sixteenth century Europe. Best of all, for our needs, he has long deplored the cozy relationship that the current Swiss regime has maintained with the Nazis. I can't wait!"

Wade looked first at Jean-Pierre, then at Georges Blanchot, "If the Colonel were here, I can hear him now; he would probably say *'Damn, boys! We just hit the jackpot!'* and I would agree."

# *Chapter Twenty-Four*

Dominique had not seen her father since the day she had left Aix to join *Les Amis*. He looked gaunt and nothing resembling the larger than life *Papa* she had always remembered. He wasn't conscious as she kneeled and gently caressed his hand, trying in vain to keep her composure.

Her mother had gotten a message to her 24 hours earlier that her father might be dying after the third of a series of strokes. Standing now at the bedside, she explained to her daughter, "He refused to permit me to *distract* you; that was his very word. He insisted that your work was more important than any one person's health, his included.

"But after the last coma commenced," she said, now sobbing, "I—I—felt that you would never forgive me if you could not come to bid him what could be a final farewell. I am sorry to use those words but it is perhaps true."

Her daughter stood and pulled her mother close to her. "*Maman,* there is nothing in Heaven or on Earth for which I would not forgive you. Come; let's have a cup of tea." As they walked, arm in arm, to the kitchen, she asked, "Does he regain consciousness at times?"

"Yes, and when he does, although his speech is not clear, he seems to be quite alert mentally; that is what I cling to for hope. But the doctor says we should be prepared for the worst, because of the history of his heart.

"Dominique, I must tell you this; the day before your father's last stroke, he gave me a sealed envelope and said that it contained an important letter to you, in case of his death. But perhaps you should have it now. I will get it, and you can judge whether to open it."

As she and her mother sipped their tea, she opened the envelope. The note was brief, but the script was as bold as ever:

*To my beloved daughter:*
*Words cannot express how proud I am of your dedicated patriotism in behalf of our great and honorable nation. With the*

*recent successes of the Allied military forces at Normandy, I now have total confidence of victory over Fascist despotism.*

*It may be the will of God that I am not destined to witness the day of final liberation, but it will surely come.*

*However, if I do not have the joy of seeing you again, I wish to caution you and your contemporaries about the very real danger of exchanging one despot for another of equal evil.*

*I refer to the threat of France being dominated by Communism after all the travails of this war.*

*I ask that you, and your generation, dedicate yourselves to opposing that great and real threat to the liberty of all of France.*

*With devotion, I am,*
*Your loving father,*
*Papa*

By the time she finished the single page, the ink was running because of her teardrops. She took a long breath and handed the page to her mother.

Sleep came fitfully, but pleasantly, to Dominique that night as she dreamed of childhood pleasures that had long been dormant in her memory, most of which she had shared with a father she adored.

The voice of her mother awakened her, "Dear, *Papa* is awake and asking for you. Come quickly, please."

As he struggled to speak clearly, it was painful for her to see the changes in this man who had always been an articulate model of quiet self-assurance.He told her that *Maman* had said that she had been given his letter, and had read it, "And do you understand how great is my concern about exchanging one despot for yet another?"

"Yes, *Papa,* I do.

"And you have my oath that I, *and*—I am certain—millions of others, have not struggled to remove the Nazis, in order to endure a different, but equally horrible, fate with *les rouges.* I promise you that also."

She left for Eze two days later, within hours of her father's burial. *Maman* had said that was what he would have wanted.

"Assuming that we find that the site is indeed on the lakeshore in or near Lausanne," Emile was saying, "I find it remarkably fortunate that Bastille Day is approaching. July 14 may well become our day of choice for a successful attack and withdrawal across *Lae Léman.*

"But, assumptions aside, I feel that the threshold task is to travel to Lausanne, contact the professor and—presumably with his assistance—

locate the bloody site. Until that is accomplished we are only stumbling in the dark."

Georges Blanchot nodded agreement, and Duck said, "'At's for damn sure, Emile; so when do we leave?"

"Also, *who* should go?" added Jean-Pierre.

Wade said, "I think we are it, with the exception of Monsieur Blanchot; obviously he is needed here. We've gotta have Duc along for his evaluation if it does turn out to be a *fort* they're in."

"I believe you are correct, Jean. Emile, do you have a way to contact Professor Clément without traveling to Lausanne?" asked Blanchot.

"It could be done, but I do not favor that. First, I think it wise to see him in person on a matter of such monumental importance; also, any other means of contact would be painfully slow. Perhaps I should explain my earlier remark regarding Bastille Day; it will clarify why I think time is so important."

He then told how surprised he had been to learn—when he lived there—that Bastille Day was traditionally a day of raucous celebration on both sides of Lake Geneva, almost as much so among the French-speaking Swiss on the northern shore as with their French brethren in *Evian-les-Bains* just across the water.

"My grapevine tells me also," he said, " that it is one place where the noise levels of the celebration have not diminished a whit during this war, and have perhaps *increased;* after all, the Swiss *people* are not pro-Nazi.

"In particular, if it should develop that our plan is to destroy the site with explosives and/or withdraw across the lake to *Evian,* the traditional high decibel levels of *le 14 juillet* could be our best ally. An additional advantage is that there will be so many other strangers in both Lausanne and *Evian* on and before the fourteenth, a few more will never be noticed."

"I should also mention that Grenoble is less than 100 miles from Lausanne, by road—less than that from *Evian*—and, thank God, it is summer and the roads are usable. We could stock, immediately, the camp at Grenoble with our arms, explosives, and the like; possibly put in place there any additional personnel who may be needed for the actual attack. Then, after our *reconnaissance* visit, we gather at Grenoble for the final planning.

"In *Evian-les Bains* I have an acquaintance who is a longtime employee at the famous casino there; he owes me a great favor, and this may be the occasion for me to cash in the chit. We shall know more after our visit."

Georges Blanchot was about to speak when there was a knock at the door of the boathouse meeting room. Isabelle said that Colonel Hebert was on the radio. Blanchot beckoned the four to follow him to the radio room.

"Well, at long last our guys came up with some better scoop on the '*site*'; we're encrypting a message to you as I speak; you'll have it pronto. It doesn't give the complete answer, but it narrows the search down a helluva lot.

"While I gotcha, tell me if Emile caught up with you O.K. at Bastia." Blanchot pointed at Emile.

"Oh yes, Colonel; I'm here, '*with bells on,*' as you chaps say. Thanks for my *deliverance,* sir. I now know how a prisoner feels when released."

"'At's good, son; didja tell Wade about the Lysander deal, yet?'

"Not yet, Colonel; we got in a bit late last night. But I will today."

"Good; I think 'at's important. Gotta go now; here comes your coded one; stand by. Bye now."

While the message was being de-coded, Wade asked, "What's that all about Emile—the *Lysander* talk?"

"The Lysander pilot who flew me to Bastia said that Colonel Hebert had requested that a tech-manual on the Lysander III be given to you. I have it in my rucksack, but thought it could wait until later. I'll get it for you after we finish here. He obviously wants you to learn something about the airplane."

"Yeah; he's convinced we will need it in this mission. But I don't know if time will allow me to go to Bastia to get even the few hours training I'd need to check out on it."

"We could get one brought in to the strip near the camp, if that would help. You could do it there. Think about it; it may be needed."

Isabelle handed M. Blanchot the message. He read it aloud: "Usually reliable source claims certainty that subject site is in one of three locations fronting on the lake in Ouchy, all very near present marina. Exact addresses listed below. All are of ancient origin, and reportedly each was originally used to house unorthodox religious sects during the tumultuous era of a religious Inquisition. Stuart now in Lausanne. He expects to furnish contact info re informant within hours. When we get it, you get it. Thumbs up, and good hunting! L.H."

M. Blanchot looked at the others, "I will pass that information on when it arrives, and I hope that is soon, because we now have only two weeks if we are to act on 14 July. You four should plan to leave for Lausanne as soon as possible.

"In the interim we need to decide two issues: Do we confide the true purpose of this operation to any others? And *who,* amongst *Les Amis,* should we send ahead to the Grenoble camp to standby? Any thoughts?"

"Yes, I've given thought to both." answered Wade.

"First, I don't think we should give the full *purpose* information to anyone else, unless it becomes absolutely necessary to secure the aid of someone who is vital to our success. That may be unfair to them, but this is too critical to take the most remote chance of a leak, inadvertent or otherwise. In our case, the Colonel had to tell us more for planning, but that's not true for the others, with the possible exception of Professor Clément.

"As for the makeup of the attack team, that's difficult to determine until we find and evaluate the site. In addition to us four, we probably will need Juan; in my view we *must* use him. He is our best hand-to-hand combatant, regardless of his political views.

"If a boat is gonna be involved, for a withdrawal or otherwise, we need David for sure. Unless you will want them here for something vitally important, we should have Isabelle and Frederic in Grenoble also—as backup—subject to what we learn at Lausanne."

"I have no disagreement with that," said Blanchot. "Regarding the personnel, nothing pending here is as important as *Top Drawer.* But, Emile, do you feel that you can secure the cooperation of the professor without revealing all?"

"I think yes. Though he is Swiss, this man is a true humanitarian, and has long detested the assistance that the Swiss politicians have given the Nazis. If I tell him simply that our target is a Nazi activity, I think that will suffice; we will soon know."

"And Jean-Pierre, do you have any different feeling?" asked Blanchot.

"No, I am in full accord."

"So be it. Now, when—and how—do we get you four on your way to Lake Léman? Time is passing."

Emile said "I suggest that we go first to Grenoble from Bastia, in the Lysander; it would be much faster. Then we could travel the shorter distance to *Evian* by road."

"Is the Lysander still at Bastia?" asked Wade.

"Yes, *Jean,* I forgot to tell you, but its pilot said that your colonel had ordered it to be made available there for our later use." Emile grinned, "I gather the colonel definitely plans for you to learn to handle it."

By noon the next day, David, Isabelle, Juan and Frederic were well on their way to Grenoble, and Wade and Duck were in their room preparing to return to Bastia on *Nicoletta II* that evening. Wade had spent most of the previous evening studying the tech-manual for the Lysander III. He and Duck were about to leave for lunch when Dominique knocked and Duck answered the door. She was visibly upset and asked to see *Jean* "*Alone,* please?"

"Course, Dom. See ya later, Wade. I'm goin' ahead and chow down; be back in 'bout an hour.

"Bye, Dom."

She sat on the edge of Duck's bunk, saying nothing, but wearing a mask of sadness Wade had never seen, before speaking, "Is anyone going to tell me what is happening? Four have gone; their rumored destination is Grenoble. Four of you are preparing to go, but none of us know *where.* Why—suddenly—are the rest of us being told nothing?"

Wade slowly stepped over and sat beside her, gently pulling her close. "Dear Dominique, you surely know how much I truly love you. But you must also know that in our work we are sometimes entrusted with confidences that we can reveal to no-one, *absolutely* no one. This is such an occasion."

"Yes, but why am only I and two others remaining here, when we have been comrades for so long?"

"Because, as you well know, in our missions oftentimes *more* is not *better.* This mission doesn't call for your skills, just as *I* could never have written your inspiring messages to your compatriots.

"Trust me; it is better for everyone that you stay. I wish I could say more, but I cannot. Come on now; let's join the others for lunch, and enjoy the few minutes we can have together; we leave at sundown."

The next day, at Bastia, the RAF pilot of the Lysander was with Major Larsen at dockside when *Nicoletta II* tied up. He was introduced to Wade as Flight Sergeant Jeremy Thompson.

On the ride to the airfield he told Wade, Jean-Pierre and Emile that his Orders stated that he was under Wade's command until he received different directions from the London headquarters of OSS or BI.

"Also, sir, I should mention that a second Lysander has already been ferried to the strip near Grenoble for your use if needed, and that I have been directed to offer you my services for your training on the Lysander. I was advised that you are qualified to fly—and have flown combat in—the *Mossie.* After that, learning to drive our slow little bird should be a piece of cake for you.

"I think we could use some work on that while here, rather than at Grenoble, if that's possible for you. We could practice freely touch-and-go landings here without fear of observation by unfriendly types.

"In any event, it would be best if we not depart for Grenoble until almost nightfall. That would give us ample time for some good instruction today in this perfect flying weather; it's still a bit iffy in the Alps, you see."

"That sounds fine to me Jeremy. It's been a while since I've been in a cockpit, so bear with me; you're gonna find me a tad rusty, but let's give it a go. I'll be ready in an hour."

By the time they had finished in late afternoon, Wade felt confident enough to ask if he could take it up solo, saying, "I love this airplane Jeremy; it looks like an ugly duckling but it makes you feel like you are *really* flying. This is the first time I've had that feeling since the Stearman; it was an open cockpit bi-plane."

"Sir, it's probably a good idea for you to do your first solo here, so why not get the landings under your belt on a good strip. By the way, your engineer chaps did a superb repair job here; I was here before them, and it was a bloody mess."

Most of the day, Duck had been watching—with some envy—from behind the fence, but had just walked out to the ramp and overheard the talk. He said, "Any chance I could ride with ya, Wade?"

Wade slapped him on the shoulder, while winking at Jeremy, "Climb in, if you're sure your insurance is paid up!"

When they took off for Grenoble that evening, Wade was at the controls, with Jeremy calmly coaching him along, saying, "You keep it until total darkness sets in; then I'll handle it the rest of the trip and do the night landing, but I'll sing out comments all the way home."

To the other passengers, he added, "Enjoy the view of the Alps while we still have light. There's no more magnificent sight that these eyes have ever seen, except for the very same scene in the dead of winter, under a full moon."

"If possible, I think we should leave for *Evian* by six tomorrow morning." Emile said to Jean-Pierre and Duck. "Guy will have the lorry ready for us, and that should put us in *Evian* before noon. My croupier friend— he *claims* to be the supervisor of all the croupiers there, but he is a world-class braggart—never rises until well after noon. I plan to go directly to his home, which is quite impressive."

"How is this casino still operating in France?" asked Jean-Pierre. "I thought most were closed."

"*Simple,* my friend. It is five miles across the lake from Switzerland, and a playground for visiting Nazi businessmen. After all, any prudent Swiss banker learns to keep his clients happy, *oui?*" sneered Emile.

"But as it has developed,' he said, "we are indeed fortunate that the casino is open and busy; otherwise my friend Arnaud would not have his grand chateau, with the enormous cellar rooms which I intend us to use for both our living quarters and as an advance command post for our mission."

Guy was waiting as they taxied in from the grass strip, an area very different from the Alpine meadow where Wade and Duck had first met Emile so many months before. This strip had permanent lights marking clearly its width and length, and it was very near the Maquis camp.

When Wade expressed surprise, Emile explained, "We Maquis have largely *owned* France from this point northward *almost* to the Swiss border, since well before D-Day, and almost completely since. Most of the Vichy-minded residents, as well as many who had collaborated passively, have long since fled the region. It has been a pleasant change."

While unloading their gear from the lorry, Emile told Guy, "We want to get some sleep, but leave at six tomorrow morning. Have you heard anything regarding the road conditions to the north?"

"Not a problem, as of today. The snow and ice are gone, hopefully until autumn. When can I expect the other four who are coming?"

Jean-Pierre answered, "Within four days, possibly three. They are coming by automobile, a battered green Citreon."

"One other question," said Guy. "We received a message from London to be prepared for a drop of explosives and related apparatus soon; do you know about that?"

Duck said, "Yeah, but I gotta figure out what and how much first; we ain't gonna know 'til me and the others git back, so don't sweat it yet."

"I understand," said Guy. "And Jean, you will be pleased to know that our lorry has been thoroughly renovated since I drove you to the south in it. It is quite pleasing how the community co-operation here has expanded as the German presence has contracted."

The drive to the town of *Evian-les Bains* was uneventful, "Just as I prefer," said Emile, as he pointed to the sign welcoming visitors there. "Now I must find a telephone cabin to call Arnaud. He is probably not yet awake, but it is important that we not miss him. We should be very near his home soon."

"Ah, there is a cabin! I will call now."

Emile stepped back to the truck with a bounce in his step, "He was not pleased to be called so early, but said he was glad to hear my voice. I've not yet told him that there are four of us; better to do that eye to eye."

"Aren't you going to have to tell him *something* about why we are here?" asked Jean-Pierre.

"I think not, given what I will be trading for his co-operation. If need be, I will explain that it is better that he does not know. If Arnaud is anything, he is the consummate pragmatist. How else has he justified his activities during this war? Regardless, it may be best if he never meets the three of you; I will deal with him alone."

Ten minutes later, Emile turned down a narrow side street, drove another half mile and stopped slightly beyond the crest of a small knoll. It was a brilliant and bright late morning as three of the group enjoyed their first view of the beautiful blue waters of Lake Geneva.

"Get out and stretch your legs awhile. I'm going to walk a few yards over to the area of Arnaud's boat dock and knock on his back door," Emile announced. "He's expecting me; I should be only a half hour or so."

All except Emile were surprised to learn that Arnaud's *cellar* was substantially mis-named; it was more like a large, plush apartment, complete with a well-stocked pantry of food and other comforts of life long forgotten by most in war-torn Europe. Emile said that it was financed by the proprietors of the casino, and laughed, "You can probably guess why the inventory includes such bizarre combinations as red cabbage, Reisling wines, and sauerkraut. But *we* have the *'lease'* now, and for an indefinite time."

While they were settling in, Emile said that he thought he should return later to the telephone booth and try to reach Professor Clément. He added, "I hope to arrange an immediate meeting with him, but I feel he would speak more freely to me alone, inasmuch as he doesn't yet know any of you. Is that satisfactory?"

"Of course," Wade quickly said. "Nothing else makes sense. In the meantime, we can use the time to practice our new identities and attire, so as to avoid looking too conspicuous when we all go over to Lausannne."

"Fortunately, that shouldn't pose a great problem," smiled Emile. "It is an historic place, once a Roman city called *Lousanna*. Of all the cities I have known, it may be the most cosmopolitan; yet it remains very low key.

"For centuries, literally, it has been a home for many exiles—including some deposed monarchs and their entourages—from around the world, together with all the other varieties of humanity that such an environment attracts. Thus the inhabitants pay little attention to strange faces, clothing, language or accents."

Professor Paul Clément's ancestors had settled on the northern shore of the lake shortly after the French revolution, during the period when Napoleon Bonaparte controlled the region.

His father had taught at the same university from which Paul had recently retired. The school traced its origins to 1537, the year after John Calvin's arrival in Geneva.

He had often thought that may have been what had fueled his longtime fascination with sixteenth century religious history. He had written dozens of papers, and lectured frequently, on the subject for years, and it was following such a lecture that he had met the interesting young language teacher who was coming to visit him that morning.

Having worked in his study since seven, the aging teacher had decided to rest his eyes from his writing for a few moments.He had pulled his shawl up around his shoulders against the cool lake breeze, and was sitting by the open window, speculating on why Emile had asked him not to mention the visit to anyone else.

He thought he knew the reason. Emile had been an outspoken and articulate French patriot during their two year friendship prior to the fall of 1939 as the clouds of war were threatening to envelop Europe. He could not imagine this courageous and sincere young man passively accepting Nazi domination.

Indeed, many times during the past four years he had vowed to himself that if only he were a few years younger he would leave Switzerland to resist, in some active fashion, the ambitions of *"those butchers."*

A few minutes later, Professor Clément felt a pleasant surge of excitement as he walked slowly to answer the knock at his door and heard the voice saying, *"C'est Emile, Professeur."*

The old man wept with joy as they embraced.

They sat with tea and reminisced for a full hour, until Emile cleared his throat somewhat nervously, and spoke. "Professor, in fairness to you, I must tell you that I have been active in the French *résistance* for a long time, at all times subject to imprisonment by agents of Vichy—and probably worse by the Nazis—if caught. And I am here, in my capacity as an active member of the Maquis.

"My purpose is to seek your assistance in what may be the most important mission of the entire conflict, not only for France but for all of mankind.

"I am not at liberty to tell you the details, but I give you my word of honor that it is not an exaggeration to say that the success of our mission here may be *essential* to the achievement of complete and final victory over Hitler and his regime.

"While the extent of your participation would be limited to a provider of information only, even that slight degree of involvement could place you at serious risk. I tell you this at the outset, in order that you may choose not to become involved in any way. If that is your decision, sir, we will understand and will pursue the matter no further."

"Emile, I have lived already far beyond three score and ten years—and a *good* life too—but I have only one major regret; I have contributed little or nothing to challenging what is undoubtedly the most evil force of this century—perhaps of *any* century. If there is something of importance I can do to assist you, I have no fear of the risk, absolutely *none*. I would treasure the opportunity to make my time on this Earth complete.

"Tell me what you need from me."

Emile told him that their mission was to find and destroy an important Nazi-sponsored activity somewhere in Lausanne, probably in Ouchy near the marina.

He showed the three addresses to Professor Clément, who immediately exclaimed, "Ah yes, I know them well. I have written of each at one time or the other. All were constructed during eras of barbarous persecutions of many dissident religious groups by the established church and when this region had become a place of refuge; there were some who called Geneva *'the new Jerusalem.'* A typical priory was what I would describe as a 'fortified church.' Those were terrible times too, but for different reasons.

"Give me a moment; I think I have something that would be very helpful to you." He disappeared for a half hour, then returned with four large and dust-covered books.

After placing all on the table, he paged slowly but methodically through one, mumbling inaudibly to himself as he did so.

At last he looked at Emile and beamed, "Yes; I thought I remembered this! I wrote this book in the early '30s, but never succeeded in getting it published. I paid personally for printing several copies and retained this one for my library. It was one I had done after visiting and cataloguing information about the then remaining ancient priories on Lake Geneva; it includes the three you have mentioned today.

"Ah; *here* is what I am searching for, the section I did on *floor plans*. I sketched, and made copious notes describing, the interior of each.

"*Look at this one,*" he almost shouted, "and notice the long and narrow parallel lines running from beneath the main rooms of the structure. They were *tunnels!*

"This was—to me—the most *fascinating* discovery! They would bury their dead brethren in small spaces carved from the walls of these presumably secret tunnels, because the raiders would often *burn* the remains of the dead when they found and entered these facilities. Some of these sects regarded that as the ultimate desecration.

"Also, they planned to use some of these tunnels to escape being captured or killed during an attack; some opened almost directly onto the lake itself, the easier to flee by boat, I assume."

At this point, Emile was more excited than his host. The drawings in the book were clear and precisely done, and to scale, as noted in the lower left corner of each and every page. When he complimented Professor Clément about that, he beamed anew, saying that was the work of his late wife, who had laboriously converted his notes into legible form.

"But," said M. Clément, "that doesn't tell us *which* of the three is the one you are after. All are on the lakefront; why don't you and I go fishing for a bit. I can identify the three for you. My last information on the three was that all were completely closed down and unused. From the water, we may discern something of value. I fish often, with little success; no one will notice us."

It was late afternoon when they tied up the small boat by the professor's cottage. They had located easily the three sites, all of which were very close to the busy Ouchy marina.

None showed signs of life to Emile's eye, but one had caught the attention of the professor. He had leaned over in the boat and spoken quietly to Emile, "Notice the faint wisp of smoke or vapor coming from the largest chimney. Even this late in the year we often have cool nights; with two to three foot thick walls the sun doesn't warm an interior rapidly; I think there is life in that one."

Emile asked if he could bring his colleagues over to see the book and sketches the next day. The professor readily agreed, and volunteered to speak to a contact that evening, regarding the site he referred to as "the wispy one," adding that, "I have been questioning everyone on this lake about these places for 30 years; they will not be curious about my reasons."

Then, as Emile was departing, he volunteered, "If and when you wish, you may have the sketches, if you need them."

"Monsieur, you are most gracious. However, for now I believe they are more secure here. Until tomorrow, *merci et au revoir.*"

Emile could hardly control his exuberance on the ferry back to Evian; the information he had gotten from the professor was more than he had dared to hope for, especially the floor plans.

He explained to Wade and the others about the tunnels indicated on the drawings for all three sites, and that the site suspected to be currently in use had a network of tunnels which ran to the edge of the lake.

# Chapter Twenty-Five

Professor Clément was watching by the window again as the four came up his walkway. He was eagerly awaiting their arrival, because he had more news for them.

He told them that a good friend of his was employed at the official agency that dealt with two utilities—electric power and water—in the Lausanne region; they had played chess almost every Wednesday evening for many years. The professor had called his friend after Emile had left the previous afternoon, and asked him whether any of the three sites were current customers of the agency. Early that morning, the friend had dropped by to say that two were not, but one *was;* and he had volunteered that the one had applied for those services only three months prior.

"The one with the *wisp?*" asked Emile.

With a sly smirk, the old professor slowly nodded his head.

"BINGO!" shouted Duck.

"Not yet," cautioned Wade. "We've got to be absolutely certain on this, before we plan an attack."

"Right," added Jean-Pierre. "Ideally, we would get someone inside the site; but is that possible?"

"Maybe," said Clément. "My friend is as opposed to the Nazis as I. While many of our politicians and bankers may have been willing to sell their souls, I assure you that most of the Swiss people do not share that shame. Perhaps he can find a way."

"Please try him, but," Wade said, "in the meantime, we could stake out the site—let's call it *Site X*—to find out if there is activity there and, if so, what kind; that may help. For now, let's study the sketches on Site X."

M. Clément laid out the sketches on a large table in his study and said, "Let me tell you more about the tunnels. You can see that *most* do not reach to the outer perimeter of the structure, and that those are much wider than the ones which *do* run all the way to the perimeter.

"The wide ones were used to bury the remains of their dead, as well as to hide any valuables of the sect or order, in the walls of the tunnel, and they endeavored also to conceal the tunnel entrances; this was done in fear of an attack and desecration of their departed or the theft of their assets.

"On the other hand, compare those with these more narrow tunnels, noting that each narrow one runs to some edge of the structure; one goes to the side away from the lake, but two of them go not only toward the lakeside of the structure, but also beyond that and almost to the very edge of the water. These narrow ones were designed as *escape* tunnels and for nothing else.

"Now, note the drawings of the living and working quarters of the site. As I have said, they were constructed as much like forts as religious facilities. This one, as you can see, has three main sections. All three sections consist of two levels, one above the surface of the earth, the other below.

"In the center section only, both levels were used by the religious community, either for living quarters or for their work. In the two other sections— one on either side of the center one—only the above-ground level was occupied, and that was by armed guards, many of them mercenaries, hired to protect the priory and its religious community. Underneath the guards' quarters were situated primitive chapels, portions of the tunnels, and the like. Supposedly, only the members of the religious community knew the details of, or had the right of access to, any of the lower level.

"As I see again these sketches, I see how the design would be perfect for a secret and guarded laboratory. The guards could be posted in the outside sections, and the work carried on in the center, exactly as in the sixteenth century.

"My God; how ironic that an ancient place of the faithful may be now being utilized by the *Nazis.*

"It may not be important, but you might note also that all three of the *escape* tunnels originate from the center section, lower level, whereas the other tunnels start from the walls of the lower level *underneath* the guards' quarters."

Duck asked, "Sir, wouldja have any kinda idea how thick the ceiling an' all wuz between the top of the lower rooms and the floor of the guards' place above 'em?"

"No, but let me check something in my book regarding this site; give me a moment, please."

He picked up the old book, and gingerly turned to the index, then carefully turned the pages and said, "Yes, here we have it. I wrote here that a great sport of the guards—at least *they* thought it was great sport—was to eavesdrop on the religious below, particularly during their chants, mimicking them from time to time. That information came from a diary found there, apparently kept by one of the few guards who was literate; actually he sounds quite literate, though arrogant and insulting to his employers.

"Here is an exact quote from the diary: 'The work in this primitive and cavelike place is boring to anyone with a decent mentality, but quite rewarding in terms of payment. The only pleasure available within these walls is to place one's ear to the floor of our wet and cold quarters and take humor from the babbling of the religious mental-midgets whom we are well paid to protect.'

"If that was an accurate statement, I assume that the distance between the floor of the guards' room and the ceiling of the room below must have been a short one indeed; otherwise the guards would have never heard a sound from below."

"Geez, I shore hope you're right. That might make this job a whole lot simpler. By the way, where'd the religious folks actually sleep, upstairs or down?"

"That I *do* know. They always used the above-ground part for their living quarters."

"When do you think you could speak to your friend?" asked Emile. "It's possible that he could give us even more valuable intelligence."

"This noon; I will walk to his office and suggest lunch."

"Fine. Jean-Pierre, why don't you and I do a stakeout on Site X this afternoon, then check back with the professor late in the day. In the meantime, Wade and Duck can stay here and study the book thoroughly while the professor sees his friend, and we can resume this meeting here early this evening."

The professor and his friend Daniel lunched in Lausanne's Old Town, near *place Saint-François.* at a tiny inexpensive cafe they had frequented often. Daniel's mother tongue was Swiss-German, but he was also fluent in German and French, and almost so in English.

He told M. Clément that, because of his language proficiency, he had been assigned the task of working with *Les Laboratoires des Sciences, S.A.* (*LLS*) when that company had first contacted the agency six months ago, and said they wished to move their small but important research lab from Zurich to Lausanne, and would need to plan for their utility needs in an ancient building they had acquired for their laboratory. He had thought it strange that, when he first visited with the company's advance team, all of them spoke only German and none spoke Swiss-German or French.

Daniel also said that because the company had made massive renovations to the interior rooms of the center section, lower and upper levels, he had been required to visit periodically to insure that their utility needs were met. In response to M. Clément's question, he said they had done little or nothing to the network of tunnels, except to marvel at what a massive task it must have been to create them in centuries past.

"There are four scientists working and living there regularly. One of them is Swiss and the other three speak only German, and I have already wondered about their nationalities; now I wonder even more. In the walls of the sections on either side of the center, on the upper level, they have constructed gun emplacements that would make our Swiss army look like a boy playing with toy soldiers. And, curiously I have thought, each of the guards who have spoken to me have spoken only German."

"Do the guards wear uniforms?" asked M. Clément.

"Never! Always it is civilian attire. But they change the personnel occasionally. Perhaps it is a regular shift change; I don't go there on a scheduled basis, and therefore it is difficult to know. However, it appears that there are four guards in each section at any given time; all of them wear sidearms.

"As for the scientists, my impression is that they are virtually prisoners; they never leave for meals or anything else; a woman comes in each day to clean and cook for the day, but she also speaks only German. Each time I see the Swiss scientist—his name is Hausler—I have the feeling that he is yearning to tell me something, but he never has done so."

"Daniel, this information is very useful, and I thank you for it. However, if possible we need some proof positive that this is a Nazi operation before a decision is made on how to deal with it. Do you think it possible to obtain some ID of either the scientists or the guards; my guess is that the guards are SS or Gestapo, but this needs verification."

Daniel thought for a minute, "I doubt that it is left lying around at the site, but at their homes they may be sloppy. Possibly I could get some residence addresses for the guards, possibly under a pretense for 'Emergency Notification' or such. After that, who knows when a thief might enter the home address?"

"Good idea! Try it, and we shall see. *Merci et au revoir, mon ami;* I shall look forward to hearing from you, soon I hope."

Three nights later, Jean-Pierre entered the studio apartment of Hans Karl Mueller, in the *Haute Ville* section of Lausanne, by way of the fire escape, the moment he heard the shower running full. He had just finished reading Mueller's official credentials as a Waffen-SS officer—which had been left on the coffee table with his wallet and pistol—when the shower noise suddenly stopped, and a tall, blonde German stepped into the room, with a towel wrapped around his waist. He yelled something at Jean-Pierre in German, and Jean-Pierre drew his long knife from its scabbard.

As the German dove for his Luger, Jean-Pierre pulled his knife in a sweeping upward arc and drove it deep into the Nazi's falling chest; then he twisted it with all his strength, before yanking it out and slashing the bleeding man's throat.

Jean-Pierre calmly pushed the body aside with his foot, wiped his hands, then his knife, with the towel, took all the money from the wallet, put the credentials in his inside jacket pocket, and deliberately dropped the wallet to the floor as he walked to the window and climbed through it—leaving the window open as would have a fleeing thief.

As he strode down the back alley toward the street, he removed the Deutschmarks from his pocket, spat on them, then dumped them into a filthy garbage can.

The same night, in Evian, they discussed a tentative plan for destroying *Site X*.

They first confirmed that all still agreed that the attack should commence promptly at 10:00 P.M. on the evening of July 14, during the traditionally boisterous fireworks displays around the lake in celebration of Bastille Day.

Wade then asked Duck for his thoughts on the use of explosives.

"I figger we're first gonna hafta blow the two wings where the guards hang out, so they wont be able to git in the way much—if at all—while we bring out the science fellas and make our getaway; and here're my ideas on 'at."

He then went on to say that the best way to do it would be to set the charges in the ceilings of the lower level rooms directly under each of the guards' quarters. "If the guards in the old days could hear the religious fellas singing below 'em, I believe we can blow 'at whole damn floor out frum under 'em, and them what makes it out—if any *do*—ain't gonna have much fight left in 'em."

"Fine," Emile smiled, "but how do you set the charges without gaining entry to the interior of the site beforehand?"

"Here's my idea on 'at. We gotta check 'is out first, but if the getaway tunnels—excuse me, the *escape* tunnels—are open enough to git through 'em, me and Juan could slip in 'ere on the fourteenth, goin' through a tunnel—frum the *lakeside* end—set the charges and timers, then git back out through the tunnel and be ready to take care of any guards who might make it through the explosion in one piece.

"Oh yeah, I thought of sumpin' else, if you wanta do it. I could also set some more charges under the main room in the center, so we could blow the hell out of the lab too, after you guys get the scientists out." Duck grinned, and continued, "It might be better not to use a timer for 'at, so if you guys are held up—findin' records or sumpin'—we wouldn't lose you, too. Colonel Hebert would kick my butt if 'at happened."

"*Very* funny," smiled Wade, "but how do we know if the escape tunnels are clear enough to use?"

"No problem; tomorrow afternoon I go find the exact spots where they end near the water, 'en go in an' explore 'em. At oughta tell us.

"Two more things—'en I shut up. Since we've decided not to go back to the camp before we do this job, I need to let Guy know what to tell OSS about what I need dropped, so Isa and the others can bring it with 'em when they come. Number two, when the guards' places blow, we oughta have Isa and Frederic waitin' on the other side, so as to take care of any Kraut guards who might make it outta the wing on 'at other end away from me and Juan."

"Your plan sounds good, *if* the tunnels are clear," said Wade. "If they turn out not to be, we will need a contingency plan. Tomorrow, we should know. *Then* we radio Guy about the drop.

"Next, let's discuss how we deal with the four scientists.

"We—by *we* I mean Jean-Pierre, Emile and I—should be poised to enter their quarters the moment the explosion occurs.

"My Orders from OSS are very specific on this.

"The four scientists are absolutely *not* to be allowed to remain free to be used again by the Nazis. We are to first assure them that we mean them no physical harm, *but* that they *must* come with us. If any one of them refuses to come—and this is the *most difficult* part, gentlemen—we are under strict orders to liquidate them on the spot. If anyone does refuse to come, we are to advise him that he has *thirty seconds* to change his mind and then—if he persists in refusing—he is to be shot on the spot; we then leave with those who are willing to join us.

"Do we all understand that, *completely?*" All three men nodded in unison, and Wade continued. "Since three of them probably speak only German, Emile will do all the talking with them. If he tells me that one of them has persisted in a refusal to leave with us, I will be responsible for the unpleasant, but necessary, task of terminating that individual, as well as any other who refuses."

"Now," said Jean-Pierre, "we must decide when to have the others arrive here, and advise Guy tomorrow when we radio him. Today is the eighth. and I think it would be best if they not arrive until about mid-day on the twelfth. That gives us a half day, plus a full day on the thirteenth, to brief and orient them to the site and area. Is there any need for them to come earlier?"

Emile asked, "What about David? I have arranged to use Arnaud's large boat all day and night on the fourteenth. Arnaud is curious, but hasn't pushed me for the reason. David will take us over on the fourteenth and return us after the attack. The boat will be one of hundreds on the lake that night, and will attract zero attention.

"The only question is whether David can handle it without prior instruction."

"I doubt that will be a problem; he is quite a competent boatsman," answered Jean-Pierre, "but we can ask David tomorrow when we contact Guy. Try to get some information about the boat tomorrow and have that ready to give to David."

"Good. Now we should discuss the withdrawal," said Wade. "I have asked Jean-Pierre to prepare a proposed plan; Jean-Pierre?"

Jean-Pierre walked over and taped a map on the wall; it showed an area from the northern shore of Lake Geneva to a point a few miles south of Grenoble.

"When we return to Evian after the attack, the lorry and the Citreon will be parked just over the knoll where we stopped the lorry on our arrival here. Isabelle will drive the Citreon and I the lorry. We will drive south from Evian on the main thoroughfare until we cross a high bridge over a very deep gorge; the bridge will be before we reach the town of *Morzine.*

"During the night of 13 July, *Duc* and Juan will have set explosive charges on that bridge.

"If there has been no sign of pursuit by the time we cross that bridge, we shall continue south as rapidly as possible. However, if we have *any indication whatsoever* that we are being pursued, we will stop after crossing over the bridge, while *Duc* runs back to detonate and demolish the bridge. In this way, if there *is* pursuit, they will be required to backtrack to *Evian* in order to continue; that should give us sufficient time to extend our advantage."

He pointed to the map. "The town of *Morzine* is *here,* roughly 40 kilometers south and directly on our route. If we wish to use an extra precaution, we could have Isabelle acquire, with the aid of the local Maquis unit near Morzine, two vans, and leave them parked at the rail station. We could then switch to those vehicles for the remaining drive to Grenoble.

"At the Grenoble camp's strip, the two Lysanders will be ready to fly us directly to Bastia. Jeremy will pilot one and *Jean* the other. Any questions or comments?"

"Only one," said Emile. "I question the advisability of involving the Morzine Maquis. While I am satisfied of their loyalty, there *have* been security leaks there before. Why take a chance of a leak in advance of the attack? Also, if there is pursuit, the destruction of the bridge should dispose of that; and if it did not, why waste valuable minutes switching vehicles?"

"Good points," said Jean-Pierre. "What do you think, *Jean?*"

Wade agreed with Emile's comments, and they decided to forget the switch.

"Done," said Jean-Pierre. "But *Duc;* is the bridge any problem? I know I hadn't mentioned it to you before."

"No sweat, podner," Duck laughed. "I remember us crossin' 'at bridge comin' up here; it's a lulu. Too bad we cain't hang around long enough to hear it hit bottom in that deep gorge!"

It was a good 30 minutes after Duck had entered the tunnel before he had finally stumbled back out into the bright sunlight, to Wade's immense relief. However it was a moment before he had been absolutely certain that it *was* his friend and comrade, because Duck was covered with cobwebs from head to toe.

After he climbed back into Professor Clément's small dory, and he and Wade had spent some time rescuing him from the cobwebs, he smiled, "Well, I just met our worst enemy yet; that tunnel's got spiders bigger'n you ever seen. They damn near surrounded me in 'ere, and I ain't kiddin' you; whew, what a mess!

"But here's the *good* news; nothin's blocking 'at tunnel, if you don't count the spiders, an' I think most of '*em* came out hangin' on to me a while ago. Boy, somebody did one more great job of building 'em tunnels; they were built to *stay.*"

"Well, they've already stayed for 300 years," said Wade. "That's great news about the tunnel; sounds as if we're in business on your plan. Was it hard to *see* anything in there?"

"Yeh; it was black as ink when you got a few feet from 'is end. My flashlight worked pretty good, but what Juan and me could use is some caps with a light on the front, like the miners use back home; 'at way your hands are free for working 'stead of holdin' a light. You reckon Isa and them could scrounge up some?"

"I doubt it on such short notice, unless Colonel Hebert could find some and include them in the drop. We'll ask Guy to request it. If you're ready to go, let's return this boat and get back across the lake."

Guy had been standing by his radio for well over an hour, when his receiver finally came to life in the Alpine night. "I have Isabelle, Juan, David, and Frederic with me," he told Jean-Pierre, and suggested that Isabelle translate for the benefit of *Jean* and *Duc.*

"First," said Jean-Pierre, "I want *Duc* to tell her what he needs from London in the drop there; afterwards, Emile will describe a boat to David—it is one we plan to have him handling during the operation—and, last, I will go over the movement from there to here."

Duck took the mike and detailed his needs for explosive and related devices, then tried to describe what he called the *"miner's lights"* he needed from London.

"I forgit exactly what it's *called,* but any miner'd know whut I mean. It's like a big flashlight, battery operated; the miner hooks the light on the front of 'is hard-hat; 'en 'ere's a wire runnin' frum the light an'down 'is back to a battery hooked onto 'is belt; 'at way he can see what he's doin' but 'is hands are free to work without havin' to hold the light. Tell 'em guys in the Colonel's office to git off 'ere butts and get hold of some Limey miner; he'd know in a minute whut I mean."

David knew the boat which Emile described, saying, "Actually, I piloted a similar boat when I worked in *Cannes.* They were originally designed and built in Glasgow; fine vessels; it will be no problem."

After Jean-Pierre instructed them on when to arrive at Evian, he added, "One last thing; *Duc* is asking me to tell you that if London *cannot* send him four 'miners' lights; then they need to send four strong *hand*-held lights. *Merci et au revoir."*

After the radio transmission, Emile said, "Let me tell you of an interesting conversation I had with the professor this afternoon. He has already concluded that we may create *'a bit of noise'* during our attack, and has an idea that he felt might help us go unnoticed by almost everyone.

"Apparently there is an old hotel very near our Site X. It's core is a tower dating back to the twelfth century, and it was once fortified. Before this war, it was a regular custom to fire operating replicas of its ancient cannon during normal and traditional fireworks displays on several holidays each year, *including* Bastille Day.

"His idea is to endeavor to have that custom reborn this year, exactly at 10:00 P.M. on 14 July. What do you think?"

"Nice of him to try to help, but I question whether one or two *'booms'* would provide much cover for our blasts that night," said Wade.

"That was precisely my reaction, *Jean,*" replied Emile. " But hear this; the custom for the 14 July celebration has always called for *14* 'booms'—seven from each of two cannons!! The elapsed time from the first to the fourteenth boom, is about one minute.

"That might make *our* booms fit in quite nicely with the celebration, *oui?"*

"Hell yeah," Duck chimed in. "These folks might even invite me back ever' year after they hear *my* booms!!"

"It certainly couldn't hurt any," Wade said. "The more noise that night, the better. But it worries me a little for the professor; he's getting deeper and deeper into this. What happens to him after we are gone, if his part should be discovered?"

Emile shrugged, "I know, *Jean.* But he truly *wants* to be involved. He is a humanitarian, and his participation in this is a great balm for his conscience. Just today, he told me that he feels that he is finally contributing something useful in this great struggle for the freedom of humankind. Unless we think it will interfere with or harm our mission, I think we should encourage him to pursue this."

"O. K. Tomorrow, tell him to try it ," said Wade. "But tell him to let us know the minute he learns it is going to be a *Go;* I don't want the sun to set on the fourteenth with any loose ends."

**London**

"Why the hell would he want *miners' lights?*" Colonel Hebert half-shouted at Joe Cassidy, after Cassidy had interrupted the meeting with Under-Secretary Hopkins.

"I don't have the foggiest idea, Louis. We've adhered strictly to your orders and scrupulously avoided direct radio contact with Wade's group since they got to Lausanne, but Guy said that Duck seemed adamant about having them if we could get 'em. We think we've already found some, and have sent two guys over to Wales to get 'em."

As Cassidy closed the door behind him, Hebert turned to Hopkins and said, while wiping his brow, "This damned waitin' is drivin' me nuts, Dick. I did order no direct radio contact with Wade and his boys once they got to Lausanne, mainly because Washington is so friggin' terrified about some jackass learning we're behind this operation.

*"God almighty!* This damned job wouldn't be so tough if it weren't for havin' to please some numbskull politician ever' time you turn around!"

"I sympathize with you, Louis. Just thank your lucky stars you don't have to stay in D.C. as much as I do. But look; the only criticism I've heard—from those who really *count*—was about putting the mission under the command of an officer as young as Wade Johns. Of course, they don't know him as we do."

"Hey, they need to wake up to reality. Damned near every combat soldier in this scrap —other than the damned *Generals*—is a *kid* by pre-war measures, but they are kids havin' to do a *man's* job; and by God, they're doin a helluva good one too. Too bad some of our piss-ant politicians cain't say the same!

"Wade and *Les Amis* had done some outstanding work before this— some of it extremely innovative—and I felt they could pull this job off if anyone could. I still believe 'at; but it's nerve-wracking to have to sit here and wait without much current information."

He then stood, stepped over to the window, and stared out into the foggy London night with his back to Hopkins. "Actually Dick, this operation is so damned important that *nobody* should have to bear the burden of responsibility for its success, but somebody has to. The great thing about these very young officers is that they seem to feel absolutely invincible, so maybe it's best they do a job like this one.

"God knows *I* feel the pressure in this; like in *nothing* we've done before, even D-Day."

Hopkins stood up, walked around the desk and threw his arm around Hebert's shoulder, "Let's go somewhere for dinner; maybe you can get this off your mind for a few hours. Just hang in there old friend; in a couple of days we'll know the results, and *I'm* betting you picked the right people for the job."

## Grenoble

It was another moonlit night as Guy and Juan gathered up the dropped items and loaded them into the Citreon. The solid black B-24 had done a sharp 180 degree turn after the drop and was passing back overhead as they were driving away; as they glanced up at it, the aircraft's wing lights blinked five times very rapidly, before blacking out again and climbing toward the west.

"*Ah bon,*" Guy said quietly, as he and Isabelle examined the drop at the camp. "These must be the *miners' lights* that Duc requested; they fit his description perfectly. And there is a handwritten note taped to this one, but I don't know the language."

"It is Welsh," Isabelle said, after studying it a minute. "I understand some of that ancient language." Then she smiled, "It says that the writer is a Welsh miner, that he knows not where his lamp is going except that he was told that a *'Yank'* soldier needed it, and that he hopes it lights his way to victory and a safe return to his home and family. How nice! I shall take this note to *Duc.*"

# Chapter Twenty-Six

The old green Citreon drew scant attention as it rattled along on the streets of Evian, even with the small trailer it had in tow. It was a few minutes before noon on Wednesday, July 12, as she slowly maneuvered the auto and trailer down one narrow and busy street. The town was already receiving a steady stream of incoming visitors for the Friday celebration, and every street was packed with pedestrians.

When she was signaled rather rudely by a police officer to wait for crossing traffic, Isabelle glanced over at David and chuckled, "Wonder what he would do if he knew that our little trailer has enough plastique in it to blow this town and all its drunken revelers into the middle of the lake?"

Emile met them at the beginning of the lane and motioned them on over the knoll, where Duck was waiting eagerly to help unload their cargo. They unhitched the trailer and pulled it behind the fence, out of sight from the lane.

"Perfect," Duck exclaimed as he examined one of the four *miners' lights,* and handed one of the miner's hats to Juan. "Here go, Juan; try 'is here hat on fer size. With these and 'is lantern, we're gonna be able to see an' work at the same time. Hope spiders don't bother you none, 'cause a main part of our job's gonna get done by goin' through a 300-year-old tunnel."

That afternoon, Wade showed the four the drawings of the interior of Site X, and explained the usage of the various chambers; then he accompanied them across the lake to see its exterior from the lakeside.

After dinner all of the eight gathered for a final briefing for the attack phase of *Operation Top Drawer.*

Standing before a blown-up map of the lake and Site X on the wall behind his left shoulder and another detailed and annotated drawing of the chambers and tunnels of the site behind his right shoulder, Wade commenced the briefing.

"Just prior to dinner, Emile familiarized David with the boat we will be using to cross the lake—and return—on Friday night. Tomorrow morning,

David will have an opportunity to take it over to the Ouchy marina for a dry run.

"At precisely 9:00 P.M. on Friday night, we will leave the dock here, cross the lake to a point on the far shore a few meters from the entrance to one of the escape tunnels—*here,* on the drawing.

"Duck and Juan will take their materials and their individual weapons to the tunnel entrance, enter it and proceed to set the charges, after which they will return to the entrance. There, Duck will stay until after the detonation while Juan takes a position near the guards' wing located on that side of the site.

"The moment that Duck signals us that the charges have been set and that he and Juan are in position, Isabelle and Frederic will leave the boat and take up positions near the guards' wing located on the other side of the site, and Emile, Jean-Pierre, and I will position ourselves near the entrance to the scientists' quarters, prepared to enter—by such force as may be necessary—as soon as we hear the blast under the guards' quarters."

He then emphasized to Frederic and Isabelle that it was vital that no guard survive the attack. "If any should survive Duck's explosion, you are to take them out at once, as will Juan and Duck at the opposite wing of the building.

"And *yes;* remember that we have decided not to use a timer for the detonations. Duck will detonate manually, from the end of the tunnel, after the *second* cannon shot from the hotel which we discussed this afternoon. If, for any reason, that cannon shot has not been heard by him by ten minutes past 10:00, Duck will proceed with the manual detonation of the guards' quarters."

"When we emerge from the scientists' quarters, we may have one or more of them as our prisoners. If so, we, together with Frederic and Isabelle, will take them to the boat, after we have seen to the collection of available records and destruction of the lab if need-be. For the latter task, I want Duck and Juan to remain with us.

"Afterwards, all of us will return by the boat to Evian and our two vehicles, which will be concealed in an area near the knoll.

"Now, I will ask David to come up and tell you of our disguises for Friday night."

David walked to the front, carrying a set of garments in each hand.

"As all of us know, Friday is Bastille Day. I don't know whose idea it was to execute the attack on that day but, in my capacity as the creator of disguises for *Les Amis,* I think it was a stroke of genius. Also, we are blessed that *this* year 14 July falls on a Friday, which means that the crowds will be much larger and noisier—and the parties more numerous—than usual.

"Emile learned also—on the first day he arrived here—that there will be several masquerade parties that night, in Lausanne as well as Evian; after all, even Vichy sympathizers still pretend to celebrate our National Day.

"Two of the larger Balls will be near Ouchy, and many guests will be arriving from Evian by boat at the Ouchy marina. Obviously, most of the costumes will be in the mode of those who stormed the Bastille in 1789, but with *masks*."

"When he radioed me about this, I had no doubt about the disguise we should have." He then held up one of the costumes. "This is an example of the men's costumes I found for the men, and the other is for Isabelle. And here is a mask of the kind you will wear.

"Of course Duc and Juan will be required to do some changes in their head-gear while in the tunnel, but that shouldn't pose a serious problem; I would suggest simply abandoning the 'miners' hats in the tunnel after they have served their purpose. Does anyone have a question?"

"Yeah," said Duck. "Them pants look kinda flimsy; howya gonna hook a pistol on 'ere—much less a grenade—an' make it stay put?"

David reached over and picked up a wide scarlet sash and started tying it around his waist, then looked up at Duck. "This is a very *wide* sash. It ties around your waist area, like this. Then you wear—underneath it—any type of firm belt you wish; it also conceals your weapon."

Wade spoke up, "Yeah, Duck; and the only occasion for use of your grenade should be if we need it to destroy the lab area. You and Juan could haul them up with you as you come there after the big blast, O.K.? Besides, we don't want to have any more unusual-sounding explosions than necessary, the better for a successful withdrawal."

"Does 'at mean no charges under the center section? I wanna be sure."

"Yes. Removing the scientists is the important objective; all else is *very* secondary."

"O.K., I gotcha.

"But fer God's sake, don't take any 'pitchers' of me dressed in 'at get-up David held up a while ago. If folks back in Pike County saw me in 'at. they'd think I'd lost it fer sure."

As the laughter in the room subsided, Emile affected a sad frown and said to Duck, very slowly, "*C'est la guerre, mon ami. All* of us must sacrifice."

Wade then said, "Finally, I think everyone is up to speed on the withdrawal plan; if so, I want to be sure about the setting of the charges on the high bridge tomorrow night. Emile?"

"All is *go*. I will drive Duc and Juan there in the lorry. Frederic will go with us; he and I will stand guard while they are working on the bridge. We plan to go shortly after midnight, when traffic at the bridge should be light."

"Sounds good," said Wade. "That's all I have; anyone else want to add something? O.K., then let's try on our new costumes."

When Wade sat down on his bedroll late on Thursday night, he had a feeling that was totally foreign to him. He was nervous—and he was frightened. The magnitude of the mission—and his responsibility for its success or failure—had suddenly rushed to the forefront of his mind.

He thought of home, and of how it seemed such an eternity ago that he and his twin had argued about what they should do in the war—and how such naive children they had been to think that they had any concept of what war was really like.

Above all he dreaded the thought that he might have to actually kill one or more of the scientists the next day.

Three hours later, he fell asleep.

Friday morning arrived on Lake Geneva bathed in brilliant sunshine. Each of the group was awake by dawn. Before 7:00 A.M. all had begun to busy themselves with the chores warriors do while waiting for battle; many of those were necessary, but others were done over and over, simply to make the time pass less slowly. By seven that evening, Duck had checked and rechecked his explosives a dozen times, and the others had detail-stripped, oiled, and cleaned their individual weapons almost as often.

At 8:30, Wade's quiet order of "O.K.; let's start loading the boat, and go *do* it," was greeted with a loud, *"Aw right!!"* from Duck, and a cheerful, *"D'accord!"* by the French.

During the trip over, they passed close to several other boats loaded with partygoers, most of whom were obviously headed to masquerade balls in Lausanne; on several occasions, David laughed from his position at the wheel, "They look so much like us that if I did not know better I would think I had also selected *their* dress for the evening ."

The lake was congested with boats, some quite loud in celebration, but David eventually worked his boat through the traffic to within an arms-length of the entrance to the tunnel. As soon as Duck and Juan finished unloading their materials and disappeared into the tunnel, David backed off a few meters, and turned up the volume on the boat's music system, shouting to be heard, "We may as well *sound* like the other craft also, although it is bedlam already!"

It was 9:50 when they saw Duck waving his red sash outside the entrance to the tunnel, the signal for the others to take up their positions at Site X.

At 9:58, they were all in position, waiting to hear the first cannon shot, when someone opened a door to the guard wing being watched by Juan. A huge man emerged in his shorts and undershirt, with a jacket slung loosely over one shoulder. He had left the door ajar.

"*Merde!*" Emile murmured to Wade. "I hope he doesn't notice something, and alert his friends." Next they saw a figure spring from the shadows; he nudged the door shut with his foot, and garroted the guard from behind, without a sound being made.

When he released him and the man slumped to the floor, Juan bent over and slashed his throat at the exact moment that the cannon boomed for the first time. At the second cannon shot, Wade, Emile, and Jean-Pierre stepped closer to the door to the scientists' quarters. A split second later each was staggered by the blasts that followed from both wings of the structure.

Wade glanced toward one of the wings as its roof collapsed, then signaled to Emile, who shouted at the door, in German, "*Open up, at once! We are not here to harm you, but if you do not open at once we shall do it for you by force of arms!*"

He waited, then drew his .45 caliber pistol in order to fire at the lock, then said, "You have ten seconds to open your door, or we shall fire it open. Please stand away from the door."

They heard some garbled conversation inside, then a German voice, "Do not shoot; we are opening."

As they stepped into the room, one quite elderly man was cowering in a corner behind three others who appeared to be in their late forties or early fifties. One of the younger men said, "I am Doctor Hauptman, Chief of this project. What is this outrage? Are you bandits? We have money; you can have it and then *go!*"

Emile ignored him, saying, very slowly and deliberately, in German: "Listen to me, and listen very carefully; we do not have time to waste with chatter. You will not be harmed, *if* you are willing to come quietly with us. If you do *not* come quietly—and immediately—it will become our unpleasant duty to terminate you here and now. Do you understand me?"

The older man stepped forward, "I am Swiss; my name is Hausler. I will go with you," he said, in Swiss-German.

Hauptman sneered, "We are going *nowhere* with you; do as you wish!"

Wade drew and cocked his pistol, telling Emile, "Time is passing, Emile. Tell them they have 30 seconds to agree or I will shoot them, here and now."

As he listened to Emile, Wade heard Juan's voice behind him, "*Jean,* if they refuse, allow me the pleasure. I *beg* you!"

As Wade counted off the seconds, one of the Germans stepped forward to Hausler's side. At Wade's nod, Juan shot Hauptman and the other German in the head, then calmly assisted Duck in setting devices in the lab facilities in the lower level, while Jean-Pierre and Emile gathered documents in the other rooms.

Isabelle and Frederic joined them outside, and they strolled casually to their waiting boat. Five minutes earlier, a Swiss police-boat had pulled alongside David, asking if he had heard an unusual explosion near the marina. David had replied, "Only the hotel's cannon and the many loud fireworks. We have *such* lovely traditions here, *oui?*"

Juan and Duck took the scientists below deck, tied, gagged, and guarded them during the crossing. Halfway across the lake, they heard fire department sirens blaring from around Ouchy. The timed incendiary devices set in place by Duck and Juan before departing Site X had ignited fully.

After they docked, they rushed to quickly load the vehicles and pull out, with Isabelle driving the Citreon and Jean-Pierre the lorry. Frederic, David, and Emile rode in the Citreon, and the others the lorry. After clearing the still busy streets of Evian, both vehicles accelerated fully onto the main highway south.

In the back of the lorry, Duck was talking to Wade about what to do if they decided not to detonate the bridge. "I unnerstand we aint gonna do it if there's no sign of us bein' followed by the time we hit the bridge, but don'tcha think we oughta stop to at least dis-arm the stuff; it wont take a minute to do it."

"Yes; I hate to take the time, but we really should do that. We're not here to hurt innocent civilians if we can avoid it. We can cover you with at least five rifles, just in case there is any surprise. Let's do it. We'll stop a minute or so when we're a few kilometers out and I'll tell the others."

They were confidant of no pursuit as they approached the bridge, with the Citreon in the lead, but as they came out of a twisting *S*-curve, the Citreon screeched to a sudden stop. In its headlights there was a two-car road block, with the bridge just behind it. Jean-Pierre pulled up beside the Citreon and shouted to Isabelle, loud enough for those in the back of the lorry to also hear him. "Follow me Isa, I'll smash an opening between those two small cars, and you can follow me through it; stay as close as you possibly can.

"We'll cross the bridge, then deploy with rifles—everyone except Isa, who will guard our prisoners. We will then cover Duck and Juan while they blow the bridge. Let's go, NOW!"

As the lorry sped full tilt toward the road block, Jean-Pierre saw the Police markings on the vehicles. He jammed the accelerator to the floorboard and split the two tiny autos' *V*-shaped roadblock as if it were a toy in a child's playpen. Duck shrieked in delight as he watched Isabelle grimly leaning over her steering wheel, staying no more than a meter behind the lorry at high speed, while Frederic and David both got off pistol shots at the Police who were diving frantically for cover.

Twenty meters past the other end of the bridge both vehicles stopped, and six riflemen leaped out and deployed to cover Duck as he ran to find the device he had concealed the previous night. He was on the bridge when the headlights of two huge vehicles rounded the *S*-curve with sirens screaming in the moonlight. Two men in some kind of uniform leaped from one car, quickly set up a tripod for an automatic rifle, and opened fire on the bridge.

When Juan saw Duck fall, he dashed to his side and flattened himself beside his friend. Duck looked up and said, "It's my leg. It aint so bad, but I aint sure I can climb down to where we hid the line and detonator an' git back up here; if you kin go git 'em, we can pull 'em back to the end of the bridge and blow 'is sumbitch."

"Done; wait for me, and keep down."

Juan reappeared within minutes; meanwhile his comrades had advanced to within better range of the automatic weapon, and had pinned it down well, except for sporadic bursts.

Juan and Duck had almost reached the end of the bridge by crawling along and tugging the line and detonator inch by inch, when Juan got impatient; he stood almost straight up in order to carry Duck more rapidly to shelter behind a wide steel upright a few feet away. As he did so, the automatic weapon swept the bridge with three long bursts; the second one found its main target, putting two slugs into Juan's temple and more into his chest cavity. As he staggered backward to the edge of the bridge he collapsed over the guard rail and fell silently to the bottom of the deep gorge hundreds of feet below.

There was an eerie silence among the stunned *résistants,* until they saw Duck struggling to get to his feet. Wade shouted, "NO, DUCK! STAY DOWN! I'm coming to get you! *STAY* DOWN!!"

Wade raced in a crouching zigzag dash to Duck, while Emile, Jean-Pierre, David, and Frederic covered him from prone positions with a barrage of rifle fire. When he reached Duck, he said, "I want you to you grab the device and line and hang on as tight as you can; then I'm gonna stay on my back and side but drag you along to where we can detonate this bridge. It's only a few feet, so hang in, old pal. Here we go."

As Wade slowly backed off the bridge, the other *Les Amis* did the same. At last, all were clear of the bridge and, from behind an upright girder, Duck pulled himself up on one knee and detonated the entire span.

Emile rode with Duck and Wade, in the back of the lorry, as they drove away from the gorge toward the town of Morzine, where Emile had said he knew a physician who could be trusted to treat Duck's injured leg.

Duck sat quietly in the corner of the truck for miles, head down as if in a daze, until he muttered, as if talking to himself, "Ya know, I never agreed one bit with 'is politics; an' he *was* a bloodthirsty sumbitch, but he shore was *my friend.* Anybody know how the Police found out 'bout us?"

"We may never know Duc," answered Emile. "It may have been only a routine roadblock, but we couldn't chance it. But let's talk about it later," he added, pointing over his shoulder at their two prisoners a few feet away.

"Yeah, sorry. But I *do* wanta talk about it later; 'cause if somebody blew the whistle on us, I owe 'em one—fer Juan."

They reached the camp at Grenoble along with the sunrise. Guy and Jeremy were up and waiting to escort them to a good meal, but Wade said he first wanted to radio Colonel Hebert, "He's probably been waiting all night."

Wade was right. Joe Cassidy was at the OSS receiver, "Damned glad it's you; the Colonel's worn the rug out pacing all night. I'll get him."

"Thank God in Heaven its you, boy!" His voice had a tone of relief in it that Wade had never before heard. "I've never sweated anything like this before. Give me some clues now, then detail me a coded one soon as you can."

"Wilco, boss. *Top Drawer* a success; mission accomplished. Site destroyed; two of four primary targets liquidated, other two accompany us south tonight. One friendly lost, one wounded. Have Joe stand by for details. Awaiting further orders.

"Over."

"Gotcha, son. Congratulations! See ya on the island—wait for me there. Will have your orders later.

"Bye."

During breakfast, Wade wrote out a detailed report for Isabelle to encrypt and send to London ASAP, "But *not* until you have finished your breakfast," he smiled.

Later on that Saturday morning in Washington, a copy of Wade's report was handed to the president as he finished his own breakfast in the Rose Garden. He smiled broadly, tapped the paper with his cigarette holder, and said to one of his closest confidants, "It's done, Harry. The Nazis are finished; this was their last hope."

# Chapter Twenty-Seven

Flight Sergeant Thompson told Wade that the Lysanders were fueled and ready to go, and it would not be a problem to fly during daylight hours, if he wished to do so. "The Allies absolutely own the skies here now; and by all reports, that is true over the entire continent, but definitely so in Italy and the Mediterranean, as well as all of France with the possible exception of some resistance the Luftwaffe has managed to muster in parts of Normandy.

"But of course that's your call, sir. I'm sure all of you are rather exhausted."

Before Wade could respond, Guy walked in and handed him a new message from OSS London. Wade read it, looked up and said, "Colonel Hebert will be in Bastia tonight, at the *Hotel de l'Ile*—not at the Army's facility—and he says we should go there, too. Two OSS agents will meet us at the airfield and take custody of the two scientists."

"Make that *one* scientist!" Duck yelled as he limped into the room. "Seems the Kraut fed hisself a cyanide capsule when we let him take a shower he'd been beggin' fer ever since we got here. He left this note, but I cain't read it. Anyway, he's dead as a doornail now."

Wade grimaced, "That's not going to please the Colonel; I'm sure he wanted to have some deep interrogation of that guy. But I think we've gotta take the body to Bastia; they'll probably want to do an autopsy. How is the Swiss behaving, Duck?"

"Fine; Emile told me he keeps sayin' he was 'ere against his will; that the Krauts kept on threatenin' harm to his kin if he didn't help 'em. Maybe he's lyin', maybe not."

Wade then turned back to the RAF pilot, "Sorry for the interruption, Jeremy. As for the flight, I'd be more comfortable doing my first cross-country in the Lysander in daylight, but after a little shuteye; how about a departure at 4:00 this afternoon? That would give me some rest time, yet get us there well before dark at this time of year."

"Good; I'll do a copy of the flight plan for each of us, with detailed checkpoints noted on your copy in case we get separated en route; but I'll plan on your following me all the way to the island. See you at 4:00."

At the strip, Duck was surprised to notice Emile, along with Guy, saying his farewells. "Ain't you goin' with us, Emile?" he asked.

"No, *mon bon ami,*" was the answer. "Guy and I leave tomorrow to join the action in the Normandy region. The Brits and Canadians captured Caen while you and I were busy in Lausanne, and your Yanks will take St. Lô within the next day or so, but there remains work for the Maquis there. *Bonne chance* to you, Duc; it has been a signal honor to serve with you in this grand adventure."

"Me too, buddy; but I want to ask you sumpin' before you git away. Member after Juan got it at the bridge, I asked if somebody had blowed the whistle on us. You said we'd talk on it later, so now's my last chance."

"I can't be sure, Duc, but the best candidate is Arnaud. He is the *only* person there who could have monitored our activities at all, and I know that he would sell his mother for a few francs. Frankly, I was blackmailing him but—and I shudder to admit this—I remember mentioning casually to him, on the day of our arrival in Evian, that we had traveled through Morzine on the way there. He may have guessed that we were returning the same way, and alerted the Police.

"After we've finished this bloody war—and I hope that will be soon, in Europe—perhaps I can learn more. But remember; the roadblock may not have been for us at all, but we simply could not chance stopping for it."

"Yeah, I know 'at. But here's my Kentucky home address on 'is paper; if I don't ever see ya agin, write me if ya find out for sure. Promise?"

"I promise."

Wade walked up, embraced Emile and Guy in turn, then said, "Sorry folks, but we've gotta takeoff now. Duck, I'd like for you and Isabelle to ride with Jeremy, and take the Swiss with you. The others will go with me, along with the corpse. And Jeremy, if we should get separated in the air, you continue straight to Bastia without worrying about us. I can get us there on my own, if necessary. See you on the island."

As soon as he was airborne, Wade banked the Lysander to the left, and glanced back down at the strip where Emile and Guy stood waving. He felt as if he had just left two *brothers* behind, and reached for his handkerchief to wipe dry his eyes.

Jeremy's plane had come to a stop with engine still running, and two men in civilian clothes were waiting nearby on the ramp as Wade taxied up beside the other Lysander. The men grasped their hats as the propwash from both aircraft blew their coats back, exposing their shoulder holsters, as well as—thought Wade—their occupations. As he cut his engine, he opened his cockpit window, and yelled, "I'm Wade Johns. Are you here to meet me? If so, back off a ways; I need to speak with you before you talk to the occupants of the other aircraft."

"Yeah, Captain Johns. Colonel Hebert sent us," one of them replied. "We'll go back to the weather shack and wait for you there."

They presented their credentials to Wade, and he laughed, "Sorry I can't return the favor, but I didn't carry any on this trip; I assume the Colonel told you that. But I do have your man, at least one of them; I need to explain that."

Twenty minutes later, after they had reached London by radio, the two agents took Dr. Hausler, as well as the body of the German, telling Wade, "We are going to take the Swiss guy to London; we're leaving within the hour. London said Louis is still in the air; should be here soon. They told us to bring the German too; they'll have a pathologist sittin' on ready to do the autopsy soon as we get there."

When the five men and Isabelle walked into the tiny lobby of the *Hotel de l'Ile,* Nadia beamed—it was more like *"gushed,"* as Isabelle described it later—from behind the reception desk, *"Bienvenue encore, Capitano Johns!* We are so happy to have you again!" She said that the very best section of the hotel had been reserved for his party, and that she was pleased to tell him also that the kitchen was now operated by *their* chef, not the American army.

After all had enjoyed their first hot bath for weeks, they met in the bar to await word on Colonel Hebert's arrival. Wade stepped back to the desk to tell Nadia where they would be if the Colonel came in, when he was surprised to see a very familiar figure standing by the stairway as if waiting for someone.

Wade blurted out, "Monsieur Blanchot, is that *you?!"*

Georges Blanchot wheeled around, recognized Wade, and began to stammer, as if embarrassed more than he was surprised. The Frenchman fidgeted for a few more moments, then abruptly excused himself, and entered the stairwell. Wade returned to the bar, and had begun to describe the bizarre scene to the others, when Duck said, "Hey, there's our boss now! Just walked up to the desk."

One would have guessed that this very large man was greeting his longlost children home, as he bear-hugged Wade, Duck, and Jean-Pierre, one by one, unabashedly weeping with joy, and then did the same with each of the other three whom he had never met.

Nadia broke the moment, saying quietly, *"Pardon, Signore Hebert,* but your private dining salon is ready for use when you wish to go there, sir."

Louis Hebert looked embarrassed as he wiped his face with his coat sleeve and, gathering himself, said, *"Grazia, Signorina,* we will go there now. I think I need a stiff drink." Then he playfully slapped Duck on the back and joked, "You got any Kentucky white lightnin' with ya, boy?"

It was a stately room that Colonel Hebert had reserved for what he had described as a "grand and joyous occasion" when his call had awakened the hotel manager that morning. The champagne was from the last case remaining in the hotel's cellar from a truly great pre-war vintage. The manager had planned to save it for V-E Day, but Louis's emotional—and persistent—Cajun pleas had ultimately won him over for half the case.

The table looked almost regal, Isabelle thought, as the Italian crystal sparkled in the flickering candlelight. As the men were having yet another glass—and getting a bit boisterous—she ambled slowly down the length of the table, admiring the silver and china, as well as the lovely linens that—she mused—only an Italian could have designed.

Only one thing puzzled her as she walked back to join the men; there were *seven* of them, but the table was set for *nine.*

Colonel Hebert tapped his wine glass for attention, and suggested that everyone find their place at the table, noting that a waiter had finished the setting of the place cards. Louis took his place at the head of the table, the others found their places, and the champagne was poured. Two chairs—one at the Colonel's left, and the other next to Wade—were marked "Reserved."

Louis then stood again, and announced, "And, oh yes; we have some 'surprise' guests whom I wish to present to you. He then nodded with a broad grin—to the senior waiter, who stepped briskly to the door, rapped on it three times, then opened it with a flourish, to admit Monsieur Georges Blanchot, clad in a formal dress suit. On his right arm was a stunningly beautiful young woman.

She was tall and slender, with jet black hair and crystal blue eyes, and clothed in a full-length snow white gown that seemed to fuse perfectly with the contour of her body as she moved quietly across the room.

Louis Hebert glowed as he watched intently for a reaction from the others, who simply gazed at his "surprise." It was only after Georges held her chair to seat her next to Wade, then stepped around Louis to take his own chair, that the spell was broken, and then only by Blanchot's cheerful, "Good evening! Has *anyone* yet noticed that *I* am here also?"

Five chairs slid noisily away from the table, and there was a rush to greet Georges. Meanwhile, Colonel Louis Hebert was thoroughly enjoying watching Wade and Dominique enjoy what he termed "the longest and best damned kiss of this war."

After all had settled down, Georges looked across the table to Wade, "Jean, I trust that you now understand why I appeared to be the complete fool today. Your Colonel had sent a sub for me this morning, with prior orders to 'bring Dominique or stay there'—as he so quaintly puts things—and he insisted on complete secrecy. I was waiting for her to descend the stairs when you appeared; it was one of the few times in my life that I was utterly at a loss for words."

"You're forgiven; this is the best surprise I could have had." He looked again at Dominique, "This was a first to see her in real dress clothes; I knew she was beautiful, but never like. . . . "

Dominique interrupted him, "Please! I feel a bit foolish in this dress; *that* was part of your Colonel's directive also, but it belongs to Bridgette, not me.

"Let's talk about important things; how bad is Duc hurt? He has a really bad limp." She stopped as she heard another tapping of Louis's glass.

"Folks, let me have your attention, please. I want to propose a toast."

He stood, holding his glass. "Six of our group here tonight have just returned from one of the most—if not *the* most—important missions of this entire war. It was so important to the security and well-being of not only my country and yours—but the entire world as we know it—that none of us may share the complete reasons for the mission—even with three of the people sitting in this room tonight who risked their lives to make it a success.

"I hope and trust that you can understand that. In the United States it has already been decreed by my government that those details shall be kept under seal and remain classified as TOP SECRET for a minimum of one-half century.

"The mission required daring and innovative decisions, made in the field without other than very minimal support from outside the group of eight who were charged with making those decisions. My only regret is that you cannot be honored *publicly,* so that the entire world can appreciate what you have done. Be assured that in time history shall record, and applaud, what you did.

"I would be remiss if I did not say a word about our fallen comrade at arms, Juan. I had serious reservations about his participation in this mission, for reasons all of you surely know. But I was wrong, and your field leaders' judgment was right. He performed with great valor and gave his life to save one of our own; no more can any man give.

"Tonight I salute you six, and I thank God Almighty for the life of our friend, Juan!"

"*Hear-hear!*" said Georges, as he stood. "And *I* have also a toast.

"It is to a man whom all of us have come to love and respect. He is a remarkable person for many reasons, but foremost in my mind is his uncanny ability and absolute courage to defy and overwhelm any and every obstacle to success.

"I raise my glass to our American friend, Colonel Louis Hebert; *à votre santé, Louis!!*"

As the dinner was winding down, Louis told the group that he wanted to meet with Wade, Jean-Pierre, Georges, and Duck the next morning at 9:00, in order for him and Georges to receive a detailed briefing of the mission as well as to review the documents recovered from Site X.

After the dinner, he asked Georges to step down to his room for a moment.

"Georges, they don't know it yet, but we're sending Wade and Duck home from here. That's one reason I made such a thing out of your bringing the girl here. A moron could tell they've both 'got it bad' as we say where I'm from, and I just couldn't send him home without them havin' a chance to see each other.

"I'd never admit to that reason to anyone else, 'cause my boss would jerk a knot in my tail for that, but that's why. I'm gonna tell Wade and Duck privately, tomorrow morning after our other session, so I hope you can stay here until after tomorrow night. That way the kids can have some time after I break the news."

"I understand Louis, but this is bad news for us. Jean and Jean-Pierre had become a superb team, and Duc is admired—and loved—by all of us!"

"Yeah, but this is not my decision to make. This is by the personal order of the president himself; he had already directed that it be done if they survived *Operation Top Drawer.* I know he wants to see them and thank them personally, and I *think* he wants to decorate them with his own hand. Plus, neither of them has had a leave for a long time.

"Who knows? Maybe they'll be back, but I don't think so. We need some veteran agents back stateside to train others for the Pacific. The Japanese are a long way from being whipped, and God help us if we have to invade the Japanese main islands; that'd make Omaha Beach look like a stroll in the park. At any rate, I thought I should tell you now."

The small hotel had only one suite; it was on the east end of the second floor, and each of the two tiny bedrooms opened onto a balcony overlooking the sea. When Wade and Dominique discovered it was theirs for the night, she broke into a girlish giggle with, "Your Colonel Hebert certainly makes a very large *Cupid.*"

Wade smiled too, then shook his head in disbelief as he closed the door to the hall and saw a magnum of champagne cooling on the coffee table. "Yeah, just look at *that*. He must have had his whole staff setting all this up *before* today; Joe and the others are probably cursing my name all over England."

They took the magnum and sat close on the balcony, chatting for hours, until she tugged on his sleeve and whispered into his ear, "*You* may not be sleepy, but I think it is time that both of us got to bed; *d'accord monsieur?*"

The next morning they enjoyed a quiet breakfast on the balcony; but the waiter who brought it said it was a shame that they had missed a *fantastic* Corsican sunrise.

Both Louis Hebert and Georges Blanchot were fascinated anew by the occurrences at Lake Geneva. It was the first that either had known all the details of what had happened there. The important part played by Professor Clément was absolutely new to both, and was described by Blanchot as '*heroic in the highest*' several times during the briefing.

Each expressed deep regret that Emile wasn't present to know their gratitude for his invaluable contribution, Hebert saying to Wade at one point, "Boy! I'm damned glad you mentioned his name 'at day in London; sounds like he was a key to the lock in more'n one way."

Louis took a quick look at the documents, noting that all were in German and would need to be translated, but said, waving a fistfull of credentials taken from Site X, "But I can tell ya—from Isabelle's notes—that these are great evidence if we ever need it. Every damned one of these birds—except Hausler—were *German,* and the sumbitchin' guard Juan croaked 'at night was *SS* too. At was damned quick thinkin' of Juan to look in the guy's jacket pocket 'at night."

It was almost noon when they finished. Colonel Hebert said, "Wade, I need you to do a formal report on this whole operation, from beginning to end; not now, but soon. Someday it's gonna be mighty useful.

"O.K., thanks, folks. That's all I have, but I do need to see Wade and Duck for a few minutes longer—just the three of us."

When the rest had left, Louis took a long drink of water and cleared his throat.

"Fellas, I want to express to you two my *special* thanks for being such a credit to the OSS and to our nation. I'm not sure you quite realize fully the level of importance of what you've accomplished, but someday you will.

"The president himself has been following closely this entire operation, and he has personally ordered that you be transferred to our D.C. headquarters immediately. That is one reason—not the only one, but an important one—that I came on down here yesterday.

"Additionally, we need to have the benefit of your experience for the training of a multitude of agents for work in the Pacific. The war here may last another year or more, but once we back the enemy up into Germany proper—and that should be fairly soon—we will no longer have the same need for your line of work here in Europe. But God only knows how long it will take to handle the Japanese, and we'll need all the skills we can corral for that task."

He paused for reaction, but got none.

"Here's some even better news. I know neither of you have had any leave since before I jerked you up and sent you to Europe. I guarantee you're gettin' some pretty soon after you get to Washington.

"Whatta ya think?"

"Colonel, sir; 'at sounds real good, but what about Les Amis?" said Duck. "We been through hell and high water with 'em. We jus' gonna leave 'em high and dry? *Their* war ain't over yet either; 'at's fer damn sure, sir!"

"You're not doin' that, son. If they need more help, I'll get it for 'em. I admire you for feeling that kind of loyalty, but we need you more in the States now. I'm truly sorry if you prefer something else, but these are my orders, so I have no choice, son."

"We understand, Colonel," Wade said. " I feel the same as Duck expressed, but if that's it, that's *it*. When do we *have* to leave? I'm sure you know that I have another reason—a personal one—for not wanting to leave at all."

"Yup, I think I do. I'm supposed to have you on your way by *yesterday,* but I've been known to find ways to slow-roll things a time or two. If you're thinking of the possibility of having a female *résistante* go stateside with you, that can be arranged," he said with a wink, "but it will have to happen real soon, within a matter of days."

"Can you give me until at least through tomorrow for an answer?"

"You got it! Now let's get some eats; lunch will be ready in exactly one hour. And cheer up, Duck; we've got plenty of work to keep you busy on the other side of the world. Oh yeah, I almost forgot," he said, reaching for his briefcase. "I brought some personal mail for both of you. Here 'tis. See ya at lunch."

Wade went straight to his room and opened his mail pouch. There were a number of letters from Polly and several more from Mama, all with old postmarks, but one with a recent postmark caught his eye, an envelope from "Capt. William Johnson and Miss Polly Hearn." The letter told of Bill's grave injuries and the long journey back from those wounds, for both him and Polly. Then it went through what had obviously been a carefully crafted but difficult-to-express apology for their having fallen in love and their plan to be married as soon as Bill was released from the hospital and placed on terminal leave from the air corps.

The letter was both saddening and truly bittersweet for Wade. He was shocked and distressed to learn of his brother's terrible injuries, but greatly relieved by the news of the impending marriage. For months he had been concerned—-and felt no little guilt—-about his love for Dominique and its eventual impact on his prior commitments to Polly. He sat down at once to compose a long reply to them, to be taken to London by the colonel for mailing.

In it he expressed his deep regrets about his brother's misfortune, but also his total confidence that Bill would never let it deter him in his future life endeavors. He added that he could not think of anyone on Earth who would be a more loving and supportive helpmate than Polly Hearn. He assured them that they had his complete blessing, understanding, and sincere congratulations on their decision to share their lives together. He finished by saying that he expected to have some leave soon, and hoped to spend it doing nothing but working with Bill in his rehab.

Wade sat by Dominique at lunch, without a word about the meeting with Louis or his letter from home, but suggested a walk down by the water as they left the restaurant.

She was clearly stunned about his orders, but said—with her head down, as they walked barefoot along a sandy stretch of the otherwise rocky beach—she understood that he was a soldier and had a duty to perform.

He said, "There's a place we can sit; I want to ask you something very important." He fidgeted a bit, before taking her hands gently in both of his and saying, "The colonel said you can go with me if you wish, and that he would arrange it. I'm trying to say that I want to spend my life with you, Dominique; I want to marry you."

There was a silence, broken only by the soft sounds of the surf, as she gazed lovingly at him; and the crystal blue eyes had become misty before she said, "I want the same. I have dreamed of it so many times since you came into my life. And I have long known that—someday—this day would come, when I must make a difficult decision. But now that it is upon us, I don't know *how* to decide.

"Jean, I love my country dearly, as you do yours; and my country still needs me; and it will continue to need me—perhaps even *more*—after the Germans are finally expelled from this land. When I was in Aix, to bid my final farewell to my father, I promised him on his deathbed, that I would never cease working to keep his—and *my*—France free from the yoke of any despot, be he Fascist *or* Bolshevik. How can I be true to that pledge if I leave now?"

Wade gazed at the sky for a long moment, and finally spoke. "The truthful answer is that you cannot, but that's a decision *you* must make. In my case, I have no real choice. Realistically, no one truly knows when this war with Japan will be finished. I may be sent to the Pacific for years.

"And, as much as I want you to come now, I certainly understand why you wouldn't want to leave *Les Amis* at this time. Given a choice, neither Duck nor I would do it now. If you can't see fit to come now, maybe you will decide to come after all Europe is free.

"Please don't say 'no' now; at least sleep on it tonight. If you don't decide to go with me, I understand that you and the others will be leaving tomorrow at noon."

That evening they dined alone at a small and intimate cafe on the *rue Dragon,* that had been recommended to Wade by the hotel manager. Wade was determined that, come what may, they would enjoy what might well be their last evening together.

Although tempted by the minute, he avoided any discussion of her decision.

As they walked, hand-in-hand, back through the *place St-Nicolas* toward the hotel, they saw Isabelle, David and Duck waiting in line for service at *La Glace Superbe,* the ice cream shop of choice on the island. Dominique blushed a deep red as Duck bellowed across the square, "Well howdy there! We been lookin' fer you lovebirds all night. Where the heck you been hidin'?"

They joined their friends, and sat at a sidewalk table to crowd-watch with them for a while, until Dominique nudged Wade, and whispered, "Let's slip away while Duck is doing his next round of party tricks for the people of Bastia. I want some quiet time to think."

She woke him early the next morning, saying she had been up since five and wanted to talk. As she led him to the balcony, her face was a mask of sadness, and he feared the worst.

He was half right.

"My dear Wade," she said, as a teardrop started to form beneath each of her eyes, "Whatever the future holds for us, I will never love another man as I do you.

"But—for the present—I must remain here, and carry out my duty to *Les Amis*—and to France. As you said last evening, you may be away, tending to your military duties, for much longer in this terrible war. How would I feel, doing nothing but waiting, if I left now, when my people still need me?

"Perhaps I will not feel the same after France is totally free of the Nazis—but perhaps I *will.* I do not want to make another promise to another man I love—*you*—unless I can find a way to keep it.

"I hope—and pray—that you can understand."

He nodded and drew her close to him. "I do understand; sadly, but I do. The truth is that all of us have promises to keep. Perhaps, some day, we can find a way to honor them all.

"When you're ready, I'll see you to the boat. But I do want *one more* promise," he said, as he wiped another tear from her face. "No more tears! *D'accord, ma chérie?*

She forced a smile, and whispered, "*D'accord, mon chéri.*"

# Chapter Twenty-Eight

**E-Street Complex; August 25, 1944**

The meeting room next to the General's office would hold a select crowd on this steamy day in the nation's capital.

They had one thing in common. They were some of the few Americans who knew that *Operation Top Drawer* had ever occurred.

Like many prior meetings in this insignificant looking old building, it was to be a secret one, described later by many of the staff as the single most guarded of the entire war. The first early arrivals were the Chief of Staff of the Army, along with the Secretary of State and his Under-Secretary, Richard Hopkins, who were discussing the news that American troops had entered Paris that morning.

Within another half hour, all the chairs were filled, except the two under the permanently blacked out windows, marked "Reserved," and two more behind the podium.

In his modest office next door, William J. Donovan, the Commanding General of the OSS, along with Colonel Louis Hebert, Captain Willard Johnson, and newly promoted Master Sergeant Luke Hatfield, awaited the imminent arrival of the speaker for the morning ceremony.

Both the younger men seemed a bit tense to Louis, but he was exhilarated in anticipation of the events of the day, and joked, "I hope both you boys understand who this gentleman's talkin' to when he calls you by your real name; it's been so damn long since I did, I couldn't remember 'em last week, without lookin' 'em up."

Will and Luke tried—not too successfully—to force a smile, and felt relieved when the general's secretary cracked the door and said, "His car just pulled up to the rear door, and they're getting him out now. Apparently they dodged the press O.K."

Colonel Hebert stood quickly, and said, "Wait here fellows; we'll go meet him and bring him in here. He wants to see you privately before the ceremony."

As the agents were lifting him from the limo into his wheelchair, he spotted General Donovan and waved a cheerful, "Good morning, Bill! Too bad we're not doing this in Paris; this morning it's *free* again! But *my* good news is that we made it across town with no fanfare. Are the men where I can see them for a moment, before we do the honors?"

"Yes sir, Mr. President. They're sitting on ready, but a tad nervous about all this, if you can believe that after what they've been through."

While they were rolling him down the hall, he looked up at the Secret Service agent-in-charge and said, "After I go into the general's office, I want you and your men to wait in the hall until after *all* the proceedings are concluded." Then he smiled, "This is a unique situation, gentlemen, so you must humor me this once."

Will and Luke snapped to attention and saluted as he entered the room, but he quickly said, "Please, gentlemen; take your seats. We're here to honor *you,* so I want you to relax and enjoy this day; God knows you've earned it."

He then leaned forward to shake the hand of each , and spoke with no little emotion. "I wanted to have the honor of meeting both of you, and seeing you privately, in order to express my deep appreciation for the selfless service you have performed for this nation. I only wish that we could be honoring you publicly—including the *reasons* for your mission—in order that all the people of our nation—indeed, the peoples of the entire *world*—could know of your deeds.

"But, as you know, we cannot do that. I felt that the next best thing would be a quiet presentation, in the presence of those few individuals who already share our knowledge of those reasons."

Immediately after leading the others into the meeting room, he rose behind the podium as he tried to quiet the applause and get the group seated again.

"Gentlemen, one of the most gratifying duties of a president is that of presenting—from time to time—to a member of our armed forces, the highest honor our nation can bestow upon such an individual—the Congressional Medal of Honor. This morning, I will present that award to *two* very deserving men, Captain Willard Johnson and Master Sergeant Luke Hatfield.

"Today's ceremony is—I believe—truly unique in the history of Medal of Honor presentations. First, it is not public, for reasons of national security that all of you in this room certainly understand. Secondly, for the same reasons, we could not have here—as I would have wished—the family and friends of these two gallant young men to share this grand moment with them."

"Rarely in the glorious history of this great nation have any individuals, military or civilian, been asked to lead a more dangerous—and more security sensitive—mission than were these young men. Moreover, they did so absolutely voluntarily, with the clear understanding that they could be legally executed if captured, and that their government would not be able to intervene in any way on their behalf.

"They, together with their equally valiant French *résistance* comrades, entered into a foreign—supposedly 'neutral'—nation; there, utilizing ingenious innovation as well as valor, they succeeded in destroying the last potential means remaining to the Nazi to enslave the free world."

He then asked, "Captain Johnson and Sergeant Hatfield; would you please come forward?"

The walls of the small chamber resonated with a standing ovation as the two strode to the front and stood at the side of the President of the United States of America.

He first draped around the neck of each man the blue ribbon from which was suspended the Medal of Honor designed to be presented to members of the Army. Then, as they stepped back and saluted him, he said, "Once again, I offer to you both my personal gratitude and my congratulations for this well-deserved honor. But before we adjourn, I want to add this: While you cannot reveal the details of *why* you wear this symbol of great valor, you most certainly have every right to wear it proudly, and *publicly,* as do the few other recipients of this most coveted of military decorations.

"In that regard, I have decided that, on my return to the White House today, I am going to direct my Press Secretary to prepare and issue brief press releases announcing these awards, along with appropriate references to the fact that the basis for the awards remains highly classified information.

"Thank you again—may God bless and protect you both."


**Atlanta; August 27, 1944**

Bill Johnson, his parents, and Polly, were just returning home from the 11:00 church service, and the phone was ringing loudly as they entered the front door. Sergeant Macdonald was half-shouting as Bill answered it. "Bill! Glad I got ya. Have you seen the piece in this mornin's paper—the one about Will?"

Before Bill could answer, he said, "It says here that the President gave him and some sergeant the Medal of Honor on Friday! Did you or his folks know that was gonna happen?"

"That's terrific Sarge! I can't wait to tell my parents! But no; he called a month ago from Washington, but not a word about that. Said he'd be here on leave soon and was gonna spend a whole month with us. What else did the paper say?"

"Not much. Says that the facts behind it are 'Top Secret.' Of course that's OSS work for ya."

"And that's our Will. As you and I have talked about so often, he always chose a different road."

# *Epilogue*

**September 2, 1945**
**Tokyo Bay**

That morning, the Japanese had surrendered formally aboard the battleship *USS Missouri,* after the Atomic Bomb had been dropped on Nagasaki on August 9.

## Pikeville, Kentucky

In the little mountain town, the recently-elected Sheriff of Pike County was packing a bag for a few days' trip to *Evian-les-Bains, France.* He had been required to take a disability retirement from the army after his injured leg failed to heal properly, and had run un-opposed for Sheriff. He was to meet his French friend Emile at the Geneva airport; from there they intended to pay an unannounced visit to the supervisor of the croupiers at the *Evian* casino.

## Eze Village, France

The young former leader of *Les Amis de Liberté* was announcing to the media—while standing on the ancient ruins at the summit of *Le Nid d'Aigle*—his candidacy for election to the National Assembly of France.

## Camp Carson, Colorado

At the OSS training facility in the Rocky Mountains, its commanding officer was answering a telephone call from Colonel Louis Hebert. "Well son, I guess you sure know *now* how important your last mission was! Think what would have happened if the damn Nazis had beat us to it! So whatcha gonna do, now that the war's over?"

Will laughed, "The first thing is that I'm going to ask *you* to expedite my discharge. Just this morning, I got a letter from Dominique. She's in Paris, visiting her cousin, and reminded me that I had offered to take them to dinner there. Can you help us, *Monsieur Cupidon?*"

"Not with a 'quickie-discharge' just yet; but sounds like what you need more is a quick leave and a ride to *Paris*. I think 'at can be arranged. Standby for an expedited TWX, with travel orders; and kiss 'er for me too.

"Bye for now."

He thought of leaving to pack, but decided to wait for the TWX, thinking, *Knowing the Colonel, he's probably dictating it this minute.*

Instead he read her note again, especially the last part.

*"When I left you at Bastia, I wept the entire voyage, and each night thereafter for many weeks. Finally I realized that if I were to have the joy of reunion with you, I must first bear the pain of missing you. I want us to discuss our 'promises' (the important ones—not your 'dinner' one!)*

*"You told me once that your brother Bill loved your American poet, Robert Frost; I do also, and he wrote: 'The woods are lovely, dark, and deep,*
*But I have promises to keep,*
*And miles to go before I sleep,*
*And miles to go before I sleep.'*

*"I think that describes us as well—those of us fortunate enough to survive the past six years of strife. All of us do 'have promises to keep, . . . before we sleep.' But my fondest hope is that we—you and I—can reconcile our promises and have also our love.*
*"Whatever happens, I will always love you."*
*Dominique*